NONE OF YOUR BUSINESS

BY

PHILIP BRYER

Johnson soon found out that the corporate world involved itself with many things that didn't have anything much to do with work at all. Things like company 'fun' days, outward bound team building events, psychometric testing, diversity audits, motivational tools and other bullshit.

None Of Your Business is a comic novel which features a rich cast of incompetents, bullies, oddballs and idiots whose influence leads to Johnson becoming increasingly unhinged and reckless.

As disillusion takes a grip, Johnson's thoughts turn to revenge.

TOWNSEND PUBLISHING

First published in 2007
This edition by Townsend Publishing 2010

Copyright © Philip Bryer, 2007, 2010
The moral right of the author has been asserted

Cover photographs copyright © Samantha Stiff, London, 2010

ISBN: 978-0-9561544-1-5

For Sandra

Without whom, None Of Your Business would have remained just so.

The Author

Philip Bryer has experienced at first hand some of the situations recounted in this book. As a result he is now dedicated to avoiding repeat performances and to carrying out random acts of revenge on anyone carrying a clipboard and occasional sabotage on those who are foolish enough to advise him to pick anything up and run with it.

None Of Your Business was his first novel.

Contents

Interview Phase I

It wasn't an unpleasant room, but the heat outside sucked clothing into soaking flesh, and the grime that wasn't sluiced away by the constant sweaty streams running over the skin felt dirty and gritty as it gathered here and there, a persistent reminder to scratch at the body and pluck at the clothing, but it was cool in here. The table, a dark-wooden one, was bare, but for a telephone and there were six matching chairs placed in regulation fashion. I sat on a pale-green cushioned seat and pushed damp, but drying hair back from my forehead, dark blond lightening as it dried. The air-conditioning was thrumming away and the breeze from the ceiling fan dried my neck and my shirt.

The floor was bare boards, but sanded and polished to a dullish sheen. A plant, a palm, six-feet high at least, sat in a terracotta pot in the corner, its fronds clacking a reminder of its presence every now and then as it was hit by the disturbed air. I fetched a bottle of water from a mini-bar style fridge and filled one of the two tall tumblers which rested on the top, bent and twisted the ice-tray until a few cubes dropped into the glass. I picked a few things out of my case. A notepad and a couple of pens, a small voice recorder, spare batteries and a camera. Although I couldn't see Johnson agreeing to photographs, I wasn't even sure about the recorder, but it was worth a try.

There wasn't a knock at the door, I didn't hear it open, but there he stood. Johnson. As old and as young as he ever was. Much taller than me. Dark hair to my fair, brown eyes to my blue. Looking fit and tanned and toned, he moved easily, smoothly, relaxed and alert, with bright enquiring eyes and clear skin with the sheen of one who looks after himself. Black trousers and a white shirt, both suitably silky and expensive looking. Unlike my jeans and sweat-stained pale blue shirt, which were both suitably crumpled and ancient. I'd rather not mention the disparity in the footwear.

I stood and offered my hand.

"Good to see you Johnson." I said.

He returned the handshake, and hinted at a smile, but he didn't say anything.

"So…" I offered.

He helped himself to water and sat down. There was a day's worth of stubble around his chin which he rubbed with the back of his hand, he sipped at the water, his eyes never left mine.

"So," I ventured, "let's talk".

"Talk?"

"Talk, Johnson. You know, have a conversation."

"About?"

"We've got plenty to talk about."

"Such as?"

He was always a contrary bastard, but I hadn't been expecting this.

"Well, let's see. The decline of the monarchy? Our chances in the World Cup? What we had for breakfast?"

"I wouldn't be too interested in any of those subjects," deadpanned Johnson.

"OK. Shall we talk about the trouble that you've caused, the trouble you've caused me, and the trouble you're in right now?"

Johnson grinned a wide, white-toothed grin.

"Oh yeah," he said, "let's talk about that."

So we talked about that, we talked about that for a long time. We sent out for sandwiches and pizza and we ate and we talked, and then we talked a lot more. About that.

He wouldn't let me take any photographs, wouldn't let me use the voice recorder, so I wrote it down in my own peculiar version of shorthand. More usually known as, 'Christ, your writing is appalling'. This, as far as I can tell reading it back, is Johnson's story.

Stepping Out

Johnson, like a lot of teenagers, maybe like a lot of people, had high hopes for the future. Some people never lose that optimism, that sense of wonder and excitement about things to come, or on another level, the feeling that things can only get better. Johnson was full of hope, at the beginning. He had done acceptably well in the exams that he had found himself taking, not spectacular results, but good enough to set him on his way. Found himself taking, because having the exam result was all that counted, the subject mattered little. A Levels or degree required. Could be in Medieval History or Marine Biology, just the ticket for a budding young banker or stockbroker. Why not skip all of that work and just go for the ones that specify a candidate of graduate calibre?

So it was that the wide-eyed young Johnson chose a career in industry. He visited employment agencies with smart reception areas and tatty interiors, and was interviewed in a similar fashion at each one, each time by a variation of the same slightly pushy young man or woman in trendy specs, hair gel and nearly the best of high street couture. He took the psychometric tests without the hint of a smirk or snigger. He was prompted to identify his strengths and weaknesses. He spoke with certainty about where he hoped to be in five years time, and the right answer wasn't 'retired'.

They sent him on interviews for positions which, he realises now, were totally unsuitable. But they coached him beforehand, they dangled the money before him, they became impatient and then cold and distant if he refused anything. You might as well go to the interview, you won't know until you've talked to them, the salary is *very* good for someone of your age and experience, you'd be lucky to get that sort of money anywhere else, well I don't know, Johnson, if you're not going to go for this one I can't see what else we can do for you. And so it went on. Commission, they screamed silently, I need my commission you little bastard, and all I've got to do for it is stick you in a job, any old job, who cares? I'll throw half a dozen of the idiots on my books at one of these jobs and one of you will stick like shit to a loafer. Just give me my commission. It didn't take too much of this before Johnson became cloaked in disillusionment and cynicism.

"It's a very interesting role, Johnson, for an oil and gas company."

"Really?"

"Now we've got you an interview at 8.30 tomorrow morning."

8.30? In the morning?

"OK."

"I'll just run over a few things while we're on the phone. Very professional outfit, quite formal, so you will er…"

"I'd always wear a suit to an interview Tara."

Tara Petherton of Bleed Employment imagined herself to be the Donald Trump of recruitment consultants. She had trendy specs in all sorts of different colours. Perhaps she was the Elton John of recruitment consultants.

"OK. Good. I knew you would, of course."

"Of course."

"Now, that's an 8.30 interview at Wink and Kinker…"

Wha…?

She gave him the address.

"With, now let's see…"

Christ, she hasn't even spoken to him, she got one of the spotties to do it.

"..Ah, yes, Mitchell Turner."

Mitchell? Jeez.

"So, strengths and weaknesses, that's bound to come up."

"Cos it's in your manual."

"Sorry, what was that?"

Ooops.

"Eh? Oh, sorry, radio. I'll turn it down."

"Now, any thoughts on strengths and weaknesses?"

"I'll come up with something Tara."

"How about, now this is a good one for answer on weaknesses, this often works, trust me on this."

"Go on."

"When he asks you about weaknesses, pause for a moment and then say, 'well I'm told that sometimes I'm too much of a perfectionist'."

10

Sweet Jesus, save me from this. And Johnson was not a religious man.

He took a breath or two, he bit down hard on his lower lip and thought of genital surgery. This drove the laughter away.

"I think that's a bit of a cliché isn't it Tara?"

"Well...."

Bit sniffy, careful.

"I just wouldn't feel comfortable with saying it. You know in an interview situation the candidate must feel comfortable, wouldn't you agree?"

"Of course."

Johnson could almost hear the grinding teeth.

"I'll come up with something Tara, just let me come up with something of my own."

"OK." said Tara, like she was on her way out of the door.

"Thanks Tara."

"Well, good luck tomorrow. Call me when you get out, let me know how you got on. You're the first one in you know."

Sending a few more are you?

"Sending a few more are you? asked Johnson.

"Well, yes, but you're the first, so be sure to call me."

"I'll call you Tara," said Johnson, and he put the phone down.

Johnson spent a quiet evening, an idle flicker between the channels. It was still an opportunity wasn't it? Tara Petherton might be a manipulative cheat and a liar, but at least she'd seen the light and given up estate agency. This was a chance to get a foot on the escalator, and Johnson had had a few wobbles so far, the interviews had not gone smoothly.

"What are your hobbies?"

"Well, I like to get down to the pub with my mates."

"Really? Do you do this often?"

"It used to be every weekend, but now..."

"Now?" Encouragingly.

"Oh, now? It's every night of the week really. We'll be in the Mulberry Bush tonight if you fancy coming down."

Or,

"Tell me what you know about Universal Fruit."

"Ha. Not a lot, I have to be honest, not much at all. Sorry. But Universal Fruit, eh? Funny."

And,

"Have you got anything you'd like to ask me?"

"No. Can I go now?"

Johnson just hadn't got the hang of this interview business. But on this occasion, he did some research on the oil company, he made a list of questions to ask, and questions he might have to answer, he had a quiet night in, he ironed a shirt for the morning, he set the alarm clock.

He rose in good time, showered, popped a couple of blackheads, pulled a few stray hairs from his nose with pinched fingernails and, when his eyes had stopped watering, he shaved carefully and emerged from the bathroom without specks of toilet paper clinging to tiny cuts. He took grapefruit juice, cereal and tea, and emerged from the flat in his best (only) dark suit, gleaming white shirt, black silk tie with a subtle pink stripe, and black brogues that he'd buffed to an acceptable sheen in front of last night's ten o'clock news. He stopped at the corner newsagent and bought a tube of mints for extra fresh breath, an FT, purely for show, and a Daily Mirror to read on the train. It was cold day and he was coatless, but he felt untroubled by the weather, he felt confident, comfortable in his own skin, and with his own abilities. Sod it, he thought, if this one goes wrong I'll get a job as a postman.

He arrived early at the swish offices of Wink and Kinker, somewhere off The Strand, announced his arrival and intentions to a receptionist who seemed to have brought the frost in with her, and waited in the reception area. He was studying the FT, having given himself the simple task of understanding just one article, but he hadn't managed to yet and was rapidly running out of pages when Mitchell Turner appeared from the lift to his left.

12

"Mr Johnson?"

Mitchell Turner. Greasy wideboy git by the look of him. Black shirt and a white tie, oh dear.

"Mr Turner. Very nice to meet you. How do you do?"

Mitchell Turner escorted Johnson to the lift and off they went to the interview.

"Hello Tara."

"Hellooo," *so bloody effusive sometimes*, "So, how did you get on?"

"Fine, Tara, just fine."

"Usual sort of thing was it?"

Hardly.

"Oh yeah"

"Strengths and weaknesses?"

You're not even close, Tara.

"That sort of thing, yes."

"So, do you think you've got a chance?" asked Tara.

"Tell me, how many more candidates are you putting forward?"

"Well, three actually."

"And I was the first?"

"Oh yes, thought I'd give you first go."

Oh did you now?

"Very kind."

"So, who did you see?"

"Mitchell Turner."

"Anybody else?"

"No, just me and Mitchell over a coffee. Nice bloke."

"Nice bloke?"

"Very easy going, I thought."

"I see."

Johnson fancied he could hear her pencil scratching across her notepad.

Johnson had walked into the interview room with Mitchell Turner. They sat him in an uncomfortable wooden chair with one dodgy leg and no arms, facing into direct sunlight, no offer of tea or coffee or water, and the chair was just far enough away from the table to preclude him from leaning on it. Across the table sat the blackshirt Mitchell Turner, to his left an HR (that's just a self-important reinvention of the term personnel really isn't it? Johnson just managed to stop himself from asking) man with a severe haircut and an ill-fitting beige woollen jacket which had a bad case of pilling. To Turner's right, an earnest looking, and judging by her clothes, just-out-of-college woman who didn't say a word throughout, but sat with her head down, features covered with the hair hanging over her face as she scribbled Johnson's answers down on an A4 pad, and she had plenty of writing to do.

After Mitchell Turner had relayed the standard history of the company, which included a large portion of the history, attributes and accomplishments of Mitchell Turner, the interview took a turn for the worse. The HR man announced that he had a list of questions, just a hundred or so. *Or so*? Questions which Johnson should answer honestly and swiftly. They came with a thickness and fastness which tallied nicely with those attributes of the average premier league winger. The two men alternating, firing another question almost before Johnson had finished answering the previous one. Name an occasion when? What did you do when? What would you do if? How did you react when? It wasn't too long before the deathly dullness of 'How did that make you feel?' came thudding through the air with all the subtlety of a darts commentary.

"So you think it went well?"

Strangely, Johnson felt exactly like that. He had belted through the questions, found he had enjoyed thinking on his feet, and in his undoubted favour, as he had decided he didn't care if he got the rotten job or not, he was totally relaxed. At least he had gone in without too many preconceptions. Unlike the other three interviewees who were about to be told to expect a gentle fireside chat over coffee with a thoroughly decent chap and a general chinwag about the bloody inconvenience of being such a perfectionist.

"I'm very happy Tara, yes," said Johnson, honestly.

"I'll give you a call."

"A call?" he queried.

"Let you know how you got on."

"Of course. Of course." Johnson was grinning, but he wasn't sure why.

"Are you OK?"

"Never better, Tara. I don't think I've ever been better. I really don't."

Tara was confused. Never mind, she had one of those other three to get through this interview. This Johnson idiot had no chance. Only sent him to make up the numbers.

"Good. I'll let you know then."

"Good luck Tara." wished Johnson.

"Good luck?"

"Yeah, all the very best to you and your hardworking colleagues. Bye."

Johnson ended the call, and walked on. He loosened his tie, lobbed the FT in a waste bin, and hands in pockets he strode up the Strand towards Trafalgar Square, whistling.

Induction

When Tara Petherton rang the following morning, Johnson was pissed. He'd spent the previous evening with a couple of friends. Friends who were already making great strides in their careers, his flatmates, Tim and Jeff. Tim was the archetypal barrow boy who they'd put in a suit and bent his talents from selling fruit and veg to trading in stocks and shares. Tim was already something in the city, Johnson mused, while I'm nothing everywhere. Tim, ordering bottles of champagne (although he preferred Stella) and peeling off a fifty from his wad of notes, with a wink to the barmaid and a keep the change love. Jeff was quieter. Did something in planning or logistics or something, he didn't really talk about it. Very boring, you wouldn't be interested, he'd say. Tim, shorter than average, dark hair already thinning, cheeky and full of chat and confidence. You could kick him, tell him to piss off, but he'd keep on coming back. Like a puppy. Jeff was more reserved, not necessarily shy, but happy to remain in the shadows. Spurning champagne and sticking to his pints of bitter, that's a proper drink, a man's drink, don't know what you're missing. Fair-haired, brushed straight back, but quite long. Lean would best describe him, yes, lean. Johnson too preferred a beer, but tonight he shared the champers with Tim as he felt he had something to celebrate, although he wasn't sure what it was yet, but he tucked into beer as well. And a few gins and tonic. Wine with dinner, and a few post-meal cognacs. Some other unspecified drinks in a club. Red wine back at the flat with Tim, he was sure about that as he knew he didn't have anything else. Jeff had made his excuses at around midnight, after the meal. But Johnson and Tim were in it for the long haul. It was daylight when Tim showered and, knowing Johnson didn't approve, snorted a couple of thickish lines of cocaine in the bathroom to kick-start his day. While Tim set off for the City, Johnson hauled himself off to bed for a few hours. Tara Petherton intruded shortly afterwards.

Johnson had been dimly aware of a noise, but he thought it was coming from the deeper recesses of his brain. Overtime in the headache area. Finally, he opened his eyes. First impressions? Ragingly thirsty and bursting for a pee. He located the bedside phone but his attempted 'hello' came out like that of a man with no larynx.

"Hello?" said Tara Petherton impatiently.

"Tara," Johnson managed to cough out four stale letters while reaching for his bedside glass of water.

"Are you alright. What's going on there?"

You're going to be tetchy and impatient on your deathbed aren't you?

Johnson took a gulp of water and decided he'd feel better if the room were to stop spinning around like that, and if only the floor would stop rocking from side to side. What was this an earthquake?

"Fine."

Johnson made his way to the bathroom.

"I've got some good news for you."

Johnson stood over the toilet and let go a steady stream of well matured, booze-laded urine directly into the bowl.

"Great, great, marvellous. Who is this again?"

Must try not to slur quite so much.

"Tara. Tara from Bleed Employment. Are you sure everything's OK there?"

"Fab and groovy Tara. Definitely F and G."

His bladder's Niagara showed no sign of abating.

"What's that noise. Is it water?"

"Yes, Tara. I'm just cleaning the windows."

"Cleaning the windows. Sounds like you're using a hosepipe."

"Good spot, Tara. It's much quicker that way. Now what can I do for you?"

Johnson was supporting his unsteady self with one hand pressed against the wall over the cistern, he kept hold of the phone with the other, the toilet bowl continued to bubble like a witches cauldron, and then he felt a sudden and undeniable urge to vomit.

"As I said, I've got some good …."

"Call you baaauuuugggh," good shot, thought Johnson as he took a breath, "Call you back in a minute."

After Johnson had evacuated his stomach he called Tara back. It turned out that he had a few days before he was expected to start work at Wink and Kinker. He was to be an account executive, very impressive, his mum would like the sound of that.

When Johnson presented himself at the offices of Wink and Kinker at 9AM on the following Monday he was ready to get stuck in to his career. He wanted to learn and to earn. To get that first foot on the ladder. The thought of picking up Tim-sized, keep-the-change-love sized bonuses was attractive, but he was also looking forward to having a meaningful role in a big and important company in the hugest of industries, maybe end up in Dallas one day, in charge, who knows? Now that he'd been given the chance he was keen and inspired again.

Mitchell Turner met him in reception. Slid over from the lift wrapped in smarm and extended a slippery hand. Johnson just about managed to hold onto it during the handshake, like a wet bar of soap.

"Good morning. Welcome to Wink and Kinker."

"Thanks Mitchell."

"Before we start, what do we call you? I don't think the agency gave us a first name."

"Johnson is fine."

"Johnson?"

"That's it."

"But, what is your first name?"

"Really, Mitchell., just Johnson."

"Just Johnson?"

"Just Johnson."

"As you wish. Now, this way."

They entered the lift, polished steel and mirrors bombarded them with images of themselves and each other and they talked inconsequential talk. They had gone up a few floors when the doors slid open and Mitchell ushered him out into the lobby. Johnson's new black loafers sank into the deep pile of the carpet and he admired the black marbled walls as they headed for an impressive pair of oak doors at the end of the hall. Mitchell Turner swung them both open with a flourish.

He's been practising that.

Johnson looked around, impressed. It was like an old library. Leatherbound (he guessed) books lined the walls, the deep pile carpet had given up to a polished wood floor which somehow had almost as much warmth as the carpet. There were beautifully framed antique maps on the walls, old seafarers charts perhaps, originals, Johnson was sure about that. Several portraits of long-dead men with stern expressions, some long-haired, piratical looking types, others wearing chalky old wigs, high-buttoned white shirts and black tunics. Thankfully none were on horses, Johnson didn't care much for horses.

They sat at an enormous table. Johnson thought, it's like a two snooker tables laid end to end, only without the green baize, or the pockets, obviously. He also thought, I'm going to like it here. I'm definitely going to like it.

They talked for a while about the company, about the role, and about Mitchell Turner.

"You've got a big chance here, Johnson," said Turner.

Reflecting his positive outlook, Johnson replied, "And I'm going to take it Mitchell. I appreciate you giving me the opportunity."

"So I want you to step up to the plate…"

What, we're in the canteen are we?"

"…and, you know, pick it up and run with it."

Run? With what? My lunch?"

"If you come to the party, Johnson…"

There's a party?

"..there's no limit, really, no limit."

"That's, er, great Mitchell. I'd really like to come to the party."

"Good man. But how much do you really want it?"

"Oh, I want it."

"But how much? You've got to show me how much you really want it."

"I'll show you Mitchell. Trust me. I'll show you."

"Good man. Now follow me."

They descended in the lift, exited the building, took a sharp left, went around the building, down a flight of external stairs, through a beaten up door which hinted that many years ago it had once been introduced to a thin coat of white gloss, and entered a long, low-ceilinged room which was full of young men in business suits, office-style shirts, ties, and black shoes. They sat in two rows along the length the room, maybe a hundred of them, a PC in front of each one.

"OK," said Mitchell Turner, "Let's find you a desk."

Johnson followed Mitchell Turner to the far end of the room. There was a small partitioned office there, with the door closed, inside was a big man sitting on a chair which was far too small for him, as was the desk. His head was supported by one meaty hand, pen poised in the other cluster of sausages as he concentrated hard on the papers in front of him. Turner didn't bother to knock, he hurled himself at the door and snapped it open.

The big man gave out a shout, and leapt and quivered in shock. Fleshy folds jumped in all directions, but soon began to settle.

"Morning Brian," Turner announced.

"Christ, I wish, I just wish you wouldn't do that Mitchell."

"Ha, man in your condition, eh?" Turner was obviously enjoying his joke, "Cardiac ahoy, eh boy? About to pay a short visit to heart attack city are we?"

Johnson noticed the remains of a sausage and bacon sandwich on the desk, still sitting in its paper wrapping, clear spots where the grease had dripped onto it, and a large mug half-full of tea or coffee, large like a pint. Faded red capitals on a white background announced that it was 'Brian's Mug'.

"Brian, this is Johnson, just Johnson. He's your new account exec. Johnson, just Johnson, this is your line manager Brian Salt," Mitchell Turner stood over Brian Salt and announced this news with a brook-no-argument style rat-a-tat-tat.

"New account exec? I didn't know about this Mitchell. I haven't even got a desk for him," Brian Salt rubbed his almost completely bald head with the wrong end of the pen that was pinned between his fingers and his cranium was tagged like a railway station wall. Johnson noticed the sweat stains under his arm.

Mitchell Turner had slid into Brian Salt's chair. He was smiling. Sort of.

"Well, that's not strictly true, Brian."

"Not true?"

"Well, you see, Brian, it's all about planning. Space for all. Come one come all. Seats in all parts. That kind of thing."

Betraying a hint of exasperation, Salt said, "If I haven't got the space, I haven't got the space have I Mitchell?"

Turner, curled his lip and wrinkled his nose, pinched a couple of grease-free areas with his fingers and slid Salt's breakfast away from him, he rested his elbows on the space he had created.

"Tell you what, Brian. I'll leave it up to you."

"Up to me?"

"Up to you."

"Well, it hardly seems fair on this young lad, does it? Johnson isn't it?" Brian Salt nodded at Johnson.

"Johnson, yes," said Johnson.

Mitchell Turner sniffed. A loud and awful catarrhal sniff, followed by a swallow.

"I'll tell you who's impressed me," said Turner.

"Who?" asked Brian Salt.

"He hasn't been here long, but he's destined for great things, you know."

"James?" Salt ventured.

"James, that's him. James Weller. Jim. Very impressed with him," said Turner. He moved Brian Salt's mug, 'Brian's Mug' to the very edge of the desk.

"He's alright, Mitchell. Lot to learn still, but he might come good," agreed Brian.

"I think he might be ready, Brian. Ready for a step up, our Jimbo."

"A step up? To where exactly?"

Johnson noticed bubbles of sweat on Brian Salt's ample forehead.

"Well, there aren't any openings in the main building, you know, with me, but I can see definite opportunities in other areas…"

Johnson watched as Brian Salt heard, maybe even felt the penny drop.

"Hang on Mitchell.."

"Maybe you're right," said Mitchell Turner, "Maybe Jim's not quite ready. Yet."

Brian Salt's relief was advertised, evident and obvious.

"You'd better free up some space, Brian. Get out there and free up some space. Johnson here needs a desk," Mitchell Turner grinned at Johnson. In the absence of a better idea, Johnson smiled back.

Brian Salt, sweat ran from his nose, a drop or two fell on the desk as he pulled open a drawer and took something out, but Johnson couldn't see what it was. Brian Salt walked a slow and measured walk from the small office to the very end of the room, he stopped and bent over the young man seated at the desk nearest the door and handed him a black bin liner.

"There's your desk Johnson," said Mitchell Turner, "Best give him a minute or two. No longer though."

"So how was the first day, then?"

Johnson was sitting at the bar of The White Lion with an unusually subdued Tim. No champagne this evening.

"It was OK, Tim," replied Johnson.

"OK?"

"Not outstanding."

"So, what are you doing exactly?" Tim asked.

"As yet, not much. Well, not much work of any description. I'm doing some research."

"Oh, yes?"

"Going through newspaper ads."

"Looking for clients you can cold call?"

"I think so."

"Thrilling."

"It's a start Tim. I'm on the Internet as well."

"Looking for..?"

"Clients..."

"...that you can cold call?"

"Pretty much. But my induction starts tomorrow. Sounds pretty interesting."

"It does, huh?"

"My boss says that they lack the inventory and skills matrices."

"Does he now?"

"They want people who can think outside the box."

Tim's eyes rolled back in their sockets.

"What does that mean, Tim?" asked Johnson.

"Bollocks, is what it means. Horrible, hairy, goose-pimpled and lumpy danglers is exactly what it means. Same as inventory and skills mattresses."

"Matrices," corrected Johnson.

"Same thing."

"Well, it just isn't is it?"

"What?" Tim swilled back the dregs of his beer and ordered two more.

"The same thing. Matrices and mattresses."

"It amounts to the same thing, matey. You'll see."

"Alright, what about thinking outside the box, then?" persisted Johnson.

"It means…well, you tell me what you think it means."

"Well, being an ideas man. Bringing something of value to the organisation. Invention."

"Invention's about right Johnson."

The barman, a toothy youth in a grimy, yellow 'I Love Bungee' T-shirt slapped two pints on the bar carelessly and Johnson withdrew his suited elbow from the puddle of beer which was spreading rapidly in his direction.

"Thank you so much," said Johnson.

"No worries," said the barman.

"No wucking furries," said Tim.

The barman swaggered away to his leaning post at the far end of the bar, eyes aimed again at the TV high on the wall. Johnson mopped up the spillage with a beer towel, then lobbed the soggy mass in the general direction of Mr Bungee. But half-heartedly, without conviction. He couldn't carry off the complete act of chucking it at Mr Bungee, so he made the gesture, but it landed only a couple of feet away, and nobody noticed. Probably just as well.

Tim hissed a quiet gynaecological term, at about forty-five degrees to Mr Bungee's station. He's as bad as me, thought Johnson.

"You seem a bit pissed off, Tim," Johnson observed.

"Yeah. I suppose I am."

"What's up?"

"I've got my appraisal tomorrow."

"Appraisal?"

"My boss and me will be going through my PDP."

"This is all new to me Tim. PDP?"

"Personal development plan."

"Oh, yes?" Johnson prompted.

"Otherwise known as the personal departure plan."

"I'm not really following you, Tim."

"In that case, Johnson, sit back and relax. Let me tell you all about appraisals."

"OK."

"And mentoring."

"Mentalling?"

"You're a fast learner, boy, I'll give you that. Out of the mouths of babes, eh? A real fast learner," Tim rocked back and forth on his stool, with his eyes shut and faint smile about his lips.

They talked for a bit.

"So, when I have one of these appraisals I get to tell my boss what I think of his performance?" Johnson asked, with an air of confusion.

"After he's had his say, yes," Tim supped and yawned a gentle yawn.

Johnson thought Tim was taking the world-weary act a little too far for one so young.

"But, that's good isn't it? I mean getting to have your say in things. In how things are run?"

"It doesn't work like that Johnson."

"But if he's asking me my opinion?"

"Don't volunteer it. Whatever you do when you find yourself in an appraisal situation.."

Johnson tried to interject, but Tim shot him down expertly.

"Shit, listen to me, in an appraisal situation, just do yourself some good and steer clear of honesty."

"In what way?"

"Oh, you know, saying things like, I think you're lazy or there's no point talking to you in the afternoons because you're too pissed, or are you banging so-and-so?"

"But he's asking.."

"Johnson, what if someone asks a question but doesn't care about the answer?"

Johnson sensed the brush of the world-weariness gene, or germ.

"So what's the point of it all?" he asked.

"Search me," said Tim, "Shall we go and eat something?"

"No, hang on. What's the answer?"

"The answer? To what?" Tim was befuddled now.

"Well, how do you handle an appraisal?"

"Turn up well-groomed and smart, and on the dot, don't complain about them wasting time which you can ill afford to lose because of the impossible workload they're responsible for having given you, nod your head, make a show of listening and paying attention, smile, make a few notes - doesn't matter what- agree with most things, disagree with a few - again, doesn't really matter which, take some water or coffee, whatever, so you've got something to do when it gets too dreary, don't doodle, tell them you're keen for this, that or the other to happen, but don't dig any graves for yourself, don't say that you want his job, or, correction, if you know he's in the crap anyway, just for the crack, say that you see yourself doing his job anytime soon, say yes to any training that takes place in a city and indoors with lunch and drinks included, make sure you get in an immediate point blank refusal to anything which takes place outdoors and in the countryside involving canoeing or climbing anything or running around in the pissing rain having to find your own dinner which some bastard's hidden under a fucking hedge and then cooking it yourself, or backing off mountains suspended from a bit of string tied to a masonry nail or anything like being elected captain of a team of arseholes, who have to get across a river for no sensible reason whatsoever other than that some twat of an instructor is waiting on the other side, with the aid of only a plank, two bicycle wheels, a bucket of sand and a paper chain."

Tim drew breath and beer. Johnson's air matched that of a child who'd just been mugged for his dinner money.

"So, when he asks me what I think about him?"

"Tell him he's doing a great job."

"Just that?"

"Wake up, Johnson. Haven't you been listening to me? What else are going to tell him?"

"Then it's pointless. It really is just a pointless exercise," Johnson sighed.

"You have been listening, haven't you? Good. Let's go and get something to eat."

They sat at small table for two in a gloomy Italian restaurant. Tim had insisted on a litre carafe of the house red, which sat on the red check tablecloth closer to Tim than to

Johnson. Tim held his wine glass up to whatever light he could find, grunted, and splashed it full to the brim, he drained half of it before refilling his glass and finally passing the carafe to Johnson. He shot Johnson what Johnson regarded as a superior look. Well, thought Johnson, he does know more about this stuff than I do. As they waited for the food, they talked. Tim talked.

"You see, we haven't got the inventory and skills matrices in place."

"Eh?"

"What I was hoping was that, well if I could leverage your influence we might be able to raise the bar."

Johnson knew he was looking blank, but couldn't seem to snap out of it.

"I'm really stuck at a roadblock here," Tim went on.

"Oh I see," said Johnson. He didn't.

"Good, Johnson. I can see you're starting to think outside the box. Out of the box thinking that's what we need here."

"I get it," said Johnson. This time he did.

"You've got to be proactive, Johnson."

"It is all bollocks isn't it?"

"Good lad. Now just one thing."

"Go on," encouraged Johnson.

"If anyone ever asks you to take a psychometric test…"

"I've done one."

"Idiot. Never mind, here's the food. We'll have lesson two some other time."

The next three months or so passed, and were relatively uneventful. Johnson had been getting on with his job, making progress, and had even been trusted with some projects of more interest. He tended to arrive early, sometimes he worked late. The induction had consisted of being shown around the building and introduced to around two hundred people in the space of an hour or two, unsurprisingly all of their names had fled his memory with impolite immediacy, but it didn't matter as he never encountered the majority of them again. Nevertheless, he felt he was making a quiet impression, and taking his first useful steps. He did, however, sometimes sense an underlying, occasionally overbearing air of crap about the place. The management-speak, the

26

corporate bollocks of which Tim had spoken, something to watch out for, he told himself.

There was a solitary e-mail in Johnson's inbox when he arrived at Wink and Kinker early that morning.

"Fun and games. On Wednesday morning work will continue for everyone as normal, doing what makes us the best damn oil and gas operation on the planet! Then at 1PM, tools will be downed and we will all proceed to the facilities of the City West College for an afternoon of (you've guessed it!) FUN AND GAMES!!!"

Johnson felt a creeping chill in his stomach. All of those exclamation marks and the false bonhomie were making him feel queasy on their own, but this had to be a joke. The e-mail continued:

"It'll be a bit of everything. Something physical, something mental, above all something challenging. Bring running shoes, comfortable clothing and your bulging brains and bodies. You have all been divided into teams, lists of which are attached. Uniforms, team songs or war cries are up to you, perhaps you'd like to get together and elect a leader of your group. The fun starts at 1PM and points will be lost if you are late, and you know what points mean!!!"

"Points mean shite if you ask me," said Johnson. This was toe-curlingly, buttock-clenchingly awful. As far as Johnson was concerned he had left primary school a long time ago.

"Sorry?"

A sharp-featured man some years older than Johnson, perhaps in his early forties had announced himself from several desks away. It was before eight and there were few people in the office, Brian Salt sat slumped in the fish tank chewing on something and tapping absently at his keyboard. Johnson had decided the best cure for his headache would be to get up and do something useful, failing that, Wink and Kinker would have to do.

"This, er, grand day out thing. I was just saying.." ventured Johnson.

"Crap isn't it? But they seem to think it works."

"They?"

"Sorry, we haven't been introduced. I'm Frank Westlake, and you...?"

"My name's Johnson, been here three months."

27

"Good to meet you Johnson. I've just been transferred over here."

Frank Westlake weaved his way around half a dozen desks en route to Johnson and held out his hand which Johnson shook in greeting. Frank told Johnson that he was forty one, had worked at Wink and Kinker for over ten years, but things hadn't, you know, really worked out for him. Always thought about moving on, but never got around to it.

"Sometimes better the devil you know Johnson, you know?"

"I know." said Johnson.

Frank's hair was mostly grey, with a few black streaks, swept straight back and he still had most of it. He had the sharp features which Johnson had noted, but also a generous smile and lines around his clear blue eyes which told that he laughed readily and easily. Like everyone else, he wore a dark suit, jacket slung across the back of his chair, and a white shirt.

"You said they seem to think it works." said Johnson.

"Mmm. Ha. Them. Us and Them." Frank grinned and ran his left hand through his hair. Johnson saw a gold ring, but on Frank's little finger.

"Are you married Frank?" Johnson surprised himself. He wasn't normally this forward.

"Mmm. I was. Mmm" Frank seemed to Mmm a lot, thought Johnson.

"Divorced?" Johnson ploughed on.

"No, Johnson, never divorced. My wife died you see."

"Oh," Johnson cursed his insensitivity. "I'm sorry."

"That's OK. It's alright. It was four years ago now. You're never over it, never get over it, but it does get easier."

"What happened?" Johnson heard the words tumble out, but didn't feel he had anything to do with them.

"Cancer. They didn't catch it early enough to do much about it, but it was early enough to give us some time together, realise a few dreams, that sort of thing, and Madeline was strong right to the end. Stronger than I was, I must say. Anyway, enough about me. So, I get the impression you're not looking forward to an afternoon of fun and games then?"

"Sounds like being back at school. Us and them, you said."

"Mmm. Bit like masters and prefects, not forgetting bullies of course."

"Mitchell Turner?"

Frank Westlake shot a look at Johnson.

"You might want to think a little bit before you say things like that, Johnson," he warned.

"I'm sorry. I just thought…"

"I'm not saying I disagree with the sentiment, but you should be a bit more careful. I might be his brother-in-law. I'm not, and should thank Christ for it every day, maybe I would if I thought it might do some good."

"Sorry."

"Not a problem Johnson, just bear it in mind. A bit of thought could save you a lot of trouble. If you'd said something like that to James Weller your career at Wink and Kinker would be notable only for its brevity. Wouldn't be a record though."

"No?"

"Leaving after, what, three months? Not a chance. Makes you seem like a bit of a timeserver compared to some. One lad, he'd been here for forty minutes or so, said he was popping out for a couple of minutes to buy a bacon roll or something, it was pointed out that there were break times for that sort of thing, but he pressed it and when it was decided he should be allowed to go providing he picked up breakfast for the rest of us, well, he walked round with a pad and a pencil taking orders and pocketing coins and fivers, making added notes like 'plenty of brown sauce' and 'no butter'. Probably took him half an hour, taking all the orders, then off he went with a big smile on his face."

"And two hundred quid in his pocket," smiled Johnson.

"Probably. But I don't think that was the intention. I think he would have happily walked out after forty minutes, that was his intention, just to walk out not to take our money, it wasn't his suggestion to get everyone's breakfast was it?"

"No. But didn't he just sow the seed of the idea? Someone says, 'bacon sandwich' and suddenly everybody wants one."

"I don't know…" Frank Westlake's face had the look it might have worn many years ago when, lying awake, he realised that the Father Christmas staggering around his bedroom was in fact his pissed-up old man with a fag in his mouth.

"Not bad money is it, two hundred pounds an hour?"

"You're very cynical for one so young, Johnson."

29

I didn't used to be, thought Johnson. A few months ago I'd never have seen that angle, it's quite possible I'm wrong, but, worryingly, I saw it and Frank didn't.

"Anyway, looking back, I sometimes wish that I'd had the good sense to sack this place after forty minutes," Frank Westlake, his elbow on Johnson's desk was rubbing at a tiny patch of stubble which had evaded the razor that morning.

"We keep getting sidetracked here, Frank."

"We do?"

"Fun and games? Us and them? Masters and prefects? Upstairs Downstairs? Cowboys and Indians?"

"My guess is that one of the directors got a book, perhaps a small child gave it to him for his birthday. A book, probably written by an American who refers to himself as a business guru. I looked it up in the dictionary once."

"What?" asked Johnson, smiling, despite sensing they were going off course once again.

"Guru."

"What did it say?"

"A spiritual leader, especially in India."

"Really?"

"Maybe it's me, but I can't see what's particularly spiritual about skinning a turd."

"I suppose not," agreed Johnson.

"Or about bullying your staff who, let's face it, have enough day-to-day crap to put up with, into running around like a bunch of ten year olds."

"The book?" asked Johnson.

"Oh, you know, management techniques, motivation, getting the best out of people."

"What, by treating them all the same?"

"Mmm." said Frank, "We're in danger of the bleedin' obvious taking over here, Johnson."

They paused for a moment. Johnson fetched two teas, the office was still fairly quiet and they continued their conversation.

"So, are you taking part on Wednesday?" asked Johnson.

"It's not a question of having a choice in the matter."

"No choice? We can't be forced, surely?"

30

"Not forced, Johnson, but it wouldn't do the old career prospects much good. Not joining in is, er, somewhat frowned upon by those that matter."

"I see."

"Not that I have much chance of progressing any further, but you're a different matter, you've just started haven't you?"

Johnson watched Frank grinning away at the prospect of his own lack of prospects.

"I suppose so."

"Might as well give it a go, Johnson."

"Yeah, might as well."

The office started to fill up. A crossword of white shirts and black suits. A mixture of groans and whooo-hoooo's greeted the Fun and Games e-mail. Johnson blamed the whoopers on daytime TV shows and the finales of shoot-em-up-save-the-world-from-aliens movies. Never films, always movies.

His PC told him that he had a new message.

"Morning team C, I suggest we get together over a cup of wake-up-juice for a little team talk and a chat about how we're going to approach this. I don't mind being team captain. Let's win this thing, guys."

And another.

"I know where we get team T-Shirts run up quickly. Probably a tenner each or so. Red, I should think, to intimidate the opposition. All we need is a name. Any suggestions? I quite like The Invincibles."

Then we're going to look like a load of pricks if we finish last aren't we? thought Johnson.

The e-mails continued throughout the morning.

"Go, go, go Team C! I think we should have a logo. I've attached a rough design. The shield and the sword signify strength and aggression. As does the hawk with the bleeding dove clenched in its talons."

He sounds sexually confused and quite possibly inadequate, Johnson decided.

"I've heard that Team B have organised superhero costumes. Perhaps we should give a thought to something similar."

Perhaps Ann Summers do something which would suit? The knobs, perhaps?

"We need to sort out who's going to be the best at the physical challenges, and

31

who's going to do the mental ones."

And exactly which one of you is going to be the first to get a kick in the bollocks.

Johnson made his way to the gents and locked himself in a cubicle. Wasn't three months a bit of a short stint, surely a bit too early to entertain thoughts of leaving? He hadn't expected work to be like this. Men didn't need any encouragement to behave like overgrown schoolboys, surely they should be inspired to act like grown ups? His thoughts were interrupted by two people entering the gents.

"Know anything about this new bloke?"

"New bloke?"

"Been here a month or two. Sits by the door. Called Johnson, I think."

Johnson sat up and paid attention.

"Haven't spoken to him."

"He's on our team. Doesn't look too fit though."

"Maybe he'd be better on the mental stuff."

"Dunno about that. Student type, wouldn't know A from a bull's arse."

"I'll have a word with him."

"Right."

"Don't want any screw-ups do we?"

The voices receded and Johnson heard the door close. A pep talk to look forward to, but for lack of something to read Johnson might have considered staying in the gents for the rest of the day. As it was he returned to his desk. More e-mails.

"Hope you look good in your T-Shirts boys, by the way, don't bother getting me one."

Johnson felt a twinge of encouragement. This Sam Goode sounded like a decent bloke.

There was another:

"To Team Who Cares? Please note: if I get any further e-mails about what you bunch of twats want to call yourselves or what sort of uniforms you sorry uniform bunch are going to wear, or anything encouraging me to go, go, go (I'll go where I please, and preferably on my own) or to 'do it' (be assured, whoever or whatever I choose to do 'it' with won't bear any relation to any of you wankers), they will be immediately deleted. I read the first few of them and won't be making the same mistake again."

32

Terry Bedford sounded onside as well.

Johnson returned to his work for an hour or so. He didn't feel confident enough to send an all-team e-mail like Goode's or Bedford's, but he could at least express solidarity with the two who had poked their heads above the parapet. He sent a brief e-mail to both of them. Terry Bedford responded to Johnson and Goode.

"Meet out the front at one."

The office began to thin out at twelve-thirty or so as people went out to hunt and gather boxed sandwiches, Johnson wandered over to Frank Westlake who sat clicking and tapping.

"Frank."

Westlake looked up and grinned.

"Mmm."

"We're having a bit of a get together in a bit."

"Oh, yes?" Who's that then?"

"A few of us, it's about the organised fun and what we're going to do about it."

"Oh, yeah?"

"I wondered, well, if you'd like to join us?"

"I don't think so, Johnson," Frank Westlake maintained the grin.

"I just thought you might be interested."

"Mmm. Interested? Interested in getting the sack presumably?"

"The sack?"

"Fired, Johnson, you know. Fired. Out of work. Big Issue, sir? Fired."

"They couldn't do that, could they?"

"They can do whatever they like, Johnson. Maybe not sack you for not joining in with the nursery class, finger painting or music and movement, or whatever other delights are in store, but those that can will always find a compelling reason for getting shot of anybody. Me? Personally, I need the job, I need the money, so, much as I don't want to play outside and I'd much rather sit here with my crayons, I have to play."

"So they could sack me then?"

"Johnson you've been here for about five minutes, they could garotte you at your desk, slit your belly open and spill your guts all over that shiny reception floor, stick your head on the coat rack, chuck what's left in the river, and even the rare sensitive

33

types we have around here wouldn't remember anything about you in the morning."

"I see," Johnson nodded, but he didn't feel discouraged.

"Mmm. Anyway…" said Frank Westlake.

"What?"

"I'm on Team B and that makes you the enemy, so piss off."

"Thanks Frank," said Johnson, and grinned back at him.

Johnson was outside the building when Goode and Bedford came out. Both had the close-cropped, borderline-male-pattern-baldness hairstyles of those too young or foolish to realise that someday pretty soon they might not have a choice in the matter, and both were chunkily built. But they were affable and welcoming to Johnson, Goode (or Bedford) suggested a beer and they crossed the road to the nearest, but not necessarily the best, pub in the vicinity. There was urgent business to attend to.

"Thing is," said Goode (Johnson had by now established which was which), "It's all crap isn't it?"

"Totally," agreed Bedford.

"Right," said Johnson.

"Total crap," said Goode.

"Right," said Bedford.

"Totally," Johnson agreed.

They stood at the bar, which was original, surveying the surroundings, which weren't. Laminate flooring and fake chrome tables topped with smoked glass. Bar stools far too high for the tables. A fine example of a ponceteria. Goode had produced a packet of cigarettes and dissuaded the others from smoking their own.

"Giving up anyway. Soon as these are gone, that's it. You're doing me a favour boys. Go on dig in, help yourselves."

"So do we turn up?" asked Bedford.

"Probably a good idea to turn up," said Goode.

Johnson stubbed out a cigarette and Goode proffered the pack again, clutched in his thick, stubby fingers. Nails bitten.

"Have another mate?"

"What the hell," said Johnson.

34

"He's a lad isn't he?"

They all agreed that Johnson was a lad.

"Passive resistance," suggested Johnson.

"Like Gandhi?" said Bedford.

"Like Gandhi," said Goode.

"Exactly. We go along, ostensibly to join in, but we do our own thing."

"Do our own thing?" asked Bedford.

"We don't act like the rest of the sheep," said Goode.

"Exactly," said Johnson, "No plans, we'll just wing it, yeah?"

"Yeah," said Bedford and Goode.

They decided that such a momentous meeting deserved a toast and so called for more pints.

"You realise," said Johnson, "That we could get fired for this, for mucking up the games."

"Sod it," said Bedford and Goode.

"The way I see it", said Johnson, "We can always go and do something else."

"Exactly," Said Bedford and Goode.

"Have you two known each other for long?" asked Johnson.

They wandered back to the office. Johnson hadn't been seated for more than five minutes when his phone rang.

"Johnson," he stated.

"You missed a team meeting Johnson."

Johnson thought the voice sounded like one of those in the gents earlier.

"Well, I was out for lunch."

"With Bedford and Goode I see."

"What of it?"

"You were e-mailed."

"E-mailed?"

"About the team meeting."

Johnson kept his head down but cast his eyes around the office. James Weller seemed to be the only one on the phone. Oh well, might as well hit the corner flag as the post.

"Is that James Weller?" asked Johnson.

"Yes, it's James Weller. As we're the only two in the office on the phone that's a safe assumption."

"What can I do for you James?"

Johnson looked across the office at James Weller who was bobbing up and down in his seat.

"Listen to me Johnson," James Weller hissed, "I am team captain…"

"Congratulations."

"…Shut up. I am team captain. My team is going to win this event. You are on my team, ergo…"

"Ergo?" enquired Johnson.

"Yes, ergo," confirmed Weller.

"What does that mean then?"

"It means, what do you mean, what does it mean?" Weller hissed a little louder.

"Er, I mean, what does it mean?"

"Alright, alright, it means, 'therefore'."

"Therefore?"

"It means, Johnson, that you will do your utmost as a member of my team to ensure that you make a full contribution tomorrow. Understood?"

"Yes, James," Johnson nodded to him.

"So, I can expect you to impress tomorrow?" James Weller sounded a little taken aback.

"You can count on me to impress, James." Although it might not be you that's impressed at the end of it. By the way, James, Johnson mused, just because you call it a team doesn't necessarily mean it is one.

Johnson got through a satisfactory afternoon by deleting unread any e-mail headed 'Team C' or 'Go for it'. He left on time and went straight home.

Let the Games Commence

The morning before the West London Olympics passed slowly. Every available thoroughfare in the office was obstructed with sports bags and stinking trainers. Sam Goode strolled over.

"We're ducking out in a minute Johnson."

"Ducking out?"

"Ssshh. Pub. You coming?" asked Sam Goode.

"Bit obvious isn't it?"

"Nah. Leave your jacket over the back of your chair. Pick up a file and walk out all busy looking, hang a left down the corridor, out the fire escape doors. See you over there."

"Have we got time?"

"Plenty. Got some refreshments for this afternoon as well."

Goode offered him one of those plastic sports drinks bottles, in an understated hot pink and purple. Johnson unscrewed the cap and took a sip.

"Wha..?" Johnson coughed violently.

"Tequila and Fanta. Mostly Tequila."

"OK," Johnson continued to cough, imagining the dislodging of scalded tissue from his throat.

"Get us through the afternoon that will."

"I'm sure it will."

If you're going to get fired, thought Johnson, why not get the getting pissed bit out of the way first?

"See you over there in five."

Johnson retrieved his wallet from his jacket pocket, fetched a few sheets of scrap paper from his bottom drawer, wrapped them in a bundle and strode purposefully out of the office.

Johnson, Goode and Bedford spent the next ninety minutes in the pub drinking vodka. Although they had decided to wing it, after all they knew little of the arrangements for the afternoon and saw little point in formulating a detailed plan, they discussed a few options. All three of them, despite the alcohol, were rather nervous.

Their first idea was to arrive at the event a good ten minutes late, to that end, they had another round of drinks and some more of Goode's endless supply of cigarettes.

"When these are gone, that's it for sure."

The second idea was not to bother changing their clothes. After a short hop on the underground, they arrived at the City West College sports grounds. They strolled towards four loosely grouped teams and took on some frosty looks and prickly comments. A further group of four, one of which was Mitchell Turner, stood to one side. This group were dressed in chinos and polo shirts with the company logo on the left breast, a winged 'W and K' shot through with a bolt of lightning. Very tasteful, thought Johnson. Green on violet, too. This group held clipboards and had whistles and stopwatches strung around their necks.

"Doesn't look like this lot are going to be getting their hands dirty," whispered Bedford.

James Weller bounded over.

"You three are late."

"Hello James," they said.

"Fifteen point penalty to Team C," announced Mitchell Turner.

"Come on Mitchell, that's not fair," complained James Weller.

"Everyone knows the rules. Penalty for being late."

"Seems fair enough to me, James," observed Johnson.

"Me too," agreed Bedford.

"Can't argue with that, mate," Goode concurred, and was then caught up in a bout of bronchial coughing. He had clearly hawked something up into his mouth which he spat extravagantly at James Weller's feet.

"Look out," shouted Weller, jumping backwards.

"Ahh, I was aiming to miss, James. Here's an idea, any games requiring accurate gobbing, and I'm your man."

"Christ, you're not in your kit either," exclaimed Weller.

"Fifteen point penalty to Team C," announced Mitchell Turner.

"No! Mitchell…," Weller protested.

"The rules are quite clear," said Turner.

"He's right you know, James," said Johnson.

"OK. Better get changed out here, there isn't time to go inside. Quickly, then," ordered Weller.

"Thing is, James...." started Goode.

"We seem to have..." Bedford continued.

"Left our kit at home, sir," concluded Johnson. He was aware that he'd laced the 'sir' with rather too much sarcasm. Johnson slumped his shoulders forwarded, slouched, and chewed on some imaginary gum.

Johnson took a sidelong glance at Mitchell Turner and saw him flip over page one on his clipboard and continue to dash off some notes.

"You know what this means don't you, you idiots?" James Weller pinged up and down like a wasp trapped in a corked bottle.

"What's that then, James?" asked Goode, coughing again. Weller took a pace backwards.

"Don't worry James, you know I'm a good shot," Goode grinned.

"He's going to give us another fifteen point penalty," Weller pointed at Turner, who had finished writing.

"No I'm not, James," Mitchell Turner assured him.

"You're not?"

"Nope."

"Well, good, because I mean, we're almost out of it anyway, before we've even started..." James Weller voice cracked a little.

"Not giving up are we James?" asked Mitchell Turner.

"No, of course not." Weller was quite red in the face now, Johnson noted.

"Not a quitter are we?"

"Absolutely not," said Weller, hotly.

"There's no place at Wink and Kinker for quitters, you know that don't you?"

"I know, I know," Weller's tone was one of rising panic.

"Particularly at the top. No-one got to the top at this company by being a big baby and you strike me as a big baby, Weller."

"I'm not," Weller spoke through his clenched jaw.

"A big baby girl."

Weller blinked a few times and swallowed hard a few more, but didn't say anything.

"A big baby girl who's pissed herself," veins stood out on Mitchell Turner's sweaty temples.

James Weller found something interesting to look at in the vicinity of his left foot.

"What's up then Weller? Bad case of nappy rash is it?"

Johnson looked around at the one or two who were laughing, but most looked embarrassed.

"That's enough of that, Mitchell," said Johnson.

Turner spun around.

"What did you say?"

"Leave him alone," Johnson was surprised at how calm he felt. Must be the vodka, he remembered.

"How dare you speak to me like that?"

"And who are you exactly, the headmaster or just one of the prefects?"

"What? What's your problem Johnson?"

"My problem? That's a good one. Beware, beware the self-aware."

"What are you talking about?"

"Just leave him," Johnson said quietly. He felt like he wasn't quite present, that he was an spectator at this fracas, looking on at himself and Turner and the rest.

Johnson had at least accomplished something, Mitchell Turner had completely forgotten about James Weller.

"You turn up late, having been in the pub on company time."

"The pub?" enquired Johnson innocently.

"I'm not stupid, Johnson. Whatever you might think."

"Lunch break," said Johnson.

"Late, dressed incorrectly, and you haven't even bothered to bring the right gear."

"True," agreed Johnson.

"Look, Johnson. What is your problem? Why won't you join in?"

"Join in?" asked Johnson.

"With the games, with the event, with your team."

"I'm sure they are all decent blokes," Johnson looked around, "Well, most of them, but don't try and put me into a team. Or your idea of a team."

"Why won't you join in with us?"

Johnson had tired of the brick wall and his head was starting to hurt.

"Because I'm a grown man, Mitchell. Look around you, we're all grown men. What is this the fucking boy scouts? Worried that I won't be your friend and play with you?"

He took a tiny step towards Turner. Turner took a larger step back.

Mitchell Turner turned away and conferred with his fellow judges. Johnson, Bedford and Goode stood in a tight circle, speaking quietly and unable to mask the odd smile.

Mitchell Turner strode back, seemingly unaffected by the confrontation.

"Right, my fellow judges and I..." The sound of barely muffled laughter greeted this pompous announcement. Mitchell Turner stopped speaking, he had the look of a man who'd hit the buffers at speed. He tried again.

"We have decided that it wouldn't be fair on the rest of you to involve three people," he turned to Bedford and Goode, "Three people?", Bedford and Goode nodded enthusiastically, "Three people who seem hell-bent on ruining the fun," the derisive snorts bubbled to the surface once more but Mitchell Turner soldiered on, like a roller-skating elephant.

"..Er, ruining the fun. So we are disqualifying Johnson, Goode and Bedford, and striking out the points penalties for Team C." The teams responded to this news with cries of, 'Oh Sir' and 'Rotten swizz, sir', and Johnson bit down hard on his bottom lip.

"The judges will now pick new teams."

A shout came from Team A.

"But we've had T-Shirts made."

Team B joined in.

"And we've got baseball caps.

Mitchell Turner was thankful that so little notice had been given and he wasn't facing the prospect of splitting up Batman and Robin, or telling Spiderman that it just wasn't going to be his day.

"Swap," he suggested.

"But we've bonded now," said someone from Team A.

It's like they've scented blood, thought Johnson, hyenas.

"What?" yelled Turner.

41

"Bonded, as a team. We're all for one. Easy, easy. Go the A team. Go Team A."

"But you've only been a team for five minutes."

"Isn't that what you wanted though?"

"Yes, well, you see.." It was Mitchell Turner's turn to blink and swallow.

"Team building. That's what you wanted."

"Look, it's only a game, alright?"

"I couldn't abandon my team mates, Mitchell, I don't know about the rest of the guys, but I just couldn't do that to these blokes. We've been through a lot together."

"Been through a lot together?" Turner's tone was incredulous, "Since yesterday?"

"Shows the team ethos has been successful, at least for us," said Team A.

"And us," chipped in Frank Westlake from Team B.

James Weller didn't say anything.

"We're like the band of brothers," said a Team D-er. "Yo!" shouted his colleagues.

"Bloody hell, this is a nightmare," said Turner, almost to himself, however, Johnson, Bedford and Goode were close enough to hear him.

"Might as well call it off," suggested Bedford.

"Go and have drink," Goode pitched in. He lit a cigarette and offered the pack around. They all took one, including Mitchell Turner, his hands shook as he held the lighter and tried to apply the flame to the tip. He wandered back to his fellow judges and they held a conversation which was urgent for a short while but soon receded into glum acceptance.

Johnson saw Mitchell Turner sidle away from the group and begin a slope-shouldered walk to the exit. One of the other judges addressed the teams. Johnson hadn't seen him before, he was ginger-haired, white as a washing machine, shifty-eyed and so rodent-like that Johnson wouldn't have been surprised to see ginger whiskers sprouting from his nose.

"Gentlemen, the judges have deemed that a number of circumstances," he glanced at Johnson, Bedford and Goode, "have made it impossible to continue with what would have been a very valuable exercise. I would have hoped that our people, of all people, would have been keenly aware of the threat from the far east, the tiger economies.."

"Who's this?" whispered Johnson.

"Colin Camper," answered Bedford, "Company hit man."

42

"Company twat," said Goode, "Ex-army."

"Rupert," said Bedford.

"Rupert?" Johnson queried.

"Army officer. Known as a Rupert." confided Goode.

"..and how we are going to face this threat.." Colin Camper continued.

"By beating them at rounders?" suggested Bedford.

"Should have them quaking in Shanghai," agreed Johnson.

"I'm sorry to say gentlemen that we seem to have lost the plot…"

"Who's he talking about?" asked Johnson.

"Management, I'd say," suggested Goode.

"..consequently I would suggest that we spend the rest of the day reflecting on the behaviour and attitude that we've shown today…"

"Well, I'm quite happy," said Johnson.

"Me too," agreed Bedford and Goode.

"…so you are not expected to return to the office…"

The rest of Colin Camper's announcement was lost among the ragged cheering and the stampede to the gates. Strangely, for the first time today, the Wink and Kinker workforce were behaving like schoolchildren. Camper glared at Johnson, Bedford and Goode, but didn't speak.

The three of them dispersed shortly afterwards. Johnson announced he was going home for a bath, and headed west, while Bedford and Goode went off to the east.

Johnson opened his front door and through the open living room door he saw Jeff on the sofa. He was with his girlfriend, Anna. Jeff and Anna had met at work two years ago. Anna's shoulder length blond hair was tied back, accentuating her finely-boned features, she was quite tiny. Whenever Johnson saw her he wondered at how it felt to go through life being so small, it helped when you were so damn attractive, he supposed. Jeff and Anna were both dressed in baggy black track pants and sloppy T-shirts, they were quite a unit, sometimes known as JeffandAnna. They were watching a DVD of some costume drama or other.

"What are you doing home?" asked Johnson, parking himself in a chair.

"Afternoon off," said Jeff, he clicked the remote control and the lakeside walk of two Edwardian ladies with hats and parasols was stilled.

"To watch a film?"

"To go shopping. Went shopping. Got bored. Came home," said Anna.

"Ah."

"Too many people about, Johnson. You know, it's French and Italian student season," said Jeff, scratching and yawning.

"Anyway, what are you doing at home so early?" asked Anna.

Johnson relayed the story of the afternoon.

"So, are you in trouble, then?" asked Anna.

"Quite possibly," said Johnson.

"You don't sound too worried," observed Jeff.

"I don't know if I am or not," said Johnson, lapsing into silence.

Jeff glanced at Anna and the two Edwardian ladies resumed their parasol-twirling stroll, casting shy glances from under the brims of their hats.

James Weller collared Johnson as soon as he arrived at the office the following day. Immaculate as ever, starched and cuff-linked, neat side-parting and a little expensively-scented cologne.

"Johnson."

"Morning, James."

"A word?"

"Sure."

"Listen Johnson, I can't condone most of what you did yesterday. But, leaving that aside, well, thanks for getting involved."

"He's a bully, that's all James. Got to stand up to him."

"Yes, but you didn't have to. So I just wanted to say thanks."

"Don't mention it. Remember, you don't have to take it from him."

"That's immaterial really, Johnson. I'm finished here aren't I?"

"Well..."

"They're not going to promote someone who bursts into tears at the first sign of trouble, are they?"

"Well, if that person was subject to a campaign of bullying and intimidation, I think

44

there are extenuating circumstances aren't there?"

"I don't know. I don't think so. You saw what happened to Turner, they pounced on him when they saw he was weakened. I can't manage people if they see me as a big baby girl can I?"

"Well…"

"Who's pissed her nappy?"

"Maybe not," Johnson agreed.

"Might be time to move on. Pity, really, I've invested a lot in the hope of getting on here."

"Take a lesson from yesterday, James. Would you want to get on in a place like this?"

"God, I don't know. I was prepared to play the games, looking forward to it really, to winning. That's what it's all about isn't it, winning?"

"If you say so, James."

"So, I wanted to say something to you, before…well, perhaps if you don't win this one, I mean, maybe winning isn't everything, not all the time."

"What are you saying to me, James?"

"You might have won the battle, but…I think you're out, Johnson."

"Out?"

"Yes."

"Have you heard anything?"

"Just a whisper from Brian Salt."

"And?"

"Turner, or maybe Camper wants to see you this morning."

"I see."

"Can't see it being Turner."

"I don't know, James. He'll want to claw back some of the credibility that took a knock yesterday. Maybe I can expect a public dressing-down?"

"Well, good luck, anyway."

"Thanks, James."

Johnson grabbed a tea and made his way to his desk, receiving various nods, winks and smirks on the way. He sat down and noticed a makeshift hangman's noose which

45

someone had fashioned from a ruler and some string and taped to the top of his PC monitor, so that it hung down before his eyes. He tapped the ruler so that it sprung upwards and downwards, and offered the room a beaming smile. Frank Westlake smiled back, but shook his head. The phone rang.

"Johnson?"

"Yes."

"Colin Camper."

"Morning, Colin," Johnson noticed ears pricking up all across the room, suited meerkats taking notice.

"Would you make your way to my office, please?"

"Sure. Erm, where is it?"

"What?"

"Well, Colin, we'd never met before yesterday and I don't know where you live."

"Fourth floor. Left through the double doors, halfway down on the right. See you in five minutes."

Johnson thought about taking his tea with him and getting a sandwich on the way, but saw little point in being antagonistic.

"See you in five minutes," he said.

Johnson looked over to Frank Westlake who gave him a rueful smile, then drew his finger across his throat and raised a questioning eyebrow. Johnson returned the rueful smile and shrugged.

Johnson spied Goode and Bedford on their way in, and intercepted them.

"I've just been summoned."

"Where, Mitchell Turner's?" asked Goode.

"No. Colin Camper's."

"Ooops," said Bedford.

"For the high jump then," said Goode.

"Have you packed all your stuff up? Ready for the move?" asked Bedford.

"Get him a bin liner," said Goode.

"Very funny. I'll let you know what to expect," said Johnson.

"If they let you back in here," said Bedford.

"Might be escorted out by security," said Goode.

46

"As I said, I'll let you know what to expect."

"Fair enough," said Bedford and Goode.

Johnson took the lift to the fourth floor. Normally he would have walked, but he didn't want to arrive sweaty and out of breath. Following Camper's directions, he found himself outside a door with a plastic nameplate, 'Colin Camper', it said, and below, 'Operations Director'. Whatever that means, thought Johnson. He knocked, heard a muffled assent, and entered.

Colin Camper sat behind a substantial desk that had been polished so hard that it looked slippery, Mitchell Turner sat in the corner, today all is slippery, observed Johnson.

"Sit down," said Camper, formalities over.

"Good morning," said Johnson.

"Morning," mumbled Camper, grudgingly.

"Morning Mitchell," said Johnson.

Mitchell Turner didn't say anything.

"Well, you know why you're here," Camper started.

"Well, I assume it's about yesterday," Johnson confirmed.

"Unacceptable behaviour on your part. Totally unacceptable."

It was Johnson's turn not to say anything.

"Mitchell, here," Camper flung out an arm in Turner's direction, "Mitchell is your boss. Your B.O.S.S., and, as such, you should treat him with some respect."

Johnson maintained radio silence.

"I expect people in your position, may I say, your lowly position, to present themselves at company events and behave like adults."

Johnson was Trappist-like.

"I'd go as far as to say this was insubordination. You were inconsiderate. You betrayed no semblance of thought for your team-mates. You did not join in. You, and you alone, were responsible for ruining the whole day for everyone. You, young man were the catalyst, the ringleader, the troublemaker. I know that there are certain people here, who shall remain nameless, who are calling for your dismissal." Camper rather ruined the subterfuge by waving an arm at Turner again. Camper's complexion, which was normally almost translucent was reddening quite alarmingly from collar to hairline.

47

Even the ears, noted Johnson, even the freckles on his ears, he looks like he's got measles.

"Mitchell?" enquired Camper, as he took a gulp of water.

"I've got nothing to add," said Turner. He looks back to his old self, no sign of a shadow of his former, thought Johnson, although that would be hard to locate.

"Now, although, as I say, there have been calls for you to be dismissed, I'm not going along with that, I cannot begin to understand your behaviour, perhaps drink was a factor, perhaps you are easily led, but surely we're allowed one mistake in life, eh? I think that, if properly channelled, your talents can be of use to the Wink and Kinker family, give us the boy and we'll give you the man, isn't it? I understand that you have worked well in your position and you were deemed to have a future here, and I have some experience in the coaching of young men, of soldiers, so I think we can get the best out of you yet. What I would like you to do is apologise to Mitchell, your boss, remember, and then we can move on. Now, going forward, I would like Mitchell to take much more of a role in your development, take you under his wing, say. You will report to him at seven-thirty each morning to review your projects, you will remain in touch on regular basis throughout the morning with Mitchell, to all intents and purposes, sitting on your shoulder, if you like. You will lunch together without the benefit of alcohol, the afternoon will be given over mainly to coaching from Mitchell, and at the end of the working day, whenever that might be, eight, nine, perhaps later, on occasion, you will review the day's progress. Now then, Johnson, when you walked through that door a few minutes ago, you probably did not expect to have much of a future with Wink and Kinker, but I think that with Mitchell as your mentor, you might just have a chance. So, you've been very quiet. Admirably restrained, even, and I don't think I'm being too optimistic when I see that as the first lesson learned, first of many, let's hope. So, young man. Speak up, you're still in a job, I see a future for you at Wink and Kinker, and Mitchell is going to be your guru, what do you think of that?"

"You must be fucking joking," said Johnson.

Johnson had turned on the worn down heel of his brogues and exited Camper's office at a fair lick, he noticed Camper's jaw dangling an inch or so above his shiny workspace and glanced at Mitchell Turner who was taking far more time than was necessary to leap to his feet. He didn't bother returning to the office, he could always catch up with Bedford and Goode and Westlake at a later date. He walked out on Wink and Kinker without regrets, and having walked out, he broke into a gentle jog until he reached the underground station.

"But what about a reference?" he asked Tim. It was the evening, and they were in the flat drinking a bottle of Aussie Shiraz which Tim had brought home.

"Don't worry about it," advised Tim.

"It seemed the right thing to do at the time. But now, well it won't look good on my CV will it?"

"So don't mention it."

"Just leave it off?" asked Johnson.

"Leave it off. Pretend it never happened. Christ, you weren't there for long were you?"

"So, I won't need a reference?"

"You won't need a reference," Tim confirmed, "Because you never worked there."

"But, if I leave it off my CV, and get another job, and I've got a P45 from Wink and Kinker?"

"Shouldn't think anyone'll notice." said Tim, confidently.

"Why not?"

"Someone interviews you, you get the job, you give your P45 to someone else and never the twain."

"I see," answered Johnson.

"So, what are you going to do now then?"

"Find another job."

"Tell 'em you've been taking time out. Travelling or something."

"Good idea."

"What were you doing before?" asked Tim.

"I had that office cleaning job, you know, when I first moved down."

Johnson had taken it to supplement a small legacy from a great uncle, a legacy which was now seriously depleted.

"Got much in the bank?"

"Not a lot."

49

"And you weren't too impressed by your first venture into commerce?"

"Yes and no. Ultimately no, obviously."

"I'll tell you the best thing you can do then."

"What's that?" Johnson asked.

"Get your pinny on and ask for your hoover back."

By the time JeffandAnna came in, jeans and white T-shirts, they had started on their second bottle and Johnson had resolved to give up smoking in the morning. He would have to be on his mettle for job interviews, so he would have to cut down on the booze as well. Tim fetched two extra glasses from the kitchen and another two bottles from the hall, "Bought a case," he explained.

"Think I'll have a day's R and R tomorrow," announced Johnson.

"Rock 'n' roll, Johnners, that's the way, rock 'n' roll," Tim advised, filling Johnson's glass to the brim. He gave Anna the third wine glass, and Jeff had to make do with the Bugs Bunny tumbler he'd brought from home. They phoned for a take-away, finished the most of the case of Shiraz, turned up the music until the evening finally wore out.

Johnson didn't do anything on the following day, Thursday, and was similarly engaged on Friday. No jobs in the paper until Monday, he told himself, anyway he didn't feel ready to go through the agency thing again, not until next week.

He sat talking to Jeff on the Saturday morning. Unusually, Anna was not bolted to Jeff's hip, she was away on a hen weekend. Johnson sipped tea in his bathrobe, while Jeff sucked on a bottle of water. Jeff had been out for a run, he sat in an impressively damp T-shirt and shorts and positively radiated good health and fitness. Johnson decided against a cigarette.

"Where is it you work again, Jeff?"

"Well, it's kind of the civil service," Jeff replied.

"Kind of?"

"Well, we're attached to the civil service."

"Attached?"

"Yeah, we are contracted to work for them on certain projects."

"What sort of projects?" Johnson asked.

"Well, Johnson, it's like this, I can't really say."

50

"Spying is it? Wow," enthused Johnson.

"No, nothing like that. But the Official Secrets Act, you know?"

"You can't tell me?"

"No. Nothing interesting, anyway." Jeff confirmed.

"Or you could tell me but then you'd have to…"

"Don't say it, Johnson," warned Jeff.

"What?" said Johnson, so innocent as not to worry butter.

"You know."

"Yeah," Johnson confirmed.

"If you had any idea how many times I hear that every day."

"Must make you feel like killing someone."

Johnson spent the rest of weekend falsifying his CV. However, this only involved omitting Wink and Kinker and, at Jeff's advice, including some more positive pastimes. Squash replaced reading, and current affairs took over from food and drink. Jeff assured him that it would make him seem dynamic and cerebral rather than solitary and hedonistic. Johnson wasn't convinced, and knew the sort of person he would rather spend time with, but he went along with it. He also checked out the internet for vacancies and employment agencies, by Sunday evening he had a list of numbers to call on Monday morning. By Monday lunchtime he had a job.

Interview Phase II

I poured Johnson some more water.

"No chance of a drink, I suppose," he ventured.

"No chance," I confirmed.

Johnson stood, he wandered around the room for a few minutes pausing at the window, which was closed. He fiddled with the catch.

"Leave the window would you Johnson?" I requested.

"Hot in here," he replied.

"We've got the air-con and the fan. They're just about better than nothing. Anyway, I don't think opening the window will help, there's no breeze out there."

"No, suppose not, could do with some fresh air though," he said.

"Anyway, we're on the tenth floor, and I don't want to lose you."

Johnson laughed.

"Suicide? I'm not quite ready for that."

"You think you might be one day, then?" I asked.

"Do me a favour?"

"That depends," I said.

"Don't try to analyse me."

"I wasn't," I insisted, "I was just asking if, someday, you might consider suicide."

"Who knows? That's not to say I would, or can see myself entertaining the thought in the future, but who knows what lies ahead?"

"Fair enough." I agreed.

Johnson abandoned the window and took a seat on the hard wooden floor.

"That doesn't look too comfortable," I observed.

"Just trying to stay awake," he said.

"Do I annoy you that much, Johnson?"

"Not annoy particularly, no. It's all a bit tedious thought isn't it, all this talk?

"Tell me more about Wink and Kinker."

"More?"

"You've told me what happened, but not much about why it happened."

"It's all there," he replied, "All you have to do is look for it."

"I'd like you to tell me." I persisted.

"Have you got any cigarettes?" asked Johnson.

"I thought you gave up," I said.

"Feel like starting again."

"Tell me about Wink and Kinker."

Johnson laughed again.

"You're a piece of work aren't you? Who'd have thought it?" he said.

"Tell me about it," I said.

Johnson said nothing, he remained on the floor, sitting forward and hugging his knees, like a junior on the school hall floor at assembly. I picked up the phone.

"Could we have some beer and cigarettes up here please? Yes, beer and cigarettes, oh, and an ashtray. No, local beer will be fine. A dozen, please. Yes, twelve, that's it. Thank you," I replaced the phone and looked over at Johnson.

"Wink and Kinker?" I asked.

Johnson got to his feet slowly, once upright he rubbed his legs vigorously.

"For a beer and a fag I'll talk about whatever you like."

"So?" I asked.

"Not being funny, but I don't see any provisions yet."

"They're on the way," I said.

"Well, you see, one thing I've learnt from all of this is to trust nobody."

"You can trust me Johnson," I assured him.

"Really? Well, no offence and all that, but it might be a trick."

"It isn't, I wouldn't do that to you," I said.

"OK, but what difference is five minutes going to make?"

"Not much, I suppose," I conceded.

"Tell you what, let's give it five minutes, then."

"Alright," I agreed, "And then we'll go through everything properly."

"Well, I'm not sure I agreed to that," said Johnson.

"You agreed," I said, "Anything for a beer and a fag, you said."

"We'll see where it goes shall we? Just don't try and organise me, I don't like being organised," said Johnson, there was mildly threatening edge to his voice.

A Fresh Start

Johnson's new job was at The Department of General Administration, a government body which dealt with all of the affairs at which other, more important, departments had thumbed their noses. He had been employed on a temporary basis to assist with clearing a backlog of something or other, no-one seemed to be too sure. He met Mr Flitch in the reception area of a poky office building on a back-street somewhere between Waterloo and London Bridge, far removed from the grandeur of Whitehall.

Mr Flitch was a tall man, but his cadaverous features and lank frame made him seem even taller. He was dressed in a dark, barely pinstriped suit which looked to have been designed, and quite possibly manufactured, in the nineteen-forties, he wore a once-white shirt with a thin, plain dark blue tie, only the top few inches of the tie were visible, the rest disappeared into a waistcoat which matched the old suit. He sat with Johnson in the reception area, and crossed his long levers. His black lace-ups, Johnson noted, rose high on the ankle, almost like bootees. Mr Flitch had a few strands of grey hair remaining which had been carefully drawn across and plastered to his scalp. His skin was not so much pale as a light shade of ashtray-grey.

"Now, Mr Johnson," said Mr Flitch.

"Mr Flitch?" said Johnson.

"We have a backlog of work, sent to us by other departments, which needs dealing with, that's why you're here."

"OK, what sort of work?"

"Oh, you know," said Mr Flitch, wearily, "Claims, registrations, applications, propositions, or more correctly, proposals, I suppose."

"I didn't expect to be propositioned on my first day, Mr Flitch," said Johnson with what he supposed to be his winning smile.

"Quite." said Mr Flitch, unimpressed, "Let's get on shall we?"

Mr Flitch led Johnson up a cramped and curving staircase to the fourth floor, to a room where two desks were joined as one. They sat facing each other.

"At least I'll improve my fitness, working here," said Johnson.

"As long as you maintain your work ethic, Mr Johnson, I shall be satisfied."

"Of course," agreed Johnson.

"This is a place of work, Mr Johnson, some might call me old-fashioned.."

"Surely not?" Johnson interrupted.

"But I have little time for small talk and chit-chat."

"Understood, sir." agreed Johnson.

"I have even less time for sarcasm."

"I'm here to work, Mr Flitch," said Johnson, "I'm sure we're going to get along like the proverbial house."

"Indeed," said Mr Flitch, unconvincingly.

Mr Flitch's desk possessed a PC, which was switched off, a large desk diary, opened at a point some two weeks ago, an A4 pad, untouched by ink or pencil, and a telephone. On Johnson's desk was a four tier in-out-pending-don't know tray arrangement which was crammed so full with papers that each of the trays stood a little prouder than the last. The top tray overflowing from every side. There were also several piles of forms and papers - a mixture of reds, greens, yellows and whites - scattered around his desk. So many that he couldn't actually see the surface, he assumed it to be the same melamine-topped affair of Mr Flitch. There was an old clock high on the wall behind Mr Flitch, it was nine-thirty-five.

"Right," said Mr Flitch, "Time to get you started."

"OK," said Johnson, "By the way, can I get a cup of tea or something?"

"Tea and coffee should be made before nine. Next break is at ten-thirty. There is a further break at three," advised Mr Flitch.

"But I was told to get here at nine-fifteen," protested Johnson, quietly.

"So you were, so you were," agreed Mr Flitch, "Just this once then. There is a room to the right with a kettle. What did you bring with you?"

"Bring with me?" asked Johnson, puzzled.

"Tea, coffee, sugar, milk, you know. What did you bring?"

"Don't you, er, provide that sort of thing?" Johnson enquired.

"We are the civil service, Mr Johnson, a government organisation. Can you imagine the outcry in The Daily Mail if it were the case that the taxpayer was funding refreshments for we faceless bureaucrats?"

"I suppose so," said Johnson.

"Do I take it then, Mr Johnson, that you have brought nothing in the way of beverage and as such are now becoming increasingly thirsty?"

"I am," Johnson concurred.

"Well, Mr Johnson, what are we to do?" Mr Flitch ran the tips of his fingers over and around his eyelids, his milky blue eyes popped back into view. Johnson pondered on the strangeness of having both milky eyes and chalky fingers.

Mr Flitch opened a desk drawer and delved into it. He produced two mugs and set them on the desk. There followed a small jar of instant coffee and a box of teabags.

"Now, Mr Johnson, I can lend you a teabag or a spoonful of coffee, which is it to be?"

Johnson played with his own eyelids for a moment.

"A teabag would be just the thing, Mr Flitch. Please."

"A teabag it is then," Mr Flitch dropped a teabag into one of the mugs and spooned coffee granules into the other. "I do hope you don't take sugar?"

"No, I don't," confirmed Johnson.

"Good, because as I don't take it either, there is none."

"That's fine, I'll go and make the drinks," announced Johnson, rising to his feet.

"I recommend, Johnson, that you visit the delightful and well-stocked corner shop during your lunch break and purchase your own box of teabags. That way you will have your own supply to hand and can also recompense me for the loan."

"Milk?" enquired Johnson.

"Milk?" queried Mr Flitch.

"In your coffee?"

"Please. And feel free Johnson to avail yourself of my milk," offered Mr Flitch.

"Why, thank you," said Johnson, with a gratitude he didn't necessarily feel was justified.

"Your turn to purchase the milk will come tomorrow. Don't buy it today as we do not possess a refrigerator."

"Right then."

"One thing Johnson, let's make this an isolated incident shall we?"

"Isolated incident, Mr Flitch?" Johnson asked.

"Drinks at, now, let's see, a quarter to ten. Best not let that happen again."

"OK, Mr Flitch," said Johnson, and decamped to the kitchen, the aged and tarnished kettle rattled and fizzed alarmingly as it stuttered towards boiling point. He returned with the drinks.

"Right then, Johnson, to work," announced Mr Flitch.

"That's what I'm here for," Johnson agreed.

"Your desk, pile of papers, all need sorting, OK?"

"Sorting."

"You'll see. Into separate piles, easy," assured Mr Flitch.

"Righto," said Johnson.

"Pick up, identify, place, repeat. See?" Mr Flitch had done just that. As there was no room on Johnson's desk Mr Flitch had placed, rather tossed a sheet of paper onto the floor, followed by another.

"One's DOT, the other's FO, see?"

"I see," Johnson agreed.

"Transport there, Foreign Office there, and so on, OK?"

"Got it," said Johnson, confidently.

"Any others, keep them separate, OK?"

"OK."

"Fresh piles."

"Fresh piles," Johnson agreed.

"Right, I have to go out to a meeting."

"A meeting? Right, any idea when you'll be back?" enquired Johnson.

"Be back?"

"In case there are any calls?" said Johnson, efficiently.

"Calls? Oh, you mean on the telephone. Don't worry about that, Mr Johnson. The telephone hasn't rung in, oh, I should say, nine months or so."

"Really?"

"Just get on, Mr Johnson, get this lot in nice, neat, tidy piles, eh?"

"Nice, neat, tidy piles, yes, of course."

"I'll see you later, then, after my meeting. You should take your lunch between one and two."

"OK," Johnson said.

"And if you'd like another cup of tea at ten-thirty, well, help yourself, eh? Just this once."

Mr Flitch handed Johnson a teabag.

"Just this once, Mr Flitch." agreed Johnson.

"You'll be buying your own teabags at lunchtime of course, so you won't be needing another, will you?"

"That's right, Mr Flitch," agreed Johnson.

Mr Flitch loped out of the office, and Johnson set to work on the sorting.

At ten-thirty, Johnson repaired to the kitchen and fetched himself a cup of tea, free milk today, he thought. There didn't appear to be anyone else in the building, no signs of anybody using the kitchen, and no sign of people moving about. He returned to the office, which by now boasted as much floor space as an Irish bar on new year's eve. Papers of all colours were arranged around the room in separate stacks, he compared them to the piles that remained on his desk, and those in cardboard boxes that lined the office, he assumed these were also his, although Mr Flitch had made no mention of them. He finished his tea, better get on with it, he decided.

Johnson spent the rest of the morning patiently constructing what were becoming pillars of paper, he paused for a moment. Transport was in the lead by a good couple of inches, environment had recently impressed with a late surge, while housing had been consistent, child support had faded after a less than inspiring start, taxation still had a lot to do, and health looked out of its depth in this company. There didn't seem to be much difference in the amount of paper on his desk, and he hadn't even started on the cardboard boxes, he resolved to try harder in the afternoon. He glanced around the office, a radio would be nice, he thought, I can't see Mr Flitch going for that, though, look at that, one o'clock already, and time for lunch.

He wound himself down the staircase, pulled open the heavy front door and stepped out into the street. A sunny day, it was definitely getting warmer. Two girls walked past, both in short skirts and skimpy tops, Johnson fancied that one of them smiled at him, but later he couldn't remember if it had been the leggy one or the busty one. Must do something about my sex life, he decided, like involve someone else in it. Still, to do that,

I need an income and prospects and all of the things that'll make me attractive to women, I'll be cool and dynamic, sensitive and masterful, and an irresistible prospect. Now, for the teabags.

Johnson wandered around for a bit, ignoring the welcoming pub signs which seemed to occupy every other building, he had decided to give up lunchtime drinking. He bought a sandwich in a plastic wrapper, a bottle of fizzy water, some chocolate, ten Rothmans and fifty finest PG Tips.

Back at his desk, the sandwich turned out to be filled with something yellow and slippery that the manufacturer had found in the factory after running out of cheese. He hoped the pickle was genuine. He placed two teabags carefully on Mr Flitch's desk, glugged the rest of the water and unwrapped the cigarettes. Mr Flitch hadn't actually *said* anything about smoking being prohibited, had he? But, being realistic, it surely wouldn't be permitted, would it? He wasn't tackling those stairs again. Johnson crossed to the window, opened it and lit up. He leant out, but the smoke just wafted back in, it didn't seem to matter in which direction he blew, the silver-grey clouds just floated back inside, and however far outside he held it, the wisps from the lit end of the cigarette weren't even making it to the open air, they flew back past his ears and gathered in a bluish haze above Mr Flitch's desk. This was no good. There was a wide ledge outside, which, as far as he could see, appeared to run along the whole side of the building. Four floors up, but it was wide enough, surely.

Cigarette clamped between his teeth, Johnson clambered out. The sill was quite low, so it wasn't difficult, although he took care not to pitch too far forward. He edged along a few feet, stopping a short distance from the next window, and sat, legs tucked up under his body as far as he could manage. Then he felt that sitting in this fashion, he might lose his balance, so he unfurled his legs and dangled them over the ledge. He puffed away, happily. Five to two, he noted, better get back.

He continued to stack during the afternoon, he broke for tea at three but foreswore another smoke. From three-fifteen to four-forty-five the columns grew relentlessly, then Mr Flitch re-appeared.

"Good afternoon, Mr Johnson," he said, announcing his arrival.

"Hello, Mr Flitch."

Johnson was on his hands and knees, crawling about in his own personal Manhattan.

"Been busy, I see," observed Mr Flitch.

"Oh, yes. I replaced your teabags as well," Johnson gestured to Mr Flitch's desk.

"Good man, good man," Said Mr Flitch.

"There's a lot here, Mr Flitch. I'm not sure when I'll be finished. Haven't started on the boxes yet."

"Oh, yes, the boxes. Well, you must do the best you can. Anyway, it's that wonderful time of the day, thank goodness."

"Mr Flitch?"

"Time to depart, young man. Homes to go to, and all of that."

"Time to go?" Johnson asked.

"Five o'clock young man. Time we weren't here."

"Five is it? Already? Right. I'll get back to all of this in the morning then?" Johnson enquired.

"Absolutely. You've done well, by the look of it. Well done."

Johnson put on his jacket and Mr Flitch ushered him out of the door, they twisted their way down and at the front door Mr Flitch said, "Goodnight then Mr Johnson, and thank you."

"Yes, thanks, Mr Flitch. I'll get the milk in the morning then?"

"Good man. Goodnight."

Mr Flitch strode away, Johnson was going in the same direction, but he followed a good ten paces behind.

The following morning, Johnson arrived ten minutes before nine. Mr Flitch was at his desk. Johnson waved a carton of milk at him.

"Coffee?" asked Johnson.

"Oh dear, that's not semi-skimmed is it?" said Mr Flitch.

"Er, yes it is actually," Johnson replied.

"Oh, dear," said Mr Flitch, quite mournfully.

"I can always go and get something else," Johnson suggested.

"Full fat?"

"Of course," reassured Johnson.

"It's almost nine you know," Mr Flitch reminded him.

"I'll be quick," said Johnson.

"Be sure you are," said Mr Flitch.

"See you in a minute," said Johnson.

Johnson returned with full fat milk, and made coffee for Mr Flitch and tea for himself, the mugs were on their desks by eight-fifty-eight. Mr Flitch sipped hard, frequently and noisily at his coffee.

"Right, Mr Johnson, I'm afraid I've got more meetings today."

"Oh."

"So, once again, you're going to be on your own for a while."

"OK."

"So, you know, just carry on. Plenty to be getting on with, eh?"

"Absolutely."

"Carry on sorting, eh?"

"Right," said Johnson.

Mr Flitch put his mug down, bade Johnson a cheerio, and was gone.

Johnson carried on sorting. He was so engrossed in his boxes that he missed his ten-thirty break, he resolved not to miss lunch, and set his phone to go off at twelve-fifty. That way, he said to himself, I'll have ten minutes to finish up.

He got the bleeped reminder and set off down the stairs at one. Newspaper, bottle of water, another ten cigarettes, but he passed on the ersatz sandwich. There didn't seem to be many more options around here. Should make my own, he thought, just a question of getting organised. Fresh, crusty bread, butter, ham carved off the bone, organic cheese, all I have to do is call in at the deli counter. Maybe I'll go shopping tonight.

Johnson wandered up a couple of side streets. The Windmill. A pub on the corner of a terraced block. Johnson walked in. Dark greenish and reddish patterned carpet, low tables and red velour-style bench seating, the nicotine stains had done an efficient dye job on the net curtains and it was hard to tell whether the ceiling had once been white or had been painted that baccy-brown colour. A chubby, mostly bald man in late middle-age who Johnson took to be the landlord greeted him with an 'afternoon, sir' and a 'what'll it be?'

The man squirted Johnson's soda water into a tumbler holding a splash of lime juice and ice. The landlord wore navy suit trousers, a white shirt picked out with navy and yellow stripes, sleeves rolled up, half-moon spectacles were perched precariously on the end of his nose.

"Any food at all?" enquired Johnson.

"Rolls," said the landlord, he pointed behind the bar at a plastic tray with a transparent lid which housed a haphazard collection of slightly filled bread rolls.

"What have you got?" asked Johnson.

"Cheese, cheese and ham, cheese and tomato, ham and tomato, cheese and pickle, ham and pickle," said the landlord, quickly, as he placed Johnson's drink in front of him.

"OK, and a, er, let's see, er, ham and tomato please."

"Right," the landlord lifted the lid and picked up a roll. He pulled it apart with his fingers.

"No, that's cheese and pickle."

He put the cheese and pickle to one side and resumed the search.

"No, ham and pickle. No, cheese and tomato. What was it again?"

"Ham and tomato, please," requested Johnson.

There were more rolls on the counter now than there were on the tray. The landlord inserted his finger in his ear and waggled it around vigorously.

"Ham and tomato, is it?"

"I think I've changed my mind," said Johnson.

"What's that?" The landlord's ears were still only operating at fifty percent capacity, as were his hands.

"Just a packet of crisps, please."

"No roll now?"

"No roll," Johnson confirmed.

"Crisps, is it?"

"Cheese and onion," said Johnson.

The landlord bent down and retrieved a bag from under the counter. He tossed it towards Johnson.

"There you go, sir," he said.

Johnson thanked him, he took a seat on a low stool at one of the tables and looked around. There were a couple of older suited types reading newspapers, and a small group in what his father used to call working clothes. Johnson assumed theirs was the ladder-adorned van which was parked outside. A woman of similar age to the landlord sat at the end of the bar, ashtray and glass of wine at her elbow, the landlord wandered over to her and spoke.

"Might have to have a bit of a rethink on the rolls, love, we've hardly sold one all week," he reported.

Johnson accompanied his crisps and water with two cigarettes, and on his way out he placed his empty glass on the bar and exchanged goodbyes with the landlord and his wife.

"See you again, sir," said the landlord, hopefully.

"I think you will," Johnson replied, "I think you will. Thank you."

Apart a brief interlude on the window ledge with a cup of tea and cigarette, the afternoon was uneventful. When Mr Flitch returned at four-thirty or so, Johnson's paper empire had risen to new and impressive heights.

"You've done well, Mr Johnson," announced Mr Flitch.

"Thank you, I've nearly finished." Johnson replied.

"I can see it's time to entrust you with this," said Mr Flitch.

Johnson was intrigued.

Mr Flitch opened a desk drawer and pulled out an ancient date-stamp and an ink pad.

"You see, you can change the date by turning these wheels at the side, you see?" said Mr Flitch.

"I see," said Johnson, "I have a horrible feeling about this."

"Now then, Mr Johnson, the thing is that we have to confirm the time of receipt of all of the documents that we take delivery of in this office and the way that we do that is…?"

Johnson blinked.

"Is..?" Mr Flitch persisted.

"We stamp the date on them?" ventured Johnson.

"We stamp the date on each one. Although, more correctly," Mr Flitch laughed for the first time that week, though he soon composed himself, "More correctly, Mr

64

Johnson, you stamp the date on each one."

"OK," agreed Johnson.

"Although, when I say each one, I don't want to mislead you."

Johnson brightened for a moment.

"Ha, ha," He was in a good mood this afternoon, thought Johnson, "When I say you are to stamp each one, I mean you are to stamp each page of each one, of course. If they're in triplicate, you stamp three times, d'you see?"

Johnson visualised his sickly bank statement and spoke positively.

"I see, Mr Flitch," he said, "In fact, I could finish the sorting tonight and start stamping first thing if you'd like?" he suggested.

"No, no, Johnson. No need for that. It's that wonderful time of the day, isn't it?"

"So it is," said Johnson.

"So let's away then, young man," announced Mr Flitch, "Let's away."

When Johnson arrived home he realised that he hadn't seen Tim since the weekend, although that wasn't unusual, and JeffandAnna were out. He mooched about the flat. He switched the TV on, but lowered the volume, and listened to some music while gazing at the screen trying to guess what was going on and where it was happening. He cooked some pasta, tossing in some slices of leftover sausage and most of a jar of ready-made-genuine-Italian-tomato-sauce, he checked the label. Made in Dagenham. In the absence of parmesan he grated cheddar over the top, liberated the remains of a bottle of wine which sat on the counter top with cling-film wrapped around the neck and over the mouth. He turned up the volume on the TV for the news and ate from a tray on his lap. At ten-thirty he went to bed in the empty flat and tried not to think about the extravaganza of date-stamping excitement which awaited him tomorrow.

The day followed the normal pattern. Johnson arrived early and by the time Mr Flitch arrived he had finished sorting the rest of the documents. He made tea and coffee. Mr Flitch announced that he would absent at meetings for a good part of the day and Johnson was to set to work on the stamping of the papers. Mr Flitch rummaged in his desk drawers for a few moments, taking things out, putting other things back, the things he took out he placed in his briefcase. He set the briefcase on his desk.

"Back in a moment," said Mr Flitch.

Johnson nodded, sipped his tea and looked at the briefcase. It was a battered, but solid piece of luggage. Shiny black in places, scuffed bare in others, particularly on the edges where the brass protective runners had become detached. Johnson noticed the monogrammed gold lettering, J.J.F. Wonder what his name is? Johnson pondered. Jimmy James? Probably not. Jackie Jackson? Wouldn't think so. Jeremiah Johnson? Wouldn't rule it out, he decided. Mr Flitch returned, snatched up his briefcase, and with barely a murmur was gone.

Johnson stamped, building up a rhythm, maintaining it for a while, then occasionally dropping into what he imagined was a jazz-drumming pattern. He kept one eye on the clock. He broke at ten-thirty and took tea and cigarettes on the ledge. For the rest of the morning he was the engine room for Elvis, Miles Davis, Led Zeppelin and Frank Sinatra. At twelve-thirty he walked to The Windmill.

"Lime and soda?" asked the landlord and Johnson was so impressed he almost concurred.

"No, Pint of bitter, please," Johnson requested.

"Drinking today then?" asked the landlord as he pulled Johnson's pint.

"Tough morning," confirmed Johnson.

"Wise choice then," said the landlord.

"And a roll, please."

Sod it.

"What would you like?" The landlord was approaching the tray of food, rolling up his sleeves.

"Could you bring them over?" Asked Johnson.

"Bring them over?"

"Over here."

"Don't see why not," The landlord shrugged. He set the tray down and lifted the lid.

Johnson took the nearest one.

"Thanks," Johnson said, "You're busy in here today,"

"Got a few in sir, can't complain. Table there in the corner's free. Your usual table, sir?" The landlord said, "Your usual table's free, sir," He laughed.

"Thank you, my man," said Johnson, joining in. They exchanged a smile and a nod, and Johnson settled at the corner table.

Johnson hadn't brought a newspaper with him, so he looked around the bar as he drank his beer and ate his ham and cheese and tomato and pickle roll, it's got a whiff of salmon as well, he thought. Tired of looking around the bar, and worried that he'd made eye-contact once too often with the scowling arrangement of singlet, muscles, body hair, and tattoos which surrounded a roll-up, he turned his gaze to the window and the fascinating brickwork of the opposite building which was broken up only by the occasional passer-by.

"Excuse me? 'Scuse me?"

Johnson stirred.

"Excuse us?" The two girls who he'd seen outside the office were standing over him. He knew it was them as soon as his involuntary glance had lingered a little too long on one's legs and then switched to the other's breasts. He cursed his cock.

"Sorry," he said.

"What for?" laughed one of them, knowingly. Johnson wasn't sure which one spoke, as his eyes were dancing around the bar, desperate not to alight on a female body part. He could feel the blood rushing up from his collar and filling his head. His red head.

"Er, sorry, I didn't hear you. Looking out of the window. Miles away."

"He didn't hear us, Nicky," said the other.

"Had a good look though," giggled Nicky, but quietly.

"Are these seats taken?" asked the other one.

"No, help yourself," Johnson offered.

"Thanks. Come on, Sue, we'll sit here with this gentleman," said Nicky.

"Alright," Sue agreed.

Well, gentleman, am I? Thought Johnson, and I know their names already. That must count as a good start.

Sue and Nicky chatted away for a good few minutes, someone in their office was getting married, was it one of them? But Johnson couldn't see any tell-tale engagement rings on their fingers. Could this be another good sign? Someone else was having a secret affair with someone, but it seemed that everybody else knew about it. The coffee machine was still broken.

Johnson tutted. He got two questioning looks. At least they weren't ignoring him.

"Sorry, couldn't help overhearing. No coffee, eh?" Even by Johnson's standards, he had to admit that this was a poor opening gambit.

"That's right, no coffee," said Nicky.

"Nightmare," agreed Sue.

"How about another glass of wine each then?" Johnson jumped in with both feet.

"Oh, we're OK," said Nicky.

"Thanks anyway," said Sue.

"Oh, come on. I just couldn't bear to think of you back at work this afternoon with everyone else getting married and having affairs and such a wonderful time and you two won't even be able to console yourselves with a coffee."

"Overheard quite a bit didn't you?" said Nicky.

"Quite a bit," smiled Johnson.

"Wine would be lovely," said Sue.

"Large ones," said Nicky.

Johnson went to the bar and ordered a pint and two glasses of wine. He checked them out in the reflection of the mirror which ran along the rear of the serving area. Sue had long, slim legs, shoulder-length dark blonde hair, blue eyes and was tall and trim. Nicky was smaller, her dark brown hair parted on the side, with a long fringe which she pushed away from her eyes every few moments. Johnson found himself looking forward to the next time she did it.

"You work round here then?" asked Sue.

"Just around the corner," confirmed Johnson.

"Saw you yesterday," said Nicky.

"Thought I recognised you" said Johnson. He was trying to slow his heart rate with surreptitious deep breathing.

"You don't work with that funny old bloke do you?" asked Sue.

"Funny old bloke?" asked Johnson.

"The undertaker," said Nicky.

"In that funny old building," said Sue.

"Yes, I do," said Johnson.

"Government isn't it?" asked Nicky.

"Yes. I'm just a temp, though. Not there for long, I don't think. Don't think I could stand it."

"Student, are you?" asked Nicky.

"Well, I was. Graduated. Looking round now, you know, for the right thing to come along."

"He should come and work with us, shouldn't he Nicky?"

"That'd be nice," answered Nicky, but she wasn't looking at Sue.

"So, where do you work?" Johnson asked.

"Cartwright Blott Spectre, but I'm leaving for another agency soon," Sue answered.

"Advertising," said Nicky.

"But, what would I do?" asked Johnson.

"Oh, they're always looking for people," said Sue.

"I could ask around if you like," offered Nicky.

"Well, that's really kind of you," said Johnson, "I'm not sure they'd be interested though, given what I'm doing at the moment."

"Graduate though, aren't you? Always need smart people at ASP," said Nicky, encouragingly.

"Good looking boy too," said Sue, pointedly, "isn't he, Nicky?"

"Look," said Johnson, "If you could ask around, maybe I could give you a ring in a couple of days...?" He left the question hanging.

"Here's my number," said Nicky, passing him a card, "Give me a call next week."

"Next week?" said Johnson.

"Next week," said Nicky, firmly.

"We'd better go, Nix," said Sue.

Johnson stood as they got up to leave.

"Manners too," observed Sue.

Nicky smiled at Johnson. He held out his hand, she shook it.

"Thank you," he said.

"Quite a catch," said Sue.

"I'll call you," said Johnson, as they left.

"Another drink, sir?" said the landlord, addressing the lone Johnson.

"No, thanks. I'd better...," Johnson checked his watch. Shit. Forty-five minutes late,

69

"…be off."

"See you tomorrow, sir?" called the landlord.

"Maybe," yelled Johnson, over his shoulder.

He was quite out of breath after a brisk jog-trot back to the office and a run up the stairs. Panting, he flung open the office door, as usual the room was deserted.

As Johnson stamped with vigour, he thought about Cartwright Blott Spectre and possibilities, about Nicky and possibilities, about getting this bloody job finished and moving on.

He continued in this vein for the rest of the week. Mr Flitch kept to his usual timetable, Johnson saw him for a just few minutes, morning and afternoon. He visited The Windmill for lunch every day, but didn't see Nicky or Sue in there. He took to calling in on the way home and, although he got to know the landlord and landlady, Roy and Vera, he didn't see the girls again.

On Friday morning, he addressed Mr Flitch.

"I've almost finished the stamping, Mr Flitch."

"Have you? Excellent, excellent," said Mr Flitch, who made a lame attempt at clapping his hands together with enthusiasm.

"I'll be finished this morning, I think," said Johnson.

"Good, good," said Mr Flitch, glancing at his watch and getting to his feet.

"So, I'll need something else to do."

"You just, er, hold the fort Johnson. That's it, just hold the fort for now," Mr Flitch had picked up his briefcase and was edging towards the door.

"You see, these piles here are completed. Sorted and stamped, whereas the few I have here still need to be stamped," reported Johnson.

"Good, good. I'll have them picked up."

"Picked up?" Johnson enquired.

"You know, collected."

"Collected?" Johnson asked.

"Yes, Johnson, collected. For processing. They will be processed elsewhere."

"But where?" Johnson felt that, in a way, he would miss his piles of documents.

"At another department, Johnson," said Mr Flitch, a touch impatiently, Johnson thought.

"You're the boss," said Johnson.

"Indeed I am. So you hold the fort. I may not be back at all today, but I feel I can trust you Johnson."

"Thank you," said Johnson.

"So, I'll arrange to have these papers collected, might be today, so be on your toes, Johnson, OK?"

"Certainly, Mr Flitch."

Mr Flitch said goodbye and wished Johnson a nice weekend. Certainly won't be back then, Johnson decided. He gave it ten minutes and switched on Mr Flitch's PC. Internet, search, Cartwright Blott Spectre.

They certainly looked to be a professional outfit. Johnson reckoned the website would have been even more impressive, but he wasn't able to see the whole show as Mr Flitch didn't have the software. Click here to install FlashSoftPlayer, or something. Better not. Advertising. Plenty of big name clients. Offices look nice. Lots of smiling faces too. Johnson pulled Nicky's card from his wallet. Nicola, funny he didn't think of her as a Nicola. Nicky, yes, that sounded right. Nicky, yes, he said aloud, Oh yes Nicky. He looked at the card for the around the hundredth time that week. Nicola Pennywell, Key Account Manager, it said in bold, business-like script, all wrapped around with a fancy logo, body of the snake curled across the top and down the sides of the card, enclosing everything within. Sexual sign isn't it, the snake? She had been quite firm about him not calling her before next week. There was a mobile number on the card. He picked up Mr Flitch's phone, it smelled of coal tar soap and something else which Johnson couldn't quite identify, and dialled Nicky's mobile number. Chest banging away, he lit a cigarette.

"Hi, this is Nicky…"

"Bloody voicemail, should've known," Johnson hissed.

"Hello?"

Oh shit, Johnson observed silently.

"Hi, Nicky. It's Johnson."

There was a pause.

"Oh, hi. I thought we were going to speak next week? I'm not in the office today,

71

you see."

"You don't mind me calling then?" Johnson asked.

There was a male voice in the background, Johnson fancied he heard a few words: who is it? Hurry up. Christ. I thought we were going out. That sort of thing.

"See you downstairs, I'll just finish up this call. Well, work darling, you know," Johnson could hear Nicky making her excuses.

"Sorry, I didn't mean to…" Johnson apologised.

"Sorry? I said don't ring me until next week, didn't I?" said Nicky.

"You're with someone. I'm sorry, I just thought…"

"Bad timing, Johnson, bad timing."

She hung up.

Bollocks, said Johnson. He brushed the ash he'd been flicking into a pile on the desk into his palm, crossed to the window and tossed it out with the butt. He stood gazing out across the rooftops for a while, but he was jolted back to reality by the door opening. Two burly men in overalls filled the door frame.

"Collection?" said one, offering Johnson a sheet of paper.

"Oh, you've come for these documents, have you?" asked Johnson, his arm described a wide arc covering most of the room.

"That's right, sir."

They proceeded to clear the office. It took a lot of trips, even with a trolley which they piled high with tumbling paper. Johnson could hear it bouncing down the stairs.

For variety, he stole a spoonful of Mr Flitch's coffee and put his feet up. Hold the fort? The phone never rings, there's nothing to do. He walked around some of the rest of the building, tried a few doors, all were locked. Haven't even got a paper. Eleven-fifteen.

At eleven-twenty-five he was sitting in The Windmill at his favourite table. Pint at his elbow, newspaper spread out, chatting idly to Roy and Vera. Shortly after noon they were busied by the lunchtime crowd and Johnson spent a lazy couple of hours drinking beer and frowning over the cryptic crossword. Roy had lent him a pen, won't be needing it for the food orders, said Roy.

Johnson considered the disaster that the morning had been. Losing a potential girlfriend and the chance of a glittering career in advertising, and only through impatience. He regarded the dregs of his ale morosely.

"Seen JJ today?" said a voice somewhere over near the bar.

"Mr F?" said Roy.

"Yeah."

"He was in the other bar earlier. Went to the bookies, I think," Said Roy.

"Or the bird's."

"No, I think she blew him out."

Johnson wandered up to the bar.

"Excuse me, Roy?" he said.

"Another one, sir? You're pushing the boat out today, I must say."

"No I won't thanks, well, just a half, then."

"Just the half, sir? Coming up," said Roy.

"Roy?"

"Sir?"

"Who is Mr F?"

"Ah, now sir, you put me in a difficult position. Never betray a confidence, that's the rule for us landlords, and journalists too, I believe. The fourth estate. Or are they the fifth? Never could remember."

"JJF? Mr Flitch, isn't it?"

"Sir?"

"Tall, gaunt, old-fashioned, like an undertaker?"

"That's him," said Roy.

"He's my boss, only I haven't seen much of him this week."

Roy laughed.

"Well, you wouldn't sir would you? Being as you're not in the pub game, or the bookmaking game, or the game game. If you know what I mean?" Roy seemed to have forgotten his vow of silence.

"So, he's, excuse me Roy, but he's on the piss or gambling or whatever, all day every day?"

"Pretty much, sir."

"While I'm doing all the work?"

"Looks like that, sir," agreed Roy.

"Well, fuck that," said Johnson, "Can I have a bottle of red wine please Roy?"

Roy set a bottle on the bar.

"Cork out, please," Johnson requested.

"Cork out, sir."

Johnson drained his beer and snatched up his wine, Roy had thoughtfully provided a Tesco carrier bag, and headed back to the office.

He entered all sorts of disgusting requests into Mr Flitch's search engine and saved quite a few revolting pictures in a folder he called 'Flitch's Filthy Favourites'. Wearying of handcuffs and chains, rubber and plastic, farm animals and scenes from public lavatories, Johnson took his wine and cigarettes out onto the ledge.

Why does it always rain on me, he wondered, as it started raining. He swigged wine from the bottle and chain-smoked. Bastards, the bloody lot of them. Bosses, prospective bosses, opportunities, women. Sod the lot of it. He had finished the wine.

Johnson shifted himself along the ledge, the rain was coming down harder now, he held tight onto the bottle with one hand, and pulled himself along with the other, as his buttocks did a shifting walk. He reached the window, but as he half-turned to pull himself in, as he'd done expertly all week, he slipped a little. Whether it was holding the wine, whether it was the drink he had consumed, maybe it was the rain, whatever it was he slipped, he dropped the empty bottle which he heard shatter a few seconds later. He grabbed hopelessly at the window sill, his hands slipped from the greasy surface and he tumbled downwards.

Oh dear, thought Johnson, as he fell, what a waste.

Johnson couldn't quite comprehend what had happened. He had fallen some distance, but he was alright, he seemed unhurt. He had closed his eyes on the way down, and had some vague feeling of landing on something reasonably soft, while all the time expecting to encounter a much harder surface very soon indeed.

Eventually Johnson felt brave enough to open his eyes. He looked about himself. He was still some distance from ground level. He was in rubbish skip. He laughed. He cried. And when he saw that he had landed in a skip-full of triplicate, date-stamped, but no longer sorted, government forms he cried some more.

74

Interview Phase III

"*So*, how did that make you feel?" I asked.

"What's this, some sort of counsellor now are you?" Johnson shot back.

"What do you mean?" I persisted.

"Come off it," said Johnson, "Asking me 'how did that make you feel', with your head tilted to one side and that stupid concerned look on your face."

"I'm just trying to understand, Johnson."

"Don't tell me, you feel my pain."

"Just building up a picture, Johnson," I said, quietly, attempting to remove some heat from the situation.

"Alright. Fair enough, but any more of that floppy-haired, moist-eyed, soft-voiced, worried-about-you bollocks and I'm resigning." Johnson seemed firm on this point.

"Resigning? Again?" I ventured.

The ceiling fan and the air-con had done a good job of dispersing the cigarette smoke, but there were still some pockets of smoke-puffs hanging around the ceiling. Although Johnson had smoked steadily throughout and I'd almost joined in with one or two, we'd hardly touched the beer during Johnson's run-through of the civil service episode, but now Johnson popped the cap from a bottle and passed it over to me. The label slipped off in my hand, stripped away the by condensation, I squeezed a little water out of it and onto the carpet, screwed it up and dumped it into the ashtray. Johnson huffed a little.

"Fag ends and matches only," he said, picking out the crumpled scrap of soggy paper which he flicked aimlessly over his shoulder.

"Getting a bit fussy, aren't we?" I observed.

"Thin end of the wedge," said Johnson, "Gotta be careful or before you know it you've got chewing gum in there."

"Chewing gum?"

"And that's not good," said Johnson.

I thought better of saying anything, and restricted myself to an affable nod.

"So, I was in this skip," said Johnson, surprising me, as so far he'd needed prompting.

I nodded.

"Until I got kicked out," said Johnson.

"You got kicked out of a skip?"

"Ah, it was already occupied, you see."

"Occupied?"

"Turns out it was this old boy's day room. Seems he used to doss down in there for a couple of hours in the afternoon."

"So, he was sleeping and...?"

"Got something of a shock, yeah, with the aerial bombardment, and all," said Johnson coolly.

"What happened?"

"Old bastard kicked me out."

"Kicked you out?"

"Yeah, I was told in the most certain of terms that it was already taken and was then summarily invited to fuck off out of it. Yep, those were his exact words."

"And after you'd de-skipped?" I asked.

"I went looking for Flitch. J.J.F."

"Did you ever find out?"

"Jayston Jonathan Flitch."

"Ah," I said, "Did you find him?"

"Oh, yes. In The Windmill. With two hookers."

"In the pub?"

"Not in the bar, as such. More sort of upstairs."

"Upstairs bar?"

"Upstairs in bed."

"In bed?"

"Well, strictly speaking, on it, I suppose."

"Busy?"

"Very much so."

"So, what happened next?" I asked.

"There's champagne, cognac, and cocaine on the bedside table."

"Bit of a dark horse wasn't he?"

"So he was," said Johnson, resignedly.

He stood, carried the ashtray to a waste bin and emptied it. He surprised me by stopping on the way to collect the screwed up beer bottle label from the floor. He rubbed it between his fingers before dropping it into the bin. He returned to his chair, lit another cigarette and continued.

"He was surprised to see me, and I was, shall we say, not happy. I asked the girls to leave, which they did, I meant no trouble on that score, not to them. He had a huge hard-on, but that didn't last long, it waved around for a bit, pointing at me, but he was the incredible shrinking man long before I gave him his trousers back. Bit surreal though, never had a cock pointed at me before."

"A loaded cock." I said.

"Loaded," agreed Johnson, allowing himself a relaxed grin.

"And after you'd disarmed him?"

"Only by my presence."

"Of course, but after that?" I asked.

"Poured myself a brandy. Sat down for a chat."

"What about the coke?" I asked.

"Flushed it down the toilet."

"Did you?" I laughed.

"Sure, told him that after I'd beaten him up that the police might become involved and I didn't want to complicate things."

"Did you beat him up?"

"No. I just wanted to know what had gone on, I needed to press home my advantage so the threat was handy to have up my sleeve." Johnson smiled and flicked a good half-inch of ash from his cigarette. He took a long pull of beer, drained the bottle and popped open another. He offered it to me, I shook my head.

"So, what had happened?" I asked.

"Oh, you know."

"I don't, Johnson."

"Money in the budget for staff. Use it or lose it. If he doesn't use it he might get a visit from someone who's full of awkward questions, like, who the chuff are you? Get me in to do something, doesn't matter what, government pays. He's on a cut from the agency as well."

"Was he?"

"What?" asked Johnson.

"On a cut."

"Never proved it, but I'm pretty sure. It was a backwater anyway, forgotten department, no phone calls, no visitors, he had a budget, but no work to do. Forgotten man. Forgotten man who found a way to make a few quid."

"And got into booze and drugs and sex because of the circumstances?" I suggested.

"Don't think so," Said Johnson, confidently, "I think he was always like that, he was just able to push the boat out and take the piss. And, boy, did he take the piss."

"Not a case of, too much time, too much money and too much freedom? We could all understand that couldn't we?" I said.

"No way," said Johnson, firmly, "A man in a position of trust abused that trust and the faith shown in him, he stole taxpayers money, both literally and metaphorically. Bad man. Wouldn't know how to go about proving it, but I think he was selling on information as well."

"What information?"

"Credit card numbers, dates of birth, names and addresses, loads of personal stuff."

"Why would you think that?" I pressed.

"The man had an expensive lifestyle to maintain."

"What did you do, after you'd spoken to him?"

"I left."

"Just left?"

"Well, I got him to sign my time sheet."

"You what?"

"Only for hours done, you understand. For what I was owed."

"Shame about Nicky, wasn't it?" I said.

"Ah, well," said Johnson, "I was upset about the phone call, of course, I admit that, but as it turned out there was more to come from Nicky. Quite a lot more, actually."

Partnerships

Johnson left Mr Flitch in the room upstairs at The Windmill with instructions not to come out for half an hour. He wanted to say goodbye to Roy and Vera.

"I didn't want to cause any trouble, you know, Roy? Vera? You do understand that?"

The three of them were sitting at Johnson's usual table and Johnson had insisted they have a drink with him.

"You're obviously upset, son," said Roy, sipping his scotch and soda..

"He looks upset," said Vera. She regarded him from over the rim of her spritzer glass.

"I don't like being taken for a ride, that's all." said Johnson, cradling a mood-calming cognac, "I didn't want to spoil things for you, you know, make things difficult."

"That's alright, we understand. He was a pain in the arse anyway. Either flat-out drunk or bouncing off the walls. Haven't a clue what all that was about, up one minute down the next," said Roy.

"But, you do know what he's been up to, in your pub?"

"He rents a room, son. He likes the ladies, and quite honestly we need the money."

"You know he's been taking drugs up there?"

"That, I didn't know. Explains a lot though. And if I had known, well, we wouldn't be sitting here now. He'd have been long gone. That's my licence we're talking about." said Roy.

"Alright, as long as you understand." said Johnson, feeling guilty, despite also feeling that he'd done the right thing.

"Your two girls were in earlier," said Vera, anxious to change the subject.

"My two girls?" Johnson asked.

"The ones you had lunch with the other day. They were down here when you were upstairs. They only had the one," Vera reported.

"I don't suppose…," Johnson said quietly, and almost to himself.

"No, they didn't ask after you, son. Sorry," said Roy.

"I'd better be going," said Johnson.

"Take care," said Vera.

"He'll be down in a minute, Mr F.," said Johnson.

"I'll get rid of him," said Roy.

"Make sure he pays you what he owes you. If he doesn't, just let me know."

Johnson caught a bus, but got off several stops early and walked the rest of the way home. He was glad of the rain, glad he didn't possess an umbrella, glad his raincoat was screwed up in a ball at the bottom of his wardrobe. He saw the people walking along with heads bowed, huddled and hunched, trying to protect themselves against a little water, as he stopped to cross the road he offered his face to the muddy clouds, tried to catch some evasive raindrops in his mouth. Not worried about the job, he thought, I'll get another one, and on Monday, too. But, what a shame about Nicky. What a bloody shame. When he reached his front door, he had a cigarette cupped in his hand, guarding it from the weather. He scrabbled in his pocket for his keys. Must have fallen out in the skip, he thought. He rapped on the door.

"Ah, soaking wet, hours late, bit unsteady on the feet, and looking a little pissed off. I'd say you've either been paid and pissed it away already or you've been fired again," said Tim in greeting.

"I've never been fired," Johnson corrected.

"My mistake," said Tim, as they retreated inside.

"I resigned from Wink and Kinker."

"Apologies."

"And now I've resigned from the civil service."

"You don't hang about do you?" said Tim, "What's the plan then? Go through the career in dog years?"

"I had good reasons," protested Johnson.

"You can tell me all about it, well, edited highlights anyway, over a drink and a hot meal."

"Drink?" asked Johnson.

"You look like you could either do with no more or another dozen. Anyway, we're eating as well."

"Eating?"

80

"We're going out with JeffandAnna."

"We are?"

"They've got news." reported Tim.

The four of them gathered around a table in the local curry house.

"I'm moving out," said Jeff.

"OK," said Johnson.

"Sorry to hear that, Jeff," said Tim, looking pointedly at Johnson.

"Of course, sorry to hear that, goes without saying," said Johnson.

"We're getting our own place," said Anna.

"Great," said Johnson.

"After we get married," said Jeff.

"That's brilliant news," said Johnson, "Congratulations. When's the happy day?"

"Tomorrow," said Jeff, "And we'd like you to be best man."

"Told you they had news," said Tim, "Right, Cobra beers all round is it? Now then, we'll have plain and spicy poppadoms, I reckon, what does everybody else think?"

Some food arrived, and they chewed away over the eve of wedding feast.

"So, when are you moving out then?" asked Johnson.

"Tomorrow," said Jeff, he was positively glowing.

"Right, I mean, erm," said Johnson, this was difficult. Unemployed, and losing a tenant all in the same day.

"I'll pay you a month in lieu, mate, and divide the bills up, of course. Y'know, take a view on it," offered Jeff.

"Yeah, fine, of course," Johnson crammed a handful of poppadom into his mouth and softened it down with a mouthful of beer.

The main dishes arrived and sparked the usual rearranging of the contents of the table-top. Everything was finally squeezed in, and Johnson, as usual, had a dish of pilau rice perched on the table edge and dangerously close to his left elbow. He picked at his food, left elbow tucked into his ribs.

"Bit sudden this isn't it?" he ventured.

"We've been together for a long time, you know," said Anna, rather too quickly.

"Pregnant?" enquired Tim, glancing towards Anna's belly.

"No, I'm not," she protested.

81

"Just seems sudden," reiterated Johnson.

"Sudden like what?" asked Anna.

"You might think it's sudden, but..." said Jeff.

"What's sudden anyway? Soulmates shouldn't leave it too late, and we're soulmates aren't we darling?" said Anna.

"No offence, "said Tim, "But would you excuse me while I repair to the gents and throw up my dinner while it's still hot?"

"Take no notice, darling," advised Jeff.

"Well...," Anna seethed, "It's supposed to be the happiest day of our lives and we thought that we'd involve our two best friends in it, and all they can do..."

"Anna..." interrupted Tim, or tried to.

"..is to make a big joke of it, just like always..."

"Anna..." tried Jeff.

"...I don't know why we bothered..."

"I just meant that being told the day before was a bit sudden, you know?" said Johnson.

But Anna had gone.

"Where's Anna gone?" asked Tim, looking up from his biryani.

"Ladies," said Jeff.

"You going after her?" asked Tim.

"No, best not to," said Jeff's voice of experience.

"Keep an eye out then?" suggested Tim.

"An eye out?" queried Jeff.

"Case she escapes." said Tim, cramming a quarter of a naan bread into a mouth that was already stuffed with chicken and rice.

"I didn't mean anything," said Johnson. He didn't feel that today was going very well.

"I know, mate," reassured Jeff, "I know."

"Why tell us so late though?"

"Thought it would be fun. A surprise, you know," said Jeff.

"But I might have been busy tomorrow," suggested Johnson.

"Yeah, OK," said Tim, glancing at Jeff.

"What's that supposed to mean?"

"What?" asked Tim.

"Sharp intake of breath, quick 'yeah OK', knowing look, and then put your head straight back into your dinner. That's what."

"Well, your diary hasn't exactly been overflowing lately has it?" Tim pointed out.

"I don't know about that," Johnson protested.

"OK. When's the last time you went out on a Saturday night?"

"Last Saturday, actually."

"Tesco's doesn't count." said Tim.

Jeff's eyes hadn't left the door of the ladies.

"Perhaps she climbed out the window," Tim suggested.

"What do you want me to do tomorrow then?" asked Johnson.

"Be there to support me."

"OK."

"Carry the rings."

"Right."

"Make a speech."

"A speech?"

"You know, Johnson," interjected Tim, "the best man makes a speech. It's kind of traditional."

"But I haven't got anything prepared," Johnson protested. He searched the empty Cobra bottles, looking for one that Tim hadn't demolished.

"Just make it so heartfelt that we weep a few touching tears and so gut-bustingly funny that we all piss ourselves laughing and you'll have done your job," advised Tim.

"Oh, thanks for the advice," said Johnson, "it was well-meant and totally useless."

"Pleasure," grinned Tim. He had a few lentils on his chin.

Anna had returned unnoticed to the table and was sitting on Jeff's knee, arms around each others' shoulders. She was distractedly kneading his crotch with her other hand.

"Can't you wait for twenty-four hours, you randy tart?" suggested Tim.

"I think he's talking to you," said Anna to Jeff.

The table was cleared. Coffees and cognacs and, for Tim, more beers arrived.

"The one time I would have expected someone to be buying champagne is tonight, yet you, who drinks it like Lucozade, isn't playing." Johnson observed.

"Champagne and curry?" Tim queried, "Are you out of your mind?"

"Getting there, I think," said Johnson.

"Any thoughts on the speech?" asked Jeff.

"Well, not yet," Johnson admitted.

"Give you a hand if you like," offered Tim.

"Alright, thanks," Johnson said, "I mean, I've never done this before. I know it should include something embarrassing about him," He gestured at Jeff, whose eyes were now quite alarmingly narrowed.

"You'd better pack it in dear," advised Tim, "Or he won't be able to perform tomorrow night. Anyway, those are his best trousers. Be a shame if they ended up with a little map of Africa all down the front."

Anna repeated the silent mantra that had got her back from the ladies to the table, 'boys will be boys', and took a break from the kneading.

"That's it, a few naughty stories from the groom's past," said Tim.

"Not too naughty, thank you," said Anna.

"No, no, no. That thought shall perish and wither on the vine, dear Anna. Trust us." said Tim.

"Hmmm," said Anna.

"How long should I speak for, then?" asked Johnson.

"A few gags, wish them every health and happiness, and that's your lot. Ten minutes should do it."

"Oh. Alright," said Johnson. He had been hoping to get away with around forty seconds.

"Don't forget the toast."

"Toast?" asked Johnson. He hadn't been to a wedding since his father had hauled him out of some semi-distant relative's affair for charging around the room and wiping out the guests with his imaginary machine-gun. His incredibly realistic sound effects had been the tipping point.

"The toast. Here's how it goes. And finally, laydeeeeeeeeez aaaannnnddddd gennnnnelllllllmeeeeen...,"

"He's not commentating on the darts, Tim," said Anna.

"He's got to give it a bit of showmanship," Tim argued.

"Not at my wedding," said Anna, firmly.

"Nor mine," agreed Jeff.

"So, how many ladies and gentlemen will be there, then?" asked Johnson.

"Let's see," mused Tim, "Full Catholic Mass."

"Catholic Mass?" Johnson said, unsurely, "I don't know any of that standing up, sitting down, call and response stuff."

"I'll walk you through it," offered Jeff.

"Who's supporting who here, then?" Tim questioned.

"I didn't know you two were Catholics," said Johnson, calling for more cognac.

"Absolutely," JeffandAnna assured him.

"How many in the church, Jeff?" Tim enquired.

"Oooh, let's see. Three hundred."

"Three hundred?" squeaked Johnson.

"Then another, what, at the reception? Two hundred?" Tim was draining another bottle of Cobra.

"More like two-fifty," said Jeff, pouring refills from a fresh pot of coffee.

"So, five hundred and fifty in all, then," said Tim.

"You don't know that many people," said Johnson accusingly.

"Anna's got a big family," said Jeff.

"Loads of them," said Anna.

"Coming over from Ireland, Scotland, Wales," said Jeff.

"Where's the reception, then? The Albert Hall?" asked an increasingly desperate Johnson. He hadn't spoken in public since reading *Far From The Madding Crowd* to the class when he was fourteen. And he hadn't enjoyed that very much either. Now this, five hundred plus, listening to his own words? He wouldn't be able to blame the author this time.

"No, we're going to The Grey Horse," said Jeff.

"The pub?" queried Johnson.

"The pub," confirmed Tim.

"The pub on the corner which holds…Oh, I see," Johnson closed his eyes.

"Told you he'd fall for it," said Tim, beer in one hand, cognac in the other.

"Priceless," said Jeff.

"The man who gets embarrassed at the head of a queue," said Tim.

"You bastards," said Johnson, "You absolute bastards."

"Sorry, Johnson," Anna apologised.

"It'll just be the four of us, and Anna's sister, Kate, and Anna's mate, Rebecca."

"Told you he'd go for it," said Tim.

"Alright, Tim," warned Jeff, "Don't go on about it."

"It's OK," said Johnson, "I'm just relieved, really."

"Just a quiet do, you know." said Jeff.

"Just the six of us. Pagan wedding service, and afterwards in The Grey Horse."

"Pagan wedding, eh? Very good, shall we knock it on the head now?" said Johnson, sitting back and relaxed.

"No, that bit is actually true," Anna assured him.

"Pagan wedding?"

"Absolutely," said Jeff.

"Bring your own nuts and berries?" suggested Tim.

"It's not in the least bit like that," argued Jeff.

"Must get my smock back from the cleaners," Tim persisted.

"Tim," warned Anna.

"It got covered in woad at the last one I went to," said Tim.

"He'll have to stop for a drink shortly," said Anna.

"Things got out of hand when the Saxons turned up."

"Won't be long now," agreed Jeff, "There's still beer on the table."

"It's always the same, those Saxons are trouble, let me tell you."

"Shall we tell him?" suggested Anna.

"What, that it's a Pagan wedding and therefore has nothing whatsoever to do with the Saxons?" asked Jeff.

"What's the point?" asked Anna.

Jeff and Johnson agreed.

"We're not religious, so…" started Anna.

"…it seemed the best way, really." Jeff concluded.

"Where is this do, then?" asked Tim.

"In the garden at the town hall." said Jeff.

"As Pagan as it gets," stated Tim.

JeffandAnna smiled as one and Johnson started to fret about his speech.

"Great, that's all settled then," said Tim, "Now then, as it's your stag night and it's your hen night, I suggest we all repair somewhere and get, like, totally shit-faced, man."

Which they did.

They gathered in the kitchen in the baleful mid-morning and swapped gazes from hooded, bloodshot eyes.

"Bloody Mary's all round, is it?" suggested Tim, to a collective and suicidal howl.

"Got to get us back on our feet, big day ahead. What time's the do?" Tim was undaunted, he pulled a carton of tomato juice and a bottle of vodka from the fridge.

"Three," said Jeff.

"Great stuff. Better get cracking then."

"Need food," said Johnson, two words being all he could manage.

"Me too," Jeff agreed.

"Anna?" asked Tim.

"I'll grab some toast or something. Kate and Rebecca will be here soon. They're going to help me get ready."

"What is de rigeur for the modern Pagan?" asked Tim, "Surely you'll be leaving the hair in that attractive just-out-bed-style that's sooo hard to achieve without getting completely hammered and having next to no sleep?"

"Something like that, Tim," agreed Anna.

"Don't suppose we've got any celery salt?" Tim asked.

"Got some fresh limes," said Johnson. He was conscious of his speech, although it was only for a small crowd.

"Right. Ice, Tabasco, limes, I think we're ready to go. Kettle on for the lightweights, I hope I won't be counting you among their number, gentlemen. Johnson, get the grill on. Jeff, bacon, sausage, mushrooms, tomatoes, whatever, in the fridge. Fresh, crusty loaves in that paper bag on the side. Get the butter out as well. Eggs. Eggs are over there, Jeffrey, dozen free range. Oh, and there's black pudding too, for those that like their frothy blood fried up with bits of fat in it."

"You've been shopping." accused Johnson, edging towards the sink, just in case.

"Went out early. Couldn't sleep." said Tim.

"This is brilliant, Tim, thanks," said Jeff.

"Wedding breakfast, eh? Couldn't let my two mates go to the gallows without a feed, could I? Get four plates out, Johnson, boy, no make it six. Got guests coming haven't we? Right, must pay a quick visit to the facilities."

Tim strode off to the toilet.

"He's a good bloke isn't he? Underneath it all, I mean," whispered Jeff to Johnson.

"He is," agreed Johnson.

"Might have a crack at that Kate later, if I don't get too pissed. Always fancied tucking a bit under there," called Tim over his shoulder.

Some time later they gathered at the town hall. The men in suits, the women in dresses. A Pagan wedding, thought Johnson, what do you wear? Traditional wedding clothes, I suppose. Perhaps we're not ready to embrace the whole Pagan thing.

The woman conducting the service had no problem with that. She appeared to be dressed in a large potato sack. A large, smiling lady, with twinkling eyes and uncomfortable-looking sandals. Maybe they're vegetable fibre, if there is such a thing, at one with nature, Johnson imagined, must be nice, to be at one with something. Or someone.

Johnson and the rest were pleasantly surprised and rather taken with the service.

"Cycles of life," mused Johnson, quietly, "And mutual respect. Flowing freely."

"The womb of time," said Tim.

"The masculine, the feminine, the great forces," Johnson continued.

"The woooomb of time," said Tim.

"One too many drinks, eh?" observed Johnson.

"Feminine forces? Wombs? Flowing freely?" said Tim, "You don't have to be boozed to enjoy this stuff, Johnson."

Johnson hushed him, they were coming to the end of the service. Johnson, Kate and Rebecca took photographs. They moved on to The Grey Horse where they sat in boy/girl order around a large table in the pub's small restaurant.

Anna's sister, Kate was, if anything, tinier than she was. Her hair was an appreciably darker blond than Anna's, she had wide blue eyes, the same fine-boned features were present, but were slightly more rounded. Kate, a little tinier than Anna, was also more slightly built. Johnson decided that if Tim got anywhere near her she was quite likely to break. Although, verbally she was at least her sister's equal, and Johnson's view was that Tim would present no threat on that score. Johnson decided that, although he had always liked Kate, she smiled a great deal and he found that slightly troubling, then he realised that he should perhaps make allowances for it being her sister's wedding day.

Rebecca was dark-haired, very dark, almost olive-skinned, with dark, slightly hooded eyes. She regarded the seated guests from underneath a protective cloak formed of a long fringe of almost-black hair and a head tilted slightly downwards. Once you'd got past that, Johnson observed, her heavy eyelids formed another line of defence. Rebecca was wide-mouthed, with a Beverly Hills-style smile and a flawless complexion. God help the spot that tried it's luck on there, Johnson thought, as he admired her from across the table.

They ate and drank for a long time, and any speechmaking seemed to have been forgotten about. Johnson looked around the table, a small crowd for two such lovely people. He knew that Jeff's parents had been killed several years ago in a car accident, but, as far as he could remember, Anna had never mentioned her family and Jeff had never talked of meeting them, or of spending one of those, oh so joyous, weekends with the partners' parents.

"Kate?"

She was sitting next to him, he leant over and spoke quietly, "Can I ask you something?"

"Sure," she smiled up at him, eyes smiling, a real smile.

"I hope I'm not, I mean, speaking out of turn…"

"Go on," said Kate, encouragingly.

"Well, it's Anna's wedding, right?"

"Right," confirmed Kate.

"There are six of us here."

Kate looked around the table.

"Yep. You're right there," she said.

89

"JeffandAnna and four guests."

"Two from six is four, yes. I've heard you've had a couple of career hiccups, Johnson, have you ever considered accountancy?" said Kate.

"No," said Johnson.

"I think you should, you show real flair with numbers, you know."

"What I wanted to ask you was…"

"Where are our parents?" asked Anna.

"Well, yes." admitted Johnson.

Kate leant in a little further.

"They don't approve," she said.

"Of Jeff?" Johnson was incredulous.

"Of Jeff."

"But he's a great bloke with a steady job and they love each other so much. I mean, they're JeffandAnna, for Christ's sake."

"I know, but, they just don't approve. Never hit it off."

"What a shame," said Johnson, sadly.

"I think they'd set their sights a little higher for their daughter."

"And for you?"

"Oh, similar, but perhaps this will teach them a lesson."

"What did they say when they found out?"

"They don't know, Johnson."

"How terribly sad," said Johnson.

The party around the table continued until the band set up in the main bar, and the six friends spent the rest of the evening drinking at the bar and increasingly interrupted by dancing to covers of Sixties and Seventies hits. The mens' moves being as foolishly overblown as ever. Their suits and wedding gowns were incongruous among the rest of the Saturday night punters' jeans and T-shirts.

JeffandAnna were spending the night at the flat, before moving Jeff's things out the following day and then flying to Paris for a few days. They left before the others.

Tim seemed to have paired off with Kate, they had danced the last few together, and Johnson was weaving around the miniscule dance floor holding on tight to Rebecca. They walked their way through 'I Heard It Through The Grapevine', and then took one of the bench seats on the far side of the bar from the band.

"Bit quieter over here," said Johnson, his arm around Rebecca's shoulders, they sat very close together, she slipped her arm behind his back. Johnson felt more relaxed now about admiring her cleavage, adorned as it was by her black, silk lacy top. Beautiful skin, he thought, she really has got the most…wonder if she's wearing a bra? Doesn't look like it, but it might be one of those stick-on things. Hard to tell.

"Can I get you another drink," he asked, solicitously.

"No, I'm fine thanks. Had quite enough."

"Oh, have you?" said Johnson, not attempting to mask his disappointment.

"For now," she tossed her head back and laughed, "For now. Could be a long night."

I do bloody hope so, observed Johnson, silently.

"Those two seem to be getting on well," Johnson nodded at Tim and Kate.

"Big Dirty Dancing fans, obviously," agreed Rebecca.

Tim was striking a pose while Kate wrapped her legs around as much of him as she could manage.

"So," Johnson nuzzled into Rebecca's thick and dark hair, searching for an ear, "So," He whispered, "Would you like to come back to the flat?"

"For coffee?" enquired Rebecca, innocently.

"Coffee? Yeah of course," said Johnson. Hope she likes instant.

"Or a glass of wine, maybe,"

"Now, wine I can do. Or cognac."

"Sounds lovely. Come on then, Mr Johnson, what are we waiting for?" Rebecca said, "Let's go."

They retrieved their friends from the dance floor and, in doing so, rescued Tim from a kicking which would have been eagerly administered by a few of the local hooligans. Their timing was on the money, as his Dirty Dancing exploits had upped the pummelling-likelihood odds from the possible to the near definite.

"Tim?" asked Johnson, on the walk back to the flat.

"Yeah?" Tim was walking, arm-in-arm with Kate, just ahead of Johnson and Rebecca.

"When we get back to the flat."

91

"Yeah?"

"Promise me something will you?"

"I always take precautions, Johnson, but thanks for your concern," said Tim.

Kate dragged him to a halt and punched him, quite hard, on the side of the jaw.

"Jesus," said Tim, shocked.

"Take nothing for granted, Timothy," advised Kate.

"OK. OK, I'm sorry," said Tim, hurriedly. Suddenly contrite.

"Just promise me one thing," continued Johnson.

"Sure," said Tim to Johnson, and then to Kate "Bloody hell, that hurts. How many rings are you wearing?"

"Just watch it, boy," she chuckled.

"No pissing about with JeffandAnna," Johnson advised.

"What?" asked Tim.

"No bursting in their room. No shouting 'Fire'. No loud talk about wedding nights and has he got it up yet? Or I'm warming up on the subs bench."

"As if," protested Tim.

"Leave them alone, alright?"

"Alright," said Tim.

Johnson and Rebecca made their way into Johnson's room soon after they arrived back, where Rebecca plucked at his shirt buttons as he searched for the fastening of her skirt.

"JeffandAnna?" asked Johnson, as they lay in each others arms afterwards. Johnson, in gentlemanly fashion, had nudged her over gently and manoeuvred himself onto the wet patch.

"Tim and Kate?" Rebecca responded.

"Could be all of them," said Johnson.

The flat was one living, breathing, throbbing sexual being. Springs squeaked in protest and headboards banged against walls, they heard a low moan, quickly followed by another.

"I wonder who's going to..." began Johnson.

92

"Stop it," said Rebecca,

"It's just a bit distracting, that's all."

"Then put some music on," Rebecca suggested.

"Good idea," agreed Johnson, "Any requests?"

"Oooh," Rebecca stretched, and as she stretched, Johnson gazed at her magnificent breasts, with nipples still proud, "Marvin Gaye, have you got any Marvin Gaye?"

"Sure," said Johnson.

"Let's Get It On," said Rebecca, "That's the one, Let's Get It On."

"I'll get it," Johnson kissed her softly on the mouth. A lingering kiss.

"Mmmm," sighed Rebecca, "And you can get me a drink and don't be long."

"OK."

"Bring some cigarettes in, too," Rebecca called after him.

In the kitchen Johnson found three-quarters of a bottle of Cabernet Sauvignon which Tim and Kate had left. He was rinsing out two glasses when Tim appeared in the doorway. Naked.

"Quite a night, eh?" beamed Tim.

"Quite a night," agreed Johnson.

"So, how is she?" asked Tim.

"Come on Tim, you know I don't give running commentaries."

"No, you don't do you? Sorry." said Tim.

Tim had crossed to the fridge and was taking large draughts from a carton of milk.

"Quite a night, though," said Tim, again.

"You're on kitchen cleaning this week aren't you?" said Johnson.

"What? At a time like this he's on about household chores?"

"You're dripping on the floor mate," Johnson reported.

"It's only milk."

"Er, Tim..." Johnson, glancing down, had to disagree.

"Ooops. Sorry. Just get some kecks on. Hang on there a minute will you?" Tim was back from his bedroom in thirty seconds or so, wearing boxer shorts. He picked up the milk carton.

"That's better, " Tim said, happily, "No more leakage."

"Listen, er, Tim…" Johnson began.

"Yes, mate."

"Well…" Johnson started coughing, Tim proffered the carton. Johnson took a glug or two, "Thanks," he said, "Now, you know I don't talk about, liaisons, you know."

"Oh, yeah," said Tim, interested.

"It's just that I get the impression that I'm expected to perform again very shortly, and…"

"The only time you feel like doing it twice is just before you've done it once?" said Tim, in a summing up kind of fashion.

"Well, kind of…"

Having trouble finishing my sentences, thought Johnson, though Tim is a born interrupter. To give him due credit.

"How about a toot?" Tim suggested.

"A toot?" asked Johnson.

"Bit of coke, mate, the old powder, you know?"

"I don't…"

"If the old chap's asleep this'll give him a wake up call, I'll tell you." Tim assured him.

"No, I…"

"You don't approve, I know."

"No, I don't. I don't think…" Johnson began.

"Little pinch on the old bell end for you, and, as a bit of a bonus, it does the lady in question quite the power of good as well, you know."

"Does it?" asked Johnson.

"Oh, yes."

"Does it really?" Johnson persisted.

"Oh, yes."

"I don't know, Tim. I've just come out here for wine and cigarettes, and…"

"It's gonna be a long night," said Tim, sagely.

"Looks like it."

"Wait here." Tim disappeared to his bedroom again.

Johnson heard renewed pounding, squeaking and squealing from JeffandAnna's room. Alright for some, he thought, what it is to be in love. How on earth does he do it?

Tim reappeared.

"There you go." Tim handed him a small twist of foil.

"Well, I'm not sure…" said Johnson, doubtfully.

"Little pinch mate, a little snort, and away you go."

Johnson nodded.

"I'll give it a go, I think," he said.

"Good man," said Tim, "See you in the morning. And, if you'll excuse, I have business to attend to."

"Of course," said Johnson, politely, "Goodnight."

Johnson put the bottle of wine, two nearly clean glasses, half a packet of cigarettes, a lighter, and a Marvin Gaye CD on a tray and headed back to the bedroom. The cocaine was in the pocket of his bathrobe. He nudged the door open, Rebecca was stretched across the bed, and snoring very quietly. Her nipples are amazing, remarked Johnson to himself, as he edged in beside her. Amazing.

Johnson dozed for a bit. He awoke, Rebecca's nipples were still calling their siren's call to him, but he was wary of disturbing her. He'd once tried the romantic wake-up with a previous girlfriend and fancied that his ears still rang occasionally with the memory of her thighs clamping shut and the sound of her crying for help. He tugged the duvet back and exposed her sleeping form, her golden thighs and her dark bush of hair. Johnson sighed, and took the wine and cigarettes to the kitchen.

He was standing in darkness by the open window, sipping wine and puffing the last dregs of his cigarette when he heard movement.

"It'll be fun," said a voice. Anna?

"Wow. Really, you think?" said another. Kate?

"Come on, they'll never know."

"Look, I need a drink before I even think about this."

"Swapsies. Come on, swapsies."

"Me and your husband? On your wedding night?"

"And me and Tim."

The kitchen light clicked on.

Johnson blinked.

Anna blinked.

Kate blinked.

Anna and Kate were both wrapped in tiny white towels. But, as they were both tiny, they were both well wrapped.

"Hello Johnson," said Anna.

"Hello," said Johnson.

"Hello Johnson," said Kate, "come on crash the wine, then."

"Sure," said Johnson, pouring.

"How's Rebecca?" Kate asked.

"She's asleep," Johnson answered.

"Cool," said Anna, "been a good day, hasn't it?"

"Yeah," Johnson, "really good."

"Getting chilly, isn't it?" Anna announced.

"Mmmm," Kate agreed.

"Going back to bed, then?" Johnson asked.

Kate and Anna laughed in unison.

"We've always shared everything, Johnson," said Anna.

"Everything," Kate agreed.

Johnson watched Kate go into Jeff's room and Anna go into Tim's. They dropped their towels on the way, as if by pre-arranged signal, and two twinkling behinds bade him goodnight.

"Goodnight," he said. What the bloody hell's going on? He thought. Funny old wedding.

Johnson didn't need the cocaine. Rebecca was still asleep when he went back to his room. Later that morning, he was awoken by the touch of Rebecca's soft lips and her tongue.

"Morning," he said, looking down at her.

"Morning," she grinned, running her tongue upwards.

He dozed for a bit after Rebecca had rolled away, then he got up, put on his robe and slipped out to the bathroom. He pulled his robe apart and regarded his flaccid manhood.

Looks a bit red, he thought, he's probably flushed with excitement. Or surprise. Haven't seen one of those in a while, that's what he's thinking.

He picked the wrap of cocaine from his pocket. Need a mirror, that's what I've heard, you snort it from a mirror. Trouble is, the mirror in here is fixed to the wall. Or a glass-topped table, and there's certainly not one of those in my bathroom. Johnson took a pinch of the snowy powder between finger and thumb and, holding it to a nostril, gave a guarded sniff. He sniffed harder and felt the jolt in his sinuses, and then rising higher and higher. Repeating the operation on the other nostril, he concentrated hard on not sneezing, dabbed the remainder on his cock and tossed the wrap into the bin.

He returned to bed, nudging Rebecca sideways as he climbed in. Trying to engage her, he wormed his hand between her thighs, she shifted slightly but did not give any indication of eagerness or even wakefulness. As the time passed, she moved in her sleep, encouraged by Johnson's hand, her thighs now gripping his wrist. Rebecca laid on top of his prostrate frame. As she stretched across him, their legs wrapped around each others, her hair, blue-black in the half-light, covered his face. He could feel her breath on his cheek. Jesus, thought an increasingly agitated Johnson, now I need a pee, like now. Rebecca snored gently in his ear. Her hair was tickling his face and, whatever he tried, a strand or two were sucked into his nose or mouth whenever he tried to breath, and he was sure he that he could feel the tiny white Colombian crystals dancing around his septum and his penis. Her weight pressed firmly on his bladder. Her hair flicked up his nose and he pulled his bottom lip over his top lip, dragging his face down and pinching in the nostrils, then he tried breathing through his mouth, but managed only to hoover up a couple of stray hairs. He risked a quiet cough, she replied with a louder snore. Johnson tried edging sideways, but their interlocking legs were firmly intertwined. He whispered her name. He whispered more loudly. Rebecca snored on, her head shifted over a little and Johnson's head was now completely wrapped in her hair. The flat was quiet. Christ, don't tell me they've all had enough, sniffed Johnson. The metallic smell of hair lacquer shot up his nostrils and exploded somewhere behind his eyes along with everything else. Although Johnson tried to stop himself, he knew it was inevitable. His body bucked like it had done a few minutes ago, violently, but the pleasurable aspects were sadly absent, he attempted to resist the urge to take in more air, but he no longer had a choice, and once it had rushed in, an opposite force took over.

"Wha...?"

Johnson's ears were ringing and his bladder was on a code red so he wasn't sure whether Rebecca had actually spoken, but it didn't seem fitting that she should fly upwards, and sideways, and floorwards in total silence.

"Sorrygottahaveapiss," he yelled on his way out of the door, hearing the thump of her beautiful, soft body meeting the nasty, hard floorboards.

The bathroom door was locked and Johnson only just made it to the kitchen sink. Sadly he didn't have time to empty it. He heard a door opening.

"Out of Fairy Liquid again, are we?" said Tim, "Never mind, I find piss works just as well, must be the acid content, just so long as you remember to rinse properly. Good man. *Good man,*" Tim was obviously mightily impressed.

Johnson had passed the point of no return back in the bedroom. All he could do was make sure his aim was good, try not hit any upturned teaspoons, and will it to be over before anyone else arrived.

"I'd only got up to wash the dishes," said Tim, "but as you've got that covered, do you want a hand with the drying up?"

"No," Johnson eased the word out through clenched teeth. Hissing through both ends.

"No problem, mate. I'll get Anna or Kate to help you."

"No need," said Johnson, "finished."

"So you have," agreed Tim, tossing him a towel.

Interview Phase IV

"*You* want to take a break?" Johnson enquired. His brush of stubble seemed to have thickened noticeably. He rubbed his eyes, they were still clear and alert, although I had a feeling that mine were looking reddened and weary.

"I'm OK," I replied. "You want some coffee or tea or something?"

"No. The tea's rubbish here."

"Still don't drink coffee then?"

"No. I know it's unfashionable of me. I don't like cappuccino or americano or any of that other stuff people are so desperate to carry around in their cardboard beakers."

"You don't care though, do you?"

"Don't care?"

"About being unfashionable."

"I don't think I'm unfashionable," argued Johnson.

"About being thought unfashionable," I said.

"No, I don't. It's all transient isn't it? Trust me, before long people will be queuing up to hand over their crispy hard-earned for a cup of orange pekoe or silver tips."

"Not PG?"

"In a proper cup too. Nothing to go soggy."

Johnson took on a dreamy look.

"Milk from a jug," he went on.

"Are you sure you don't want to take a break?" I asked again.

"My mother never liked the milk bottle on the table, you know. Even if we didn't have guests, even if it was just the family, you know, sitting down for tea."

"Tell me about your childhood," I said, unwisely.

"Bollocks," said Johnson. "This, whatever *this* is, has nothing to do with my arse being smacked too hard by the midwife, nothing to do with having to eat all of my greens, or some bastard flushing my head down the toilet on my first day at school, nothing to do with burying my dead hamster in a shoebox, or my parents coming home early from visiting my granddad and interrupting me mid-shag with Amanda Metcalfe."

99

"So, your hamster died?" I asked.

"I was thirteen."

"When you buried the hamster?" I ventured.

"When I was stuck up Amanda Metcalfe and the folks walked in. Idiot."

I opened two more beers and passed one to Johnson.

"You didn't hear them?"

"Had some music on. Something loud, you know. Something heavy."

"Very romantic."

"Well, it kind of fits at that age doesn't it?"

"I guess so."

Johnson tilted his chair back, eyes pointed to the ceiling, lost in the memory.

"Was she in your class?" I asked.

"No. She was eighteen," he grinned.

"Eighteen?" I exclaimed, "you ...."

"Yeah. I know," his grin showed no signs of dimming.

I left Johnson to his memories for a while. He was rocking back and forth on his chair. I walked to the window and looked down through the haze of heat and pollution at the people and the traffic. The bright blueness of the sky had faded and it had taken on a smoky hue, it still looked steamy out there, though, and we still had a lot to talk about.

"Go and freshen up, Johnson," I suggested.

"I told you, I'm OK," he said levelly. He snapped his chair back to an upright position, ran his fingers through his hair again.

"Yeah, but I'm not," I announced, "I could do with a shower and a change of clothes."

"OK," Johnson agreed, with apparent reluctance.

"You OK with that?" I asked.

"Just want to get it over with."

"I know, but let's take an hour's break, freshen up, then we can get on."

"If you say so," said Johnson, suddenly seeming tired.

"There's a lot to get through yet."

"Is there?"

"I think so, Johnson. From what I've heard, I know so."

"Alright."

"Going to be a long night. Go and take a rest."

I saw Johnson out of the room, and followed a few minutes later.

After an hour we were seated again. Johnson had changed into a black T-shirt and loose dark grey cotton trousers. I had found something clean but scruffy in my suitcase. He had shaved, we had both slicked our hair back, it was still damp from our showers, and we gave off a rare mix of soapy odours. Herbs and coconuts and probably jojoba. I could feel the gritty residue of toothpaste in my mouth. At least toothpaste still tasted like toothpaste and not like an exotic salad.

"Beer?" asked Johnson.

"Water," I replied.

Johnson poured water for me and flipped the cap from a beer for himself. He lit a cigarette and tossed the pack over. The herbs, coconuts and jojoba were soon overwhelmed by the reek of smouldering tobacco.

"So what happened with Rebecca?"

"You don't want to know about that," said Johnson, resolutely.

"No, I do," I assured him.

"Well, I don't really want to talk about Rebecca."

"You don't?"

"Not right now, no."

"I just wondered, you know, after you'd dumped her on the floor. Was she..?"

"Was she what?"

"Wounded in any way."

"Wounded?" cackled Johnson, "wounded?"

"You know, hurt," I persisted.

"No mate," said Johnson, "she wasn't hurt."

"Good."

"And that's enough about that."

"For now?" I asked.

"Maybe," allowed Johnson.

"Alright. As you wish."

101

"I do. I do wish," said Johnson.

"So what next?"

"Next, my little interrogator, next, I went into recruitment."

"Recruitment?" I said, surprised.

"As you well know."

"Tell me about it."

Recruitment

Johnson and the rest said goodbye to JeffandAnna in the morning. Rebecca didn't have much to say to Johnson. She wasn't particularly cool, Johnson decided, but not amazingly you-were-fantastic effusive either. However, they were all feeling a little jaded.

"We have to go," Rebecca announced. Johnson bounded over to her, put his hands on her shoulders and she pecked him on the cheek. He didn't let go, and she allowed him a kiss on the mouth which wasn't quite lingering, but wasn't discouragingly brief either.

Tim was slumped untidily across an armchair. Kate wandered over and scrunched the toes of his right foot together in her hand. She maintained the pressure until he yelped.

"Reaction. That's good. See you, wankpot," she said.

"Bird," said Tim, by way of romantic acknowledgment.

Johnson sensed wedding bells.

"Rebecca, I'll see you outside," said Kate.

"Outside?" Rebecca queried.

"I just want a word. See if you can hail us a cab."

"Right," said Rebecca, heading for the door. Johnson gave her rear what he imagined to be an affectionate squeeze as she left the flat, and she smiled, briefly, mouth semi-hidden by the curtain of hair.

Johnson made for the kitchen, but Kate was right behind him.

"I thought you wanted to talk to Tim," he said.

"Him? You won't get any sense out of him today, and probably not tomorrow either," said Kate.

"You're probably right," agreed Johnson.

"You're out of work again?" said Kate.

"Yeah," agreed Johnson, rubbing his eyes, "thanks for reminding me."

Kate wrote something on yesterday's front page.

"You want a job. Call me," she said.

"Really?" said Johnson.

"Really," said Kate, "but don't think for one minute that you can fuck me about."

"No. I wouldn't. I've just had a bad run, you know."

"Alright. You want a job. Call me. Got to run."

Kate kissed him on the cheek and skipped out of the door.

Johnson picked up the newspaper. There was a phone number and a name, Locked-In Recruitment.

Johnson cooked up the remains of yesterday's breakfast for breakfast while Tim remained in the lotus position, or at least the version that might be practised by inhabitants of a parallel universe.

"What the hell is this?" asked Tim as Johnson handed him a plate.

"Well, the blackened strips are bacon, those charcoal lumps are sausages, the hard black bits are mushrooms and the rest of it is other stuff."

"Any baked beans?" Tim enquired.

"Ahead of you," replied Johnson, pouring half a saucepan-full onto Tim's plate. Tim mashed it all together, and Johnson followed suit. They watched an old American comedy show, which seemed to be on a permanent loop, and ate down to the pattern in virtual silence.

"I was in that pub the other night," Tim began, when they had finished eating.

"Which one?"

"Never could remember the name of it. You know it. Duke of something. Out East, just when you're going out of the City."

"Yeah, I know it," agreed Johnson, not sure, but happy for the story to move on.

"You know that barman?" Tim went on.

"Barman?" I don't even know where we are, let alone who pulls the pints or pours the drinks, thought Johnson.

"Twat with a beard," Tim reported.

"Of course. Twat with beard," Johnson agreed.

"So, I'm in there the other night and he's on a break. Sat down next to me and he's rummaging in a carrier bag. Big bag full of books."

"Oh, yes?" said Johnson, encouragingly.

104

"His girlfriend walks in. She's wearing some Hippos-R-Us denim dungaree things. Think she works for the council. Sewers, I reckon, human drain-rod. Anyway. Any drink going, boy?"

Tim gestured towards the kitchen with his dark eyebrows. Johnson got up.

"What do you want?"

"Lager. Any lemonade? I'll have a shandy, if we have. There's some fags on the side as well."

"Feeling better then?"

"Coupla shandies. Nothing outrageous. Ah, nearly forgot, how did you get on then, young man?"

"Get on?"

"Hokey cokey."

"Oh, I didn't need it."

"Didn't need it, eh? That's the fellah. I'll have it back then."

"No, you can't."

"No?" queried Tim, "whaddya mean, no?"

"Well, I…"

"You might need it? Might as well keep it then, mate. Now, pinta shandy, lovely. So, where was I? Oh yes. Barman twat."

Tim's mouth was engulfed in a good two inches of shandy head.

"Sorry, I didn't pour it too well," Johnson said, contritely.

"No, no, that's sweet mate. Can't beat a bit of head, you know?" Tim gurgled.

"Twat," said Johnson.

"Ah, yes. He's got the bag of books, or two bags, if I remember right. Yes, two bags. Two carrier bags."

"Full of books," said Johnson, encouragingly.

"Full of books, right. The girlfriend plonks herself down next to him. He's on a break, right? Did I mention that?"

"What?" asked Johnson, sipping his shandy.

"That he was on a break?"

"You did," confirmed Johnson.

"Right. We're all set up then."

"That's good," said Johnson.

"So, he's the barman, right?"

"Got it."

"He's on a break."

"I'm with you."

"Girlfriend turns up."

"I can almost see her."

"Trust me, you couldn't miss her."

"And what happened, was?"

"What you got there? she says. Cookery books, he says. Really? Yeah, got ten for two quid I did, that's ermm, twenty pence each ain't it? Sounds about right, she says."

Johnson was used to Tim, but the last twenty-four hours had been quite surreal.

"What's that? she says. What, this picture here? Mixed grill, says he. A what? Mixed grill. Then, Johnson, then he runs his finger along the top of the page and says it again. Mixed grill."

"What did she say?"

"Mixed what?"

"Mixed what?"

"Mixed what. Then he moves across to the picture and he points and he says look, there's a sausage. Oh, she says. Bacon there, look, bacon. Oh, she says. There's a mushroom. Oh, she says. Look, a tomato, he says."

"Oh, she said," said Johnson.

"She did. But then he pointed, and he looked, and he stops, and he says…"

"What?" asked Johnson, perplexed.

"Don't know what that is."

"He said, I don't know what that is?"

"He did. Then he said it might be a chop. But he wasn't sure."

"Then what happened?"

"He said, anyway, that's a mixed grill," said Tim

"What did she say?"

"Mixed grill. Sounded right keen on it though."

"Is there a point to this story, Tim?" asked Johnson.

106

"Well, he's a twat isn't he?"

"He's a twat?"

"That's the point. I seem to be out of shandy my old fruit."

Johnson and Tim watched TV for the rest of the day. Tim decided that the TV newsroom must have been particularly cold as he could see the newsreader's nipples were peeking through.

"You're sick," decided Johnson.

"I can still see 'em, chapel hat pins," insisted Tim.

"It's a bloke,"

"I know it's a bloke. That Welsh one. Bricklayer's thumbs he's got on his chest."

"You're the one who's checking out a bloke's tits, though."

"Talking of Welshmen, did I tell you about the two geezers from the office?"

"What's that then?" asked Johnson.

"I'm with these two and I said, look there's Taffy over there should I get him a drink?"

"A Welsh colleague," said Johnson.

"A Welsh colleague," Tim confirmed.

"You're in a pub?"

"In a pub. Should I get him a drink, I said. Who? They said. Taffy, I said."

"And they said?" prompted Johnson.

"They said, we don't call him Taffy anymore. No? I said, what do you call him then? We call him 'that Welsh bastard', they said."

"I don't think you can get away with saying that sort of thing nowadays, Tim."

"Funny thing is, they're both Welsh as well. See?"

"I suppose so."

"So then, Taffy says to the landlord, did I fall over outside here last night?"

"Yeah? What did the landlord say," Johnson asked.

"He said, no, he didn't think he had."

"What did your mate say?"

"Must have been somewhere else then. Laugh? Showed us his bruises. Cuts all down the elbows, all down his arms. I'll find out where it was, he says. Like it matters."

"Like it matters," Johnson concurred.

Johnson phoned Kate on Monday morning. It was almost an afternoon call, as he had sat up late the night before with Tim, and then they had gone out to a club.

I've got to stop this, he thought, as the dialling tone parped in his ear. He wasn't sure that Tim had slept at all. Be alright when I get back to the flat, Tim had said in the taxi. Something about sulphate, which confused Johnson, as he could think only of his childhood chemistry set. Oh, chemicals, of course, he said to himself as he was drifting off to sleep.

"Locked-In?" queried a voice.

Now, let's start as we mean to go on, decided Johnson, no mucking about.

"Hi, Kate Ash please," said Johnson, with a confidence that would have been instantly betrayed by sight of his shaking hands. No more pissy Sundays, he resolved to treat it as a day of rest in future. Definitely.

"Johnson?"

"Hi Kate," he replied.

"So, how's it going?"

"Alright you know. Good weekend wasn't it?

"Yeah. How's Tim?" asked Kate.

Well, he was trying his hardest to cop off with two Australian backpackers at two o'clock this morning, but I think he must be over getting knocked back by now.

"He's fine," Johnson assured her, "How's Rebecca?"

"Haven't spoken to her."

"I hope I didn't... I mean, I hope she wasn't upset or anything," Johnson stumbled.

"No, don't worry. She didn't say anything. Wouldn't get your hopes up though."

"Really?"

"You know, Johnson, she's not in it for the long haul."

"Absolutely," replied Johnson, "me neither."

"Good. Wouldn't get too attached, OK?"

"Fine," agreed Johnson.

"So," said Kate

"So," said Johnson, "you said there might be some work in the offing?"

"Right," Kate replied.

"So, what is it then?"

"Here at Locked-In, of course."

"Oh. Doing what exactly?" Johnson asked.

"Recruitment, of course. As a recruitment consultant."

Fuck, thought Johnson, am I that desperate?

"Sounds great," he said.

"Right. Get yourself down here this afternoon. I've already spoken to Richard. He can see you at four."

"Richard?"

"Richard Nork. He's our boss."

"Your boss?"

"Well, he's not the absolute boss, but he heads up the consultants."

"I see."

"Like a team leader."

I don't think I'm going to enjoy this, Johnson thought.

"I'll be there at four," he said.

Johnson decided to try and calm his jitters by having a steamy bath. He put a Frank Sinatra CD into the machine, stripped off, and began to climb in. The scalding heat of the water bit at his feet, and he lifted one out for a few moments, then repeated the operation as his body adjusted to the temperature. Needs to be hot, he told himself, so I can sweat it out. He lowered himself in, aware that the one-foot-in-one-foot-out manoeuvre was not something that could be replicated with his testicles when they hit the liquid, which was by now feeling more like volcanic lava than water. He let go of the sides and dropped hard into the bath. The tide rode up his back and made an almighty splash on the floor, and then repeated the operation at the other end. It washed back and forth for a bit, but Johnson was much too busy worrying about his burning skin to pay it much attention. Sweating is good, he said, sweating is good, sweating is good.

Johnson hauled himself out of the bath forty minutes later. He felt decidedly weak and feeble. As he dried himself, he bent over to reach down to his feet and his head began to swim alarmingly, a helix of black spots spun before his eyes and he steadied himself by placing his hands flat on the wall. His towel dropped to the floor, and he regarded himself in the mirror. His face was boiled-lobster-red and beads of sweat popped up on his forehead. As soon as he spotted one, another leapt the surface, and another. It gathered in rivulets and began to run down his face, down his cheeks, stinging his eyes. Shit, he said, sweating is bad, I've got to cool down. Sweating is bad, sweating is bad.

"That's a new one mate. Cooling the old cock down are we? Burning sensation? Who'd have thought it? Looked a nice girl too, that Rebecca. Never can tell though, I'm alright though, touch wood. Bit more classy though, Kate, I'd have thought."

"Tim. What are you doing home?"

"Afternoon off, boy. Knackered, I have to say. Got to slow down a bit. Can't go on like this."

"Me neither," agreed Johnson.

"Can I just get in there?" Tim asked.

"What?"

"Want some juice."

Johnson, naked, and draped over the open fridge, with his head wedged into the ice-making compartment at the top, stepped aside.

"What you doing, anyway?" Tim enquired.

"Getting ready for an interview," said Johnson, picking up his towel.

Richard Nork was tall and, even to Johnson's untrained eye, expensively, possibly Italian-suited. He swept into the reception area, Armani vents flapping in his wake, heavy gold links winked from his Savile Row cuffs as he shot his hand out to meet Johnson's in a firm, clean grasp.

"Johnson," stated Richard Nork, pumping his hand. He didn't speak in a questioning fashion, he was sure, and Johnson was sure that this was a man who knew all of the answers before he'd even had a glimpse of the questions.

"Mr Nork," Johnson replied, pumping back as hard as his dehydrated arm could manage.

"Right. Follow," announced Richard Nork.

Johnson strode along behind, and as hard as he tried, he found it hard to draw alongside Richard Nork. He trotted amongst flapping suit and in the wake of a pricey after-shave.

They were walking through a sixties office building which had been refurbished like a Scandinavian sauna. The wood panelling on the walls echoed the boards on the floor and the ceiling. Isn't it good? thought Johnson.

"What are you doing at the moment?" asked Richard Nork.

"Job hunting," replied Johnson, "I mean, I took some time out after graduating and now I'm sorting out the career," he said, correcting himself hurriedly.

"Right. Sales floor through there," Richard Nork waved at a large door inlaid with a pair of small, wire-threaded windows, Johnson glanced in as they sped past. Everyone seemed to be on the phone, but they do have wide-screen TV, he noted.

"OK. In here. Interview room. For candidates, normally."

Richard Nork opened a door, indicated a chair and took the other. There was a heavy duty, hessian-type carpet in the room, a certificate of some sort on one wall which Johnson couldn't quite make out, and, on the other, a framed and faded Monet print.

"So, why recruitment?" asked Richard Nork.

Johnson felt confident that he'd done enough of this interview business in recent months to sail through this one without a hitch.

"I'm not sure I'm getting the hunger from you," said Richard Nork after twenty minutes.

Oh no, thought Johnson, another arsehole.

"I'm hungry alright," said Johnson, truthfully. He'd felt sick all morning, and worse since getting out of the bath, but now the nausea was abating, and for the last ten minutes he'd had a real problem in concentrating on anything other than a grilled mature cheese sandwich with beefsteak tomato.

"I'll make it clear Johnson," said Richard Nork, frowning. "Our people make their money, no, to be perfectly correct, the good ones, that is to say, the really good ones, make their money, good money, let me remind you, good money, by putting the hours in, by tenacity, by attitude. Without attitude, Johnson, you will not attain altitude."

Fuck me, he is another one. He might be the worst one yet, mused Johnson.

"Hunger. Hunger, Johnson, is the key. Have you got hunger?"

Toasted sandwich, a little burnt on the edges, cheddar, the best aged Canadian, oozing out of the sides, the bread slathered with olive paste and layered with hot sliced tomato. Johnson could almost taste his reward.

"I'll show you fucking hunger," he said, hammering his fist on the table and leaping to his feet. "You think you've seen it with those people out there? Hunger? They don't know fucking hunger, just you wait, I'm ready to step up. I'm raring to go, I've got the matrices going on. You just fucking watch. Just you fucking well watch me. You've seen nothing, you ain't seen nothing. Nothing," as Johnson grimaced the final 'nuthin' he feared he might be giving it a bit too much Brando, but it was too late to stop now, he was in character. He was grasping the edges of the table, a vein bulged impressively on his temple, and he could feel the blood careering around in his head. Bad for morale, thought Johnson, if I were to have a stroke right now, or perhaps it might be good for morale. See what this man was prepared to go through to make it? Death, that's what. Might be an angle for someone's next motivational talk. Something to think about, anyway. Johnson continued his tirade.

When he'd given the table another belting to signal the end, Richard Nork said, "Anger. Attitude. I like that. Bit of hunger, I like that too."

A bit? thought Johnson, a bit of hunger? I'm drained, I've got nothing left to give after that performance. This is going to be harder than I thought.

"Come with me. I'll show you where you're going to be working."

"Oh," said Johnson, "working?"

"Congratulations," said Richard Nork, offering his manicured hand again, "you're in, and I don't say that very often."

"Oh," Johnson gave a strangled choke, "thank you very much. When do I start?"

"Give you a trial right now, I think," decided Richard Nork.

"Now?" queried Johnson. What about my toasted sandwich?

"Yes. Get you out on the floor, see what you can do."

"Right," said Johnson.

"What is it now, five?"

"Five o'clock," confirmed Johnson. Be home by six.

"Gives you a good three hours then."

"Three hours?"

"At least. Right, with me."

Richard Nork sprinted away again and Johnson scrambled along after him.

"What's with the TV's then?" asked Johnson.

There was a widescreen TV at each end of the sales floor. Both tuned to the same satellite rolling news station.

"Well," said Richard Nork, "we tell clients that it's to make sure our consultants are totally up to date with world events, current affairs, currency markets, you know? Keep ahead of the game."

"You tell your, sorry, our clients that?"

"Yes."

"But in reality?"

"I think they look good. Big TV's, and they're just for show, really," said Richard Nork, "top of the range, all the channels, watch the football in the evenings if you like, we have some lively nights when there's football. Play and record. Pause the live action. You know the sort of thing. All the channels."

Johnson had a feeling that people were ducking imperceptibly as Richard Nork passed by them. That's ridiculous, he decided, it's not a schoolroom is it?

"Now, I'd better take you to meet Simon," announced Richard Nork.

"Simon?"

"Our MD. Very important man."

"Right," said Johnson.

"I'll drop you into Simon, and by the time you've come back we'll have sorted out a space for you, OK?"

Simon was fresh faced and had short curly fair hair. The sort of look that meant he would always look rather too much like a baby to be taken completely seriously. Johnson decided he was probably around forty and obviously successful, but perhaps the scrubbed pink cheeks, cherubic features and the spirals of blond locks which seemed to count against him meant he had really come up the hard way. Not to be underestimated, Johnson decided. Office dead opposite the ladies and gents, though, that's hardly pole position.

Simon Hart gave Johnson the usual talk on the history of the company. Johnson glanced casually around the office as Simon Hart was speaking. Smoked glass windows and table tops, muted lighting, expensive electronic equipment scattered around, a Bang and Olufsen in the corner, playing Kenny G by the sound of it, oh dear. Easy chairs - leather slung low over chrome, and a lot of self-help-psychology-management-style books, with titles like, 'How To Hurt The People Who Hate Winners By Winning In Style!', 'Finished Second? You Loser!', and 'Go For Gold'.

"I like to think of us here as a family," said Simon Hart.

"Oh, yes?" Johnson grinned his Goebbels-family-cyanide-grin.

"And once you're part of the Locked-In family, you know what?"

"You're locked in?" suggested Johnson.

"Exactly," Said Simon Hart, returning Johnson's grin.

Simon Hart was absent-mindedly pushing a pen around his desk.

"Should get yourself a choo-choo train," said Johnson, riskily.

"What? Not a bad idea, that. I like a good idea. A choo-choo train eh?"

"Yeees," said Johnson, cagily this time.

"Now, you're backtracking now, I can sense it. Word of advice, shouldn't backtrack on a good one. You think it's a good one then pick it up and...."

"Run with it?" interrupted Johnson.

"Give it some air, I was going to say," said Simon Hart, sounding a little hurt, "Pick it up and give it some air. Fly it like a kite out in the big blue sky and, you know what? Then you might see some real blue sky thinking."

"Alright," agreed Johnson.

"But I like your idea of picking it up and running with it."

"You do?"

"Certainly do," said Simon Hart, "must write it down."

Simon Hart leapt to his feet and crossed to a white laminate board which was mounted on the wall behind Johnson. A black marker pen squeaked across the board as he wrote 'pick it up and run with it'. He turned around, baby-cheeks flushed with colour.

"Motivation."

"Oh, yes," said Johnson, fervently.

"Like a bit of motivation."

"Great."

"Have you had a look in the gents?"

"For what?" Johnson asked.

"We have a board in there, just like this one," said Simon Hart.

"Right," said Johnson.

"I like to sketch the odd motivational thought on there from time to time."

"You do?"

"Helps keep up the old morale."

"It does?" asked Johnson, trying to button down the sarcasm as he wondered, whose morale are we talking about here, exactly?

"I might put up the odd quiz thing now and then."

"A quiz?"

Simon Hart wandered around the office until he reached another stretch of smoked glass, this time it was serving as sliding doors atop a mahogany cabinet.

"Drink?" suggested Simon Hart.

"Scotch, thanks," Johnson replied, quickly.

"Water, still or gassy, cola or grapefruit juice."

"Nothing in it thanks. Certainly not grapefruit juice."

"What?"

Finally, Johnson sighted the man-trap, he hoped he wasn't too late, and hadn't already blundered in.

"Sorry, didn't hear you. Water would be fine."

"Still?"

"With gas, thanks."

Simon Hart poured fizzy water from two tiny bottles into two impossibly tall and heavy tumblers, the water barely reached a quarter of the way up the glass. Johnson took his glass and had to tilt his head back a long way before the gassy liquid reached his mouth.

"So, you do the quiz questions then?" Johnson enquired.

"Just on the board. Bit of fun, you know."

"Bit of fun," said Johnson.

"Yes. Winner gets a bottle of fizz,"

"Perrier?" asked Johnson, innocently.

"Oh no. No, no, no. Moet."

"Of course," said Johnson.

"I think I mentioned the family aspect of what we do here?" began Simon Hart.

Oh bollocks, said Johnson into his Sahara of a glass.

"Now, do you have any issues?"

"Issues?" asked Johnson.

Johnson regarded Simon Hart's chubby cheeks and blond curls and wished he'd brought him a lollipop.

"Home, relationships, personal life, you know."

Well, I feared I couldn't get it up the other night but I got away with it, although I understand she's unlikely to want to see me again, I'm drinking far too much, I can't hold a job down, I'm worried that I might have an attitude problem, I've got about four quid in the bank and the rent's due, my best friend - I suppose he's my best friend as no-one else seems to like me - seems to be intent on supplying me with class A drugs but the saving grace is that having tried them, I don't think I enjoyed the experience very much. Yet. I haven't spoken to a member of my own family in weeks, and this career stuff is just getting me down. You understand, man? It's getting me down. Maybe I'm heading for a breakdown.

"I'm all sorted, Simon," said Johnson.

"You are?"

"Life is good," Johnson reiterated.

"Really?" Simon Hart persisted.

"I'm the happiest, most well-adjusted, level-headed, potential recruitment consultant you'll ever meet."

"I'm sensing a contradiction here, Johnson," said Simon Hart, "Just haven't worked out what it is yet. You'll have to leave it with me."

"Right on Simon. Now, can I go and do my trial?" said Johnson, barely re-hydrated but somehow energised.

"OK. I like that. Moving forward, eh?" Simon Hart picked something from his drawer.

"What's that?" asked Johnson.

"This is Teddy," said Simon Hart.

"Your teddy bear?"

116

"Oh yes. He was a present from my grandmother. His name is actually Teddy," said Simon Hart.

"Teddy?" asked Johnson.

"Couldn't think of anything else," said Simon Hart, rubbing Teddy against one of his chubby pink cheeks.

"I see," said Johnson, rising from his chair.

"Johnson. One thing before you go. Teddy and I won't be very pleased if you don't make your targets in your first month."

Simon Hart's baby's eyes went from silk to steel, and Johnson was stilled in his tracks.

"One month. Alright?"

"OK," agreed Johnson. This can't be for real, he thought.

"I actually thought he'd packed in the Teddy routine," said Kate. Johnson was sitting next to her at a desk on the sales floor.

"Routine?" asked Johnson.

"Oh, you know. Something to throw people off kilter. I thought it had gone a bit stale, but he obviously doesn't."

"So, he didn't get Teddy from his grandmother?"

"No," said Kate, laughing.

"And he doesn't talk to Teddy?"

"Oh, come on," said Kate, laughing harder.

"And if Teddy's not happy that doesn't mean that the rest of us are in trouble?"

"Don't be silly Johnson."

"That's a relief," sighed Johnson.

"Remember though, it's not a good idea to upset Simon."

"Why's that," asked Johnson.

"How can I explain it? I'd say that Richard Nork is a bastard, but he's also a bit of a wanker."

"Which takes the edge off," said Johnson.

"Exactly. Takes the edge off. He's supposed to be the hard man, so if you go along with it, it helps him to maintain the image, even if we all know he's beating himself

117

blind every night over pictures of farm animals or boy scouts or whatever."

"Is he?" asked Johnson, incredulously.

"It'll do for me," said Kate, firmly.

"And Simon?" asked Johnson.

"Simon is a right bastard," said Kate.

Kate showed Johnson the ropes. Calling old clients, calling new clients. Interviewing hopers and no-hopers, usually after hours. Trying to slot curiously-shaped pegs into regulation holes. Persuading the candidate that this is the role they've been waiting for, cajoling employers into giving a someone a chance. Johnson tripped downstairs to the gents. Simon Hart's door was opposite and open. Simon Hart was alerted by Johnson's footfall on the stairs, he glanced up as Johnson passed, and made a show of checking his watch. Johnson nodded in passing at Simon Hart, the smoked glass, leather and chrome, and shut and locked the door. Johnson unzipped and as he streamed forth he checked the board which hung to his right.

Get out there and sell, people. Because we all know what awaits people who don't sell, don't we? Long lazy afternoons on the dole.

Johnson pondered this wisdom while his bladder emptied.

He picked up the black felt pen which hung from the wall on a string.

Sounds fucking lovely, he wrote, *Bring on those lazy afternoons.*

Johnson re-zipped, unlocked, nodded to Simon Hart, who was re-checking his watch, and trod his way back up the stairs, back to Kate and the phones. Seven PM.

Johnson and Kate stopped for a quick drink after work.

"Thanks for that," said Johnson, as they found a leaning-post in the shoulder-to-shoulder bar.

"That's OK," said Kate, "I know how hard it is when you're starting out."

"Yeah, but you gave me that booking. I'll earn for that and you won't."

"It's only for a week, Johnson. Anyway, you can do the same for me sometime."

"Deal."

"So," Kate was running her finger around the rim of her gin and tonic, and looking thoughtful, smiling, wide blue eyes fixed on the ice and lemon, "how's Tim?"

"I saw him earlier, Kate."

"You did?"

Johnson took a good pull of beer.

"You know what you said to me about Rebecca?"

"Yes?" said Kate, uncertainly.

"Look, the same goes for Tim. You know?"

"I do?"

"Commitment issue, yes?"

"Not good with commitment?"

"Not good," said Johnson.

"Good shag, though," said Kate, "get him to call me will you? Right, the time is...? Ooops, gotta run."

Kate drained her glass and ice tinkled against her teeth.

"Mmmm," she swallowed, "see you in the morning."

"OK," said Johnson.

She brushed her lips against his cheek.

"Seven-thirty, OK?"

"Seven-thirty?" said Johnson, "where?"

"In the office, you idiot."

Wow, thought Johnson, I've got almost eleven hours, and all to myself. In need of the air, he walked the streets for a while. It was never quiet here, he thought, even on a Monday evening. The pubs he walked past were all full, with punters wedged up against windows and doorways. Johnson heard the occasional burst of music as doors swung open as he passed by and people strode in thirstily, or weaved out, laughing too loud. He marched on.

"Hey, Johnson," a shout reached him from across the road and he half-turned.

"Johnson," came another shout, slightly different to the first. Johnson peered through the traffic, squinting against the yellowish glimmer from the streetlights.

"Over here, mate. We're coming over."

Sam Goode and Terry Bedford ran and dodged like prop forwards through the traffic which protested with honks and hoots and one clear shout of 'wankers'.

"Must be a cabbie," said Johnson, quietly.

Bedford and Goode reached the kerb.

"I'll have a quick drink", said Johnson, resolutely, and pressed between Bedford and Goode up against a mirror in the first pub they came across, "but I've got an early start tomorrow."

"No problem," they said.

Johnson filled them in on his movements since the Wink and Kinker walkout.

"So, how's it going there?" Johnson asked.

"They organised another activity day," said Bedford.

"Oh, no. They didn't, did they?"

"Oh, yes," said Goode, mournfully.

"You didn't?" Johnson paused, "you didn't take part did you?"

"It was put to us, Johnson, that it may well not be of benefit to our careers if we didn't," Bedford replied.

"You've got careers now?" observed Johnson, with a drop of sarcasm..

"We have since they got rid of you," said Goode.

"I resigned," insisted Johnson.

"Not what we heard," returned Bedford.

"Listen, I quit on the spot," Johnson said.

"You did? Why?" asked Goode.

"Because if I stayed there, at Wink and Kinker, I was to have Mitchell Turner as my shadow, my mentor, my permanent, prickling pain in the arse," said Johnson.

"Fair one," agreed Terry Bedford.

"Couldn't argue with that," said Sam Goode.

"I leave on a point of principle, and you two end up playing their game. That's what I can't get over," mused Johnson.

"There was a promotion in the offing," said Goode.

"Two promotions," Bedford reminded him.

"So, you took a bribe then? said Johnson, "I have to say I'm disappointed in you."

"Two bribes," corrected Goode.

"Strictly speaking," said Bedford, "it would be two."

"Two bribes taken," agreed Goode.

"So, didn't you get hauled over like I did? You didn't get a dose of Colin Camper?"

"The ginger whizz?" said Bedford.

"No, we didn't," Goode concurred.

"Why ever not, I wonder?" said Johnson.

"We were seen as mere foot soldiers," said Bedford.

"The poor bloody infantry," agreed Goode, "whereas you…"

"You were the ringleader. The bad apple. The capo di capo. The pirate king," said Bedford, getting carried away.

"Really?" said Johnson, struggling, and failing, to hide his pleasure.

"The donkey leading the lions," observed Goode. "But that's not the story."

"Alright then," allowed Johnson, "deflect the pressure. What's the story?"

"Salty bought the farm," said Bedford, sadly.

"Poor bloke," agreed Goode.

"Salty?"

"Brian Salt, you remember," said Bedford.

"Yes. Of course, I remember Brian Salt. He was alright."

"For a man living in perpetual terror he was," said Goode.

"What happened," asked Johnson.

"Last game of the day. Elect someone on your team to run twenty yards to a pole, hold on to it, run around it twenty times while you're holding on, let go of it, try to run back the twenty yards to where you started, fall over dizzy, everyone pisses themselves laughing, have to crawl to the finish line 'cause your brain's spinning round and round the wrong way in your head and that makes you go all over the shop," Bedford reported.

"And?" asked Johnson.

"Turns out Salty had a heart attack as he swung off the pole and hit the deck," Goode was shaking his head.

"And everyone thought it was all part of the game?" asked Johnson.

"Oh, yeah, all the crawling," said Bedford.

"And the gasping," continued Goode.

"And the collapsing into a heap," said Bedford, "and the turning blue."

"What about the calling of the ambulance? Everyone have a good laugh at that, did they? The resuscitation? The body bag? I'm surprised you didn't all go along to the funeral to poke fun at his family."

"It was bad alright," said Goode.

"I'll be in touch, lads," announced Johnson, suddenly, trying to find a space for his empty glass before finally setting it on the floor.

"We were as upset as you Johnson, you know?" said Bedford.

"Right," said Goode.

"Yes, sorry. I know. It's not you that needs....." Johnson paused, "look I'll give you ring, OK?"

"OK," they said.

"We'll get together," said Johnson.

"Under happier circumstances," said Bedford.

"Trust me, they will be," said Johnson, as he turned and left. He stopped at the door, turned and walked back.

"What's up?" they asked.

"Ever thought of growing your hair?" asked Johnson.

"Eh?" they replied.

"Growing the hair? You know, not having it razored back to the skull every two days."

"Can't say I have," answered Goode.

"Me neither," said Terry Bedford, "not recently, anyway."

"OK," said Johnson, turning for home again.

"This might sound like a silly question..." began Goode.

"But why do you ask?" completed Bedford.

"The world's full of silly questions isn't it?" said Johnson, "Haven't you noticed? Sometimes it's all there is, all that you see. Silly questions. You try to make sense of them, but is there any point?" said Johnson.

"Search me," said Goode.

"Ditto," said Bedford.

Johnson said his goodbyes, and made it out of the door.

"What was all that about, then?" asked Sam Goode.

"Haven't a clue, mate," said Bedford.

"He's a nice bloke and all that," said Goode.

"Oh, yeah. Nice bloke," agreed Bedford.

122

"I reckon Wink and Kinker are well shot of him though," said Goode.

"Mmm. You're probably right," agreed Frank Westlake.

"Where did you come from?" asked a visibly startled Terry Bedford.

Frank Westlake found a narrow shelf on which to set his tall tumbler of vodka, lime and soda.

"Just having a quiet drink. Saw you two lads talking to our erstwhile colleague, thought I'd wander over. Sadly Mr Johnson had gone by the time I arrived."

"Pity," agreed Goode.

"Yeah," said Bedford. He had backed away slightly.

"So, what was he talking about?" asked Frank Westlake.

"Talking about?" asked Goode.

"Who?" asked Bedford, a little nervously.

Frank Westlake took a sip of vodka and regarded Goode and Bedford over the rim of the glass. Goode and Bedford stood shoulder to shoulder, although Goode had to take surreptitious hold of Bedford's trouser thigh between finger and thumb to discourage him from retreating further. Frank smiled the familiar Westlake smile and the lines crinkled around his merry blue eyes.

"Don't muck me about, boys," said Frank, quietly. "So, here it is. You tell me, and I'll decide. How's that then boys? Agreed? Good," Frank Westlake drained his glass. "Now, you," he thrust his empty tumbler into Bedford's hand, "you can get me another drink while me and your friend here go and bag that table which has fortuitously just been vacated."

"So it has," said Sam Goode, "right stroke of luck that, Terry, eh? Now go and get the man a drink and I'll have a large one of the same, alright?"

Interview Phase V

"I found out about this conversation later on, of course," said Johnson.

"I wondered if you were hiding somewhere," I replied.

Johnson gave his scalp an exaggerated two-handed scratch, and I was pleased to see his aura dented by the light dusting of dandruff which gathered on the shoulders of his black t-shirt. He struck a match and touched the flame to the tip of his nth cigarette of the day. I heard a slight crackle as the dry tobacco caught fire.

"You're killing yourself, you know that?" I remarked.

Johnson shrugged and expelled smoke in powerful streams through his nose and mouth.

"I know," said Johnson.

"And it doesn't worry you?"

"I've heard it described as a slow form of suicide."

"Yes?" I said, encouragingly.

"That'll do for me," he said, inhaling sharply.

"A painful, lingering death? Coughing your lungs up?"

"No," said Johnson, sharply.

"So the thought of death frightens you?"

"Frightens everybody, doesn't it?"

"I suppose it does. Unless you're devoutly religious," I said.

"Well, as you know, I'm not religious."

"But you're keenly anticipating your own demise through self-inflicted means, aren't you? 'That'll do for me', you said."

"You should ask your people to send you on a course - How to Avoid Jumping to Conclusions and Become a Property Millionaire in Just Six Months. I was just agreeing with the observation. Smoking being a form of suicide that proceeds at the pace of a state funeral," Johnson smiled, "and then we end up talking about my impending self-doing-in-fest. Again."

"Sorry," I said, contritely, "beer?"

"Beer," confirmed Johnson.

I passed him one, and opened one for myself. It was hard not to, when you were with Johnson.

"So, did you see Rebecca again?" I asked.

"Off limits," Johnson replied, pointing his bottle of beer at me.

"We've got to go through all of this, Johnson," I said, firmly, "it's the only way. Everything out in the open."

"I guess so," he said, resignedly, "I guess so. But the subject of Rebecca is off the agenda for now, OK?"

"OK," I agreed, readily. Knowing that we would get there eventually. "Frank Westlake though, turning up like that. You must have been surprised?"

"What, good old Frank? Got to watch these smileys, you know. Always gotta watch 'em, the smiley ones, or the bastards will show their true colours one day and they'll have you, if you're not careful."

"So, you had an idea about Frank then?" I asked, "from before?"

"Not a clue mate. Not a clue. Come on, I was a child, a baby. What did I know?" said Johnson, shaking his head, and for the first time I saw real sadness in his face.

"What did I know?" he asked me again, his eyes shimmering with tears. He coughed hard, swallowed, and blinked. He sprang from his seat and gave the room a couple of circuits, coughing all the while, and rubbing his eyes while his back was turned to me.

"You alright?" I asked, as he resumed his seat.

"Sound as mate, sound as," he flashed me his up-yours grin.

"Where were we?" I prompted.

"Locked-In," said Johnson.

"Oh, yes. Locked-In Recruitment," I said.

"Recruitment? I suppose so," said Johnson, "fucking locked in, anyway."

Sky-Diving

Johnson had got home, the place was really empty nowadays. No JeffandAnna curled up on the sofa. No fun observing Jeff's keen mask of fake enjoyment at Gone With the Wind or Notting Hill, a gem of artful construction maintained for up to three hours for the major features. Tim was out.

Johnson found some salami, cheese and tomatoes in the fridge and, along with some sliced bread, concocted a mock pizza. Tim's fast-rotating wine cellar provided a glass or two. He watched some TV, but couldn't get his mind off Brian Salt and his pointless demise. Johnson realised, despite the jibe at Goode and Bedford, that he didn't even know if Brian had had a family, or a wife, or girlfriend, or both, or a boyfriend. In truth, he hadn't had much to do with him. Knew he caught a train out east, but not where he lived. Knew he was a rugby man, not a football man, but apart from that, he knew next to nothing about the departed Brian Salt. But Brian had always been affable, helpful, hard-working and, as had been pointed out, for a man in constant fear of the boot, he was 'alright'. Bloody hell Brian, said Johnson, aloud. Bloody hell. Is that it? That's supposed to be a life, a few people remembering you as 'alright'? I'm so sorry, Brian, sorry I didn't make the effort to get to know you, sorry you didn't make the effort to know me. You were probably as scared and screwed up as the rest of us, and none of us bothered and you didn't bother. What the hell's going on? It's still going on. That's the thing, with whoever's sitting in your old fish tank, nothing will have changed, you know that? Nothing. And those twats who killed you? Because they did, Brian, there are guilty people who are still there, still picking up the wages, still spouting the same old crap and putting the rest of us through it, and getting fucking paid for it. Johnson heard the sound of his voice growing louder and he stopped abruptly.

He sat in the gathering gloom for a long time and finished the wine.

"Are you alright?" asked Kate, the following morning.

"Yeah," Johnson assured her, "didn't sleep too well, that's all."

"Empty flat?" suggested Kate.

126

"Yeah. Jeff's gone, of course, so no JeffandAnna anymore, and Tim was... Oh, I get it."

"He stayed at mine," smiled Kate.

"I guessed," said Johnson. "He's my mate, you know, but just..."

"Just having fun, Johnson," she assured him.

They got on with their phone calls. After an hour or so, Johnson heard a cry from the adjacent bank of desks.

"Yeeessss," yelled a mouth set beneath an unreasonable amount of hair product, upper body encased in a white shirt with bold royal blue stripes, "Oh yeessss. Come to me baby. Come to daddy."

"What's going on?" enquired Johnson.

"Placement. Big one," Kate replied.

"We've placed someone in a permanent job, you mean?"

"Yeah. I'd say a senior position, for a big salary by the look of him. We get a percentage of that as our fee and the consultant, in this case Sebastian, gets a big commission."

"Oh, right. Richard Nork told me about this yesterday, I think."

"Here we go," said Kate.

"What?"

"Watch," said Kate, urgently, "you don't want to miss this."

Sebastian rose from his chair and, clutching a sheet of paper, strode confidently across the sales floor to Richard Nork's desk. He handed Richard Nork the paper and spoke to him quietly. Richard Nork stood, smiled and shook Sebastian's hand extravagantly. Then he resumed his seat and reached under his desk. Johnson's head exploded, his ears were bleeding and his eyes forced back in their sockets, he leant forward in his chair and clung on to the edge of the desk with both hands. The Klaxon rang out four more times and by the time it had finished Johnson couldn't hear anything. Kate hauled him to his feet and he looked around at the rest of the consultants who standing, applauding, cheering wildly (he guessed, from the sight of open mouths), some were standing on chairs, some on the long desks, stamping their feet. Open-mouthed, Johnson clapped his hands mechanically.

"What the hell was all that about?" he asked.

"Ssshh, Johnson," hissed Kate, "no need to shout."

"I'm not shouting," yelled Johnson.

"Hush. Look, come with me."

Kate took hold of Johnson's hand and tugged him to his feet.

"Come on," she said, dropping his hand, "just need to speak to Richard first."

"Right," Johnson shouted.

"Jesus," sighed Kate.

"What was that?" asked Johnson.

They approached Richard Nork's desk. He glowered at them. The smiles were obviously strictly rationed.

"Richard. Just need to take Johnson outside for a minute. Explain things," said Kate.

"Five minutes, no longer," he barked, "you know the rules."

"Right," said Kate, "no longer."

Kate ushered Johnson into the corridor.

"What was all that?" asked Johnson.

Kate flicked her hair back and looked up at him.

"Big sale Johnson. Big sale, big commission, big fuss. You know make an event of it. The Klaxon was Richard's idea."

"Klaxons? Frightened the life out of me. Thought I was having a cardiac. What's all that about?"

"Told you," said Kate, "big fuss, big noise, they reward success here."

"By blowing your fucking brains out? Funny reward."

"Sorry, forgot. How is the hearing?" she asked.

"At about thirty percent, I reckon. Better than it was five minutes ago."

"At least you've stopped shouting."

"Sorry about that," said Johnson.

"There'll be drinks tonight," Kate announced.

"Oh, I don't know," demurred Johnson, "I was going to go straight home this evening."

Kate shot him a serious look with her wide blue eyes.

"You don't really have a choice Johnson," she advised him, shaking her head.

Oh, bloody hell, thought Johnson.

"I don't have a choice? What do you mean? Me, a grown man, an adult, doesn't have a choice about how he spends his free time?"

"Not if you want to make it at Locked-In, you don't," said Kate sharply. "I stuck my neck out for you Johnson."

"I appreciate that, Kate," he replied.

"I put myself on the line for you. Got them to give you a chance. Don't chuck it all back at me, Johnson."

"I'm sorry," he said, "I won't let you down."

"You'll come tonight. For drinks?" she asked, pleadingly.

"Of course," assured Johnson, "I'll be there."

"People can really make it here Johnson, and you'd be silly to pass up a chance like this, you really would. The rewards are great, just great. Work hard, play hard. The social side is brilliant. And the activities, well the activities are something else. They're fun really, ultimately. Tough though, I won't lie to you. Well, you don't get something for nothing do you? And it's fantastic here Johnson, it really is. We're all together, fighting for the same cause, for Locked-In, for Simon and Richard and for each other. Like an army."

It seemed to Johnson that Kate's lovely wide blue eyes, and probably her brain, had been infiltrated by some kind of evil corporate zealot, and the creeping chill that he thought he'd banished from his Wink and Kinker memory had made an unwelcome return in the region of his bowels.

"Activities?" he asked, numbly.

"Oh, you know the kind of thing. Teams and teamwork. Winning points, and you know what points mean!" Kate laughed in a way that worried Johnson. "It's a bit of everything. Something physical, something mental, above all something challenging. Bring your bulging brains and bodies. You're divided into teams, you get to choose your own uniforms, team songs, even war cries," Kate's eyes shone with vigour, and belief, thought Johnson, she really believes.

"Tomorrow belongs to me," he observed.

"What's that?" asked Kate.

"Tomorrow belongs to me. It's the title of a song from Cabaret. The Nazis..." he began to explain.

"That's it Johnson. You've got it. Tomorrow belongs to me. If you make it here, then it's possible," she grasped his hands and fixed him with the wide-blue laser beams. "Tomorrow belongs to me," she continued, "I like that, I think Simon and Richard might like it too. Have you got the CD? Bring it in. I think a company song's a terrific idea."

"Terrific's the word," said Johnson, "definitely the right word. Come on, our five minutes must be up." He tried to banish the vision he saw reflected in Kate's eyes of buildings in flames, of tanks, and rubble, and endless chains of refugees, as he guided her back to their desks. The rest of the morning was Klaxon-free. After a couple of hours Johnson excused himself by rising to his feet and nodding at Richard Nork as he headed for the gents. The originator of the line about long lazy dole-driven afternoons had replied to his light-hearted comment in angry capital letters:

YOU ARE QUITE OBVIOUSLY THE SORT OF PERSON WHO HAS A BIG FUTURE IN STAFF MOTIVATION (NOT!).

In red ink too, noted Johnson approvingly, must have hit the spot, to make the effort to go and fetch a red pen, the only one in here is black, and the 'not' reference tells one *so* much about the author, he smiled. He read on:

IDENTIFY YOURSELF!!

Three exclamation marks in two short sentences. Very poor, remarked Johnson to himself. He picked up the dangling black felt pen and wrote one word:

Shan't.

He flushed and washed and left the cubicle. Simon Hart was not in his office, so there was no-one to clock him out. Later, while Kate was on the phone, he slipped out for a solitary lunch. Later, he made his calls, he even made a little money, but not enough for a blast from the Klaxon. However, someone else did, and mid-afternoon he found himself on his feet clapping and pretending to cheer. He interspersed his calls with covert glances at the nearest giant, silent Sky TV screen.

News Alert, announced the thick red and white banner at the bottom of the screen.

What's this? he thought. Looks like something big. Probably a natural disaster, or a terrorist attack, he decided.

Film Star Has A Baby.

Johnson rubbed his eyes, no, he hadn't imagined it. He shook his head and concentrated on reaching his target quota of phone calls. He applied himself to the task vigorously. The thought of renewing conversation with the diminutive Nazi by his side was ample motivation, and he had tonight to get through yet.

Richard Nork sounded his Klaxon at seven-thirty, and the entire sales floor rose as one. Jackets were slung on, some of the men untied their ties but then re-draped them, untied, around their necks. Don't get that one, thought Johnson, some just popped open their top shirt button. He left his tie defiantly knotted and top button secured.

"Alright Johnson?" asked Kate with a sweet smile.

So nice, who would have thought it? mused Johnson, although I expect she's only following orders.

"Fine," he replied.

"You've had a busy day," she remarked.

"Oh, you know," he replied, "I thought about what you said earlier, you know, about making the most of this chance you've given me," he said, convincingly.

"That's great Johnson, you won't regret it."

"No, I'm sure I won't," he said, less convincingly. "Which pub are we going to?"

"Pub?" Kate laughed.

"Yeah," said Johnson, baffled, "which pub?"

"Locked-In don't hold their formal events in pubs Johnson," said Kate, disdainfully.

"They don't?"

"Certainly not."

"Where are we going then?" he persisted.

"The Palomino," replied Kate.

"The Palomino? What's that?" asked Johnson.

Kate tutted and sighed.

"Where have you been? It's about time you stopped hanging out in grotty pubs."

"You go to pubs," rejoinder Johnson, accusingly.

"I never stay for long. I go purely for the sake of social expedience."

"Social expedience?"

"A meeting place. One drink. Move one somewhere a little more classy, or for a nice meal, perhaps."

"Right," sighed Johnson. "So this Palomino, it's a right classy gaff is it?" he said, trying to needle her.

"It's the coolest new bar," said Kate, "fantastic cocktails."

"Has it got a pool table?" Johnson asked.

"No."

"Can't be very cool then. What about a dartboard?"

"No. It hasn't got a bloody dartboard. This is not one of your usual haunts, so don't be stupid, Johnson," warned Kate.

"Alright. Sorry. What are we doing for food?" he asked.

"Grab something on the run, eat later, whatever," sighed Kate.

"I'll get a couple of cheese and pickle rolls or some pork scratchings in this Palomino place," remarked Johnson.

It was hard to establish the size of The Palomino. The place was full of mirrors and reflective silver surfaces, Johnson resolved not to drink too much as he feared the real possibility that later in the evening he might attempt to strike up a conversation with himself. Kate ditched him as soon as they arrived, she would have done so sooner but he had tagged along determinedly all the way from the office, trying to establish whether he would be able to get a brown ale or a barley wine at The Palomino.

Johnson waited for an age while the barmen tossed bottles back and forth, poured luminous liquids into glasses from great heights, and fannied about with fruit and frivolities. He propped an elbow on the bar and held aloft a ten pound note.

He watched as it took three people ten minutes to serve two drinks. They wouldn't last five minutes in the Grey Horse, he decided.

"Cocktail, sir?" a barman surprised him by wandering over.

"Me?" asked Johnson, "already?"

The barman smiled, shrugged, and walked away, and Johnson spent another ten minutes watching two drinks being prepared.

"Cocktail, sir?" another barman had approached.

"Pint of bitter please," said Johnson.

"Sir?" asked the barman.

"A pint of your finest draught bitter please," said Johnson.

"No draught," said the barman.

"No draught? said Johnson, "funny old pub."

"Sir might like a bottled beer."

"I might," agreed Johnson, "what are the choices?"

"We have Bishop's Finger, sir."

"Anything else?" asked Johnson.

"Just the Bishop's Finger, sir."

"Alright. Nun's Delight it is then," agreed Johnson, "in a jug."

"Sir?"

"In a jug. A glass with a handle. Not a straight glass."

"I don't think…" demurred the barman.

"There's one behind you look, said Johnson, "it's got matchbooks in it."

"Sir, I couldn't…"

"It's fine," said Johnson, "I'll have it. Pint of Nun's Delight in that glass over there, and if you won't give it to me then I demand to see the manager."

"What about the matches?"

"The matches? Bloody hell. Well, why don't you stick them in one of your funny straight glasses?"

"Right sir, good idea." said the barman, "coming up."

"Thank you," said Johnson, "could bring me two of those bottles, please?"

"Another glass, sir?"

"Just the jug will be fine," said Johnson.

Johnson found a leaning post and a shiny ashtray and stood alone surveying the scene. He was sure they were nice people, these brayers and gigglers and shouters, underneath the veneer of bravado. Some of them had packed in too much strong liquor in too short a time and were a little unsteady, a little sweaty about the brow, and a little too, well, *forward*. Some looked overanxious as well. Loud music played without variation, the relentless and ultimately harrowing sound of James Brown. Johnson shifted along a burnished shelf and positioned himself a little further away from the speakers.

"You did good work today," said Richard Nork, appearing at his side and draping an designer-clad arm over his shoulder.

"Er, thanks Richard," said Johnson, edging sideways, "sorry, if you don't mind, I'd prefer that you didn't touch me."

133

"No problem," said Richard Nork, removing his arm. "Just a gesture you know. Gesture of comradeship. Welcome you to the family. Make you feel like you belong. Nothing in it."

"No, I'm sure there isn't, Richard," said Johnson, apologetically, "it's just me, I'd just prefer you didn't. That's all," Johnson supped his beer, fingers wrapped through the handle of the chunky jug.

"No problem," replied Richard Nork, "not having a cocktail? I can recommend their rusty nail."

"No. I'm not big on cocktails, thanks," said Johnson, burying his face in his glass.

"Like the glass," said Richard Nork, enthusiastically, "where on earth did you get it?"

"Here," said Johnson.

"You can't have done. It's not very Palomino is it?"

"I did," Johnson assured him.

"Doesn't fit the image of The Palomino, though. How did you manage it?"

"I insisted," said Johnson, "I saw it behind the bar and I insisted on having it."

"You saw something you wanted and you went for it?"

Oh dear, thought Johnson.

"I did," he replied.

"That's good work again, Johnson," said Richard Nork, approvingly, "I'm impressed with that sort of thing."

"Are you?" said Johnson.

"Certainly am. Let me tell you, after the work you've put in today, we notice that sort of thing at Locked-In, you know, the work you put in during the day," Richard Nork was swaying a little and his breath reeked of scotch, "and I can tell you somebody else who would be impressed," he continued, "and here he is now."

Johnson looked up to see Simon Hart's baby features framed by his crown of blond curls. He was cradling a glass of champagne.

"What's this then, Richard?" said Simon Hart, "talking up the new blood, eh?" Simon Hart landed a crisp punch on Johnson's bicep, and Johnson spilt a little beer on the floor. Simon Hart laughed, and Richard Nork joined in shortly afterwards.

"Sharpen up, eh, Johnson?" said Simon Hart, "spilling your drink's not the Locked-

In way, you know."

"I'm sure it isn't," agreed Johnson.

"Not the way at all, eh, Richard?"

"Certainly not, Simon," said Richard Nork, slurring both the 'certainly' and the 'Simon', and not making much of a job of the 'not' either.

"Just to change the subject for a moment," suggested Simon Hart.

"Sure," said Johnson.

"You a bit of a writer, Johnson?" asked Simon Hart, sharply.

"A writer? No," Johnson assured him.

"Or a wit? Fancy yourself as a bit of a funny man, do you?"

"Can't say that I do," said Johnson.

Simon Hart was cold-eyed for one who was blessed with such otherwise angelic features, and Johnson felt a definite blast of the chill from Simon Hart's eyes.

"I understand that you've made a good start, Johnson, and that's to your credit."

"Thank you, Simon," said Johnson, draining his beer and snatching up the second bottle in one smooth manoeuvre. Before he had finished swallowing, he was refilling his jug.

"So, no playing silly buggers, eh? There's a good lad," Simon Hart's mouth was smiling at Johnson, but the eyes remained Arctic-cold.

He knows, thought Johnson, he knows. Well, it can't have taken much working out. I'll just have to be more careful in future.

"Simon," Johnson assured him, "I'm not a silly bugger."

"Would you like to get us some more drinks?" said Simon Hart, in a tone that made it clear that this wasn't a request.

"Sure," said Johnson, "champagne, rusty nail, beer."

"Champagne, water, beer, I think," said Simon Hart, glancing at Richard Nork.

Johnson talked the barman into preparing three simple drinks without tossing any of the glassware around, and returned to Simon and Richard, who had ousted some underlings and taken occupation of three seats and a table. Johnson fancied that he felt envious eyes on his back as he carried the drinks over.

"So," said Simon Hart," as Johnson took his seat, "are you looking forward to our little weekend away?"

Johnson regurgitated a little bitter into his glass.

"Weekend away? What, us three?" he asked, a little agitated.

"Us three?" Simon Hart was laughing, "away for a weekend together? That's good. No, no, that really is good."

"Obviously hasn't checked his e-mails," said Richard Nork, who was slumped a long way back in his seat.

"E-mails?" said Johnson, "well, I haven't looked since this morning, to be honest. Been so busy."

"No excuses, Johnson," said Simon Hart, "think of a suitable punishment will you Richard? For dereliction of E-mail duty?"

"I'll get on to it first thing," said Richard Nork, eyes closed.

"Make it suitably harsh and painful, eh?" smiled Simon Hart, "something nasty."

Richard Nork appeared to be asleep.

"He's a good man, Richard," said Simon Hart, "but he can't hold his drink, Johnson, you see?"

"I see," agreed Johnson, pouring from his new bottle.

"Now, to business."

Johnson sat up attentively.

"Our little weekend away. Coach arrives at the office at nine-thirty next Friday. We all pile on with our kit for the weekend. Coach all the way east, cross to France, get the tents up, all set for the activities," Simon Hart sipped his champagne and sat back in his seat. "Pencil you in can we?" he asked.

"Kit?" asked Johnson, faintly.

"Got a list here somewhere," said Simon, hunting in an inside pocket, "here we are, two pairs thick socks, running shoes one pair, walking stroke climbing boots one pair, shorts pairs two, swimming gear, T-shirts at least two but recommend more, sweatshirt or rugby shirt, casual wear for the evening, oh, and a flower and a hat. Prepare to get wet, to get shouted at, to get bloody exhausted, and let's not forget, to have a whole barrel-load of Locked-In fun and laughter."

"I'm busy that weekend," said Johnson, forcing beer into his mouth through the gaps in his gritted teeth.

"Disappointed in that, Johnson, I have to say. Disappointed. After such an impressive start too. I understand you've really hit the ground running."

"Well, there we are," said Johnson, keen to be making his way home, risking a mugging.

"What are you doing, then?" asked Simon Hart.

"When?" Johnson replied.

"Next weekend," said Simon Hart precisely, as if addressing a child.

"Usual stuff. I'm busy most weekends," said Johnson, adamantly.

"It sounds to me Johnson," said Simon Hart, "like you're being a little more evasive than is necessary here." He made a gesture with his hand and a bottle of beer and a glass of champagne arrived within thirty seconds. "If you're planning a weekend at home watching nauseating television programmes or consorting with some of the more repulsive members of your friends or family then you only have to tell me. I won't hold it against you," said Simon Hart, reassuringly, but in a voice which didn't seem to Johnson to drip with empathy.

Johnson took a steadying pull of Bishop's Finger, Simon Hart had succeeded in rattling him.

"As a matter of fact," said Johnson, rolling the words around his lips, "I'm going sky-diving."

"Sky-diving, eh?" said Simon Hart, "how exciting. Tell me all about it," he smiled, encouragingly, folding his arms and affecting an interested look.

"Sorry?" said Johnson.

"Tell me about it. Sky-diving. I want to know what you do."

Johnson gained a little thinking time by pulling out a cigarette. He placed it in his mouth and fiddled in his jacket pocket, he found the lighter, but brought out an empty hand.

"I'll just get some matches from the bar. Seem to have lost my lighter," he announced.

"Use mine," said Simon Hart, leaning forward and proffering a slim gold affair.

"Thanks," said Johnson, forcing a smile, "I didn't know you smoked."

"Oh, I don't," said Simon Hart, "I used to, but I stopped some time ago. I was always attached to this lighter, though, so I never stopped carrying it around. Filling it up, replacing the flint, cleaning it and so on. Comes in handy too, means people don't have to disappear when they need a light. If they do you can so easily lose the thread of the conversation, don't you find that? I do."

Johnson, inhaled, exhaled and nodded.

"Now where were we?" asked Simon Hart.

"Oh. I'm not sure," said Johnson, "now then, what was it…?"

"I know," announced Simon Hart, banging on the table and making Johnson jump and waking Richard Nork, who greedily gulped down all of his glass of water.

"You do?" asked Johnson, sounding depressed.

"Our activity weekend in France," said Simon Hart, proudly, "see, I remembered."

"So you did," agreed a happier Johnson, "France, of course."

"And then you were going to tell me all about sky-diving," said Simon Hart.

"I was, wasn't I? How about another drink?" Johnson asked.

"Just got one, thank you."

"I think I might get myself another one," announced Johnson.

"You've got a full one there."

Johnson had drained his jug before Simon Hart had finished the sentence. A little beer ran down his chin, but most of it was racing to join the rest, settling in his near-empty stomach.

"I'll get another," said Johnson, rising to his feet.

"No need," said Simon Hart, "here's the waiter. Another beer over here please, and you'd better bring him some more water," he gestured at the red-eyed Richard Nork.

"Thanks," said Johnson.

"So," said Simon Hart, expectantly.

"So," said Johnson.

"Sky-diving. Take me through it."

"Well," Johnson screwed up his eyes, this shouldn't be too difficult, "A group of us are going to meet on Saturday morning, at the airfield, and we're going to get on a plane, which will take off from the land and go up into the sky." Johnson's right hand did a useless imitation of an aeroplane.

"With you so far," said Simon Hart.

"And then we all jump out," said Johnson, triumphantly, "the end," he took a self-congratulatory gulp of beer.

"And that's it?" asked Simon Hart, puzzled.

"That's it," concurred Johnson.

"Well, I have to say, you're very cool and calm about something that always terrified me," smiled Simon Hart.

"Sorry?" Johnson choked out the word.

"From my days in the paras."

"The paras, really?" Johnson felt hot and flushed.

"Then it was all safety checks. Thorough, methodical, potentially life-saving safety checks. You didn't say anything about checking your 'chute, or anything else."

"I didn't want to bore you with mundane details."

"I see," said Simon Hart, "and which airfield do you use?"

"Which one?"

"Yes. Which airfield do you fly out of?"

"It's to the north," said Johnson. James Brown pounded on in his ears.

"To the north? To the north of what?"

"North London," said Johnson.

"Called?"

"I always get a lift," said Johnson.

"And you've never noticed where you're going?"

"Usually asleep in the back, you know."

"Or the name of the place once you're there?"

"Put it down to adrenalin," explained Johnson, "I'm just focussed on the moment. I'm in the zone, that's what we call it you know, the zone, we call it being in the zone. When you're in that hyped-up state unimportant details just don't register."

"Of course," said Simon Hart, "I understand. What's the bird?"

"Eh?" asked Johnson.

"The plane. What is it?"

"Oh, I'm not good on that technical stuff," said Johnson.

"You don't know what sort of 'plane you fly in?"

"Nah," said Johnson, "I'm only interested in getting up there and jumping out as quickly as possible."

"I see," said Simon Hart.

"And then going home again," said Johnson.

"I see," repeated Simon Hart.

"I mean I get the underground at least twice a day but I've no idea who makes the trains," said Johnson, confidently. He felt that he might have weathered the storm.

"Fair point," said Simon Hart.

"Cheers," answered Johnson.

"Listen, I have to circulate," said Hart.

"Of course," replied an understanding Johnson.

"I've enjoyed talking to you, it's been most interesting. Not to say enlightening."

I wouldn't have said it was particularly enlightening either, thought Johnson.

"Likewise," said Johnson, waving his jug in acknowledgement, "catch you later, Simon."

Simon Hart disappeared into the crowd and Johnson abandoned the still sleeping Richard Nork at the table. Johnson headed for the corridor and, after a brief detour to the gents, which bore so much resemblance to a hall of mirrors that in the confusion he pissed on his shoes, he made his escape to the street.

Johnson bought a bag of chips, which he sprinkled with a heavy dose of salt and vinegar, and a couple of hot sausages. He ate as he walked, licking his greasy lips and fingers, he hadn't realised how hungry he was until Simon Hart had abandoned his interrogation. Greedy and overeager, he burnt his tongue on a sausage. After he had finished eating he carried the empty wrapping paper for a long time, rubbish bins having joined the list of endangered species. He rubbed the sore spot of his tongue against his bottom teeth. Seem to have got away with that, he thought, although he knows that it was me who wrote on his stupid notice board. Have to be more careful in future. Johnson's route had taken him back to the offices of Locked-In. He paused at the black railings, taller than he, he rested his chin on the topmost crossbar and, with spikes on either side of his head, he looked into the faintly lit offices. One smocked woman was pushing a vacuum cleaner around the floor, he saw another spraying a heavy mist of furniture polish onto the screen of Kate's PC. Johnson mounted the short few steps to the front door, pushed in his entry code and walked in.

"Good evening ladies, good evening," he announced himself.

140

"Hello," said the polisher, the vacuumer hadn't seen and couldn't hear him.

"Nothing to worry about. Quick cleaning audit," said Johnson, confidently.

"What's this?" the vacuumer had switched off the machine.

"Cleaning check," said Johnson.

"This is a new one," said the polisher.

"New one on me," agreed the vacuumer

"New procedure, sorry, it seems you haven't been informed. You should have been. Questions will be asked." said Johnson. "I must say it looks like you're doing a fine job. Although, if I had a point to make, well, it's nothing, really," he looked at the polisher.

"What's the problem?" she asked.

"It's not that important," said Johnson.

"No, go on," said the polisher, encouragingly.

"Well," confided Johnson, edging a little nearer, "there is just one thing."

"Is it the vacuuming?" asked the vacuumer.

"No, no," Johnson assured her, "it looks absolutely perfect underfoot. I'll be putting in a favourable report on the condition of the flooring."

"Thank you," said the vacuumer.

"It's something else then?" said the polisher.

"If I had a criticism," Johnson began.

"Yes?"

"I would say you could get away with using a bit more furniture polish on the PC screens, and maybe leave it to soak in a bit before you polish it off."

"On the what?" asked the polisher.

"Here," Johnson pointed.

"Oh, on the tellies," said the polisher.

"That's it," said Johnson, brightly, "as much as you like on the tellies. The more the merrier."

"Got it," said the polisher.

"Now, if you'll excuse me, I've just got a few more things to check. You just carry on like I'm not here."

Within half an hour Johnson was on the train home. He finished the evening with a pint of water, three Nurofen, a couple of multivitamins and, on the basis that it probably wouldn't do any harm, a capsule of evening primrose oil which Anna had left in the bathroom cabinet. He set the alarm forty minutes earlier than normal and, apart from a short intermission at four when his protesting bladder nudged him awake, he slept without stirring.

Early the following morning Johnson walked onto the Locked-In sales floor, which he was pleased to see was deserted. He had awoken five minutes before the alarm was due to kick in, and had washed and dressed quickly, but unhurriedly. The train into the city was quiet at that time of day and he took advantage of the rare chance of a seated journey. Once in the front door, apart from a triangular detour from kitchen to a desk and then to his own desk, he soon settled himself in front of his notes and his PC and prepared for the day.

People nodded and wished him 'good mornings' as the space began to fill. His phone rang. Early for a punter, he thought. It was Kate, calling in sick.

"Shouldn't think that'll go down too well," he said, sagely, "place like this."

"I know, I know. Just can't do it today Johnson," she groaned.

"You know best," said Johnson.

"Just tell Richard for me would you?"

"You're supposed to report to him direct aren't you," said Johnson. I shouldn't be enjoying this quite so much, he thought, guiltily.

"Please, Johnson, just tell him."

"It's in the staff handbook isn't it? Let me have a look, ah, yes, I thought so, page thirty eight."

"Finished?" asked Kate.

"What?" Johnson replied.

"Had your fun?" she said.

"Yes thank you," said Johnson, considering it more even more fun to stop now, "what do you want me to tell Richard?"

"What?"

"About your illness."

"Food poisoning?"

"Useless," stated Johnson.

"It is isn't it? OK, I left the party and went for a Chinese and…"

"Sickness and diarrohea?"

"No good?"

"Firstly, I couldn't spell it, and secondly, it's another crap excuse, and thirdly, he won't believe you."

"Right…" said Kate.

Here it comes, thought Johnson.

"Tell him…"

Tenner on the nose, he said to himself.

"I've got…"

To win.

"Women's problems."

Bingo.

"That's it?" he said, "women's problems?" That's the best you've got?"

"It's the best there is Johnson," said Kate triumphantly, "the absolute and unimpeachable best, you just make sure you tell him."

"Alright," agreed Johnson, "I'll see you tomorrow."

"Tomorrow," agreed Kate.

"Depending on the state of your ovaries," said Johnson.

Spare seat next to me, he observed, that's fortunate.

Tales of drunken foolishness, of vomiting and of tickings off for pissing in the street developed into comparisons of headaches and nausea and the dry horrors. The water cooler, three-quarters full when Johnson had arrived, was almost drained. He walked over to it and was changing the bottle when Richard Nork arrived.

"Water, Johnson, water," he said.

Johnson smiled at him. Richard looked annoyingly healthy.

"How are you feeling, Richard?" he enquired solicitously.

"Me?" said Richard, surprised, "absolutely fine."

"Really?" said Johnson, "that's good. Considering you were pissed out of your mind not twelve hours ago."

Richard Nork paused while refilling his plastic cup.

143

"Point one, Johnson. You do not speak to me like that. Ever. Point two. I was not rendered immobile by alcohol."

"Not the whisky?" asked Johnson, innocently.

"Certainly not. Painkillers."

"I see," said Johnson, thoughtfully, sucking in his cheeks and biting both of them at once, "painkillers."

"Word of advice Johnson."

"Richard?"

"Remove supercilious look from face, remove arse from my vicinity, and go and get some bloody work done."

"Got it," said Johnson, keenly, deciding to bite his tongue. "My mistake."

Johnson strode back to his seat.

Few people noticed when, at eleven o'clock, the rolling news channel disappeared from both of the TV's. A few more began to take notice when the replacement programme flashed up, and when the titles announced the next feature to be, "Up the Anal Canal - A Dutch Barge Holiday", Johnson observed that the whole floor was paying attention.

Johnson watched Richard Nork scrabbling in his desk drawer for the remote control. Wasting his time, thought Johnson. Point one, Richard. That's the old remote from my flat, and let's not forget point two, I took out the batteries this morning. Howzabout point three, then Richard, my old mucker? Your remote, the one that works, is currently stuffed down the front of my trousers. Johnson watched the two men and two women on screen going through their carnal gymnastics. It's very clever, he thought, but are they having any fun? Alright, maybe the bloke who looks like he's just relieved himself of a whole large carton of double cream, he certainly looked like he enjoyed that last bit. That'll take some mopping up. And I moan about my career. Johnson looked around, everyone was silent, no fingers tapping at keyboards, nobody writing, all phone calls terminated, which, in view of the moaning and grunting noises emanating in crystal-clear surround sound, was probably a good idea.

The amusement, of course, lasted only until Richard Nork turned off one TV manually and raced to the opposite end of the office to terminate the other. Having done so, he spun around and gave the sales floor what he imagined to be his do-I-sign-on-

144

here? look. He turned and walked towards the door.

"Impressive bit of sprinting there, Richard," observed a voice behind his back.

"Surprised he could stand up," said another.

"Me too, said the first, "that fellah nearly hit the lens."

"Hit the spot, you reckon?"

"Did for Richard."

Richard Nork didn't pause on his short trip to Simon Hart's office.

Johnson gave it five minutes and wandered out to the reception area. He took an unusual interest in one of the many copies of *Recruitment Now!* while he waited for a call or a visitor to distract Sally the receptionist. He didn't have to wait long, a couple of short trills signalled an incoming call, and Johnson was able to surreptitiously stash Richard Nork's remote down the back of a squashy, bright orange sofa. He pushed down hard to ensure that it wouldn't be accidentally discovered, got to his feet, nodded and smiled at Sally, walked to the window, rubbing his chin thoughtfully all the way. Suddenly, he turned with renewed purpose, giving, he hoped, the impression of a problem solved, he smiled again at Sally and marched back to work. He had not been seated for long when Richard Nork reappeared.

"Right. Listen up," Richard Nork announced in a loud, clear voice. "Those of you who are not on the phone are to pay attention and not to make any calls for the moment. I have asked Sally not to put anyone through until I have finished. If the person next to you is in the middle of a call then they are to proceed with it and you are to tell them what I've said afterwards," Richard Nork had his thumbs tucked in his dinky waistcoat pockets and was pacing the floor. "Clear?" he asked. "Do I make myself clear?"

There was jumbled assent from the floor. Yes, sergeant-major, said Johnson, almost silently.

"OK. I have just spoken to Simon about the, er, incident of this morning. So, so that you know, Simon is aware of events, OK?"

A few people OK'd together.

"Simon is inclined to put this down to high spirits. Perhaps someone had a few too many last night and thought they'd have a bit of fun. We don't mind fun here at Locked-In, you know that, people. We encourage fun. For God's sake, we organise fun. For the team. For the Locked-In family."

Johnson watched Richard Nork spreading his arms as if to envelop his audience, like a TV evangelist.

"So, if the person who is responsible for this would like to make themselves known, we'll say no more about it."

Johnson joined everyone else as eyes were cast around the room, heads shaken, shoulders shrugged.

"Come on," encouraged Richard Nork, "you're only making things harder for yourself in the long run."

Don't think so, thought Johnson, you haven't got a frigging clue.

"Johnson!" barked Simon Hart.

Suddenly everyone's eyes were pointed at the doorway where Simon Hart stood, unannounced. Then Johnson felt the roomful of eyes swivel back to him.

Much as he felt compelled to, Johnson was careful not to rub his nose, or scratch the back of his head, or offer up any other tell-tale signs that he might not be about to tell the truth. He spun his chair slightly so that he and Simon Hart were exactly face-to-face. Maybe thirty feet separated them, but Johnson felt it was a necessary gesture.

"Morning Simon," said Johnson, confidently.

"Johnson," said Simon Hart, thoughtfully, "enjoy yourself last night?"

"Thank you, yes, I did," said Johnson. "Good few drinks, thanks for those. Thanks to the Locked-In family. Or to the daddy, I suppose."

A muffled snigger or two rattled around the room. Simon Hart nodded without expression.

"Get up to anything last night?" asked Simon Hart.

"To be honest Simon," Johnson replied, "I can't remember a bloody thing after we finished our little chat."

"Pity," said Simon Hart.

"Absolutely," agreed Johnson.

"Well, never mind," Simon Hart reassured him, "doesn't matter for now."

"Right," said Johnson.

"Better get your act together though."

"Simon?" said Johnson, puzzled.

"Little surprise for you, team," announced Simon Hart, turning through the degrees

146

to address the floor.

Surprise? thought Johnson, I'm not sure that I'm that crash-hot keen on surprises.

"In four weeks time, young Johnson here is not going to be a recruitment consultant anymore," said Simon Hart.

"I'm not?" said Johnson, slightly alarmed, "why not?"

"Because you're going to be a sky-diving instructor for the day," said Simon Hart, exultantly.

Johnson drove one of his few fingernails of any length hard into the first inner joint of his thumb and held it there, willing the pain to take over and take his mind off the situation.

"Really?" he said, "that's fantastic. How exciting." He found a soft part of inner thigh with his other hand and pinched himself so hard that it felt like someone had applied a pair of pliers to the flesh.

"I'm just sorry we have to put it off for four weeks," said Simon Hart, unapologetically.

"Never mind," said Johnson, "It is a shame though, because I'm just so excited that I wish it was this Saturday."

"Sadly, it's the trip to France, Johnson," said Simon Hart, "and then I'm busy for the next few weekends."

"Pity," agreed Johnson.

"I know," said Simon, "when it's your chance to show us what you can do, to pass on your expertise, to be top dog for the day, and now you've got to wait."

"Ah, well," said Johnson, philosophically.

"Builds up the tension though, doesn't it?" suggested Simon Hart.

"It does," Johnson agreed.

"On the plus side…" Simon Hart began.

There's a plus side? No, I don't expect there is, thought Johnson.

"It gives you plenty of time to prepare."

"Oh yes," Johnson concurred.

"To really think about it," said Simon Hart.

"I'll be doing that," said Johnson, "don't you worry."

"I'm glad I've given you plenty to think about, eh, Johnson?" Simon Hart departed quickly, leaving Johnson to field a volley of questions about sky-diving.

"Is it scary?" asked one.

"Yes."

"Will I throw up?" enquired another.

"Quite probably."

"This is going to be such a buzz. Do you get a huge rush every time you do it?" asked an action man.

"To be honest, it gets a bit dull after a while."

"How exciting is this?" observed an excited Australian, going up the scales as he brought the sentence to its conclusion.

"Not very."

"You'll look after us all won't you? I mean from a safety point of view. Make sure nothing can go wrong?" asked a nervous patient.

"Personally I find that if you want a real buzz, a man-sized buzz," he nodded at action man, "it's a laugh if you skip a few of the safety checks."

Johnson noted that his colleagues' enthusiasm had been suitably dampened, and he made his excuses and went out for lunch. On his calm and measured walk out of the office, he asked himself a question. It was roughly along the lines of, what the hell am I going to do? I'm a dead man, he decided.

Locked-In had been careful to inform Johnson that drinking at lunchtime constituted gross misconduct and was one of the offences for which the sack would be the sole and swift reward. Johnson sank four large vodka and tonics in a suitably out of the way, and, he considered this to be the clincher as far as his colleagues were concerned, down-at-heel pub. In consideration of Locked-In's rulebook he called into Boot's on his way back and bought a small bottle of mouthwash, most of which he swilled around his mouth while walking, swallowing around half of it, the slight peppermint tang overwhelmed by an aftertaste of chemicals. Probably not supposed to swallow it anyway, thought Johnson. He checked the label. The only words he could make out while walking were, DO NOT SWALLOW. At least it might get me out of teaching sky-diving, he told himself, while performing a complicated walking gargle and drinking the rest of the bottle. He followed the mouthwash with two wads of strongly-flavoured menthol chewing gum.

Johnson had almost made it back to the office with thirty seconds to spare when the heavy vibration of his phone gave him a jolt by jumping to life in his inside pocket. He paused by the front door and took the call. JeffandAnna would be coming round this evening to pick up the rest of their things. Johnson said he would see them later. Around eight. Anna said to make sure that Tim was there as well. Could be interesting, thought Johnson, hope it isn't though, I hope it's a boring, uneventful evening. Johnson cruised through the afternoon, keeping his head down and deflecting any questions about sky-diving. He called Tim.

"Great, I'll be there," enthused Tim.

"Just er, you know," said Johnson.

"What?"

"Oh, it's, well, I mean. Difficult, could be."

"Not too clear on what you're saying there, my friend," said Tim.

"That thing, you know, after, er, oh, night." Johnson barely continued.

"Yes. Still not getting through. Why don't you try stringing some words together in an order which might make a bit of sense?" suggested Tim.

"You sleeping with Anna a few hours after she got married," said Johnson, forcing the words out.

"Oh, that," said Tim, in recognition.

"What do you mean, oh that?" asked Johnson, "Oh that? Like it wasn't on your mind. Sleeping with the bride on her wedding night while the groom was next door?"

"Fucking her sister," observed Tim.

"Well, I suppose.."

"Things got a bit out of hand, Johnson, you know, but no harm done."

"No harm done? You're not worried about the effect on their relationship?"

"Never bothered them before," said Tim.

"Before," exploded Johnson, "you mean this wasn't the first time?"

"Nah. Don't get me wrong, it wasn't a regular thing either. But they like to swing a little from time to time, JeffandAnna."

"They do?" asked Johnson, incredulously.

"Yeah. But they're very discreet."

"I had no idea."

"Like I said, very discreet," said Tim.

"Weird though, isn't it? I couldn't imagine carrying on like that," said Johnson.

"Horses for courses," said Tim.

"I find it faintly disgusting though, don't you? No, well you quite obviously don't do you?"

"Not a bit," Johnson could see, no, he could hear Tim's grin stretching across his face.

"Just one thing, though," mused Johnson.

"What's that matey?" asked Tim.

"I can't believe they never asked me."

"You what?" laughed Tim.

"I must confess to feeling a little bit hurt."

"Because you weren't asked to participate in something that you would certainly have turned down because you find it faintly disgusting?"

"Would have been nice to have been asked, that's all," said Johnson, finally.

"Mate, it was a gag."

"What was?"

"Those two, wedding night, knew you were in the kitchen, there wasn't any swapping, ducked in the opposite rooms in the dark and then ducked straight out again after you'd gone, just a joke, worked like a charm though, didn't it?"

"So JeffandAnna don't swing?"

"Well, if they do they've never asked me," reported Tim.

"I'm going to need more proof than that," said Johnson.

Jeff was already at the flat when Johnson arrived home. He was sitting on the floor, sorting through a pile of CD's.

"How was Paris?" asked Johnson.

"Great," replied Jeff, "just perfect. Is this mine or yours?" Jeff held up a CD.

"How dare you?" said Johnson, "that's definitely yours."

"Is it?"

"Duran Duran is certainly not mine," said Johnson, firmly.

150

"Must be Anna's," decided Jeff.

"Yeah, OK," grinned Johnson. "So, married life is good?"

"Yeah, it really is."

"Does it feel any different?"

"I don't know Johnson. I told someone that it did and they told me that it shouldn't. So, the next person who asked, I told them it didn't and they told me that it should."

"But what do you think?" quizzed Johnson.

"Truthfully?"

"Of course."

"I don't know. Is this yours?"

"Must be Anna's," said Johnson, glad to be rid of a Bee Gees album he'd bought while romantically confused. "Where is she, anyway?"

"On her way. Where's Tim?"

"Who knows? Get you a drink? Glass of wine?"

They squatted together on the floor and gradually decided that they didn't have enough of the 'right' sort of music.

Tim pitched up soon afterwards. Seems about four pints to the good, thought Johnson. Tim fetched a tumbler from the kitchen and filled it with most of the rest of the bottle.

"Cheers all," he announced. "Got any photos of your Parisienne honeymoon then?"

"Yeah. Haven't got them with me though," Jeff replied.

"Just keep it that way and we won't have a falling out," said Tim.

"Tim!" protested Johnson.

"Nothing so boring as other people's holiday snaps. Here's one of me on the beach, here's one of me eating my dinner, here's one of me having a fuck," said Tim.

"Here's Anna," said Johnson.

Anna looked good, thought Johnson, smiling, slightly tanned and fit. She kissed Tim on the cheek, bent down and did the same to Johnson.

"What about the old man, then?" asked Jeff, good-naturedly.

"You've had quite enough of that," said Anna.

"All finished now is it? Now you've trapped him?" asked Tim.

"Correct," said Anna. "From now on, he's on strict rations."

"Quite right too," said Tim, "filthy little bleeder. Get him to concentrate on doing some work for a change."

"Making some money," said Johnson.

"Gonna need it," said Tim.

"Kids to put through university,"

"What?" protested Jeff.

"Need a cash mountain for that, you know, "tuition fees, books, living expenses, and that's not until later on is it Johnson?"

"Absolutely. Load of expense in the first eighteen years. Clothes, toys, bikes, holidays," said Johnson.

"School trips, pets, uniforms, food," Tim continued.

"Food?" said Anna, "food?"

"Got to feed the little buggers well, else they won't make it into Cambridge will they?" said Tim.

"Cambridge now is it?" asked Johnson.

"You have to aim high, Johnson, shoot for the stars and you might just hit the moon."

"Wise words," said Johnson, "listen to this man."

"Trying not to," said Anna, "trying really hard."

"Seriously though, when are you going to start knocking out some kids?" asked Tim.

"Still got a lovely way with words hasn't he?" observed Anna.

"It's one of his gifts, the sweet turn of phrase," observed Johnson.

"My advice is, don't leave it too long," Tim persisted.

"Why's that?" asked Jeff, who had been sitting quietly in amused bewilderment.

"Well, the university thing. Don't want to be putting them through uni when you're retired or nearly retired," said Tim.

"Retired? Jesus, give us a chance," protested Anna.

"Be around sooner than you think," said Tim.

"The clock is ticking," said Johnson, almost to himself.

"What was that, J?" asked Tim.

Johnson seemed to rouse himself from a daydream.

"I said the clock is ticking," repeated Johnson, glumly.

"So that's it," said Tim later, "the end of an era."

JeffandAnna had made their slightly tearful departure, and Tim and Johnson sat together, paying little attention to a film, which was playing out quietly.

"Yes," said Johnson, "won't be the same without them."

"Do you think they'll be OK?" asked Tim.

"Marriage, you mean?"

"Yeah, marriage. Think they'll make a go of it?"

"I think so. Hard to tell though isn't it?"

"It's a bit of a lottery," observed Tim.

"Do you think you'll ever get married?" asked Johnson.

"Who knows? Meet the right one, time to settle down, mortgage, kids. I'd like kids."

"You would?" said Johnson.

"Yeah, I'd be a good dad, I reckon."

"I think you probably would," agreed Johnson.

"You?"

"What, kids?" asked Johnson, "I don't know. The thought doesn't really appeal. I'm not sure it would be fair to pass on all my hang-ups to the next generation, better to leave them to wither and rot, anyway, I think I'm probably too selfish."

"Yes," agreed Tim.

"What do you mean, yes?"

"I think you're probably too selfish."

"Don't know about marriage though."

"You're probably too selfish for that as well," said Tim.

Johnson was early for work again. He went down to the gents and read the notice board.

Mystery Prize to be Won, read the heading. *How much money are we going to make this week? Enter your guess and your name below and the nearest one will be the lucky winner. Be a winner!*

One pound twenty pence, Joe Stalin, wrote Johnson, and went back to his desk for the day. He was interrupted at four by a call, he looked at the phone display. Simon

Hart. Summoned.

"Come in Johnson. Sit."

"Thank you."

"Now, straight to business," said Simon Hart, brusquely.

"Right," said Johnson. I hope this isn't about sky-diving, he said to himself.

"Sky-diving," said Simon Hart, "lot of nonsense. You didn't fool me."

"I know," admitted Johnson, keen to cut his losses.

"Gave you a fright, I hope."

"Oh, yes," agreed Johnson.

"Sleepless night?"

"Absolutely," said Johnson.

"Mission accomplished then," said Simon Hart, happily.

"Mission accomplished," Johnson concurred.

"Good man," said Hart, "good man for coming clean. No more nonsense then, OK?"

"Right," said Johnson, "you can rely on me."

"We've looked at what you're doing, and you're doing it well, so keep on doing it."

"I'll keep on doing it," Johnson assured him.

"Coming to France?"

"No thanks," said Johnson, "I'm busy."

"Alright. I won't ask what you're doing. I find scuba-diving so dull, d'you see?"

"What about the staff?" asked Johnson.

"The staff? What about them?" asked Simon Hart.

"Won't they be expecting sky-diving lessons?"

"They might. One or two of them, but most of them will be relieved I should think."

"You know that they don't want to spend their weekends away from home doing company stuff?"

"Of course," said Simon Hart.

"So, why do you force them?"

"Because I can," said Simon Hart, cheerily, "because I haven't got much else to do, I employ Richard to run things, I've got you lot to do, if you'll excuse me, the donkey work, and because I can."

"I see," said Johnson.

154

"Got to get my kicks somewhere. Right. Job done. Time you were back at your desk, Joe Stalin."

"Now that wasn't me," said Johnson, calmly, "I've seen it, I'll admit I thought it was funny, but hand on heart, I swear it wasn't me."

"Look me in the eye, Johnson," said Hart, "and tell me again."

This takes me back to mixed infants, thought Johnson, and I could get away with it then as well. He fixed Simon Hart with a steady gaze, eyes slightly narrowed, jaw set firm.

"I swear Simon, I'll swear on whatever you like, that I did not write that stuff on the notice board."

Simon Hart held his gaze and was silent for thirty seconds.

"You know what Johnson?" he said, "I believe you. Now bugger off back to work."

"Another cleaning audit?" said Bliss. Johnson had established that she was from Sierra Leone.

"Nothing to worry about, ladies," Johnson assured them, "just routine."

"You sure?" asked Shakira. Johnson hadn't managed to find out her origins and suspected she was an illegal.

"Strictly random," he said, "strictly random. Couple of things to look at up here and then I'm going to have a look around the rest of building. So, if you'll excuse me?"

Johnson had spent an hour walking the streets after work before returning to the office. When he left the building shortly afterwards he had his prize in the carrier bag which was tucked under his arm, and when he got home, he set to work.

He heard a whoop the following morning. An excited striped-shirt bounded over to Richard Nork's desk and thrust a sheet of paper at him. Nork took it, he read it, he looked up and smiled his non-smile. The sales floor were rapt in anticipation, some already poised for the climb onto the tables. Richard Nork reached down and pressed his Klaxon button. Silence. People looked from face-to-face. Silence. But now there should be an ear-splitting racket, and applause, and cheering, and dancing on tables. Johnson looked as surprised as his colleagues, even though he had spent two minutes last night under Richard Nork's desk with a screwdriver, disconnecting the two slim wires.

Johnson watched as Richard Nork stepped onto his desk and announced, "Slight technical hitch, ladies and gentlemen, slight technical hitch. Normal service will be resumed as soon as possible, but I'll have to fill in for now…"

Johnson cringed.

"Hurrroooogah," squeaked Richard Nork, in a no way even barely passable impression of a Klaxon, "Hurrroooogah," he squeaked again.

Johnson rose numbly to his feet, and clapped his hands together gently. The rest of the sales floor were similarly underwhelmed. Just goes to show, thought Johnson, how the lack of proper equipment can undermine things.

Johnson was fairly relaxed about his little campaign of terror. Locked-In had a high turnover of people, another two or three had come and gone since he'd started. As far as Locked-In were concerned it could be any one of the staff, so there was no particular reason for the finger to be pointed in his direction. The conversation with Simon Hart had helped, coming clean right away had enhanced his credibility and, probably more importantly, he was making money for them. He went home that evening and composed a letter, which he slipped onto Simon Hart's desk the following morning.

Johnson was a little surprised at the lack of response to his note. He had expected a full-blown inquisition, perhaps he had worded it poorly. He thought back on what he had written.

We've got your bear. If you want to see it again, do not contact the police. Await further instructions.

He signed it:

With love from The Popular Movement for the Liberation of Innocent Bears from Capitalist Pig Slavery.

Seems OK, he thought, nothing to misconstrue there. Perhaps Simon Hart was waiting for the kidnapper to make a mistake? I suppose he could actually be awaiting further instructions couldn't he? Right then, if the ball's in my court I'm going to have to hit it. Johnson waited a couple of days before sending his next communication.

You have failed to contact us. Here is notice that you should take us seriously.

Johnson employed a bread knife to saw off the bear's ear. The one with the button

156

sewn into it. He dropped it into a jiffy bag with the note and mailed it from a post office not far from Locked-In's offices. Let's see if that gets any sort of reaction, he thought. For a fleeting moment he also thought, why am I doing this? But, deciding he was stumped, he concentrated instead on his next move. He went home that evening, took the bread knife from the kitchen drawer, and carefully dismembered the rest of Simon Hart's teddy bear. He packaged up the pieces. The one-eared head in one, two arms in another, a package each for the legs, and so on. The next day he dropped the arms into the post.

A couple of days later, an e-mail summoned all of the staff to the conference room for a meeting. Johnson trooped down with the rest of them. Down the short staircase with its slatted wooden steps they marched, along the wooden corridor, into the wooden-floored and walled meeting room, with its large wooden table. Easier to set fire to the place, thought Johnson.

When all were seated, Richard Nork picked up the phone from the small table by the door, pressed three keys and spoke briefly. Simon Hart appeared shortly afterwards.

"What's all this about, I wonder?" asked Kate, who was seated next to Johnson.

"Dunno," stated Johnson. "Anyway, how are you feeling?"

"Much better, thanks," she replied.

"Over the ovaries?"

"Very funny," said Kate, clicking her tongue.

Simon Hart click-clacked across the floor to the far end of the table and stood at its head. He was carrying two packages, which he placed on the table in front of him. He shook his head vigorously, as if trying to hurl invasive insects from his ears, and his curly blond mane wafted around for a moment. His cheeks had taken on a deeper shade than their usual soft pink.

"Jokes," announced Simon Hart, "I like a joke, I really do. I appreciate that some of you might find the idea that I have a fantastic sense of humour hard to swallow. You might think that, as head of this organisation, I must be a terribly serious fellow, forever wrapped up in commerce and interest rates and expansion and the financial markets, as I try to take Locked-In Recruitment, this great creation of mine, to greater and greater heights. To, perhaps to some you, an almost unimaginable level in the corporate

157

firmament."

Modest and with a sense of humour, observed Johnson, silently.

"But when something like this happens," Simon Hart tipped Teddy's buttoned ear and his two ragged-ended arms onto the table. "When something like this happens," his voice rose quite alarmingly, "my sense of humour takes a walk. You got me?"

Johnson mused that perhaps Simon Hart had once worked for the Chicago Police Department. On the Urban Bear Patrol, perhaps.

"The bear is a joke, OK?" Simon Hart went on, "I'm not attached to the bear, I don't care about the bear, cut the bear up if you like, whoever you are. And I know it's someone sitting in this room right now." Simon Hart's blue-pink eyes took a slow tour around the assembly. Some looked at the floor or the table or the ceiling, some preferred an indeterminate centre-space gaze, as if daydreaming, others took on Simon Hart eyeball to eyeball. Johnson chose a space halfway between a black and white print of the London skyline on the wall opposite and the edge of the table.

"I know that owning up would be beyond most of you," he continued.

And he has the nerve to have a go at my motivational skills? exploded Johnson, but silently.

"So this is what will happen. No more parcels. They don't worry me, they cause me no concern, so don't bother sending any more. Understood? Conversation over."

Like a forensic scientist, Simon Hart re-bagged Teddy's bits and everyone waited until he had left the room before rising to their feet.

"You alright, Kate?" asked Johnson as they re-climbed the short flight of stairs.

"Yes," said Kate, curtly.

"OK, I know I took the piss a little. Didn't mean anything by it, you know?"

"I know," sighed Kate, "you don't have to apologise."

"It's just that I don't want to upset you, OK?"

"You don't seem to be taking to this like I hoped you would."

"Taking to what?" asked Johnson.

"The job."

"I thought I was doing my job pretty well," Johnson protested.

"You're doing the *work* pretty well," said Kate, precisely.

"That's what it's all about isn't it? The work?"

"It's only part of it, Johnson," said Kate, as they resumed their seats, both nudging a mouse to make pictures miraculously reappear.

"Surely that's it. Turn up on time, do your job to the best of your ability and go home at reasonable hour to enjoy the fruits of your hard labour," said Johnson, "that's all anybody wants isn't it?"

"Johnson," said Kate, patiently, and too patronisingly patient for Johnson's taste, "I haven't seen you networking. I haven't seen you really trying to build client relationships. I think you have the ability to communicate at all levels, but I don't see you applying it. Or stretching your boundaries, you know, pushing the envelope. Do you want to know what I think?"

"I'm sure," Johnson checked himself, "I'm sure it will be useful," he smiled.

"I think you're in the comfort zone."

"What? What bloody comfort zone?" Johnson shot back.

"See, there you are, that's another thing. The moment anyone tries to help you, you just go on the defensive."

"It's just the crap filter kicking in."

"Or sarcastic."

"Alright then, for the sake of our friendship, I apologise. Alright? Will you tell me about the comfort zone if I apologise?"

"Apology accepted," said Kate, sweetly.

I could really punch her when she's like this, thought Johnson. Not that I would, he told himself, hurriedly.

"What comfort zone?"

"You've got it too easy," said Kate, smoothly.

"In what way do I have it too easy?" asked Johnson, staccato.

"You're in the comfort zone."

"I'm not getting this," said Johnson, shaking his head in frustration, "I'm really not getting this at all. From six in the morning to nine at night, fifteen hours a day, give or take, I'm either crawling out of a soft, warm and, I'll admit, invariably empty bed and getting ready for work, or I'm trying to dodge whatever screw-up that London Transport have cooked up for the day and get myself into work, or I'm struggling to get myself home again and I'm climbing back into a freezing, and still frigging deserted bed, and when I'm not doing all that, and when I'm not waking up at three in the morning worrying my tits off about this bastard place and the wankers within it, I'm actually sitting here and doing the fucking job and waiting for my bollocks to hit the ground," Johnson paused to suck in some air, "you're my friend Kate, and I know I can speak freely, so maybe you'd like to tell me what's so fucking comfortable about that?"

Kate looked at Johnson, she smiled one of her regulation smiles, and gave him a resigned shrug.

"Strive, Johnson, strive."

"What?" asked Johnson in frustration, disappointed that his monologue had passed with so little effect or reaction.

"There is always room for improvement," said Kate, slowly, "for personal betterment, remember that. There's a life coach I could recommend, if you like."

"I'm going out," announced Johnson, "can I bring you back a sandwich?"

"It's not twelve yet," advised Kate.

"Got to get out," said Johnson, tensely.

"What about Richard Nork?"

"Think I should get him a sandwich?"

"Don't be flippant," said Kate, "this is what I've been saying to you, don't you see?"

"I see it Kate," said Johnson, breathing deeply and trying to calm himself. "The thing is, I can cope with the work. That's the bit that's alright. I've just got a problem with all of the bollocks that seems to go with it."

"You're going out then?" asked Kate.

"Got to," affirmed Johnson.

"And what do I tell Richard?"

"Tell him I'm attempting to stretch the boundaries of my morning, so that they collide with lunchtime that much more quickly. Something that can only be for my own personal betterment, and if he doesn't swallow that, then try the envelope pushing thing," Johnson slipped on his jacket. "Sandwich or a salad?"

"Wait," said Kate, "I'll come with you."

"Are you sure?" asked Johnson, suddenly concerned. "Just because I'm…"

"Because you're what?" enquired Kate.

"Because I'm, I don't know, because I'm whatever I am, doesn't mean that I should

160

drag you into it."

"See you outside," said Kate, "go on."

Johnson glanced back as he left the office and saw Kate bending over and speaking to Richard Nork at his desk.

They walked across the road to a sandwich bar and perched on stools at a high table in the sunny window with bottles of sparkling water and good, crisp ham and salad baguettes.

"I don't get you, Johnson," said Kate, "you're a good bloke, quite charming when you put your mind to it. And as you point out, quite rightly, you're good at the job, but you're not prepared to put in that little bit extra."

"No I'm not. But you are aren't you?" said Johnson, firmly.

"Sure I am."

"Why do you think you're like that?"

"Because I want to get on."

"And that's the only way?"

"It might not be the only way, Johnson, but at the moment it's the only way I know."

"You scared me a bit the other day, you know," Johnson ventured.

"I scared you?" laughed Kate, "How?"

"Oh, you know, the mad look in the eyes, the fervour, the company song, wanting to run off and tell Simon and Richard about it."

"Just trying to get on."

"So you don't necessarily believe in it?"

"I believe in the rewards."

"Anything else?"

"I like the money Johnson," said Kate firmly, "and if I have to play their silly games to get what I want...well.."

"You'll do it," said Johnson.

"Why not?" shrugged Kate, "small price to pay."

"Is it?" queried Johnson, "is it such a small price?"

"I think so. Listen, Johnson, it's hard out there. Out there? Here I mean, here is where it's bloody hard, and I'll do what I have to do."

"I don't know, Kate," said Johnson, resignedly.

"I don't understand," said Kate, "what's so wrong with it?"

Johnson chewed steadily for half a minute, assuring her with his eyes that he had an answer for her, he swilled back some water and swallowed the resultant mush.

"There's a bloke I see some mornings, most mornings, actually, on the station. He's there early in the morning, sometimes late at night, freezing his knackers off in winter. He's got his notebook, his pencil, wears an anorak, you know the type?"

"Sounds like one of those trainspotters."

"Right, don't think he works. Seems to have a lot of free time."

"Doesn't work?"

"Well, I think, from speaking to him, he's not quite, you know."

"Oh, OK."

"So, I've always been a bit sniffy, you know, when he tells me that this one coming in is his favourite train, or what the signals are doing, and why the train's stopped outside the station, and the loop line, which actually is quite interesting.. ."

"Go on," Kate directed him.

"The other night I saw him there, chatting away, smiling, writing his numbers down."

"And?"

"I thought, look at him. What makes me any better than him? He's happy, he's always smiling, he's got a purpose in life, he's harmless. Why should I think that I'm so bloody superior? What makes me so special?"

"Well, to start with, you're not a wanky train spotter are you?" said Kate, confidently.

"So what's the point?" asked Johnson, "Of the story? I mean, I'm not sure, but I know it means something to me. I just don't know what."

"Well, if you don't…"

Johnson screwed up the tail end of his lunch in the paper bag and knocked back the last of his water. He looked at Kate steadily.

"Kate, do you ever feel that you're not really here?"

"What do you mean, here?"

"Or not really there?"

"Not really there? Asked Kate, sounding confused, "Or here?"

Johnson took a breath, sniffed and gave his head a brief shake, "Sorry, he said, "I'm not explaining this very well."

Kate sucked iced coffee through a straw, and gave him a glint of her wide blue eyes. She slurped and swallowed.

"Go on," she encouraged.

"Like yesterday, I was at Richard's desk, talking to him about something. I was saying things, and I could hear what I was saying, hear what he was saying, but it was like I was standing a few feet away and watching the conversation."

"Weird," decided Kate.

"Alright, it is weird," agreed Johnson.

"You are," said Kate.

"No, I…"

Kate picked up on Johnson's frustration. He had the look of a schoolboy who'd just discovered his PE kit floating in the toilet five minutes before the lesson.

"Sorry, Johnson," she reassured him, "hey, come on."

Johnson's shoulders heaved as he gave out another quiet sob.

"Come on," she stood and put an arm around his shoulder, "come on, big boy, no tears."

"Shit," sniffed Johnson, "I'm sorry."

"Alright, it's alright. You're not weird. I don't think you're weird."

"Thank you," said Johnson, gratefully.

"Are you OK now?"

"Fine, I'm absolutely fine, don't know what came over me," Johnson assured her, "do you ever worry that when you're walking down the street and thinking about something that you've actually been talking out loud?"

"Errm, possibly," Kate replied.

"You don't do you?"

"No," said Kate.

"You never feel that you're not really here either?"

"Or there," said Kate.

"Maybe it's just me," said Johnson.

163

"Have you thought about, you know, seeing someone?" Kate suggested, "about these feelings?"

"Seeing someone?"

"Well, a doctor. Your GP, perhaps."

"My GP?" said Johnson.

"To start with, anyway," said Kate, "just to get a referral to a specialist. Come on, time we were getting back."

Johnson had finished dinner. Earlier, he had walked with Kate to the station, glad that they were friends again, although he now felt a little disadvantaged. The bloke who cries at lunchtime and has strange visions. The oddball. He was listening to some old rock and roll, drinking water, and singing along.

"Feel like jumping, baby won't you…"

"Very noisy in here," said Tim, collapsing into an armchair.

"Didn't hear you come in," said Johnson.

"Not surprised. What's this? Return of the Teds?"

"Oh, you know,"

"Bad day?"

Johnson decided not to mention his lunch with Kate. Tim wouldn't understand.

"Went out for lunch with Kate and burst into tears," Johnson blurted out.

"Did she?" asked Tim.

"Not her," Johnson figured that when Tim eventually found out, as he surely would, it would be immeasurably worse, so he decided to be first with the story.

"What do you mean, not her?" asked Tim, "Who, then?"

Johnson said nothing, just raised his eyebrows and looked across at his friend.

"Oh, mate. Don't tell me you've been sacked again?"

"I've told you, I told you last time, I've never been sacked."

"Well, not officially," agreed Tim, grudgingly.

"Not bloody unofficially either," said Johnson, heatedly.

"Alright, alright," said Tim, calmly, "so why the blubbing?"

"Oh, I don't know," said Johnson, sounding unconcerned, "it was nothing."

"Fine," said Tim, glad to be excused counselling. "Drink?"

"No, I wasn't going to tonight," said Johnson, "anyway, how was your day?"

"Have a drink with me and I'll tell you all about it," offered Tim, bounding off to the kitchen.

The music had finished, four unopened beers sat on the table, two opened ones in their hands.

"Fired?" said Johnson, incredulously.

"Undoubtedly," belched Tim.

"I don't understand," said Johnson, "you were doing so well."

"So it seemed," said Tim.

Johnson walked across to the stereo. This called for a bit of Coldplay.

"Fuck. Are you trying to finish me off?" asked Tim, after a few of bars.

"Sorry," Johnson apologised, "I'll change it," he rose to his feet.

"No, no, leave it. Not listening anyway."

"What happened?"

"New system, you see. Implemented a new system, they did. Teams, always had your teams, but now it seems to be that the idea is that the team competes against itself."

"Doesn't sound like a team to me," Johnson offered.

"You're not wrong," Tim took a long draught and shook a cigarette from his packet.

"And?" prompted Johnson.

"Mmm," Tim exhaled. Satisfied, he swallowed, and continued, "so we find out that this is the new deal. Based on the results, the point scoring and all the rest. At the end of the quarter there's some twat does a calculation of all our performances."

Tim lapsed into silence.

"He does a calculation," said Johnson.

"Who?" asked Tim.

"Some twat."

"Correct," said Tim.

"And then what happens is…"

"Sorry, lot to get my head round," said Tim.

"You seem a bit distracted," agreed Johnson.

"Yeah. Apologise. Right. Calculation. Top twenty five per cent get a bonus, bottom twenty five per cent get shown the door."

"What about the other fifty per cent?"

"They get to be ever so grateful that they're still in work."

"Unlike you," observed Johnson, and regretted it immediately, "sorry."

"Can't argue with the facts, can I?" said Tim, ruefully, "nail on the head, dear boy, that's what you've just hit, nail square on the head.

"What are you going to do?"

"You don't follow the football anymore do you? But you must remember enough, I'm thinking that you must, remember enough, I mean. I'm like the England coach at the moment."

"Resolute?" suggested Johnson, uncertainly.

"Fucking clueless."

"Fancy going out?" asked Johnson.

"You know," said Tim, "I don't. Funny, I don't have to be up in the morning, or for who knows how many more mornings, and I don't want to go out. When I had to be in work at seven I'd be happy on the pull and the piss until four or whenever, as long as there was a party going on I was going along with it, but tonight? Tonight, when I can, when maybe I should, what I want is a quiet night in with my old mucker, just the two of us. What's on the box, dear boy? Tell you what, you get the kettle on, I'll have a strong tea, drop of milk, no sugar, and while you're brewing up I'll find us a nice film to watch. Whaddya say?"

Although they had both seen it before, they watched Robert de Niro and others in Ronin.

"I remember watching this with," Tim paused, puzzled, "what was her name?"

"Don't know, Tim," said Johnson.

"Steph, that was it, Stephanie," announced Tim, triumphantly.

"Stephanie?" queried Johnson, "you couldn't remember Stephanie's name?"

"Got there in the end," mumbled Tim, defensively.

"The Stephanie you were engaged to? Your fiancée Stephanie?"

"Well, yes," agreed Tim, arms folded across his chest, "but we weren't really engaged, not as such."

"You weren't engaged?"

"No," protested Tim, "like I say, not as such."

166

"So, the ring you bought her, you remember, the one she went around showing off to total strangers."

"Yeah?" shrugged Tim.

"An engagement ring?"

"Yeah, well," Tim screwed up his eyes, his face, in protest, "didn't count."

"What do you mean it didn't count? You gave the girl an engagement ring."

"Didn't count," maintained Tim.

"Why ever not?" asked Johnson.

"Well, I had no intention of getting married."

So," Johnson reached for one of Tim's cigarettes, "why get engaged?"

"She wanted to."

"Engagement leads to marriage, Tim," advised Johnson, "it's called being engaged to be married."

"Not in my book."

"So that's why it finished."

"Yeah, I told her I didn't mind being engaged, quite enjoyed being engaged, but marriage? Forget it."

"Forget it?"

"Had to tell her."

"To forget it?"

"Pretty much," said Tim, "anyway, we're getting off the point."

"Sorry to interrupt you with trivia," said Johnson, heavily.

"That's alright," said Tim, "don't worry about it. So I hired this film, Ronin. After twenty minutes she's up getting a drink, want me to pause it? I said, she says, no, that's alright. Then she's up getting a book, doing her nails, putting the rubbish out. Want me to pause it? No, she says, this is terrible. Terrible? I said, two hours of gunfights and car chases? What's not to like?"

"I see," said Johnson.

"You do? You can see that we were incompatible? Funny, a little thing like a film can tell you so much, can't it?" Tim settled back happily in his chair. "This is a good bit," he said.

"So you'll be job hunting then?" asked Johnson later.

167

"Hard to get up for it. You know I was talking to someone lately who went through five interviews."

"Five different job interviews?" enquired Johnson.

"No, not exactly. Five interviews with the same organisation."

"For the one job?"

"For the one job," stated Tim, with a knowing look. "The one job for the one person."

"Seems a bit OTT. Not seeing the same person five times, surely?"

"No, no. See someone, then an HR person, then someone else a bit more senior, then two together, then maybe finally a board."

"What, and then they blindfold you, and strip you naked, and abandon you in Glasgow and you've got to find your way home with no money?"

"It's probably coming to that," said Tim, "and I don't know if I can be bothered with it all."

"But you're good at it Tim. You've been doing this for a while now and you've made the bonuses and earnt the good money," protested Johnson, "why give up now?"

"The bullshit, my old friend, I'm tired of the bullshit. They might think they're making things better but all they're doing is alienating the workforce. They have these arseholes sitting in their little cabins dreaming up crackpot ideas to motivate us and to spur us on. What do they fucking know? They're not at the sharp end. Like you say, I've been doing this for a few years now, I'm good at it. I know I'm an arrogant dickhead, but I am good at it, I know I am. Funny, isn't it? That all their plans to motivate and inspire have exactly the opposite effect? Have you noticed," Tim paused for tea and nicotine, "have you noticed that these pricks aren't judged the same way as we are, are they? How would you reward someone who'd managed to destroy everyone's morale and desire and drive and hunger?"

Johnson knew that interrupting Tim in full flow was likely to be fruitless.

"I'll tell you how," Tim continued, "they want to sack the fuckers. All of 'em."

"They can't all be bad," offered Johnson.

"All of 'em," said Tim adamantly, "sack the fuckers. Get 'em cleaning up after the rest of us, shit-shovelling, something like that. Least they'll have had some practice."

"So," Johnson paused, "what do you think you're going to go for?"

"Not sure I am. Might try something else. Go on the markets with my brother, he's got a few stalls."

"Seriously?"

"Yeah, why not? Mate of mine's a plasterer. Serious money to be made plastering let me tell you."

"Yes, but," said Johnson, "you're a city trader."

"So?" asked Tim, "so all of a sudden I'm something else, aren't I?"

"Seems a pity to throw it all away, that's all."

"Pissed off with it. Like I said, too many people with not enough to do, throwing their weight around, trying to make waves, you know, get themselves noticed, by pushing their looney-tunes theories. What is it? They're just justifying their own existence, aren't they? All well and good, but don't fuck up mine on your way through. I'm pissed off Johnners, had it with all of it, and let me tell you, I ain't the only one. It goes on like this, more and more are going to bail out and then where are they going to be?"

Johnson shrugged in encouragement.

"Up shit river without a frigging boat. That's where."

"I know what you mean," said Johnson.

"It'll happen," said Tim, ardently, "I mean it, man, people have had enough. Wouldn't take much to tip them over the edge."

"You think so?" said Johnson.

"I know so, boy."

"Mmm," Johnson thought of the rabid look in Kate's eyes, of the Klaxon, and of Richard Nork and Simon Hart, and the notice board, "I'm not so sure," he said.

Interview Phase VI

"*You're* looking very fit, Johnson," I observed.

He looked down at his body. Then held each arm out and gave himself a slow inspection.

"Cheers," he smiled.

"For someone who drinks as much as you do."

"Oh, you know how it is, seeking solace in the bottle."

"Solace?"

"Yeah, well. It's not a rosy outlook is it?" he gave me a wry smile, "I'm not sure that my future prospects are looking too hot. Might as well make the most of it."

"I'd just like to.." I started.

"No pictures," said Johnson, sternly, "so put the camera down."

"Just for the record," I tried.

"Put it down."

There was a definite edge to his voice. I put the camera on the table.

"In the bag, please."

"Oh, come on Johnson…"

"Bag," he said, simply.

I put the camera in the bag.

"Is your little recorder in there too?" he asked.

"Yes," I said, "but it's not switched on."

I couldn't have stopped him, he reached quickly under the table and seized my bag, and as he gathered it up I could see that he had already picked out the tiny red glow of the recorder's light. He held it up so close to his face that I saw the reflection of the crimson dot in his eye.

"Naughty," said Johnson, simply.

"Can't blame me for having a go," I said.

"Suppose not. Apart from you betraying my trust, I'm quite happy."

"I'm sorry," I said.

"Right, how do I get the tape out?" he asked, fiddling with the casing.

"There isn't a tape, Johnson."

"Don't give me that, you were recording me weren't you?"

"It's digital. It all goes on the hard drive."

"No tape?"

"No tape." I confirmed.

"Wipe it," he said, offering the recorder to me.

I leant forward to take it.

"Wait," he said, "you show me."

I held his hand as it held the machine. He was trembling slightly.

"Are you alright?" I asked.

"Fine," he said, "just wipe it."

I pressed keys with my other hand. Showing him what I was doing.

"Look. Menu. Delete. Delete current recording. Are you sure? Yes."

"Play it back," ordered Johnson.

"Play it back? But there's nothing on there, I just deleted it all."

"Play it."

I pressed the play button.

"I knew he was bad news," said the voice, "not the moment I saw him, I couldn't claim that, but pretty soon afterwards. I just had a feeling that this one might be a stirrer."

Johnson nodded for me to stop the playback.

"When did you speak to Frank Westlake?" he asked.

"Little while ago."

"Why did you speak to him?"

"He's part of the story, Johnson. He's part of your story."

"He's a little rat," said Johnson, with venom, uncapping another beer.

"He can be quite charming," I pointed out, "as you know."

"I thought," said Johnson taking a draught, "to start with, that he was a friendly bloke, you know, a good sort. Made the effort to talk to me, to make me feel at home. And, of course, I felt sorry for him because his wife had died and he was on his own. Still do feel sorry for him for that."

"His wife isn't dead," I interrupted.

"Ahh," sighed Johnson, "there we are, another one. A-bloody-nother one. Is it any wonder?"

"Is what any wonder?" I asked. "Do you want a coffee?"

"No, thank you, to the coffee. Cigarettes and beer are running dangerously low."

"Don't you think you've had enough for today?" I asked, foolishly.

"Enough?" Johnson rose to his feet, "Had enough? Do I think I've had enough? No, I do not. Am I not lucid? Am I not my usual entertaining and beguiling self? Do you see any hint of aggression or nastiness? You don't? Shall I tell you why? Because, firstly, I can hold my liquor. And secondly, when I get to the stage where I can hold it no longer, I am a sweet and gentle drunk."

"Good," I said, quickly.

"Unlike some."

"Unlike who?" I prompted.

"Oooh, let me see now," ruminated Johnson, gazing around at the ceiling in an exaggerated arc, rolling his neck about his shoulders. "Richard Nork," he decided, finally, "how about the old hooter-honker himself?"

"Bad drunk?"

"The worst kind. Likes a drink but can't handle it. The very worst. Can get nasty too."

"Nasty?"

"I haven't seen you placing the order," Johnson observed.

"Refreshments?" I asked, beaten.

"Refreshments," agreed Johnson, standing and stretching. Arms above his head, palms linked together. No sweat patches under the arms, I noticed, while I'm sitting here lathering up like a pig in heat, how does he do it?

"Getting tired?" I asked.

"No. Let's crack on. Get on that phone for beer and cigs."

"Water?"

"Yeah, water, please, and some of those little iced towels if there's any going."

I crossed the room and phoned, adding sandwiches and coffee to Johnson's list.

"Bit of history with Richard Nork is there?"

172

"Sorry?"

"You said he was a nasty drunk."

Johnson laughed.

"You could say that," he said.

"What happened?" I pressed.

"Oh, standard thing. Company do. Can't remember what it was for. Celebrating Simon Hart getting a hand job from one of the boys probably."

"I didn't know he was gay."

"Nor did I. It doesn't matter, hand job from one of the girls then. Whatever, it was another excuse to get everyone together and stick them under the microscope. For this one they organised drinking games. Got us all into a bar, split us up into teams."

"How did that make you feel?" I asked.

"I told you," said Johnson, sharply, "no counselling manoeuvres. Head up straight and level, please, and no 'how did you feels?'"

"Sorry," I said, swiftly, "I meant the concept of being forced into a team?"

"Crap. I wasn't playing. You had to down a pint in a race with someone else. One-on-one, while the rest looked on, waiting their turn."

"How did you handle it?"

"Here's the refreshments," said Johnson, responding to the sharp knock at the door, he stood.

"Sit down," I said, "I'll get it."

"Sure, whatever you say," he said, holding up both hands in a contrite gesture. He sat while the table was replenished.

"How did you handle it?" I asked again.

"Stood there, waited for the countdown, took a sip, placed my glass on the bar, watched my opponent spilling ale all down his nice smart shirt, shook his hand, bought my own drink and went and sat down."

"Didn't go down well?"

Johnson raised his eyebrows, shrugged, and took a bite from a beef and mustard sandwich.

"These are good," he observed, "don't know why they cut the crusts off though. Best bit."

"No they're not," I laughed, "it's like when your dad would say the fat's the best bit, or the skin on the fish, and you were mad for leaving it."

"Fair one," laughed Johnson in agreement.

"Richard Nork?"

"Oh, yeah. He got pissed in five minutes as usual. We were talking to a couple of the girls. Me and Adam. Aussie bloke, he was. Nice fellah, actually. Definitely one of the good guys. Bit one-eyed about his cricket team, but there you are, Aussies eh?"

"Tell me more."

"So, Richard comes over, uninvited, I have to say. And he's groping the girls and slobbering all over them and, I don't know, not being a gentleman, you see?"

"I think so."

"And it's difficult for them, he's their boss, and they're shit-scared about losing their jobs so they don't want to knee him in the bollocks 'cos they might get fired for it, you see? And he's talking to them, and it's filth, it really is horrible stuff, about what he'd like to do to them and what he's seen in a porn film and re-enacting it, you know the three of them, and they're uncomfortable and offended, so when he asks them to go on somewhere else with him they turn him down."

"What did he do?"

Johnson was animated, picking agitatedly at his fingernails, twitching in his seat.

"Got nasty. They were bitches. Dirty bitches. Bet they did all that for their boyfriends, why was he any different. He was sweating and dribbling, spitting. Pissed up, angry, aggressive, not a nice situation."

"Sounds difficult."

"He turned away for minute to talk to someone, just turned his back for thirty seconds, maybe a minute. I shoved the girls away. Bit of a shove, but it was needed, to get them moving, to get them away. Off they went, he turned back and they'd gone. He kicked off again, so I suggested he went to the gents."

"To calm down?"

"No. Worst thing I could have said, calm down. Just setting up the argument aren't you? I'm perfectly calm, don't you tell me to calm down, calm down yourself. I told him he had some dirt on his face, little smudge of something. He tried rubbing it, but I said it wasn't coming off."

"Nothing on there?"

"Of course not, it was just a ruse to get him away."

"So he went to the gents."

"Oh yes."

"What did you do?"

"Followed him."

"Right away?" I asked.

"No, no. Gave him a bit of a start."

"And then?"

"Walked in after him. No-one else in there which was handy. For me."

"What was he doing?"

"Bent over the basin, washing his face," grinned Johnson.

"What happened next?"

"I walked up behind him, on my toes, not that he'd have heard me, and his head was down, you see? Wasn't looking in the mirror."

"What did you do?"

Johnson stood and demonstrated.

"I punched him in the kidneys, with the right hand, first of all, you could hear the air shooting out his lungs, whoosh," he swung his right fist in a loop, "then, as he started to keel over, I smacked him in the other one with the left," Johnson swung his left fist across and slightly downwards and stopped it on imaginary impact.

"Was he hurt?"

"Well, he dropped, his chin hit the surround of the basin, which was a bonus. Crack! It went, and then he went down properly. Slumped on the floor, out on the tiles."

"And then you left?"

"Yep. Right after I'd kicked him in the nuts."

"I see."

"Don't get me wrong. You know I'm not a violent man, but I have to say," said Johnson, "that was the only company do that I ever really enjoyed.

Johnson chuckled to himself and looked across at me, smiling, but flinty-eyed.

"You're not a violent bloke are you?" I observed.

"Just said so," he replied, yawning and stretching.

"But you enjoyed beating up Richard Nork?"

"Well, it wasn't exactly what you'd call beating up, was it?"

"Well it certainly sounds like it."

"One, two punches and a kick?" Johnson gave a slight shake of the head. "Not a proper shoeing is it?"

"I wouldn't know," I said, removing a strip of fat which was hanging out of my sandwich. I looked at my greasy fingers, not wanting to lick them.

"Napkin?" offered Johnson.

"Thanks," I said, taking the papery square from his outstretched hand and wiping my hands.

"Jack Sprat are you?" he asked.

"Something like that."

"How long have you been doing this, then?" he asked.

"Doing what?"

"I don't know what you'd call it, I'd call it interviewing, I think. How long have you been, um, interviewing people like me?"

"I'm not sure I've ever interviewed anyone like you Johnson. I'm also not sure if interviewing is even the right description for what I'm doing, or if I've ever done it before."

"What do you do usually?"

"Usually?"

Johnson tugged at an ear lobe and leant back in his chair, lifting the two front legs off the ground.

"You'll break your back if you fall," I advised.

"Did your teachers tell you that as well?"

"Yes," I smiled, "all the time."

"So, is this a normal day for you?" he persisted.

"No such thing as a normal day."

"I'm just another assignment?"

"Yes. Sorry if it dents your ego. But you're just another problem that I've been told to deal with."

"It's not an ego thing. I thought you'd have realised that by now."

"Fine," I replied.

"Where are you based?"

"All over."

"You do a lot of travelling?"

"What's a lot?" I asked.

"Been doing it long?"

"What's a long time?" I asked.

"Interesting work is it?"

"Depends how you define interesting," I replied, sipping lukewarm coffee. The white cup was stained around the rim and trails of brown liquid formed puddles in the saucer.

"I knew it," announced Johnson, "I knew it, but thought I should confirm, you know, for both of us. So we know where we're going.

"What's that?"

"I'd be no good at your job. Best you go back to asking the questions and I'll keep coming up with any old bollocks that I think you might swallow. I think I'm OK at the interrogation bit but I have to say, you're crap at coming up with interesting answers."

"Deal," I agreed. "Didn't Richard Nork suspect anything?"

"No. Far as he was concerned he'd overdone the scotch again and taken a dive, or upset someone and they'd taken a pop at him. Whichever it was, he wouldn't remember, couldn't remember. Happened all the time."

"He'd come into work with marks, cuts to his face after nights out and no-one would notice?"

"Make-up."

"Make-up?"

"He wore make-up to cover up the evidence. Kate told me."

"How did Kate know?"

"You're asking me how a woman spotted that someone, that someone being a man remember, was wearing make-up? Perhaps we should swap places again," said Johnson, his laughter subsiding into a heavy cough.

"Cigarette?" I offered.

He looked up, eyes brimming with water, the last few coughs sounding more like hiccups, shoulders heaving in unison.

"Cheers. Won't pass up a free fag. And beer, more beer over here my dear, if you please."

"This is going to stop, you know," I advised him, "and pretty soon."

"Don't spare the horses," he coughed.

"You're going to have to get yourself together," I said.

"Damn the torpedoes."

"Reality check," I said, sternly.

Johnson puffed and swigged on. He swung forward, levelling his chair, placed his elbows on the table and gave me the full intense benefit of his cunning brown eyes.

"You see, I worked it out," he said, carefully, "it took me a while, but in the end I figured it out. As far as reality's concerned, my considered position is that it's hugely overrated."

"We're all subject to reality, Johnson," I argued.

"We are, are we?" he said, "I'm not sure that's right. I agree with what you say, that we're all subject to it, but I don't think that's a good thing, necessarily, it's not so much being subject to it as adhering unquestioningly to the norm. Because everyone else does it that's what makes it reality, isn't it?"

"Is it?" I asked.

"Oh, I don't know," Johnson replied with a frustrated edge to his voice. He seemed to be in the grip of another bout of weariness, but I pressed on.

"Well, it's an interesting point you make," I said, encouragingly.

"Really?" he said, sarcastically, "shame it's not one that's worth any gravy."

"Isn't it?"

"Sounds like a bit too much philosophy bollocks to me. Too deep."

"Too deep?"

"In too deep," he said, sombrely, "now then, did you lead me into that or was it just a happy accident?"

"I can't put words in your mouth, Johnson. I realise that much."

"I'll tell you something," he said, suddenly brighter, his eyes clear again, "about reality."

"Go on."

"Bloke I worked with somewhere, can't recall where exactly. Mervyn, Mervyn something. Doesn't matter."

"Bet he was known as Merv the Swerve," I ventured.

"Only by those with no wit or imagination."

"What did you call him?" I said, opting for clumsy flattery.

"Me being blessed with both," he said, seeing through me, "I called him Merv the Twat."

"Almost Wildean," I said.

"Thanks." said Johnson. "Anyway, Merv, Merv the Twat was one of those blokes, who are on the short side, not tiny, but a few inches shorter than the average. Balding, advanced hair loss actually, bit left round the base but nothing from the eyebrows up, barren all the way over the crown until you hit the thin strip of draught excluder at the back of the neck. He had a beard too, full set. You know the type?"

I nodded.

"He always, but always, wore grey trousers, slacks he called them, slacks! There's one for your granny. Grey slacks and a navy blazer, double-breasted, with brass buttons. Liked a beer, you know, but it had to be the right beer. Real ale. He could tell you where it was brewed, where the water came from, and the hops, the whole lot. I think he even belonged to that outfit, you know, Campaign for Retching and Stonking Headaches, or whatever it is."

"You paint an irresistible picture, but where are we going with this?" I asked, now feeling jaded myself.

"You see Merv was one of the angriest, most belligerent, argumentative little sods I've ever crossed bar stools with. You'd offer him the packet and say, 'Cigarette?' And he'd snap back at you, 'What do I want one of those for? Got my own, haven't I?' A simple, 'No thank you,' wasn't an option for him. 'Watching the football tonight?' I might say, he'd come back with, 'So? So? Football? Football? What do I wanna watch that for?' You see?"

"With you so far," I replied, "I can see the garden path, that might be a flock of wild geese up ahead, and red herrings, look, red herrings swimming in the pond......"

"Stick with it. Although if you want to do all the talking I'll just sit here and listen for as long as I can stay awake."

"Please, go on."

"You get the picture with Merv," stated Johnson, "he's an angry, beardy, little baldy man who's still wearing the clothes that his mum bought him. Same style anyway. The point is, here's the point, there are a lot of these geezers around, same profile, same temperament. Trust me, if you get talking to someone in a pub and he's quaffing real ale, if he's all slacks and shiny buttons, dazzling lights bouncing off his dome and every time he takes a drink he looks like he's drowning a weasel, and if you have to bend down to hear what he's saying, there is trouble ahead."

"How can you say that?"

"'Cos it's true. Voice of experience. Listen to me and you might learn something that could, just quite possibly could, keep you out of A&E. Those glasses with the dimples and the handles and big and thick and heavy. Looking at plastic surgery, I should think. I don't want to be too unfair though."

"You don't?" I raised an involuntary eyebrow.

"No. You see, it's generally the ones who've got hair of a fairer shade that are the troublemakers."

"What's left of it."

"Good spot. What's left of it," Johnson smiled, "the dark-haired ones are less of a problem, as a general rule of thumb."

"I'll try to remember that."

"However, last word of warning, if he's a ginger one," Johnson wagged a finger at me, loosely, "run for your life. Put your glass down, don't even think about finishing it, don't bother with goodbyes and niceties, I've seen an attempt at a friendly handshake with a ginger turn the quietest country inn into Celtic against Rangers, just get out of there with everything intact."

"What is all this about, Johnson?" I pleaded.

"These blokes, they are a recognised type. A sub-species, are they? I don't know. But, as described, they share these traits. Oh, probably got quite rosy cheeks too, quick to flush, that's the beer and the blood pressure, I suppose."

"And?" despite myself, I was leaning forward, interested.

"What's their reality like?"

"Reality's reality, Johnson, it's not negotiable," I said, sinking back again.

"But it is," he said, firmly, "it is. Their reality, the way they live every waking minute, is battling perceived slights with aggression and hostility. They're at war and the enemy is everywhere. I couldn't live like that. That's not my reality, it's not yours, and you're a liar if you try to tell me any different."

Johnson sprang to his feet, energised, he paced the room determinedly, swinging around as he reached the walls, continuing to expand on his theory. Me? I felt like the marrow had been sucked out of my bones.

"How about a comfort break?" I asked.

"A what?" Johnson exclaimed.

"A comfort break."

"In English please."

"You know what I mean."

"In English," Johnson enunciated and projected the two words like Al Pacino at his most Oscar-winning.

"A toilet break?" I said, caving in.

Johnson was still striding around the room.

"I've enjoyed our little chat," he said, "good to talk, got a few things off my chest. Enjoyed having a few beers with you too, toilet break's probably a good idea," he slipped the words out amid a hiccup.

"Come on then."

We walked the short distance down the hall, and while I was waiting outside the door for him I got a nudge from my phone. Text message.

Going OK? Need me yet?

I had just hit the key to send *Fine talk later* when the door swung open and Johnson appeared, hair slicked back and face shimmering with water.

"Got a message?"

"No," I said, "well, usual rubbish, you know."

"Nothing important then?" he said, leaning over and peering.

"No," I said, pocketing the phone, "not at all."

We walked back to the room.

"How are you feeling?" I asked.

"Alright," replied Johnson, "bit tired of this bloody room, to be honest. It's OK

181

being kept stocked up with the old refreshers, but it's been a bit of a trek hasn't it?"

"Yes," I acknowledged, "tell you what, we won't do too much more tonight."

"Great," he said with relief. His hair and face had dried off already, and beads of sweat were springing up on his forehead.

"You must be tired," I observed.

"Yeah," he said slowly, drawing the word out.

"Few drinks today."

Johnson exhaled a succession of confused breaths, which culminated in a clearing of the throat.

"You kept bringing it on," he said.

"Just trying to make things convivial."

"Loosen the old tongue, more like."

"Making the whole process as painless, as easy as possible. I don't find this easy either."

"I'm fine," said Johnson, popping open another. He offered it to me but I gestured to the cold pot of coffee. "Suit yourself," he said.

"You didn't always drink quite so much?" I suggested.

"Well, I drink more than I did when I was fourteen. And there's not many kids in their twenties who can say that with any honesty nowadays are there? I'm above twenty-eight units a week, if that's what you mean. Had a row with the doctor last time. Well, not a row exactly. Said I was borderline. Can you believe it? Couple of beers and a glass or so of wine a day?"

"What did you say?"

"Said it wasn't heavy drinking. She should get her tweedy ass down to the Grey Horse on a weekend and watch the real pros in all their raging glory, I didn't actually say that last bit, but I did say that while I of course respected her opinion that I had to disagree."

"Got a telling off did you?"

"Not really. I was just advised. Advised that my consumption was at a level likely to encourage the old cirrhosis."

"How did that make you feel?"

"Made me glad I hadn't told her about the spirits."

"Much in the way of spirits?"

"No," Johnson protested, "not really. You know how it is. Little nightcap now and again, a scotch or a brandy. Gin and tonics before lunch on a Sunday. Bloody Mary's anytime at all, all you have to do is call."

"You don't think you have a problem then?" I asked.

"No, I don't," he said, deliberately. "But it confuses me sometimes."

"How?"

"Back then, well, I say back then but I still do it now. I'll stop drinking for a few days, a week, two weeks, haven't managed a month in a while, but hey, pressure, you know? So, I'll stop, and I'll feel fantastic. Fit, and full of piss and vinegar. The little chap waking me up on the hour through the night, you know?"

"Really?" was all I could offer.

"Really. And then, after, whatever, let's say just the three days, and like I say, I'm full of energy and oxygen and muscle, the body's alive, eyes are bright, skin's glowing, busting out, and I know I'm feeling like that because I haven't been on the piss."

"What next?" I encouraged.

"I think," Johnson stopped, he picked at a strand of loose fingernail and took a thoughtful breath. "I don't know why, I say to myself, I feel great but with three or four pints and half a packet of fags inside me, I'm going to feel so much better."

"And do you?"

"What?"

"Have the drinks and the cigarettes."

"Of course," Johnson rolled his eyes and regarded me as you might the village idiot.

"Does it make you feel better?" I enquired.

"For a while," Johnson replied, "for a while. But then you just feel like shit again. Like pigeon shit, actually. Sloppy old pigeon shit."

"Pigeon shit?" I asked incredulously.

"The worst, obviously."

"It is?"

"Consider the diet."

"Does it always work like this?" I asked.

"Every time."

"Every time?" I queried.

"Never fails," Johnson replied, "sometimes I wish I had a compelling reason for giving it up altogether. The routine visit to the doctor that ends up in the last reel with him telling you that you've got six months, tops."

"Six months?"

"If you don't pack it in," said Johnson, confidently.

"That would be a good thing?"

"There's an element of choice there."

"Stop or die," I said.

"Yes. But there is the compelling reason. You wouldn't be doing it because you've got humdinger of a head one morning, or it came back to you sometime during the afternoon that last night you called your best mate a tosser or ruined your chances of getting in someone's knickers because you were rude to them because they were dancing with someone else."

"Something you want to talk about?" I asked.

"Disallowed on the grounds of irrelevancy."

"I'll decide the relevance," I said, bossily.

"Not this time," said Johnson, bossing me back.

"So, you'd like someone to give you a compelling reason?"

"Certainly. Stop or die."

"Stop or die."

"Or don't stop," Johnson smiled.

"I'm not going to play this time, Johnson," I said, returning the smile.

"As you wish."

"Do you think you've got a drink problem?"

"Walking a fine line, I suppose," he replied, "lot of people flirt with it, don't they? What does it take to swap your business suit and your office for a pitch under a bridge somewhere? Happens to people, you know. It happens. Unbelievable, really. Why aren't you writing any of this down? You've been scribbling away all day."

I didn't answer him, and suggested we call it a night.

"Not now that I've got my second wind, surely," Johnson protested.

"I think we're both tired. We'll go back to our rooms. Order yourself something to eat if you like. They'll bring it."

"Whatever you like," said Johnson, agreeably.

"I'll see you in the morning, then," I said, picking up my bag and calling down to ask for the room to be cleared of its litter of empty beer bottles, sandwich crusts, coffee cups and cigarette ends. Maybe they could give it a good airing as well. Stale air hung heavy in the heat.

"Time?" asked Johnson.

"Nine, no, eight I think."

"Eight? You are joking? Doesn't leave much time for breakfast."

"See you at eight in the morning, Johnson," I said, "we'll have breakfast sent in."

"You're the boss," he said.

I flicked up the latch when I got back to my room and made a call.

"If he should order any food tonight," I said, "he's not to have any more alcohol."

"No alcohol for Mr Johnson."

"Soft drinks or water only."

"Understood."

After a good twenty minutes under the powerful jets of the shower, I wrapped myself in a thick, soft white bathrobe and emerged from the steam. Immediately starting to sweat again, I made another call.

"Hi, it's me," I announced.

"What's happening?"

"We've finished for the night."

"I thought you'd have things wrapped up by now?"

"That was the plan," I conceded, "but I need a bit more time."

"It's going alright though?" the voice, betrayed a slight air of concern.

"Oh, yes. He's talking. Talkative, even. Not all of it's worthwhile, but we're getting there."

"Is he drinking much?"

"Constantly, but it doesn't appear to affect him much. Regular, but not heavy. Loosens him up."

185

"But making sense?"

"Yes, overall," I said, "he gets to a level and seems to stay there."

"OK, same again tomorrow, but just keep an eye on it."

"Right."

"How are you feeling?"

"I'm pretty tired now. But he seems to go through peaks and troughs. One minute I think he's almost ready to collapse, the next he's up and bouncing of the walls."

"Drugs?"

"No access to them. He can't have had the chance."

"Sure?"

"Absolutely. He's pretty much anti, anyway."

"Manic depression?"

"No. He's just, I don't know, up and down. Stars or gutter. It's not chemical or medical, I'm sure of that."

"Alright. Carry on as you are then. When do you resume?"

"Eight tomorrow."

"What are doing now?"

"Lying on the bed. Going to skip dinner and go to sleep any minute, I should think," I yawned, ready to shut down.

"I'll let you go then. Rest up and we'll talk tomorrow. You'll be finished by then won't you?"

"I think so," I said, unsurely, "but I don't know how much more he's got to tell."

"Sleep well," said the voice.

Johnson sat behind a huge plate of sausages, crispy bacon, tomatoes, mushrooms and hash browns. He was lathering butter onto a thick slab of crusty bread, a steaming mug of dark brown, treacly tea at his elbow. He had specified a side order of boiling water and a stack of teabags and had brewed his own.

"Eggs?" I offered.

"Spawn of the devil," he replied.

"Sorry?"

"Don't eat them. Horrid runny things, and even if they're solid they're just eggy

186

aren't they? With an eggy smell. Who could like that? Disgusting. And when you burst that one I'll have to look away."

I looked down at my own breakfast. Two thin rashers, a solitary tomato, and an undercooked fried egg. Raw albumen shimmered between yolk and shimmering white.

"You might have a point," I said, "I'll put it back."

"Don't," yelled Johnson, "you'll…too late."

"Ooops, broke it,"

"I know," said Johnson, covering his eyes with his slightly hairy hand.

I put the egg-soaked plate outside the door and served myself an egg-free replacement.

"Better?" I asked.

"Thank you," said Johnson, working his way steadily through the pig.

"How are you feeling this morning?"

"Fine. Bright-eyed and up for it."

"Headache?"

"No. Didn't have a drink last night."

"You didn't?" I enquired. I knew that he'd ordered wine, but had been refused.

"Didn't want one."

"Very commendable," I complimented.

"Not after you'd put the block on it, I didn't," Johnson smiled.

"Looking after your interests."

"More like yours."

"You want to be sitting here with a headache and talking to me for hours, answering more questions?"

"Guess not," he said, mashing a tomato into red slush and scooping it up with a little spoon of bread crust.

"It's a bit cooler today, I think, should be rather more comfortable," I stated, "we'll get started when you've finished breakfast."

"I'm done," he said, pushing his plate away, some fresh tea would be nice, can we get that organised? Great, I'm ready then."

"You weren't at Locked-In for much longer were you?"

"No," he said, reflectively. I hoped that we weren't going to begin the day with one of his depressive bouts.

"Last days?" I encouraged.

"So they were," Johnson replied, splashing muddy tea into his cup from the pot which he was holding much higher than was necessary.

"Carry on like that and we'll be having an unscheduled comf..," I paused and corrected myself, "toilet break."

"Right on," agreed Johnson, "sorry. Last days of Locked-In."

Follow the Bear

Johnson made the call from a phone box on the way into work.

"Simon Hart please."

"Who shall I say is calling?" asked Sally, the receptionist.

"Personal call," said Johnson, affecting a Scottish accent.

"It's just that I have to announce you sir."

Johnson watched the hurried, worried masses passing him on the street. It's not Revenge of the Zombies, Death of the Zombies maybe. Morning of the Living Dead. They all look dead. Do they know they're dead? He liked Sally, he tried some old-fashioned Scottish charm.

"Aye well, hen, y'see he and I were at school together, old friends yae know? So this is like a wee surprise for the wee feller. A voice frae the past eh?"

"Well I never knew," said Sally.

"What's that m'dear?" asked Johnson.

"That Simon went to school in Pakistan."

"What?"

"Pakistan?" enquired Sally, "or did you go to school over here?"

"I'm speaking in a Scottish accent," protested Johnson.

"A Scottish accent?"

"I mean, I'm a Scotsman."

"You don't sound like a Scotsman."

"I've been on holiday," said Johnson, "is he there, or not?"

"Putting you through," said Sally, sweetly.

Johnson listened to the tone chirruping a few times.

"Simon Hart," answered Simon Hart.

"About your bear," said Johnson, lapsing into cockney.

"Have you got him?" whispered Simon Hart.

"Well, what's left of him."

Johnson replaced the receiver and headed off to the office. He didn't want to miss

189

this.

"Hi Sally," he announced, as he walked into reception.

"Can you do a Scottish accent?" asked Sally.

"No. No good at accents," said Johnson, hurriedly, "why?"

"Oh, nothing really."

"OK," said Johnson, keen to move on, "could you let me know when the post arrives?"

"Expecting something?"

"Oh yes," said Johnson, "see you later."

When Sally buzzed down to Johnson with the news, he took a break and walked downstairs to the bathroom. He drew a large cock and balls arrangement on the notice board, colouring in the head in a rich shade of purple with a pen he'd bought that morning, and waited for a few minutes until he heard Simon Hart's mail being delivered, then he positioned himself against the wall outside Hart's office.

He'll open the parcel first, Johnson decided. We'd all open a parcel first. Especially one marked, 'Private and Confidential'.

Johnson hadn't quite expected such a teeth-rattling scream of anguish. He flattened himself against the wall and took a few deep breaths, and when Simon Hart had stopped screaming, he heard him moaning and weeping.

"The growl. Teddy's growl. The bastards. How could they? The bastards."

Johnson shook his head in wonderment, smiled to himself, and tiptoed up the stairs, back to work.

Johnson didn't much care for the culture at Locked-In. The bullying, the manipulation, the forced activities, but he was swayed into sticking with it by the money. He had now had a couple of Klaxon blasts and the effect on his bank balance meant that he didn't have to re-let Jeff's room if he didn't want to. He decided to concentrate on the work, on making money, and to attempt to, if not ignore, that wouldn't be possible, let the rest wash over him without too much disturbance. He knew that Richard Nork didn't like him (and this was without knowing who had punched him

190

to the ground in a gents toilet), but even he had to admit that of late Johnson had been King of the Klaxon.

· Johnson reclined in his seat, one leg resting across the other knee, phone tucked under his chin, and hands clasped behind the head, gently nudging and cajoling a client into the corral. His eyes flicked around the room, as he listened to someone trying to shave him of two and a half per cent. Two and a half per cent which would come straight out of his commission. Johnson stood firm, ready to threaten, in the most diplomatic fashion, to pull the plug on the whole deal. No-one was going to get away with bilking him of his hard-earned. Johnson brought the call to an abrupt end, with a promise to call back soon, and dived under the desk. He knew he hadn't been mistaken. He had seen the large lady in the bright, flowery smock with the wide, engaging smile. Her colleague, smaller, with lightly tanned skin and angular features, dressed in plain dark green, stood next to her as they spoke to the office manager. The large black lady from Sierra Leone and her possibly illegal co-worker. But what the bloody hell were they doing here during the day? Would they think it funny that the man from the cleaning company who checks their work in the evenings has a desk job here during the day? Worse, would they acknowledge him?

Johnson stuck his head out and peered around his chair.

"You OK, mate?" asked Aussie Adam, swinging around on his chair, bright and cheery as ever.

"Yeah, just dropped something," said Johnson.

"Can't find it eh?"

"You got it."

"No, mate. Don't even know what it is you've lost."

"Don't worry about it," Johnson assured him.

"No worries, mate," said Adam, "reckon it'll turn up."

"Wise words," said Johnson, crawling back. He had seen Bliss and Shakira working their way along the bank of desks, spraying and wiping PCs (approved anti-static spray, Johnson noticed, with a gulp), sucking up dust from keyboards with hand-held, mini-vacuums, they were still twenty or thirty feet in the distance. Johnson considered, and swiftly discarded the idea of putting his waste basket over his head and walking out like he had every right to do so. He stayed on the floor, under the desk, searching for

191

inspiration. Then his phone began to ring. He poked his head out again and saw Richard Nork semi-rising from his seat, half-sitting, half-standing.

"What are you doing?" hissed Kate, having finished a call.

"I'm in the shit," whispered Johnson.

"What's wrong?" Kate had swung her chair round and was leaning over him.

"Can't explain now, do me a favour and pick up that call would you?"

Richard Nork was on his way over. Johnson could see the polished brogues, kissed by flapping trouser cuffs, as they marched towards him and disturbed specks of dust from the floor, he looked up and saw the flapping of Nork's silky suit jacket, a little further up and he caught sight of Nork's frowning brow.

"Kate, Kate!" said Johnson.

"What? What?" Kate replied.

"Diversion."

"What?"

Richard Nork was almost upon them. Johnson could smell his after shave. He imagined he could almost smell the shoe polish.

"Get me out of here," said Johnson. "Quick. Sorry about this."

He shot out from under the desk, grabbed hold of Kate, and roughly scooped her up from her chair. The chair spun around and Johnson kicked it into Richard Nork's path. Holding Kate in the air, he clutched her to his hip, making sure that her head was between his and the sightlines of Bliss and Shakira, the careering chair crashed into Richard Nork and smacked him smartly on both kneecaps. Nork cried out and tipped forward, He yelped louder this time as his knees hit the floor first.

"Sorry Richard," barked Johnson as he hotfooted it away from the danger area, "Kate's not well, just taking her to the ladies see you in a bit."

Johnson sped from the office with the protesting Kate in his arms. He carried her down the wooden staircase, trying to avoid her flapping fists by ducking his head this way that, although she scored a few points by catching his testicles a glancing, yet painful, blow with a flailing knee.

"This had better be good," Kate shouted. "Will you put me down now?"

"Sssshhh," insisted Johnson.

"Don't fucking shush me you wanker."

Johnson decided to put her down. Johnson, bent almost double, facing the wall, both hands pressed to it, breathless. He tilted his head and, convinced that Kate was about to land a decent punch, sprang to one side.

"I'm sorry," he said quickly, "emergency."

"Emergency," said Kate, "would you like to tell me what sort of fucking emergency justifies you carrying me off and flashing my stocking tops to the whole fucking office?"

"Stocking tops?" asked Johnson, dully.

Kate hoisted her skirt. Sure enough, black stockings, white thighs, lacy straps.

"Are those French knickers?" asked Johnson.

"You fucking idiot."

"I'm sorry. Emergency. I didn't know about the stockings. Do you always...?"

"No I fucking don't. I've got a date tonight. I certainly don't wear them all the time."

"Well, that's OK then," said Johnson, uncertainly, "if it's just a one off."

"No, Johnson, actually it isn't fucking OK."

"It isn't?" enquired Johnson.

"No, and do you know why?"

"I don't," confessed Johnson.

"Because everyone who works here, all the pervy men and all the bitchy women will think that I do."

"Oh."

"Oh."

"At least," bumbled Johnson, "at least there are a few out today, at meetings and things."

"What, and you're sure that nobody's going to enlighten them as soon as they're back? They're probably calling and texting right now. I'm finished here, you know that? Finished. To think I got you through the door here, put myself on the line for you, and this is the way you thank me?"

"Kate," said Johnson, "I'm really sorry. You never know, perhaps it'll add something to your reputation. You know, foxy."

Johnson looked at Kate chewing furiously on her bottom lip, at her flaring nostrils and blazing eyes.

193

"Foxy," she said, in a voice that was doing its best to remain calm. "Foxy."

"Sexy and sophisticated," said Johnson, blundering on.

"The tart."

"Tart's a bit strong," said Johnson.

"All the blokes will think I'm fair game and all the girls will agree with them. Don't you see, I'll be a target for the men and a threat to the women. They'll eat me alive."

"I think you're judging us men a bit harshly," said Johnson, reassuringly, "eat you alive?"

"I'm talking about the women, Johnson," said Kate, "men I can handle."

"Kate, I'll make it up to you," said Johnson.

"Like how? Anyway, I know I'll regret this, I just know it, but what was all that about?"

"Had to avoid some people."

"What people?"

"Cleaners," mumbled Johnson.

"Cleaners?" repeated Kate, "cleaners?"

"Well, I've been having a bit of fun, you see, in the evenings."

"Take ten minutes, no, take fifteen, Kate, to sort yourself out and then get back to work," said Simon Hart. "Johnson, I'd like a word."

"Say, two this afternoon?" Johnson suggested.

"Let's say right now shall we?" said Simon Hart.

"Sorry Kate," said Johnson to her departing frame. She didn't respond. Simon Hart ushered him into the office.

"Sit."

"Thanks," said Johnson.

"You're good at what you do Johnson, you know that? Yes, I imagine you do."

Johnson smiled modestly and nodded.

"But you're not that good, you're not great and you're certainly not outstanding. If you were outstanding I'd be prepared to put up with some of your nonsense."

"Nonsense, Simon?" asked Johnson.

Simon Hart had risen from his desk. His whole face flushed with a shade of strawberry under his creamy curls. He picked up something from his desk, a metallic box, petrol blue, the size of a matchbox.

"Know what this is?" Simon Hart enquired. He showed it to Johnson, but didn't hand it over.

"Box of fancy matches?" asked Johnson.

"Good guess."

"Close?" asked Johnson.

"Not really," said Simon Hart, "a better guess would have been, miniature digital video camera."

"Oh dear"

"Oh dear, indeed," said Simon Hart. "You have been a busy chap haven't you?"

Johnson shifted in his seat. He coughed, he gaped, he blinked.

"Got many of those things have you Simon?"

"Enough."

"Must have cost you."

"Money well spent, I'd say."

Johnson, hands linked and resting in the lap of his expensive new jet-black suit trousers, blinked some more and nodded.

"Thing is, Simon," began Johnson.

Simon Hart interrupted him.

"The thing is Johnson, this is the thing, the important thing from your point of view, you are going to be leaving us."

"I am?" said Johnson. "Soon?"

"Soon is a good choice of word Johnson. These two gentlemen will escort you directly from my premises."

Simon Hart crossed the floor and opened the door, where two of the largest of the New Zealander temps stood in attendance.

"I see," said Johnson, wearily, "you've brought the All Blacks."

"If you have any personal possessions here, or in your desk perhaps," Simon Hart continued, "then tough luck, you're not getting them back."

"Tough," agreed Johnson. Let's hope they don't find the prawn sandwich for a while.

"Give me your pass."

195

Johnson slipped it out of his pocket and dropped it from height onto the desk where it bounced here and there before landing with a plastic clatter.

"The entry code will also be changed so don't waste your time in returning here."

"It's been an absolute pleasure, Simon," beamed Johnson, rising to his feet and offering an outstretched hand.

"Take him out the back way," said Simon Hart, turning his back, and Johnson was led from the premises with as much gentleness as two front row forwards could muster.

"Have you visited Wales since you've been over?" said Johnson, pitching his head left, towards a cauliflower ear.

"Nah," said prop number one.

"Pity. I reckon you'd like it," said Johnson, as they reached the end of the fire escape.

"Any good is it, eh?" said number two, as they released their steady grip from his elbows.

"Beautiful country," recommended Johnson, kindly.

"Oh, yeah?" said number one, as if squeezing out the syllables.

"Much to do is there?" asked number two.

Johnson eyed the alleyway ahead, twenty yards or so, dotted with overflowing wheelie bins, leading to the street. He could see the streams of people walking, power-walking, in each direction, criss-crossing his line of sight. Shirtsleeves, bare arms and shoulders, short skirts. It was relatively cool in the alley but he was prepared for the feeling of the heat beating back at him from the pavement and the buildings. There had been several days of searing heat in the city.

"I'd say you'll be kept busy," said Johnson, rising onto the balls of his feet.

"P'raps we'll give it a go, eh, Damon? Wales, eh?" said number one, scratching something that might once have been a neck. Johnson couldn't decide whether it was head or shoulders. Head, he decided, it being hairy.

"Aaw, I'd say so, mate," said number two, "see if we can get booked up on the train, eh?"

"I wouldn't leave it too long," advised Johnson, edging towards the street.

"Oh, yeah?" said number one.

"Why's that?" continued number two.

"Piece of advice," said Johnson, putting some alley between himself and his escorts, "if you don't get there quickly all the good-looking sheep'll be taken."

Johnson sprinted away, hearing two sets of heavy footsteps behind him, but he had a valuable start and they weren't gaining.

"Don't forget your Velcro gloves, you sheep-shaggers," he yelled over his shoulder.

"Arsehole," came the cry from behind him, "you wait you bastard."

"Or your wellies," he shouted as he rounded the building and hit the street.

Johnson cannoned off several pedestrians before re-grouping and choosing the bus lane as his escape route. He ran and ran, overtaking Sixty-Threes and Forty-Sevens, deaf to the helpful advice of the drivers. He ran for a long time after all danger was passed.

When Johnson arrived home, Tim was sitting at the dining table, in scarlet boxer shorts, pen in hand, situations vacant flattened out in front of him.

"Don't tell me you've been sacked again?" asked Tim.

"Jeez, how many times?" said Johnson, "I've never been sacked."

"What you doing home then? Afternoon off?"

Johnson paused.

"Well, on this occasion, there might be some truth in what you say."

"Fired?"

"Yeah," confirmed Johnson, pursing his lips.

"Seems like we're in the same boat then Johnners. Tell you what, I've got an idea."

"Tim," protested Johnson, "look, no offence, but if it involves getting pissed, or wasted or whatever it is, or going out somewhere and wasting time trying to get off with Scandinavian student girls, then…"

"Now," said Tim, "there's an idea. Better than mine."

"Tell me yours," said Johnson.

"We're in the crap, right? Both of us."

"Yes."

"No money, and no money coming in."

"I did OK at Locked-In, you know, I'll be OK for a while."

"I did OK as well, J," agreed Tim, "did very well, actually. Fair enough, I spent a lot of it, but I've got funds. The wolf isn't quite hammering on the door, if you know what I mean?"

"So, we're going to be alright for a bit then?" asked Johnson, seeking reassurance.

"Life lesson, Johnson."

Here we go, thought Johnson, he's going to get all world-weary and knowing on me again.

"Alright," Johnson acquiesced.

"Life lesson. If we fiddle and fart about on what we've got, if we take some time out, what we've got ain't gonna last long, trust me."

"So what's the plan?"

"Do you want to rent out Jeff's room again?" asked Tim, drawing inky boxes on the margin of the paper.

"Want to? No."

"Right, do you need to?"

"Well," Johnson sat down, "not at the moment, but…"

"Exactly. So, we neither of us want to go back to the, shall we say, unique pressures of the high-powered corporate existence? Am I right? I'm right now, aren't I?" Tim leant forwarded and nodded his encouragement.

"I'm not sure I'm cut out for it," agreed Johnson, rubbing his thumb against the fraying edge of the table.

"So, get the kettle on lad, and I'll tell you all about it," smiled Tim.

"Can I ask you something Tim?" Johnson enquired.

"Surely," said Tim, affably, leaning back now, hands behind his head.

"What do you do for food and drink when I'm not around to get it for you?"

"Fact of life. Hard one," said Tim.

"And what's this latest gem?"

"I'm not the housewife any more."

"What?"

"And you're not the hard-working husband coming home expecting a hot meal and his slippers laid out for him."

"You never did anything like that for me."

"I would have done, if only you could hold down a steady job," said Tim, "I'd have done anything."

"I hope this isn't going any further, said Johnson.

"What I'm saying, dear boy," Tim rose to his feet, "stay there, I'll make the tea, what I'm saying is, that right now we are both the housewife."

"Right," said Johnson, uncertainly.

"And if we piss about even for a day or two, you know, oh let's have a couple of days off and think about it. Not good. A couple of days becomes a few days which turns into a week, a fortnight and a month or more, and we've gone nowhere. If we don't get sorted, and do it now, then a pound to a pinch of shit says that before you know it that old wolf will be knocking seven bells out of your front door."

"I see it's suddenly my front door."

"And he'll have the bailiffs with him too."

"I see," said Johnson, soberly.

"Anyway," Tim protested, eventually, "it is your front door, you pillock."

"So it is," Johnson concurred, "you're just my tenant."

"So I am," grinned Tim, "and I'm the tenant who's going to sort your life out."

Over tea and Bensons, Tim showed Johnson the ad that he had circled.

"Is this it?" asked Johnson, "this is a joke, right?"

"What's the problem?"

"Out of all the ads in that paper? This?" continued Johnson.

"Let me explain," said Tim, rummaging in his boxers without inhibition. "Biscuit?" Tim offered the raggedly torn pack, fingers lifting the top two digestives from the pile.

"No, thanks," Johnson replied, with curling lip.

"Other hand," protested Tim, "I was scratching the 'nads with my other hand. Sometimes I think you think I've got no manners."

"Sorry," said Johnson, "the fact that I don't want a biscuit has nothing to do with them being in close proximity, not touching, I understand that, but in close proximity to your sweaty bollocks. Nothing at all."

"Fine," said Tim, biting into a three-layered Hob-Nob sandwich.

"The job?" prompted Johnson.

Tim brushed the dusting of crumbs from the paper.

"You can hoover up later," said Johnson.

"Sometimes," said Tim, slowly, and a touch menacingly.

"OK, as we're both housewives now, I'll do it."

"You'll do it?"

"Bloody hell, Tim, this job? Talk me into it."

Tim spoke eloquently, persuasively for five or ten minutes. He pitched the idea to Johnson, he outlined the benefits and demolished the pitfalls, he skywrote the advantages and laid waste to Johnson's demurrals. Tim talked him into it.

"Customer services? Well, I'll give it a go," said Johnson, eventually.

"Keep the W from the D, dear boy," advised Tim. "Give us some income, keep the funds topped up, bit of living expenses, whatever. Less pressure anyway, dealing with a few punters' problems. Be a breeze. We can earn some pocket money while we take stock and have a bit of a rest. It'll be good. Looking forward to it. Can't wait to start."

Johnson fetched two beers and two glasses from the kitchen and placed them on the table.

"Let's not get ahead of ourselves here Tim," he advised, "we're not in yet. Haven't had an interview or anything."

"Well, I'm in," said Tim.

"What do you mean, you're in?"

"Start Monday."

"When did you have the interview?"

"Haven't," said Tim, "they do it on the hoof, apparently. Sort of a working interview on Monday morning. Couple of hours. Do enough to impress and you're in, you know the kind of thing."

"Right," said Johnson, "so what about me?"

"I'll give them a call in the morning, recommend you, put you on the phone, and I reckon we'll be starting there together Monday morning."

"Alright," said Johnson.

"Sort that out first thing, things to do tomorrow."

"Busy are you?" asked Johnson.

"We are, Johnson, that's us."

"We?" asked Johnson, "Us?"

"Going racing aren't we?"

"Racing?"

"Horse racing, you know, racing," said Tim, cheerily, "Kempton."

"How exactly does this slot into your strategy to conserve our resources?" quizzed Johnson.

"Treats."

"Treats?"

"Got to fit in some treats along the way. Otherwise it's all drudge and no fudge."

"All drudge and...never mind," said Johnson, beaten, "I'm going to have a bath."

Tim launched himself at the sofa, its frame protesting as he landed. "Ooops."

"There's nothing in the budget for new furnishings either."

"Sorry," said Tim, pulling open a packet of peanuts and spilling half of them on the carpet. "Ooops," he repeated.

"Ooops indeed," said Johnson, heading for the bathroom.

He languished in the chin-high water until he felt it cooling. He pulled the plug, let some out, and replenished it with a blast from the hot tap. Steam billowed around the bathroom and Johnson breathed in deeply, feeling like it was cleaning his insides. He wasn't sure that working with Tim was the greatest of options, but, in the absence of an alternative, decided he had little to lose. At least it would be fun, and he'd have a ready-made ally. He could hear Tim laughing at something on the television, it sounded like a Warner Brothers cartoon, it would be fun, alright.

They caught a train out to Kempton late the following morning. Tim was studying the racing pages as they trundled through the suburbs. He was dressed in fawn trousers which hung high on his waist, a checked, predominately dark green shirt, light green patterned tie and a loud, checked sports jacket, layered with large squares of red and light-grey, these were split by thick dark-green bars. At least his shoes are relatively normal, thought Johnson, although the tasselled black loafers hardly matched the rest of Tim's outfit.

"Are you sure about that get up?" asked Johnson.

"What get up?"

"The wardrobe, Tim."

"It's my racing outfit. Got to look the part."

201

"Not the hat, please," protested Johnson.

Tim took a tweedy-looking, flat peaked cap from his pocket and set it carefully on his head. It also had a check pattern. Tim checked his reflection in the window, made a minor adjustment or two and nodded approvingly.

"Nice," he announced.

"You have to be joking," laughed Johnson.

"Least I don't look dull and boring."

"That you don't," agreed Johnson, "and if I look dull, well I'll settle for that, better than looking like an idiot."

Johnson wore navy cotton trousers, white shirt with a button-down collar and a blazer. Tim had insisted on ties as he was intent on paying for entry to the premier areas which enforced a dress code. Johnson had gone along with his friend's wishes and had a thin, silk navy tie knotted loosely around his neck. His top shirt button remained resolutely undone.

"I don't know why you bother with that," observed Johnson.

"What?"

"Reading the form. Turning it over in your mind. Weighing up the odds."

"It's an art, that's why," Tim replied, indignantly, "an art. Or is it a science? One of the two anyway, or possibly even both."

"It's all fixed," stated Johnson, firmly.

"It is not," argued Tim, "not every race."

"So, you'll admit that it's fixed?"

"I agree that sometimes things might not be what they seem. Certain parties might not be trying their hardest. Working out who's up for it and who's not, that's part of the challenge, part of the art."

"Or science," suggested Johnson.

"Or science," Tim concurred.

The carriage was reasonably full. A few city types in pinstripes fresh from a morning's work and with ready amounts of cash to donate to the trackside bookies. Intense- looking men in their thirties and forties in jeans and leather jackets, reading the papers dedicated to racing, to gambling. Inky fingers adorned with chunky gold rings, thick identity bracelets dangling from their wrists as they read and frowned and

202

scratched notes in the margins. Johnson watched much chewing of bottom lips, tugging of ears, scratching of thinning scalps and screwing up of eyes. This isn't fun for everybody, he thought, not for these guys, this is fear and adrenalin and despondency and excitement. It's like watching a carriage full of junkies. They're praying for the big win, but they must know that as soon as they get their hands on it they're going to blow it soon afterwards. Johnson noticed that there were no women in the carriage. Women have too much sense to be fooled by all of this, he decided, if the odds-makers had to rely on women they'd be out of business in a week.

"You should do what I do," Johnson advised.

"What's that?" asked Tim, glancing up from the racing form.

"Back something that's about four-to-one in each race. Means it's got a chance and you might get a fair return on your money."

"Too hit-and-miss," said Tim, impatiently.

"As opposed to you scratching your head all morning and afternoon trying to make sense of something you don't understand?"

"Tell you what," said Tim, "we'll see. Your system against mine."

"This afternoon?"

"Of course," said Tim, suddenly animated. "My science against your, your, I don't know what you'd call it."

"System?"

"Wouldn't call it a system," said Tim. "That's the game then, my selection plays your selection, winner takes all. Then we'll see who comes out on top."

"Winner takes all?"

"Whoever picks the most winners is the winner. Loser pays for dinner tonight."

"Done," said Johnson, extending his hand. "Oh no, please don't spit." He withdrew his hand.

"For luck, come on," urged Tim.

"Wipe it off first," insisted Johnson.

Tim drew his hand across his thigh and offered it to Johnson. They shook.

"Where are we?" asked Tim, feeling the train judder to a halt, but not looking up from the paper. His concentration levels appeared to have tripled.

"Hampton, couple of stops to go," said Johnson, looking out of the window.

"Wonder how many pubs in the country are called The Railway Something?"

"Yeah," murmured Tim without interest.

"Thousands I should think," considered Johnson.

"Yeah."

"There's one over there, look," said Johnson.

"Yeah."

There was silence for a few moments.

"Do you think there's one near every station?"

"Yeah," Tim sighed.

"I think there's one called The Railway Bell around here as well. Think it's near here."

"Uh huh."

"That must be unusual," continued Johnson, "two railway themed pubs in close proximity, don't you think?"

Tim sighed deeply and rapped the paper against his knees.

"I wonder if it is?" mused Johnson, "can you think of any other derivatives? The Railwayman, I suppose, any others?"

"I know what you're doing Johnson."

"Doing?"

"Don't be a knob."

"A knob?"

"You're trying to disrupt my reading of the form, and it won't work. I've made my selections and you're a dead man."

"Oh, you bloody think so?"

"I bloody do think so," Tim replied.

"Right."

"Right."

"We're here," announced Johnson, "come on."

They disembarked and trekked along the platform to the course.

"This way," ordered Tim, "we're in this bit."

They mounted a staircase, flashed their badges to the uniformed attendant and were waved through. Johnson fiddled with the badge strings, looping them through his buttonhole and tying them off.

"Two pints, please," ordered Tim, having led Johnson to the Guinness bar.

"We'll have Guinness then, shall we?" asked Johnson.

"It's very good here," Tim advised, "I hear they ship it in from Dublin."

"No they don't," said Johnson. "Anyway, I might have wanted something else."

"You want something else?" asked Tim.

"No," said Johnson, "but I might have done."

Tim shook his head and watched the barman finishing off their pints with a swirl of the glass under the beer tap.

"Lucky shamrocks," said Tim, sucking it into his mouth.

"Lucky for some," said Johnson, propping an elbow on the bar and regarding the room. "I though you said this was the premier, members area or something?"

"It is," Tim replied, removing white foam from his top lip with the back of his hand.

"Ties and jackets?"

"Yes."

"No jeans, trainers or sportswear?"

"Yes."

"Turn round Tim."

"Oh."

"Are you sure we're in the right bit?"

"Yeah. Absolutely."

"Looks like a fire risk to me. All of this man-made fibre on show, rubbing up against each other. Have you checked where the exits are?"

"Don't understand," said Tim.

"Did they specify, ripped jeans only?"

"No."

"Or only dirty old trainers?"

"Course not."

"Glad we made the effort," said Johnson, "you look very smart, I must say. Rather out of place, but very dapper."

"Cheers."

"This is like any town centre you care to name on a Saturday night."

"Yeah, alright."

"Chavtastic."

"They sell the tickets but don't enforce the code, I reckon."

"But that's not right," Johnson protested, "not while we've made the effort."

"Got a point," conceded Tim.

"I'm going to complain," announced Johnson.

"Do me a favour, would you?" asked Tim.

"What's that?"

"Shut up for five minutes and concentrate on the racing. You want to complain? Do it afterwards, write a letter. They're not going to kick all these people out, or issue them with Marks and Sparks' finest for the afternoon are they? We'd be the only two left in here. Let's just get on with the racing."

They left their half-finished drinks with the white-shirted, black waist-coated barman, giving him a few coins to look after them. The young man smiled and placed them behind the bar.

"You look a bit like a pint of Guinness yourself," observed Tim.

"Congratulations, sir," said the barman.

"What? Have I won something then?" asked Tim.

"Just my undying admiration sir."

"Eh?"

"For being the first today to make that comparison."

Tim paused, and picked at his tie.

"Must hear that a lot do you?"

"Only all the time, sir, only all the time," the barman replied, applying his white cloth to a glass. "Good luck with the first race."

They cruised the bookmakers' stalls, Tim comparing odds, Johnson looking for something which would satisfy his four-to-one criteria.

"What are you doing in this one?" asked Johnson.

"Tell you later," Tim replied, ducking into a queue and pulling notes from his wallet.

Johnson chose a queue at random.

"Number six. Five pounds to win," he announced to a tall dark-haired man who wore a camel-hair coat and dark brown trilby with a black band.

"Number six a fiver," the man repeated to his colleague, an acned youth who punched a keypad, the machine clicked and whirred, and spewed out a ticket which was handed to Johnson. Johnson turned, found Tim was a few feet away, and they walked back to the grandstand.

"What did you do?" asked Tim.

"Tell you later," Johnson replied.

"No, no. Now's the time to front up. Cards on the table. What have you backed?"

"Running Mustang," said Johnson.

"Shit," said Tim, "so did I."

"Told you that paper was a waste of time, didn't I?" said Johnson, happily.

They watched the horses being ridden onto the course as the crowd pressed in around them on the concrete terraced steps. It was another hot day.

"You must be hot in that jacket," observed Johnson.

"I'm alright," Tim replied, looking into the distance. "There he is, there, look. Red silks with a blue sash, red and blue quartered cap. Looking good. Fit looking horse isn't he?"

"Says here it's cerise," said Johnson, showing Tim the programme."

"Cerise?" Tim replied, not taking his eyes from the course.

"Cerise and azure."

"Red and blue," said Tim, "like I said."

"What did you put on?"

"Fifty."

"Fifty?" exploded Johnson. "Fifty pounds? Have you gone completely frigging bananas?"

"Without the speculation there can be no accumulation, Johnson, surely even an equine virgin like yourself can work that out?"

"An equine…?"

"Equine virgin, good one, eh?"

"And where did you find that little gem?"

"In my paper," said Tim, breezily, "good one, eh? Equine virgin. What are you in for?"

"Fiver," said Johnson, quietly.

"Fiver? Surprised they took it," sniffed Tim.

After the race they retreated to the Guinness Bar.

"Running Mustang, was it?" asked Tim, draining his pint and ordering two more before he'd replaced his glass on the bar.

"That's the one," replied Johnson, pulling the betting slip from his pocket and dumping it in an ashtray.

"Shame nobody bothered to teach it the fucking running bit."

"Seventh," announced Johnson.

"Seventh," repeated Tim, mouth turned down at the corners, dimpling his jowls, he shook his head ruefully, "can't believe it. Seventh."

"What happened to the form book?"

"Can't explain it, all the signs were there, was looking good, looking great actually. All the tipsters said so."

"You didn't work it out yourself then?"

"What?"

"You followed the tipsters."

"I made an informed decision based on the weights, previous form over the distance and the course, the trainer, the jockey, state of the ground, time of year, distance from the home stable to the course."

"And then you picked the one that everyone else had gone for."

"I made an informed decision."

"Which cost you fifty pounds."

"Still, I bet I'm not the only one who got it wrong." Tim shook himself out of his depression. "What's next?"

"What's next?" asked Johnson.

"In the next race, my idea is, that I'll tell you what I'm going to back and you choose something else."

Johnson held his glass to his lips and felt the head of the stout gathering around his top lip. He took a gulp.

"No."

"What do you mean, no?"

"Well, no. We choose independently or else there's no point. If we back the same horse, then so be it, proves we're both geniuses. Why should I give you first pick?"

"You can have first pick next time," replied Tim.

"What about your system?" Johnson pointed out, reasonably. "You've spent all that time choosing where you're going to lose your money, making an informed decision, and then I say you can't have that one? Won't work."

"It won't work, will it?" Tim conceded.

"So, as you were. You choose yours, I'll choose mine, and we'll show our hands when the money's gone on. Deal?"

"I guess so," said Tim, "come on, time for the next one."

They walked down to the course, placed bets, watched the race, walked back.

"So, mine was second and yours was fifth," Johnson reported.

"So I saw, yes," said Tim abruptly, "so I saw."

"Do I get anything for that?" asked Johnson.

"If you backed it each way, then yes you do," advised Tim, "under the terms of our bet, then no you bloody don't."

"Fair enough," said Johnson, "I'll take a moral victory."

Tim was chewing determinedly on a biro's end and holding his quartered newspaper close to his face.

"Drink?" enquired Johnson.

"Not now son, no," replied Tim, "got an important choice to make here."

"Two more, please," ordered Johnson, "I got you one anyway, might help you think. Tim, I said, I've got you one anyway, might stir up the creative juices, you know, help you pick the right one. A winner, you call it don't you, you racing folk? Tim?"

Tim lowered the paper a quarter of an inch and revealed his small, dark eyes. He took an exaggerated breath. In, out. Pause. Another breath

"I heard you the first time. I am trying to concentrate," he said, enunciating each syllable.

"Sorry," said Johnson, "thought you couldn't hear me. Here's your drink, anyway," he offered the brimming dark glass to Tim who was already holding a drink, a newspaper, a pen, a cigarette, and a tweedy cap.

"I can't, can I?" protested Tim, attempting to gesture with his shoulders.

"Oh, no. You can't can you?" agreed Johnson, "I'll just put it here, look, just here on the bar, for when you want it."

"Thank you," said Tim, pedantically patient. "Now, if you don't mind, I'd like to spend five minutes with the paper."

"Of course," assented Johnson, "of course."

"Thank you," said Tim.

"Do you want anything to eat?"

Races three, four and five passed without much conversation and, more importantly, without either of them paying a return visit to collect any winnings.

"Last one," announced Tim.

"Last one it is," agreed Johnson, "how much are you down?"

"Not a subject I wish to discuss," said Tim, firmly.

"Our systems aren't going so well are they?" ventured Johnson.

"No."

"So, how much are you down?"

"Johnson," warned Tim.

"Your tipsters must have lost a lot as well."

"Suppose so," admitted Tim, grudgingly.

"As much as you, do you think?"

"You can be an annoying little tit Johnson, you know that?"

"Just amusing myself," said Johnson, "I've lost as well, you know."

"Yeah," agreed Tim, charitably, "you have, haven't you?"

"Twenty-five pounds."

"Right then," barked Tim, "two beers over here, please barman. One race to go. One favour to ask."

"Of me?" asked Johnson.

"Of course, of you."

"We stand here, quietly, and drink our Guinness. I read my paper, uninterrupted, read the form, until I have made a decision. I might even smoke a cigarette. But

210

whatever happens, we do it peacefully."

"What about me?" asked Johnson.

"You be quiet."

"Quiet."

"But I've got no-one else to talk to," protested Johnson.

Tim regarded him calmly.

"I don't have a lot of time here, so I'll make this quick. I like you Johnson, you're my mate. But if you don't stop getting on my tits, then I'll hit you. I don't want to hit you, I really don't, you know why? Because I like you. But if you push me just once more, once more, sunshine, and I promise you that I will hit you."

"Right," said Johnson, uncertainly.

"I mean it," said Tim.

"I don't doubt it," agreed Johnson. "Do you want a ..?"

Tim loomed up at Johnson and suddenly seemed a foot taller and twice as wide.

"What?" barked Tim sharply, "do I want a what?"

"Sorry, nothing. Nothing at all," said Johnson swiftly, "I'm going for a pee."

"Stroke of luck that was," said Tim, later. They had hung around at the course for a while, avoiding the exodus to the railway station and, considering six or maybe seven and possibly eight pints to be an inadequate number, had decided to have one for the road. Tim reclined on the bar, both elbows resting on it, he faced outwards. Johnson stood a pace away, free hand in his pocket, rustling paper. The large room was already being cleared of its punter-dropped garbage. Glasses ranging from the full to the empty. Who buys a pint or a glass of wine and abandons it straight away? mused Johnson, they must have known a race was coming along any minute while they were standing at the bar, ordering, mind you, he said to Tim, who grinds their lighted fag ends into what might once have been a perfectly decent carpet? Racing papers and ketchup-dripped polystyrene boxes were bundled into bin liners, discarded betting slips swept up into piles of disappointment, the occasional hat or jacket retrieved. When the vacuum cleaners appeared Tim and Johnson beat the retreat.

"Winner in the last," agreed Johnson.

"At fours too," said Tim, approvingly, "didn't quite cover the day, didn't cover the bets even, but got us out of trouble."

"There's a train in about ten minutes," reported Johnson, studying the board.

"So, who's buying dinner?" Tim enquired.

"Dinner?"

"The bet."

"All square aren't we?"

"Yeah," smiled Tim, "all square."

"Your system came good in the end then? The form I mean. Time well spent with the paper and the tipsters. Studying the ground and whatever else it was you said," said Johnson.

"Yeah," agreed Tim, "it did, didn't it? Told you, didn't I? Don't mess with the man."

"Do not mess with the man!" shouted Johnson, jabbing a finger at Tim.

Three bored adolescent boys, sitting on the opposite platform with two girls of the same disposition regarded them with the practised cool distaste of the teenager.

"Do not mess with this man!" repeated Johnson, raising both arms, "He is the man!"

"Alright mate," said Tim quietly, "easy."

"Those kids?" laughed Johnson, "Don't be silly. They're no bother. You're no bother are you? You kids over there. Hey!"

"Not them mate, you're worrying these nice people over here, on our side."

Johnson looked along the platform at the not-quite-elderly couple who had been sitting unobtrusively not ten yards away, and were now preparing to move to the very end of the platform.

"Oh, I'd better…" began Johnson.

"Stay there big boy," advised Tim, "you go staggering over there shouting and I reckon they're likely to take their chances on the rails."

"Right," agreed Johnson, leaning back on the red-brick station wall, now keenly aware that the five hooded teenagers had spotted that he was, for now, alone. He watched Tim stroll calmly along the platform, exchanging a few words and shrugs. Tim laughing and pointing back to where Johnson stood. Handshakes were exchanged, even a peck on the cheek, Johnson fancied he even heard a 'naughty boy' in there somewhere, and Tim wandered easily back as the couple re-seated themselves. He really was a charmer, thought Johnson as Tim returned to his side. A train stopped on the opposite side, pulled away a few minutes later and when Johnson observed the empty platform he relaxed visibly.

"You OK?" asked Tim casually.

"Yes. No," Johnson said, "You never know do you? Nowadays. Nowadays, I sound like my dad. I've never been, you know attacked. Man found with serious injuries after an apparently unprovoked attack. But I could have got us into..."

"Don't worry about it," said Tim, "you've nearly been chinned once today already. Perhaps you're on a mission, I don't know. Wouldn't have been unprovoked attacks would they? I'll tell you that much. There was never any bother going to come from over there though."

"Chinned once? Oh you mean you."

"Yes," said Tim.

"You would have?"

"What?"

"Hit me. Punched me in the face. Given me a nosebleed, a black eye, a split lip, knocked some teeth out."

"Yep," confirmed Tim, staring into the distance.

"Really? But why?"

Tim turned around slowly, one hand rubbing his eyes.

"Don't tell me you don't know."

"What?" pleaded Johnson.

"Like I said, you can be such an irritating little wanker sometimes."

"I can?"

"Trust me," confirmed Tim, with widening eyes, "Oh yes. You see, you push it and push it, and don't tell me you don't know what you're doing, then you push it some more, and I swear that one day you will be going home in a fucking ambulance."

Johnson banged his head backwards quite firmly, feeling the rough brickwork scuffing into his scalp.

"I do know what I'm doing, Tim" he said, "you're right so far. At least I think I know, or I think I realise what it is that I'm doing. But it's, I don't know, sometimes it's my way of getting through the day, of having a some fun, or sometimes it's calculated. I won't, I can't deny that. There are times when I think, I know what'll really annoy this person, really get under their skin, so I'll say it just to see what happens. Now and again though it's because I can't actually think of anything else to say."

Tim flicked his eyebrows upwards, took a last drag and tossed the butt onto the rails.

"Train's coming," he said.

"Do you understand what I just said?" asked Johnson, "It'd be nice to have some sort of response, you know, I feel like I've poured my heart out there, and all you can say is, train's coming."

Tim pressed the button to open the train door.

"I'm glad it's not me inside that head of yours," he said, "come on, let's get you back to the unit, doctor will be wondering where you are."

Johnson sucked in a mouthful of soupy air as he opened the front door of the flat.

"Jeez, it's hot in here," remarked Tim. "Open some windows, will you mate?"

"While you recline on the sofa? No problem."

"I'll get the drinks," offered Tim, quickly on his feet again.

"No," said Johnson. "Just water for me. Big glass of water. With ice."

Interview Phase VII

"*M*ore ice?" I asked him.

"Thanks," said Johnson, pushing his glass across the table. I dropped in a chilly handful of slippery cubes. "Hope there's no egg on your fingers."

"No egg," I promised.

"Thanks," said Johnson, sucking in half of the liquid in a couple of gulps. He coughed a sliver of ice from the back of his throat and crunched it noisily. He had shaved this morning, though his hair looked a little greasy-damp it was hard to tell whether that was down to hygiene or the heat. He was dressed in yet another crisp, clean shirt and smooth, light cotton trousers.

"Not drinking today?" I asked.

"Oh, you know. It is a little early isn't it?" sighed Johnson, indifferently, he was gazing, unblinkingly at the ceiling, executing his rocking back-and-forth on the chair movement, testing the angles. Such a show of boredom and weariness so early in the day didn't seem to be a good omen.

"Fancy a walk?" I asked, brightly.

"A what?"

"A walk, you know," I struggled, "A walk."

"Get out of this room for a bit?"

"Why not?" I smiled.

"Are we allowed?" he asked, seeming suddenly cowed. Back to the person he was long before any of this happened.

"Of course," I assured him, "of course we are. I'm in charge here, you know."

"You are?"

"Come on," I said, "before I change my mind. Hang on. You wait here. Just got to make a call."

"You're in charge though?"

"Yes, Johnson," I said, "I am, and don't think for a minute that you can pull one on me, alright?"

215

"Because you've got help?"

"Exactly. So don't be a …"

"Clown. I know," said Johnson. He added, "Don't worry, I won't give you any trouble. I've got nowhere to go."

We took the lift down to the ground floor and walked across the expansive reception area and through the atrium. Plants towered over us like huge umbrellas, fifteen, twenty-feet high and in terracotta pots as wide as I am high. Our footsteps hit the cool marble as we passed the desks, the staff, the security. Refusing the offer of a car and driver, we felt the goodbye-blast of the air-con and the cooling electric fans on our backs and walked out onto the street.

Released from our cocoon, the pure daylight was blinding, the heat, track-stopping, the noise hit us from all sides, an intense wall of sound. Suddenly there were other people on the planet. Real people, not just characters in Johnson's story. I'd lost track of the hours, forty-eight? More than twenty-four, certainly. I couldn't see much smoke, a few slim twirls here and there in the distance, but the smell was everywhere. Not the smell of cooking or of fuel being burned for heat, God knows, more heat wasn't needed here, no, this was the smell of burning garbage, of smouldering tyres and plastic and shit. The humidity meant that it hung around the face and you pulled it into your body with each struggling breath, and with each step breathing became more of an ordeal.

"Let's go down to the harbour," I suggested after we had walked for a hundred yards or so, bumping through the crowds, determinedly not buying anything despite the pressure.

"Taxi!" shouted Johnson.

I looked at him sharply.

"Sorry. Don't mean to take over. I mean, you're in charge and all that. But, honestly, fuck this. I mean, fuck it over up sideways down. How do people cope with this all the time? How? Paradise. Some people at home, offer them the chance to live somewhere like this and they'd think, I'll have some of that, tear your fucking arm off, they would. But, honestly. Look. Feel. Christ. It's bloody unbearable. I feel like one of those blokes hundreds of years ago, you know, press-ganged. One minute you're having a pint in your local in the Yorkshire Dales where it's pissed down forever and you've been cold all your life, this is before the invention of the umbrella of course. Although I grant you, you might have looked a bit of a twat herding up your sheep in a smock and a brolly. Next minute, alright, couple of months down the line, on some ship being flogged and buggered all the way, or is it sodomised rather than buggered? I'm never sure of the distinction. You're being bitten to buggery, buggery again, see? Bitten to soddery by these monster flies that don't bite like that back home, no way lad, not in't Yorkshire, and you've got sunstroke and sunburn, and all your clothes have rotted away, and you're permanently thirsty. You've got a crazy itch in your nethers because you've caught a social disease from the bastard who was there before you. Shit, and now your descendants are doing all of that for fun. Taking a year out. Backpacking. The great adventure. I'm a traveller, not a tourist. All that crap."

Johnson was laughing. His face already bore traces of sweat-streaked grime and his shirt and trousers were spotted with dirt and speckled with damp.

"Are you getting in this cab or what?" he asked.

We found a harbour-side eating and drinking place, although eating looked to be a dangerous option. Anyway, it had a stretch of tatty but pretty, red and white-striped awning which was cool underneath, and we took a table near the rail and overlooking the water. Two impossibly large, and frosted with the cold, bottles of beer arrived together with two tiny glasses.

"Did I ask for mouthwash?" remarked Johnson, quietly, the waiter long departed.

"You're not so brave after all, are you?" I said.

There was a welcome breeze zipping gently off the water and we sat in comfortable silence for a while, watching the disorderly river traffic. Johnson smoked constantly, but called for water with the next round of beers.

"Bit dehydrated," he explained, removing his sunglasses and wiping the lenses on his cottoned thigh.

"After yesterday's intake?"

"H2O's the way to go."

"The, er, Big Red Book," I ventured.

Johnson replaced his shades and turned his head back to the water.

"Not the time."

"Why not?"

"Structure."

"Structure?"

"Dramatic tension."

"What?"

He turned his head back to face me, rested his elbows on the table and his hands assumed a praying position. He rubbed the tips of his fingers along his jaw line, hands still pressed together.

"A story has structure. I mean, I don't want to take the wind out of your sails or anything, or upset how you want to structure things, but we're going forward here in a certain fashion, we're at a particular point in the story. OK, I'm taking the mick when I say 'dramatic tension', but it all leads to that thing."

"That thing?"

"You know."

"The book? The Big Red Book?"

"Of course."

"I've seen it you know. The book."

"I guessed you had. You had to, didn't you?"

"Is that the only one?" I asked.

His fingers reached up behind the sunglasses and gave an exaggerated rub and dismissed a loitering waiter with studied politeness.

"Now, you know there's more than one, so don't."

"Don't do what?"

"Make it harder than it should be. Don't take me for an idiot. Don't make me out to be some sort of prize prick. And don't play the innocent by asking and prompting and nudging and wheedling, bloody wheedling, that's what you were doing, trying to get under my skin."

"I did though, didn't I?"

"Get under my skin?"

I nodded.

"Yeah. Just for a minute," grinned Johnson, "just a tad. It's a good job we get along isn't it?"

218

"It is," I agreed.

"Right," he said, "let's get on, then."

"If we can't talk about the book yet, that's OK. How about this thing you did with Tim? The complaints thing?"

"Alright," he assented.

A canopied craft slid past and hit the horn or hooter. Johnson and I both leapt a foot into the air, and I spilled beer down my front.

"Let me get that," offered Johnson.

"I'm OK."

He reached forward.

"It's no trouble. We'll get some water and just mop it off."

"Leave it, Johnson, please," I said, "I'm OK." I pressed my back into the seat and crossed my arms in front of my chest.

"Fine," he said, "just trying to help."

"I know, just leave it, it'll dry soon enough."

Although the side on which we sat was populated with old-style low, mainly wooden, buildings, there were some modern high-rise buildings across the water. We watched besuited staff on their lunch breaks streaming out of the office buildings.

"Think I'd stay inside," mused Johnson, "next to the air-con. Spent all morning cooling off then you dive out for lunch and end up all sweaty again. Makes no sense."

"Get some fresh air, I suppose."

"Fresh air?" he replied. "Fresh exhaust fumes, maybe."

"Fair point."

"Do you think any of this stuff in the air is carcinogenic?" asked Johnson, firing up another Rothman.

"What difference would that make to you?"

"None whatsoever," he smiled, expelling a grey funnel of fumes from his mouth. "The way I see it, my cigarettes are affording my lungs valuable protection from these thousands of noxious pollutants."

"Protection?" I protested. "That's a new one."

"Through years of dedicated smoking, I have formed a protective barrier around my airways and thus no nasties can find their way in," he said happily.

219

"I suppose they get stuck on the tar."

"It works for me."

The waiter had been zig-zagging his way across the floor to our table. Finally he reached us, with two menus tucked under his arm and an expectant look on his face.

"We'd better order something," I decided.

"He's not going to take no for an answer is he?" observed Johnson.

The waiter stood still, His glum expression accentuated by his floppy dark hair, long face, and a droopy moustache. I reached out and took a menu, Johnson took the other.

"Fancy anything?" I asked.

"Another drink," said Johnson. "You know what they say, one of the rules of foreign travel? Never eat anywhere which has pictures of the food on its menu."

"Better than drawings," I replied. "Just order something, you don't have to eat it."

"Cheer up, squire," Johnson addressed the waiter. "I'll have this thing that looks like it might be chicken. What is it anyway?"

"Chicken," said the waiter.

"Two of those, thank you," I said.

"Big mistake," offered Johnson. "Might be awful. If it's awful then we're both stuck with it. If, on the other hand, you order something different, then that might be OK and we can share yours."

"Or vice versa."

"Or vice versa."

"Can I change my mind?" I asked the hovering waiter. "I'll have this fish dish. That is fish isn't it?" I asked, pointing.

"Chicken," said the waiter.

"Do you have any fish?" I asked.

"Today we have chicken."

We settled on two chicken dishes and another round of drinks.

"The job with Tim?" I prompted, when we were alone again.

"As you know," Johnson began, "it was dealing with complaints from all sorts of nut jobs. Not all nut jobs, I suppose, but after a while..." he tailed off and took on that worrying gaze that might mean we were in for half-an-hour of meanderings.

"Doing what exactly?" I asked, sharply, anxious to keep him from straying.

"Taking calls, correspondence, writing letters."

"Who was this for? Which company?"

"It was centralised operation. They handled complaints for all sorts of places. Supermarkets, airlines, travel agents, railways, you know."

"These places have their own departments for this sort of thing don't they?"

"You'd think so, wouldn't you? But, no, dealing with disgruntled punters has become very specialised. People are such arseholes now that they go on holiday with a notebook and a camcorder specifically looking for problems, all they want is to screw themselves a few quid in compensation. It means they're not appreciating the natural beauty of the place, or enjoying dinner in the hotel restaurant. They're picking holes in the local driver or guide and hunting under the table for cockroaches. Greedy, ignorant bastards. So a lot of places farm these things out to the professionals," Johnson started laughing.

"You and Tim being the professionals?"

"Yeah," he laughed louder, "can you believe it? To start with we were committed and diplomatic and did all that was asked of us."

"But then you started writing letters like this?" I handed him a slim ring-binder containing twenty of the choicest, and he recited the first one.

Dear Mr Gallimost

Thank you for your letter in which you claim (in your rather simple, child-like fashion) that you have reason to be dissatisfied with the service you have received from Jammesters Supermarket.

We at Jammesters Supermarkets are committed to providing top-flight service and high-quality products at competitive prices to our valued shoppers. Unfortunately, judging by your sketchy command of the English language, your atrocious handwriting, and your grubby notepaper which was covered in dirty finger marks, you are not the sort of person with which Jammesters Supermarkets wishes to be associated. Our new mission statement makes it perfectly clear that one of our main aims is to keep the riff-raff out of our stores. As we deem you, Mr Gallimost, to be riff-raff of the very worst kind, we have no interest in dealing with you or discussing your rather laboured points any further. Your letter has been consigned to the waste-paper bin, perhaps you will come across it in the future on one of your scavenging trips to the local dump.

Yours sincerely

Jammy Jammester

Chief Twat Co-Ordinator

Jammester Supermarkets

Johnson's eyes misted over with tears, and his laughing-cough rattled its way around the patio and across the water.

"I'd forgotten that one," he said, eventually.

"Was that one of yours, or Tim's?"

"Joint effort, as I remember. I think he gave me the riff-raff line, oh, and the bit about the local dump was his too. Very good."

"Why did you go down this route?"

"It was a horrible, horrible job," he spat, venomously. "We started out with all the best intentions. Talked to the unhappy, talked them down, all of those angry people. Reached agreement, compensation, or not. Wrote the letters, took the flak. We were tactful, diplomatic. But the money was crap and it was no way to earn a living, you know? I just wrote one of these letters one day as a private joke. I showed it to Tim. He looked at me and there was never any question of not sending it. We'd both had enough, and it seemed like it might be fun."

"Fun?" I queried. "Surely you knew it couldn't last?"

"Of course," he said, pushing away the plate of pale and anorexic chicken which the waiter had just placed before him. "Looks nothing like the picture," he explained, "looks more like an insect."

"So why not just leave?"

"This way was just more fun. Shake up some of these tossers who had nothing better to do but piss and moan all day. Shake up the companies too, give their precious reputations a bit of a caning. They're no better. They're out to screw the punter and I guess you can't really blame the punter for trying to get something back."

"So the complainer is in the right?" I asked through a mouthful of gristle and bone.

"No."

"The company?" I spat the disgusting lump into a napkin.

222

"No. They're both wrong."

"What's the answer?"

"Haven't a clue," replied Johnson, "but it was up to me and Timothy to chuck a stick in the spokes."

"For the greater good?"

"Not really," said Johnson, "for a bit of a laugh. I'd forgotten this one," he said as he turned the pages

"I'm not surprised," I observed, "you managed to bang out quite a lot in your last three days didn't you?"

"Timed it around a Bank Holiday. Though it would give us an extra day or two before the first of the letters hit the doormats and by then it would be too late," said Johnson, smugly. "Here, look at this one." He passed the folder back to me and I read:

Dear Mrs Swottley

Thank you very much for your letter regarding your apparently less than rewarding holiday. I hope you will excuse as, handicapped by the sole option of using mere words from the English dictionary, like, we cannot quite convey to you the mounting levels of our excitement and eventual hilarity as we read through your interminable and dreary list of small-minded, petty gripes and whinges. While you undoubtedly raise some points of interest, sadly I have to report that they are of no interest to us in the least.

May we respectfully suggest that when the benefits office next gives you a fortnight off that you spend the time at home, thereby giving the civilised population of the world a well-deserved break from you pissing all over it and generally polluting it with your stench.

I remain, your obedient servant,

Jack Off

"Wanker by Appointment"

Toss-Off Holidays Inc.

"I wasn't sure about the name, but Tim insisted," grinned Johnson, "Jack Off. Quite funny I suppose."

"And this one?" I asked. "To a Mr Smith?"

Oi Smiffy

Why don't you fuck off and die?

Yours truly

The Customer Service Team

"Because you're not worth it"

"Perhaps we were running out of ideas by that stage. Got a bit boring."

"I'm getting the impression that you're easily bored."

"We knew the game was up. Tried to get our point across succinctly towards the end."

"I've heard some of the phone calls."

"Oh, that's true is it?" asked Johnson. "Calls may be recorded for training purposes?"

"Oh yes."

"I wouldn't mind hearing some of those," he suggested.

"Well, I haven't got them with me, they're all back at…"

"Fine. Fine. That was right at the end, of course. Just before we got fired. Probably wouldn't add much to my life right now, would it? Hearing them again?"

"Apart from the nostalgic value? No."

"Ice cream, dessert, fruit salad?" asked the waiter, who had slid up to the table unnoticed and was clearing away the barely touched main courses.

"He's kidding isn't he?" asked Johnson, nodding first at me and then at the droopy waiter. His eyes were masked by his shades, but I knew he was winking.

"Just some more water and another beer, please," I looked questioningly at Johnson, who nodded his assent.

"Everything was fine?" asked the waiter.

"Absolutely delicious," Johnson replied, "so beautifully presented and delicious that we didn't want to spoil it by actually eating anything."

"Thank you sir."

"Please be sure and present our compliments to the half-educated toss-pot who threw this abomination together and expected us to eat it," grinned Johnson, winningly.

"Thank you sir."

The waiter returned quickly with our drinks and the bill. I settled it while he waited, placing a few worn, moist notes on the table.

"We'll have these and move on, shall we?" I suggested.

"Sure," agreed Johnson, pouring my water.

"Fancy a walk?"

"Why not? I was getting far too comfortable sitting here. Must be time to lose a few litres in sweat."

"You don't have to," I said, I was just trying to make things a little less tedious, get us out of the dreaded room."

"That's fine," he said, amenably, "appreciate it."

We stuck to the riverside, seeking out the odd patches of shade. From time to time we sat on benches or steps. Johnson had bought a local newspaper.

"Best insight you get into a new place. That and going for a drink," he said, fanning himself with the paper as we sat in an adjacent park. A small, recently constructed area with a few trees, some concrete seats and a pond which was spanned by a low, narrow stone bridge.

"These seats are comfortable aren't they?" observed Johnson.

"Must be to deter the rough sleepers," I said.

"Brilliant idea, concrete seats. Surprised they didn't add a little broken glass."

"So you and Tim got yourselves fired," I said.

"Yes," Johnson replied, standing and stretching.

"Was he still seeing Kate?"

"Do we have to?"

"What?"

"Go through all of this detail?" Johnson asked, hands on hips.

"For my notes," I said.

"But you know this bit, at least."

"I need to get all the details down, put everything in order, there are things you or I might not see as being relevant. But when they appear as part of the bigger picture they might, do you see?" I explained.

"If you say so," he said, petulantly.

"Was Tim still seeing Kate?" I persisted.

Johnson sighed deeply.

"Don't pout," I advised him, "it makes you look like a spoilt little schoolgirl."

"They saw each other on and off but not for long. They weren't really much of a match. Tim, you couldn't expect Tim to have a proper relationship with anyone. As soon he was out of their sight he was out marking his territory like a tomcat, sniffing around. And he wasn't fussy either. You know, if he hadn't pulled by two AM or so, then anything, absolutely anything would do. It was like a horror film at the flat some mornings."

"That's awful," I said.

"Awful's the word, some right old nightmares."

"I meant that was an awful thing to say."

"Oh, right," said Johnson, "true, though. You never saw the aftermath."

"Right," I said, "you were out of work, without money or any income, and without anything to recommend you to a prospective employer. What did you do?"

"I made a phone call."

Advertising

"What are we going to do now then?" asked Johnson.

The day after their sackings he was settled in the living room with Tim, the radio played in the background.

"Friday afternoon," reported Tim, "Can't do much in the way of job-hunting on a Friday afternoon."

"It's a beautiful day out there in the city and it's our favourite day of the week, guys, you know why? Because the weekend is nearly upon us. Oh yes, here comes the weekend," said the voice from the radio.

"I don't know why this bloke gets so excited about the weekend," said Johnson, "he works all bloody weekend doesn't he?"

"Mmm," agreed Tim.

"Saturday and Sunday."

"Yeah."

"So, are we going to start looking for something on Monday?" asked Johnson.

"Listen Johnson, I've decided I'm going to go on the markets with my brother."

"Really, why?"

"I've had enough of this crap, mate. Make a nice change to deal with some real people."

"Are you moving out?"

"No, no. I'd like to stay if that's alright."

"Sure,"

"Good money my brother makes too. If you need a bit of help, you know?"

"Thanks Tim," said Johnson, "I hope it won't come to that."

"I'll be working Saturdays and Sundays, funnily enough."

"Of course," said Johnson, quietly.

"I'll try to be quiet, you know, getting up early at the weekend. Try not to disturb you."

"Appreciate it," said Johnson, suddenly feeling alone.

"So what are you going to do?"

"I haven't a clue," said Johnson, simply, "not a clue."

"I'm going to start with bruv tomorrow," announced Tim, "so I'm going over to his place this afternoon, sort a few bits out."

"Alright," said Johnson.

"Cheer up, mate," said Tim, "something'll come up. Take the weekend off, make a few calls next week. Take a flyer. I'll see you later. Well, probably not 'cos I'll be back late and off early in the morning. Might see you tomorrow night? We'll go out for a drink, yeah?"

"See you," said Johnson, and he heard the closing of the front door.

Unsurprisingly the contents hadn't changed at all when Johnson inspected them on his fourth visit to the fridge. Increasing hunger dictated that he must eat something. He sniffed the bacon guardedly. It had been bought from the local butcher and as there was no sell-by date he had to be guided by his nose. I can always throw it up later, he decided, slapping the remaining four rashers onto the heated grill pan where it sizzled and spat as it landed. He scraped a little mould from the edge of the cheese and sliced the rest, to grill with the last two slices of bread. Sadly, the only patches on the three tomatoes which weren't leaking were covered in white fur. He removed them from their lonely position on the centre shelf and lobbed them into the bin, although one hit the edge and bounced back, finishing itself off on the floor. Johnson knelt and mopped and scraped, trying to pick up tomato pips between his fingers. Bugger this, he decided, perhaps I do seek solace in the bottle, but is it any bloody wonder? Do you drink alone? Certainly, and I love it. Other solitary pursuits are far more dangerous to the health. He took a bottle of red from the rack and poured himself a glass while he finished off the cheese and bacon. The kitchen was filling with the delicious aroma of the sweet-cured meat, the melting mature cheddar and the toast, slightly burnt around the edges, as it should always be with cheese.

Sated, he smoked a cigarette and topped up his drink. He wouldn't be going out this evening, so what to do? He picked up the phone.

"Nicola Pennywell," announced Nicola Pennywell.

"Hi, Nicola, this is Johnson. We met a little while ago and I called you and it wasn't

....sorry, if this is a bad time as well..."

"Hello Johnson," she said, Johnson thought she sounded pleased, "I'd almost given up on you."

"You had?"

"Last time, you called me at a bad time."

"I think you were with someone, weren't you?"

"Yes, I was," she said.

"I'm sorry, I..."

"I may have given you the wrong idea," said Nicola, matter-of-factly, "I was with someone, but it was our last weekend together, I'd only gone along to break up with him."

"Wouldn't it have been easier to break up beforehand and save the bother of going away?" said Johnson, reasonably.

"I owed him that much Johnson. We were happily married for a little while."

"Married?" said Johnson, the surprise evident in his voice. "I had no idea."

"Let's face it, you wouldn't would you? We don't know much about each other at all, do we?"

"Agreed," said Johnson. "How long were you married for?"

"Do you want to meet up?" asked Nicola, suddenly. "I mean we could talk about all of this over the phone if you'd prefer it that way, but it's not like having a conversation face-to-face is it?"

"I'd like that," said Johnson, honestly.

"I know it's short notice, but I don't have any plans, I don't know about you - you're probably doing something, but how about this evening?"

"Great," said Johnson, looking doubtfully at his stained T-shirt and cut-off denims.

They agreed on a pub that was familiar to both of them, and agreed to meet in an hour. Johnson was in the shower before the phone had settled back into its cradle.

Cleaned and pressed, Johnson had managed to nick himself only twice while shaving, despite his excitement and air of anticipation, and was striding through the Friday night street people trying to remember when he had last been on a date. Despite the ending, JeffandAnna's wedding didn't count, as there had been little employment of the standard dating rituals. He seemed to remember a disastrous evening where his date

229

had gone off arm-in-arm with someone else. A man, at least I think it was a man, he thought, perhaps I put her off men for life. Not that he could blame her, try as they might, they couldn't find a single thing they had in common, eventually Johnson had tried to balance this out by agreeing with everything that she said, which only served to irritate her further.

Johnson was pleased to note that he had arrived a few minutes ahead of the scheduled meeting time, and first. You couldn't blame a woman for not wanting to enter a pub alone only to find that her date was not waiting for her. All the leering "hello luv's" and "Here, let me get that, darlings" that the lone female still had to put up with must make it more akin to an ordeal in the monkey-house than a pleasant night out. Johnson ordered a beer and stationed himself at the bar, in plain sight of the door. Nicola arrived ten minutes later. She had allowed her dark brown hair to grow out a little, but retained the businesslike parting. She was dressed simply in black trousers and a loose cream silk blouse. She walked confidently up to Johnson.

"Hi," she beamed, leaning slightly upwards to brush his cheek with her lips. "Good to see you."

What on earth's going on? Thought Johnson. Look at her, look at those eyes. Brown, hazel, maybe, flecked with a little green. What's she doing here with me? On a Friday night?

"Come on," she said, "aren't you going to buy me a drink?"

Johnson paid for the vodka and tonic from his meagre funds and they took a seat in a quiet corner. The Friday night crowd of on-their-way-home drinkers were finally on their way home and the pub was more a mix of theatre or cinemagoers, or people on their way to a restaurant.

"I should explain," began Johnson.

"Explain?"

"Well, things haven't been so great on the work front, and, you see at the moment," he paused.

"You're out of work and broke and worried that you're going to spend your food budget for the week on buying me drinks all night with quite possibly no prospect of whether you're going to get your money's worth at the end of it?" said Nicola, smiling.

"Nicola," he protested.

"Nicky, please," she said.

"Nicky, then," Johnson took a steadying pull on his pint. "I just wanted to make you aware of my situation, that's all."

"That's fine," she reassured him, "the next one's on me."

"I didn't mean…,"

"Enough," she said, firmly, "nothing more to discuss. Tell me what you've been doing."

Johnson filled her in with tales of his recent history, taking care to leave out the bits that might make him look bad. Like stealing and mutilating Simon Hart's teddy bear and carrying out acts of general sabotage about the office.

She nodded, she laughed, she shook her head in sympathy. And all at the right moments, thought Johnson, in wonderment.

"You have been busy," said Nicky.

"I wonder if I'm cut out for it, a career in commerce, industry, whatever it is, perhaps I'd be better off driving a bus or being a postman."

"It happens," Nicky reassured him, "it can take a while to find your feet, to settle into something that you're good at. Find something you like and something that likes you, that's important."

"I have an attitude problem," confessed Johnson.

"You do?"

"People say I have an attitude problem. I'm perceived like that."

"Why do you think that is?" asked Nicky.

"I have a problem with authority."

"You don't like taking orders?"

"It's not quite that. I realise that most people out there are more experienced than I am, smarter than I am, I just have a problem with, I don't know, it's not exactly with being told what to do. It's when I think they're wrong."

"And you find it hard to bite the bullet and go along with it?"

"I do. But it's the associated bullshit that I find really hard to accept."

"Sometimes you have to," Nicky advised, "if you want to get on."

"I know," admitted Johnson, "I know, I just don't find it easy."

231

Nicky picked up their glasses.

"Same again?"

"No, it's my turn, surely," protested Johnson.

"It all evens out," she said, "don't worry about it. Same again?"

"At least let me go to the bar and get them," he said.

Nicky assented and gave him a ten pound note from her purse, which was worse than having her fetch the drinks, he felt like he was drinking with his mother.

"How long were you married?" he asked when he returned.

"Actually, I am still married," she pointed out. "Ten years."

"Ten years!"

"I must be ancient mustn't I?"

"I didn't mean that."

"Got married young. Too young."

"What happened?"

"The usual, just grew apart. The person you were at eighteen is very different to the one you become at twenty-eight."

Twenty-eight, eh, mused Johnson. Older woman.

"Drink up," said Nicky, "and I'll buy you dinner. You can fantasize on the way."

Johnson felt the heat rush to his face and knew he was reddening, but Nicky didn't comment. As they walked the length of the street Nicky linked her arm through his, and Johnson again wondered what was happening to him.

"Chinese?" she suggested.

"Fine," agreed Johnson, "I feel really bad about this, you know. You buying me dinner."

"You can owe me one," said Nicky. "Here we are."

"Looks expensive," said Johnson, pausing at the window. He watched the lobsters sitting in the tank, awaiting the fate that hotter water would bring.

"Come on," she insisted, dragging him through the door.

After sharing what seemed like the entire contents of the kitchen spread over their huge round table and two bottles of hot sake both Johnson and Nicky were suitably satisfied, although unable to risk too much movement just yet.

"That was fabulous," he said, sipping his green tea.

"Told you it was good here."

"Thank you."

"Enough of the thank you's," she said.

"Sorry," he replied.

"And stop apologising."

"Right."

"Drink up and then we can go back to your place."

"My place?"

"We can't go to mine, my husband, you know?"

"Still living there?"

"Separate rooms, it's quite amicable, but it wouldn't be right for me to bring someone back for the night."

"For the night," said Johnson.

"You look shocked," said Nicky.

"No, I ...."

"We like each other don't we? We get on really well, I think so, I hope you do too?"

"Of course," agreed Johnson, enthusiastically.

"So what's the point in hanging around, playing games? Life's too short for all that nonsense, Johnson, all that fencing. Come on let's go to bed."

"To bed," agreed Johnson, rising numbly to his feet, and beginning to wish that he hadn't eaten quite so much.

"Brisk walk and you'll be fine," said Nicky, firmly, "come on."

"Can I ask you something?" asked Johnson, naked, standing in bedroom doorway.

"Sure," agreed Nicky, sleepily. She was stretched out naked across Johnson's bed, her heavy breasts lolling back on her chest. "Did you get the water?"

"Yes," said Johnson, offering her the glass. He stole a look at her dark, damp bush as she manoeuvred herself upright. Why am I stealing a look? he thought, when I've just had a close-up? An eyeful, a tongueful, a mouthful. Stop it, he said, silently.

"Ooh, wet patch," she exclaimed.

"Sorry," said Johnson.

"There you go," said Nicky, "apologising again."

233

She drained half of the glass of water and held it out to Johnson.

"Thanks," he said, draining the rest and going back to the kitchen for more.

They laid together on the bed, an ashtray resting on Johnson's chest. Nicky holding her cigarette in her left hand and Johnson in her right. Johnson smoked right-handed while the middle finger of his left hand described tiny, idle circles.

"You wanted to ask me something?" Nicky ventured.

"I wondered," said Johnson, "well, what you're doing here?"

"I should have thought that was obvious," she said, "Ooh, I think I've found some life down there."

Johnson gave her a sidelong look and saw that she was flushed around her neck and shoulders. He continued his finger's orbit but increased the pressure a little.

"What I mean is," said Johnson, while Nicky was dragging her fingernails gently up and down, "why me, why now, why tonight, what's it about?"

"I like you," sighed Nicky, "I liked you when I first saw you, fancied you."

"Well, so did I. Fancy you, I mean," replied Johnson, feeling the blood flow as Nicky pushed and squeezed.

Johnson saw that her nipples were erect and looking like overripe, black grapes, about to burst through their skins. He took her cigarette and placed it in the ashtray with his own, then he leant away from her slightly to place it on the bedside table.

"I'm no catch," said Johnson, giving a jolt as a fingernail snagged on his foreskin.

"Sorry," said Nicky, "are you OK?"

"Oh yeah," Johnson assured her, with some urgency, "just don't stop."

"God, men and their willies," laughed Nicky, twirling her fingers, "a girl's got to be so careful."

"It's fine," gasped Johnson, "absolutely just completely fine. Just don't stop."

In the morning Nicky, deciding that Tim's eggs were the only safe things in the fridge, cooked omelettes. Johnson, not wanting to spoil the mood by admitting to his dislike of them, swilled his down with large draughts of mahogany-coloured tea. They showered together, then sat at the dining table, Johnson in his robe, Nicky dressed in one of Johnson's plain navy-blue T-shirts. He had watched her moving barefoot around kitchen while she cooked, toenails painted red, her breasts swinging free under the cotton, the sunlight catching the soft hair on her legs. She had wiggled her rear at him as she bent over the fridge and caught him looking, she looked over her shoulder and laughed, a free, untethered laugh, and he had laughed along with her, opening his robe and waving his penis in greeting.

"I think he needs some refreshment," she said, gravely, "poor little chap looks quite exhausted."

"He does, doesn't he?" said Johnson, moving his member this-way-and-that and carrying out an inspection.

"He needs a good shot of protein and a dose of vitamins," announced Nicky.

"Sounds great," said Johnson.

"Eggs. I found some eggs. Just the thing."

"Great," said Johnson, attempting to sound enthusiastic.

"Omelettes?"

"Just a small one," said Johnson.

Nicky curled up on the sofa while Johnson cleared the table.

"Tired?" he asked, joining her.

"Tired," she agreed, tucking herself under his arm.

They snoozed away the morning together, occasionally waking to see the progress of the sun across the window. Eventually Johnson slid his arm out from under her shoulders, he had felt the pins-and-needles long ago and now it was completely lifeless. He stood up, waving the limb and shaking his hand from side-to-side, wincing as he felt the circulation's surging return.

"Get that blood moving," said Nicky, one eye narrowly open, "you might need it later".

"Do you want a drink of anything?" he asked.

"Just tea or water. Tap water," said Nicky.

"Right," said Johnson, "think I'll have a beer."

He returned with drinks and sat at the table, smoking and pouring his ale. Nicky regarded him thoughtfully.

"If you want me to go…." she began.

"To go?" Johnson replied, incredulously, "go?"

"It's just that, when I said you might be needing, you know, blood flow, you wanted a drink and went off to the kitchen and when you came back you sat over there."

"Over there?"

"At the table," said Nicky.

"I'm just sitting at the table."

"It's not because you don't want to sit next to me?"

"Of course not," said Johnson, rising to his feet, "I'll come over."

"No, no," protested Nicky, "if you're comfortable there."

Johnson stopped between sofa and table.

"I don't know what to do now," he admitted.

"Sit where you're most comfortable, I'm just teasing."

"You are?" asked Johnson.

"I am," she confirmed. "But if you want me to go, I'll go."

"Not at all," said Johnson, "not in the least."

"I don't want you to feel like I'm making assumptions, about staying."

"I'd like you to stay," Johnson confirmed.

"You would?"

"Most definitely."

The front door crashed open and Tim followed a split-second later.

"Although this might make you change your mind," advised Johnson.

"I see," said Nicky.

"Hello mate, fuck me, oops, sorry love, didn't see you there. Although how I missed someone like you I don't know, haven't I seen your picture in a magazine? You are a model aren't you?" Tim carried an overnight bag and looked in need of a wash and a change of clothes. His fine strands of hair were uncombed and wayward.

"Turn it off, Tim," advised Johnson, "this is Nicky."

"Hi Tim," waved Nicky.

"Hello darling," said Tim, "where have you been all my life, then?"

"Turn it off, Tim," said Nicky.

"Righto," agreed Tim, "just off for a quick wash and change. I'll tell you nothing prepares you for a day on the markets."

"Hard work?" asked Johnson.

"I stink of fried bastard onions, that's what, and greasy gristle-burgers and oily old

236

chips. Spent yesterday surrounded by vans frying up crap, and wankers buying it too, couldn't get enough of it, queuing up for the shite. I'm in the wrong game, I swear, I've got to get myself one of those vans. Had a big night last night, like yourselves, it would seem, went in this morning slightly, er, unwashed you might say, stinking of last night's ale and all, smelly old ale and fags, that's horrible isn't it? Don't you think so, Nicky? Couldn't stick it anymore. I'm on a break, so I thought I'd have a quick flit home and a clean up," Tim was stripping off his shirt as he edged his way towards the bathroom. "Hard work as well, though, you're right there, buddy," he added, hurriedly.

"That was Tim," Johnson summarised, returning to the sofa.

"I gathered," Nicky replied, laying her legs across his.

"He won't be long," said Johnson, hopefully.

"We could go out," Nicky suggested, "a walk, a film, drinks, dinner."

"How about a walk?" Johnson suggested.

"You're not still going on about money?" said Nicky, exploring his ear with her tongue.

"It's a worry," Johnson protested. "Doesn't feel right."

Nicky placed her palms on his cheeks and turned his head to face hers.

"For the last time," she said, "right now, I'm paying, it's my turn. When you get yourself sorted out, and it won't be long, I know that, then it'll be your turn. You can take me out somewhere really expensive and treat me."

"I can?" asked Johnson.

"Promise," she said.

They could hear Tim splashing around and swearing in the bathroom.

"Have you got his fucking-bastard razor?" asked Nicky.

"Don't think so," Johnson replied, "it'll be where he left it."

"And where would that be?"

"Behind the toilet, last time I saw it."

"You could lend him yours," Nicky suggested.

"Don't think so," Johnson replied, "he made sure that he used mine when he decided to remove all of his body hair."

"He did?"

"It was fashionable for a while, wasn't it? That's what Tim told me, anyway, the

237

smooth-chested look, for men, I mean."

"I think the smooth-chested look has been quite the thing for women for a while now, you know," said Nicky.

"Tim couldn't stop though, didn't know when, or where, to stop. Shaved his chest, arms and armpits, legs, feet."

"Feet?"

"He is a spectacularly hairy chap."

"He didn't do the back, sack and crack?"

"He couldn't reach his back, and I certainly wasn't going to offer to help with that, or with anything else."

"So, the crack would be impossible, wouldn't it?" asked Nicky.

"That's a wax job, surely?"

"Otherwise it would need at least two of you."

"Of course, someone to hold the cheeks apart."

"And another with a razor," decided Nicky.

"He did have a go at the sack, though," said Johnson.

"He didn't!" exclaimed Nicky.

"He told me," said Johnson, "some time later."

"How did he get on?"

"Not good. Said it was taking forever, he couldn't stop his hands from shaking and eventually he got pissed off with sitting in a cold bath that was full of floating body hair."

"Eurgh."

"I know," said Johnson, wearily, "he pulled the plug, went out and left the dregs. I walked in later and thought there was a dead bear in the bath."

"Shall we get dressed and go for that walk?" Nicky suggested.

"When Grizzly Adams has gone."

Tim made sure to give them both a glimpse of his rear end as he crossed from bathroom to bedroom.

"Are you in tonight, Tim?" called Johnson.

"No mate," came the reply, "you have the place to yourself, or yourselves, I'm guessing. Are you sure you're not a model, Nicky?"

238

Nicky walked over to Tim's room, reached in for the handle and pulled the door shut.

"That's better," she smiled.

"Tranquility," agreed Johnson, "but it'll never last. Listen, if he's out tonight and we've got the place to ourselves, why don't I cook dinner for us?"

"You seem a bit short of, what's that essential ingredient I'm trying to think of?"

"Food?" suggested Johnson.

"That'd be it. OK, if you're doing the hard bit, the cooking, then I'll do the easy bit and pay for it. Get yourself ready, let's go shopping."

They took an unhurried walk along the riverside. It was another hot afternoon, and Johnson stopped at a van to buy ice-creams.

"Two ninety-nines please," said Johnson.

"Two ninety-nines," the ice-cream man repeated, holding two cones in one hand and filling them with twists of creamy-white.

"And I'm not a tourist," Johnson said, firmly. This was Tim's method.

"You what, mate?" asked the ice-cream man.

"I said, Two ninety-nines please and I'm not a tourist," repeated Johnson.

"I don't care where you're from mate, the prices are on the board," he slipped a tiny chocolate flake into the top of each cone.

"I don't think so," said Johnson, he was now keenly aware of Nicky's presence at his shoulder. "I'm not paying tourist prices."

"It's alright," interrupted Nicky, "I'll get them."

"No," protested Johnson, "you don't understand."

"These are not tourist prices," said the ice-cream man, "these are the prices. See?" he pointed at the board.

"How much are they?" asked Nicky.

"Just a minute," said Johnson.

"That'll be ...." the ice-cream man began.

"I said wait a minute," said Johnson.

"Sorry, how much?" asked Nicky. Then she whispered in Johnson's ear, "Listen, I'll get them, we don't have to go through this silly money thing again."

"It's not that," said Johnson.

"It's not what?" said the ice-cream man.

"That's not the point," said Johnson.

"Of what?" said the ice-cream man.

"Come on Johnson," said Nicky, "they're melting." Fingers of watery ice cream were beginning to trickle down the tops of the cones. "How much?"

The man told Nicky and she handed over some coins.

"Call this a flake?" observed Johnson.

"What?" said the ice-cream man.

"I said, call this a flake?" Johnson repeated, pulling out the chocolate. "It's only a inch long."

"Why don't you run along, sonny?" suggested the ice-cream man.

"What?" asked Johnson. "What did you say?" He glanced behind him and saw that Nicky had walked away and was leaning on the rail overlooking the river.

"Piss off, son," he advised. "You don't want to upset your mum do you?"

"She's not my mother," hissed Johnson in protest, "I'll have you know there's only a few years between us."

"Alright," conceded the ice-cream man, "so don't go upsetting your big sister."

Johnson walked away, call this a flake? he said to himself.

"It was the principle," Johnson explained, joining Nicky at the rail.

"Sure it was," she said.

"It was."

"OK."

"The principle."

"That's fine, don't worry about it."

"I don't like eggs," announced Johnson.

"What?" asked Nicky, laughing.

"I wasn't honest with you this morning you cooked omelettes and I ate them and then I said I liked them and I don't I can't stand them," said Johnson, rattling out the words.

"Why didn't you say something at the time?" asked Nicky.

240

"Because," began Johnson, "because you looked so good and we were having fun and we'd had a great night and I didn't want to spoil anything."

"I understand," said Nicky, licking her sticky fingers before taking his hand.

"You do?" asked Johnson.

"Certainly," Nicky assured him, "and I'm glad you've told me now."

"You are?" asked Johnson. "That's great."

"You were a pillock back at the ice-cream van, though."

They continued on the riverside trail and stopped for a drink. Although the pub was almost empty inside, they carried their drinks outside and edged their way through the quietly-seated and shouldered a path through the altogether more raucous standing element, eventually parking themselves on a step by the pathway.

"Better start thinking about dinner," decided Nicky.

"You're so organised," said Johnson, admiringly, resting his cheek on his palm, "so..."

"That's enough of that, Johnson," she replied, "I can smell it a mile off, so watch it."

"Right," said Johnson, "I just meant..."

"Enough," she advised. "You obviously know your own mind, you don't take crap, willingly or otherwise, so you don't have to try and cover me with it either. You don't have to be any different with me than you are with anybody else, now do you?"

"No."

"Be yourself. Don't be deflected from that. Be natural. Go with your instincts, you do it with everyone else so why not do it with me?"

"I..." began Johnson.

"Just be," said Nicky, "just be."

On the way back they bought a fresh chicken, red and green chillies, a knob of ginger, Chinese noodles, green beans, baby corn, some fruit, and two bottles of dry white wine.

"Not chardonnay, please," insisted Nicky, "I don't care if I never touch it again."

"Bad experience?"

"More like over-exposure," said Nicky. "A few years ago it was harder to get a glass of water than a chardonnay.

Nicky called into her place for change of clothes while Johnson insisted on waiting around the corner.

"Are you sure?" asked Nicky. "You can come in you know, he won't mind, even if he's in, which I doubt."

"No," said Johnson, "no point in rubbing it in, antagonising the situation, you know."

"Fair enough," nodded Nicky, thoughtfully. "Fair enough. Won't be a minute."

Johnson loitered guiltily on the corner. Imagining twitching curtains, he checked his watch constantly and gazed purposefully into the distance at regular intervals while pacing up and down and shaking his head. This was a man with an appointment and a good reason for hanging around outside your house. Nicky was at his side within ten minutes. Johnson glanced at the small overnight bag she was carrying.

"Just a few bits," she explained, "make-up, underwear, couple of tops."

"Fine," said Johnson, "it's not a problem. More convenient, isn't it?"

"Rubber bondage outfit, giant strap-on dildo."

"And what did you bring for yourself?" asked Johnson.

Back in the kitchen Johnson jointed the chicken.

"You're good at this," Nicky observed. She was perched on a stool in the doorway, legs loosely crossed. She had changed into a pair of jeans that had almost faded to white, but still wore Johnson's old T-shirt. A glass of chablis dangled loosely between her fingers which were looped around the stem.

"Had a bit of practice," Johnson replied, easing the breast meat from the carcass.

"Was your mother a good cook?" asked Nicky.

"Useless," said Johnson.

"Really?"

"Yeah. Dad was better."

"Your father taught you?"

"No, not really," Johnson paused. "Ex-girlfriend. Carol, her name was. The thing with Carol..."

242

Johnson's brief experience of relationships had taught him that prospective partners, partners, partners even of the long-term persuasion, were usually mightily unimpressed by tales of previous loves. But this time we were being open and honest, unafraid of the sordid past or of the raw truth because this time it couldn't hurt us. He was with a mature female who had no interest in embarrassing mental or physical fumblings. He was beginning to think that this might be the start of his first proper relationship with a grown woman. Everything would be out in the open. They would expand on the exploration of their bodies, they would delve deep into each other's minds, there would be no taboos, there could be no secrets.

"What's this CD?" asked Nicky, turning her head towards the speakers.

"Should have got chicken pieces, really," Johnson observed, shearing flesh from a leg and quickly dropping Carol from the agenda.

"Is it Nick Lowe or Nick Drake? I always confuse those two."

"Chicken pieces would have been easier, just means that I've got to cut it up and stir fry it," said Johnson. "Nick Lowe. The Convincer, it's called. By Nick Lowe."

"It's very good."

"He is good isn't he? Great writer," Johnson slid his stack of separated meat across the board with the blunt edge of the knife.

"Yes, he is, I love this one. At least by getting the whole chicken, we know it's free range."

"Yeah," said Johnson, "that's good too."

"Are you OK?" asked Johnson.

"Yes," said Nicky, "stay like this for a bit longer."

"Do you want me to move yet?" asked Johnson again, after a good number of minutes, biceps and triceps aflame.

"Not yet," said Nicky, tilting her head back further so that her hair was brushing against the sheet.

"We're going down," he announced, lowering her gently onto her back and rolling away.

They sat in bed munching on and cherries and grapes, each occasionally feeding the

243

other. Johnson had brought in two huge balloons of armagnac which he held flat to his chest as Nicola placed cherry stones in a ragged line down to his groin. She reached for a glass, took a sip and leant down to Johnson, who was trying to sit upright. She pressed him back firmly with the palm of her hand and, finding his mouth, trickled in some of the warm spirit. Johnson struggled to separate the sensations. Her searching lips, her probing tongue, the dribble of alcohol, the smell of her hair, her sweat, and her sex.

"I should be getting back," said Nicky.

It was late on Sunday afternoon. They had walked in the park, lunched at a pub, and now sat sprawled on the sofa idly reading through the thick wedge of newsprint that supplemented the news on a Sunday.

"You don't have to," suggested Johnson, hopefully.

"Busy day tomorrow. Got a bit to do tonight."

"Work?" asked Johnson.

"Work."

"I've had a great time you know, this weekend," said Johnson.

"Me too," Nicky replied.

"Like to do it again sometime?" asked Johnson, cautiously.

"What are you doing tomorrow?" asked Nicky.

"Oh, job hunting, I suppose," said Johnson, audibly falling to earth.

"Evening?"

"Oh, I don't know," said Johnson, "no plans yet."

"If you don't want to…"

"It's not that."

"It's not a problem."

"It's just that…"

"What is it Johnson?"

"I don't know how I'm going to keep up. You, you're a, what are you? Account manager for this sexy advertising agency. Going to glitzy media parties and things, you make good money in an interesting job, must meet all sorts of wealthy and successful men. How can I compete with all that? With my prospects?"

"When I'll be off with the first greasy media type to offer me a glass of warm chablis and a tumble at a Travelodge?"

"Yes. No," said Johnson.

"It'll work out for you," said Nicky, taking hold of his hands, "I know it will."

Johnson shrugged.

"Want to feel my tits for luck?" asked Nicky lifting her top.

"Might not work," said Johnson, weakening.

"Worth a try," said Nicky, with a shimmy.

"Wouldn't hurt, I suppose," said Johnson, reaching out.

"Now, Don't get carried away, because I really do have to go," said Nicky. "Quick rub and that's your lot."

"Deal,"

"Right," announced Nicky, "put your thumbs away. I must go."

"Is it cold in here?" asked Johnson.

"Stop it," Nicky replied, pulling her top down. "Or else I'll never get away."

Johnson slid a hand between her thighs.

"I'm warning you," said Nicky.

"Funny, it seems much warmer down here," said Johnson.

Nicky wriggled to her feet with difficulty.

"Tomorrow," she said, "would you like to? Meet up, I mean?"

"Great," said Johnson with enthusiasm, rising to meet her. "I'll have to call you, I don't know where I'll be, you see."

"Call me anyway. Call me in the morning. I might be able to help."

"I don't know, Nicky," said Johnson, warily, "working together? In a relationship and working together? If we are in a relationship, of course, I mean, are we?"

"I'd say so, wouldn't you?" said Nicky, looping her arms under his and resting her hands on his shoulder blades. "Early stages, of course, but I'd say so."

"So would I," said Johnson. "I've had a fantastic weekend, I think we're…"

"What?"

"I think," said Johnson, "that in addition to you being beautiful and sexy and classy and clever and funny and full of life, that, that we're good together."

"You know what I think Johnson?" said Nicky, heading for the bathroom, "I think you're right."

"About what?"

"All of it. Particularly the bits about me."

Johnson walked Nicky down to the street.

"I'll get a cab," she said.

"You're sure?"

"Just go back up."

"I can walk with you, or wait with you."

"I'll be fine. Go on you idiot. Go home."

"Alright," said Johnson, leaning in.

"We did the passion indoors, Johnson," said Nicky, "let's not carry it out onto the street."

He held her tightly in his arms and kissed her gently on the mouth, lingering a little.

"I'll call you," he said.

"Like I said, call me in the morning about work," said Nicky, "I know you dodged the issue just now, but it wouldn't be working with me, or for me. Might not even be with the same people."

"What sort of thing?"

"Advertising," said Nicky, "definitely advertising."

Johnson took the walk back upstairs, did some rudimentary tidying of the kitchen and went to bed early. He didn't want to leave it too late and find that the bed had given up her smell before he'd had the chance to luxuriate. He put on some music and laid there in the dark, on his belly, head buried under the duvet. Stretching his hands upwards under the smooth cotton of the pillows his fingers met different fibres. How sweet of her, he thought, to leave me her knickers.

At some stage he heard Tim rolling in, but he wasn't aware of the time, he soon drifted off again, with Nicky in his arms, underneath him, wrapped around him.

"Morning."

Hearing the voice, Johnson struggled to extricate himself from the bedcovers.

"Tea?" said the voice.

246

Eventually Johnson surfaced, pulling the duvet away from his head, rubbing his eyes, scratching his head.

"Christ, it's certainly been a while hasn't it?" said Tim. "Taken it out of you, right enough."

Tim placed the steaming mug on the bedside cabinet.

"Morning. Thanks. For the tea. Great," said Johnson.

"Where is she then?"

"Gone."

"Don't tell me you've stuffed up another one?"

"No, no," protested Johnson. "She went last night."

"Screwed this one up early did you? Early, even for you."

"What?"

"Didn't even get to stay the night."

"No, she had work to do."

"Work was it?" said Tim.

"She did," said Johnson, "and if you must know, we're seeing each other tonight."

"Whoa," said Tim, "Monday night date? So soon? Someone's got it bad and I hope it ain't you."

"What do you mean, you hope it isn't me?"

Tim sat, none too carefully, on the bed. Johnson felt the reverberations and spilled a little tea on his chest.

"All I would say is, that you've had your share of disappointments lately. Hate to see you take another hit."

"I'm not going to take another hit."

"You wouldn't be the first."

"The first what?"

"Beautiful girl like that. Beautiful woman, even. Has a dirty weekend with a young fellah then she ditches him after she's had her bit of fun," said Tim.

"She hasn't ditched me, and we both had fun," said Johnson.

"You don't know that yet. I'm sorry, mate."

"What are you sorry for?" Johnson protested. "We're going out tonight."

"Alright, alright," said Tim, "I'm just saying, be careful, that's all."

247

"Well, do me a favour and don't," said Johnson, "thanks."

"Fine."

"What time is it?" asked Johnson.

"Ten," Tim replied. "Thought I'd better give you a shout, you being someone who's unemployed and should be out job hunting at this time on a Monday morning."

"Shit," said Johnson. "Ten o'clock?"

"In the morning," said Tim.

"I'd better be getting on then," said Johnson. "So if you don't mind?"

"Mind?" queried Tim.

"Leaving the room, doing your own thing somewhere else, you know Tim, in a general kind of way, fucking off elsewhere while I get myself tuned into the frigging day."

"Mate, I apologise," said Tim, "thoughtless of me. I'll be off now."

"That's OK," Johnson conceded. "I just want to get on, you understand? In private."

"I'd take those frillies off your head before you think about going out anywhere, though."

Half an hour later, Johnson was shaved and suited and on the phone.

"Nicola Pennywell."

"Hi Nicky," Johnson had been practising deep-breathing exercises, but as she answered at the beginning of an inhalation his reply sounded breathless and nervous.

"Are you alright?" she asked.

"Just ran up the stairs," said Johnson.

"Take a minute, get your breath," she said. "I'll talk for a moment, how's that? I think we can get you in with another agency. So it won't be with me, that's better isn't it? These people are Cartwright Blott Spectre. They can start you as an account exec, soon as you like, really. All you've got to do is pop along first and have a chat to Brian Rossi."

"Brian Rossi?" asked Johnson, breath regained.

"Yes, he's one of the big boys there, director level. He's OK. Owes me one. Well, when I say he's OK, oh, never mind."

"What do you mean, when I say he's OK, oh, never mind?"

"He's a bit of a tit, Johnson, but whaddya know? He works in advertising. He's got a hugely inflated opinion of himself, but they're all the same in this business, all cock and no balls."

"You say, go along and have a chat," asked Johnson, "but what is this, an interview? Do I take a CV with me? What about preparation? What?"

"Blag it," said Nicky.

"Blag it?"

"Bullshit him."

"Won't he know?"

"Of course he'll know."

"And that's a good thing?"

"Definitely," said Nicky.

"How come?"

"Because he's a cunt."

"Is he?"

"Come on, he's in advertising."

"So how do I play it?" asked Johnson.

"By being slightly less cuntish than he is."

"OK," said Johnson.

"You're seeing him at three," said Nicky.

"I'll be there."

"Ring me afterwards," said Nicky, "and we'll sort out what we're doing this evening as well."

"Not working today?" asked Johnson, over tea and cold chicken and noodles.

"On a Monday?" exclaimed Tim. "On the markets?"

"I don't know, do I?" said Johnson, sucking in a stray noodle.

"Should have heated this up," Tim observed.

"Quiet day then, a Monday is it?" Johnson persisted. "On the markets?"

"Nothing doing mate. Bruv's out doing some buying so I've got the day off."

"You'll be involved with the buying though, sooner or later?"

"Oh, eventually, yeah," said Tim, chewing confidently, "he just feels that my skills would be best deployed in the area of sales at the moment. At the sharp end. Ensuring client satisfaction, maximising turnover, increasing margins, you know."

"Oh, I know," said Johnson, ruefully. "He hasn't got a bell has he?"

"A bell?"

"Or a Klaxon?"

"It's not like that, Johnson, there's none of that crap you're talking about. I'm my own boss, master of all I survey."

"Which is?"

"Household goods stall."

"Household goods?"

"Little packs of screwdrivers, with four different heads, you know? Handy item. Tea towels, can openers, kettles from Korea, set of knives including the block for nine-ninety-nine."

"I bet they're good."

"Good value, yes, "asserted Tim. "We're doing a lot of trade in plastic boxes right now. For storage."

"Nothing dodgy then?"

"No."

"No fake DVDs or CDs?

"You're kidding aren't you? The gangs have got that sewn up. No good for us. Margins, you see? Margins."

"I admire your principles," said Johnson, sucking on his last piece of chicken.

"Guess who I saw last night," offered Tim.

"I don't know," said Johnson.

"Go on, guess."

"Who?"

"You'll never guess."

"Correct."

"Come on, who do you think it was?"

"Just tell me, Tim," pleaded Johnson, "it'll be so much better for both of us."

"Tranter."

"Oh, yeah," said Johnson. They used to hang out with Tranter, although he was more one of Tim's friends than Johnson's. Tranter had melted away around twelve months ago. One Friday he was there, flat out on the carpet in some seedy pub at last orders, calling from the floor for another round, and next week he was absent, and had not been seen since.

"Walked into The Albert, out east somewhere. There he was."

"Really?" said Johnson, attempting interest.

"Know what he said to me?"

"What?"

"Soon as I walked in?"

"What?"

"After a day's graft on the stall?"

"What?"

"Am I glad to see you, Tim, he said, I can hardly fucking stand up."

"That was nice."

"Nice?" Tim spluttered. "Oh, I see. No, it wasn't nice at all, you're right, son."

"So, how is he?"

"Haven't a clue, mate," said Tim, draining his mug of tea, "propped him up in the corner while we had a couple of drinks. He wasn't exactly capable of joining in with the conversation was he?"

"You didn't leave him there?"

"No, no," Tim protested, "put him on a train, didn't we? Not a complete animal am I?"

"You got on a train with him?"

"Sadly, no," admitted Tim. "In view of the fact that he lives out east and I live out west, there didn't seem to be any other option. He was legless though, paralysed, what a laugh. More tea?"

Johnson announced that he had to leave and, pausing to give his teeth a final brush and to take a swig of mouthwash, he took himself off to meet Brian Rossi at Cartwright Blott Spectre.

Brian Rossi was a tall, chunky man. A man with the sort of hair that, no matter what he did with it, save shaving it all off, would protrude in heavy fronds from the crown.

251

He wore glasses, unusually for someone in advertising, they were clunky and old-fashioned, reminding Johnson of the sort of eye-furniture that might have been worn by one of his old teachers. He wore a gently amused look as he regarded Johnson from under his greying palm tree.

"Well then, Mr Johnson. Tell me about yourself."

Johnson potted his history and meandered around the truth.

"Good. Now tell me why you want to work in the wild and wacky world of advertising."

Johnson thought of Nicky and did his best to answer.

"I'll be honest," said Brian Rossi, "Nicky's recommended you, she's a good girl, Nicky, I value her opinion. I know she's good at what she does and if she says you're the man for us then I'm going to go with that. Don't really care about your history, I'm going to take a punt on you. Thinking outside the box, that's what we do here, you'll come to understand that, and that's what I want to see you doing from day one, from when you kick those starting blocks away. Let's think outside the box, what do you say?"

"I'm your man," said Johnson, smoothly.

"You don't seem too excited."

"Make me an offer."

"Gonna make you an offer you can't refuse," Brian Rossi startled Johnson by singing at him in a vague approximation of a falsetto voice.

"Stylistics," said Johnson.

"Gonna put my finger on you," sang Rossi.

"Very good," said Johnson.

"Actually, it's Jimmy Helms," said Brian Rossi. "Common mistake."

"Is it?" asked Johnson. "Is it really?"

"Jimmy Helms. Start tomorrow?"

"Tomorrow?"

"Yeah, yeah," said Brian Rossi. "In principle, start tomorrow, yes? I've got some figures here, salary, bonus, benefits, take a look. I'll be back in five with tea, coffee?"

"Tea, thank you," said Johnson, catching the sheet of paper which Rossi had tossed in his direction.

"It went really well," said Johnson, cupping his hand over the earpiece.

"You liked him, Brian?" asked Nicky.

Not sure, thought Johnson, turning to the shop fronts, trying to deaden the traffic noise.

"We got on, yeah,"

"When do you start?"

"Tomorrow,"

"That's great," cried Nicky.

She sounds really happy, thought Johnson, here's responsibility right in my face and giving me a smack in the mouth.

"I'm in," said Johnson, simply. "Thanks."

"Meet me outside my office in, say," Nicky paused, "yes, half-an-hour."

"Right," agreed Johnson, seeing her checking her watch.

"This calls for a celebratory dinner."

"Right."

"Somewhere that's suitably posh and outrageously expensive."

"Oh," said Johnson.

"It's still on me until you're earning, OK?"

A Rembrandt of a martini winked in the light as Johnson raised it to his lips.

"Good?" asked Nicky.

"Bombay Sapphire," replied Johnson, simply, pulling a cigarette from his packet and sliding it between his lips. A waiter stepped forward from the shadows, flicking a lighter into action. Startled, Johnson shrank a little from the sudden movement and the flame. Holding the cigarette between two fingers and a thumb, he took the light. The waiter returned to the shadows.

"I hate that," Johnson announced.

"What?"

"Lighting your fags like that, as soon as you get one out. Makes me feel like I'm being watched."

"They would be watching, wouldn't they?"

253

"I suppose so," agreed Johnson.

"All part of the service, isn't it?"

"I just don't like it."

"Well, next time, you could suggest, politely, that you would rather cater to your own needs."

"Sorry?"

"And light your own."

Johnson took another sip from his monster martini, this time pulling in an olive which he squeezed and mashed against his teeth.

"You look great," he said.

"Thank you," Nicky leant forwards, elbows poised on the table and held her drink between the fingertips of both hands. Her hair, which had been tied back, or pinned or chopsticked, when he met her outside her office was now loose, framing her face and draped around her shoulders.

"You know, my dad had just a couple of stock phrases when he went to an Italian restaurant," said Johnson

"Which were?"

"First one: Tournedos Rossini."

"There's an old favourite."

"A classic."

"My father liked that too."

"Funny isn't it?" said Johnson. "I never saw my dad eat anything else when we went out to an Italian, which I have to say wasn't very often, the odd birthday maybe, after he decided the time was right to upgrade from the Berni Inn, but when it came to the menu he never strayed from the Tournedos."

"What else was he comfortable with saying?"

"That's it," agreed Johnson, vehemently, "it was about comfort wasn't it? I don't know the language, don't know what these odd looking words are trying to tell me, so I'm bound to order something that I won't like. Took us long enough as a race to entertain thoughts of garlic without running screaming for the hills or hunting down a Catholic for the bonfire. Fear of embarrassment too."

"The English disease," Nicky nodded.

"Ever been to Waterloo Station?" asked Johnson. "The bar opposite the Eurostar terminal?"

"Maybe," shrugged Nicky, "not sure."

"You need to be there when the visitors, the tourists, are leaving, waiting for the train back to Belgium or France. Never fails, if it's a married couple, or even just a couple, the man sits down tells the woman what he wants, food or drink, whatever, and she goes to the bar and places the order. Brings it back, sets it all down in front of him. Be it beer, coffee, cognac, or disgusting sandwich that if you tried feeding it to your dog he'd be off to live two streets away."

"Chauvinist culture," said Nicky.

"Sorry," said Johnson, shaking his head, "but you're wrong there."

"Wrong am I?" asked Nicky, slowly arching one eyebrow in a way that Johnson found immediately arousing.

"Yep," said Johnson, squeezing his thighs together, "fear."

"Fear?"

"The man is frightened. He's not on his own territory, his grasp of the language, well, even if it's rudimentary, he fears the error that he might make. He'll do anything to avoid the situation."

"The woman?" asked Nicky. "Isn't she frightened?"

"Woman are smarter," said Johnson. "They know that life's too short for such nonsense. Particularly those who've had children."

"Do you feel like this?" asked Nicky. "Like these men?"

"I don't care really," said Johnson. "I once ordered a round of drinks very confidently in an Italian hotel. Word perfect, I was, half a dozen drinks tripped off my tongue like I was born to speaking this unfamiliar language."

"That's great, though."

"Brilliant," agreed Johnson, "Even I was impressed with my urbanity, my suaveness, my command."

"So?"

"Turned out I'd said the whole lot in Spanish."

"Embarrassing?"

"Funny."

"Not embarrassed?"

"No, the barman knew, he had a laugh with me. A wink and a nod, you know?"

"He thought you'd had a go and gave you credit for trying?"

"Exactly. Well, I guess so. Maybe he thought I was a prick. Maybe he loaded the bill. Anyway, I can make a tit of myself without really trying, so trying every now and again ain't going to make much difference is it?"

They ate meat from obliging soft-shelled crabs and a salad which went the distance in giving the whole green-stuff-on-the-side idea a good name. The wine was crisp and dry, and, when needed, a waiter refilled their glasses. Johnson had succeeded in batting away the fag-lighter but the wine-pourer was made of tougher teak.

"I almost forgot, what was your father's other stock phrase?" asked Nicky, as their plates were cleared. "In an Italian restaurant?"

"Oh, I don't know that I want to tell you now."

"Come on."

"This is embarrassing."

"Good," said Nicky, "go on."

"He would say to the waiter, actually to all of the waiters in turn, he was very democratic in that respect."

"Yes?"

"Are you Mafioso?"

"He'd what?" exploded Nicky.

"And if they were non-committal he'd spell it out. Mafia. M-A-F-I-A. Are you Mafia?"

"What happened?"

"They got to know him after a while. They'd say yes and he'd promise to behave himself."

"That must have been embarrassing."

"Somewhat. Even for a twelve-year-old."

"Your Tournedos Rossini, madam, sir," said the waiter, slipping plates in front of them.

They chewed their way down memory lane and left without tasting coffee or liquers.

256

Later, Nicky tied Johnson to the bed, mounted him and bucked up and down with vigorous enthusiasm, before announcing that she had an early start in the morning.

"And so do you," she said. "Good luck tomorrow."

"Thanks," said Johnson, aiming a contented smile at her.

Nicky dismounted and was dressed in seconds.

"I'll just call a cab," she announced, leaving the bedroom.

"Fine," Johnson replied, hearing her make the call.

"Five minutes," said Nicky, reappearing in the doorway.

"Right," said Johnson.

"Looking forward to it?"

"I wish you didn't have to go," said Johnson.

"Never mind that, time to focus your mind on the job," said Nicky.

"Mind on the job," agreed Johnson. "Focus."

"Call me when you can tomorrow, if you have time. Do you know what you're doing yet?"

"Induction, Brian's going to show me around, meet some people, I think I might be sitting in on something in the afternoon, a meeting or a presentation or something."

"A pitch?"

"Yeah," said Johnson, "that was it. A pitch."

"You'll be fine tomorrow," she reassured him, she was looking into the bedroom mirror, rearranging her hair, eyeing his reflection, "be yourself, don't let yourself get worried by the bullshit, and, trust me, there will be bullshit, but don't let it faze you, just do what I know you can do. Get on with it. Concentrate on the work and don't be distracted. Let it wash over you. See it as a means to an end. You'll be good at this, I know," she was interrupted by the door buzzer. "Car's here, that was quick. Right, promise you'll call me?" Nicky's lips brushed across his, right to left, and then returned with more purpose.

"You couldn't untie me before you go, could you?" asked Johnson.

Brian Rossi had recommended that Johnson arrive at Cartwright Blott Spectre at nine-thirty in the morning. Johnson was in the slightly cluttered reception area at nine-fifteen. A loose gathering of cardboard boxes was stacked against one of the walls. On

257

closer examination, Johnson discovered that they were company brochures. *Going Forward with Cartwright Blott Spectre*, they announced, in aggressive, in-your-face, type. Brian Rossi, hair askance and spectacles gleaming, grinned at him from the bottom right hand corner of page three.

"Morning, morning," said Rossi, in greeting, bustling in and grinning at him in weird unison with the picture Johnson was examining.

"Morning," repeated Johnson, holding the brochure at head height and making an exaggerated comparison.

"Reading our brochure, I see," said Rossi, unnecessarily. "I always find it comes in handy if you can't sleep at night."

"Quite a good likeness," said Johnson, accepting the invitation for some early morning humour, "although obviously taken some time ago."

"No, no, you're wrong there," said Rossi, correcting him, "that piccie was definitely taken this year. For insomnia, you see? The brochure? Interesting read? So interesting that, in fact, it has the opposite effect. See?"

"Right," nodded Johnson.

"Don't worry, you'll get used to my sense of humour."

"I'll give it my best shot," said Johnson.

"That's what we like," said Rossi, punching Johnson on the bicep, "people who come out fighting."

Johnson rubbed his arm ruefully and considered returning the punch with interest before following Brian Rossi up the stairs.

"Right then," said Rossi, puffing hard as they reached the landing at the end of two flights of stairs, "recruitment ads, that's where I'm going to put you. You don't know anything about recruitment advertising, I hear you say."

Johnson shuffled from foot to foot, poised to follow Brian Rossi through the double doors, he could see people in there, people working. On the phones, at the water cooler and the coffee machine. Let's get on with it, he thought, fifty people in there, let's go and meet some of them, let's get started.

Brian Rossi's grey spider plant wobbled on his head as the fluorescent light bounced off his glasses, hands placed on hips, tongue resting on his bottom lip, he spoke again.

"I don't know anything about recruitment advertising," said Rossi.

That makes two of us, then, you fuckwit, Johnson nearly said. Instead he repeated Brian Rossi's words.

"I don't know anything about recruitment advertising."

"In that case," said Brian Rossi, now bounding through the doors, "I'm your man, in fact, in here, I am the man. Watch closely, pay attention and you might learn something. Read 'em and weep. Come on in and meet the team. My team, my boys and, let's not forget, how could I? My girls. On pain of equal opportunities, let's not forget my gorgeous girls. Love 'em. Love 'em all," Brian Rossi placed his arm around Johnson's shoulders and almost managed to tuck Johnson's head into his shoulder.

Fucking hell, remarked Johnson, with only the thought of Nicky tying him to the bed again enabling him to keep his words to himself. He wriggled free from Brian Rossi's grasp.

"You'd better introduce me to my new colleagues, Brian," said Johnson, encouragingly.

Brian Rossi bounced around the office, making introductions, like everyone's best mate, thought Johnson, observing the smiles and nods that greeted Rossi and taking note of the occasional curling of the lip and masturbatory gesture that signalled the turning of his back.

"Here we are Johnson," said Rossi, "we'll put you here, I think, in the very capable hands, and they are capable hands aren't they? Or so I've heard."

The seated girl with the dark blond shoulder-length hair and blue eyes looked up at him at smiled.

"It's Sue, isn't it?" ventured Johnson.

"That's right," she nodded, maintaining the smile.

"You know each other?" exclaimed Rossi. "Well, well, well, small world or what? I was only saying the other day…"

"You're Nicky's friend," said Johnson, "we met in the pub, way back."

"You're Nicky's friend too, I hear," said Sue, swinging round on her chair and crossing her long legs.

"Of course, of course," interrupted Rossi, his gaze straying up her thigh, "didn't spot the connection."

"How is she?" asked Johnson, stupidly.

"You tell me," Sue replied, shifting in her seat and hitching her skirt a little higher.

"Sue," announced Rossi, "show him the ropes would you? I'll be back shortly," Rossi marched away.

"Never fails," said Sue, smoothing her skirt down to a modest level.

"Never fails?" asked Johnson.

"He can never meet your eyes, never look you in the face because he's always looking at your tits or your legs, so all you have to do is make it too obvious for him to be comfortable hanging around. Have a seat."

Johnson slid in beside her.

"I see," he said, "but how do I get rid of him?"

"Give his knackers a squeeze, I should think, that might work," said Sue. "Right, let's talk about the exciting world of recruitment advertising."

"Better make some notes," said Johnson, "can I use this pad?"

Sue nodded and passed him a pen.

"We might have a request from a client to run a campaign for new staff, doesn't matter what for, just to give you the picture, although it doesn't matter what for anyway, to be honest, but we try and avoid that, the being honest part. Say it's a rural council. Our creatives, you know, the creative department will invariably put together something that reads like, let's see, "Think you're fulfilled at the moment? Reached all of your goals? But have you ever paused to consider the work-life balance? Here in Dreamshire we've got it all, forests, wildlife, community spirit, a more relaxed way of life where you'll be surrounded by jolly locals and rosy-cheeked children, and we're only twenty minutes from the coast". It goes on like that for, well, too bloody long actually, and is accompanied by a picture of some woods or a lighthouse or a sheep-covered hillside."

Johnson scribbled away dutifully as Sue continued.

"The alternative, for an urban council, would be, "Think you're fulfilled at the moment? Time for you to slow down? Then maybe you're not right for us. If we seem too edgy for you, then stop reading right now, go back to your milky drink, and have another early night. On the other hand, if you're up for a challenge, then why not come and work for us right here in Shitborough? We're not saying that dealing with challenging issues will be easy, but we don't deal in easy. You'll be based on the fringes of the city in a vibrant and exciting environment. We want your brain, we want your talents, what Shitborough doesn't want is your preconceptions". This'll be accompanied by a picture of some high-rise flats in front of a sunset, or a cool-looking teacher in front of some attentive kids, there's a laugh, or some skateboarders toting aerosol paint cans, that's a recent favourite."

Sue shrugged and looked questioningly at Johnson.

"You run just the two ads then?" he asked.

"Pretty much," she confirmed.

"A vibrant and exciting environment. Reminds me of a holiday I once had in Kenya."

"The trip to the local market?"

"Exactly," said Johnson. "Although, as I remember it, that was described as colourful rather than exciting."

"And was it?"

"It was all of those things," said Johnson, suddenly reminded of the offer he had once had in the market in Mombasa to trade his girlfriend for a sack of hashish, "but mainly, it was shitty and dangerous."

Johnson was pleased that he was under Sue's wing. She seemed good-natured and friendly, although he was wary about her friendship with Nicky. Did she know that he had been strapped down last night, for instance?

"I don't want to tie you up," said Sue.

"What?" asked Johnson, feeling the flush to his cheeks.

"In too much detail," said Sue. "Are you alright?"

"Oh, yes," said Johnson.

"You look a bit hot and bothered."

"I'm fine."

"If you're sure? OK. You do look hot. Would you like some water? No? OK. As I say, you're right, it is basically two ads that we run, and they fit where they touch. Idiot-proof. Good enough for the idiots anyway. You know what they say? If you can't do then teach, and if you can't teach then find yourself something else to do in the public sector. So, you'll be dealing with publications, papers, magazines, creative and production departments, proof-reading, get you sitting in on a few presentations as well, to start with."

261

"Great," said Johnson.

"I think Brian's lined up some induction stuff for you today, going round the different departments and finding out what they do, he's on his way over, actually."

Johnson followed Sue's gaze and saw Brian Rossi striding in their direction and, on his way, waving distant high-fives to the uninterested office.

"OK," said Johnson.

"Nicky's really happy right now," said Sue, quickly.

"That's brilliant," Johnson replied.

"I hope you're going to…."

"What?" asked Johnson.

"She's a good friend," said Sue.

"We're having a good time, I think," said Johnson.

"I don't want things to go wrong for her again."

"Trust me," said Johnson. "Hooray, here's Brian."

"Oh, bollocks," said Sue, rising slightly from her chair and yanking up her skirt.

"Don't worry," Johnson assured her, getting to his feet, "I'll meet him halfway."

"Thanks," smiled Sue.

"We don't want him jizzing in his Y-fronts do we?" Johnson stated.

"You're leaving me with that image are you?"

"It'll be a tough one to shift too, I should think," said Johnson, backing away. He turned to face the approaching Brian Rossi.

"Brian," said Johnson, baldly.

"Getting on OK are we?" asked Rossi.

"Fine," Johnson assured him, "just looking at some ads. Examples, you know?"

"Of course," said Rossi, breezily, "of course. Now we've just got time for a couple of induction briefings, with production and creative, I think, then I've got you booked into a short diversity awareness session."

"Short, you say?" asked Johnson.

"Couple of hours or so."

"Couple of hours, eh?" Johnson said through the chewing of his bottom lip. "On, what was it again?"

"Diversity awareness," said Rossi, shepherding Johnson towards the door.

"Which is what, exactly?" asked Johnson. Steady, he told himself, steady.

"What?"

"Diversity awareness."

"You're asking me what diversity awareness is?" Rossi came to a halt. "You're asking *me*?"

"Er, yeah," said Johnson, "I'm asking you."

"Awareness, Johnson," he began, "of diversity issues will be fully covered in your session with our HR team this afternoon. I wouldn't want to cramp their style, and, avoiding treading on others' toes being my mantra, my vision, indeed my target, that means that you should be asking them and not me."

He doesn't know, thought Johnson, he's got all the jargon but none of the bottom. All style and no substance.

"You don't know," said Johnson.

"I'm sorry?" Brian Rossi began to bristle and bridle.

"You don't know where I can get a cup of tea, do you?" asked Johnson, sweetly.

Brian Rossi gave a nod, a shake, and finally a twist of his grey spikes.

"Follow me," he said, the sucking in of his belly was followed by the inevitable, inelegant hitching up of his trousers as he walked past the desk by the door which housed four female staff members.

Johnson sat and listened with some interest as the creative and production functions of the advertising business were explained to him. However, he had a feeling that the day was not going to improve. He was right.

Interview Phase VIII

"*S*he sounds nice," I ventured.

"She was. Is," Johnson replied, correcting himself.

"Was? Is?"

"She is, er, nice. For want of a better word."

"Give me a better word," I said.

"Beautiful. Talented. Charismatic. Elegant. Sexy. Gorgeous. Charming. Fun. Interesting. Classy, Exciting," Johnson recited.

"That's a lot of better words," I said.

"Exciting," said Johnson, firmly. "If I'm only allowed one, then that's it. Exciting."

"What does the future hold?" I asked. "With Nicky, I mean."

"I don't know," said Johnson.

We had returned to our original room. An enamel pot of tea, a milk jug of the same silvery sheen and two cups, thankfully not made of metal, sat between us. I poured. The room had been cleaned and the wearying fug of stale tobacco had almost been eliminated. Johnson flicked his lighter into life and touched the pristine end of another cigarette. He puffed and inhaled deeply two or three times, exhaling through his nose and mouth. The smoke was caught and exaggerated in the sun's rays which were shafting through the window.

"No ashtray," he said, it was more of a statement than a question.

"No," I concurred.

"Never mind," he said picking up his cup, "I'll use the saucer." He tapped the first few draws of embers into the makeshift ashtray.

"What about Nicky?" I persisted.

Johnson cupped his tea in both hands, cigarette protruding from the first and second fingers of his right hand, rocking back and forth. He looked like he was engaged in some sort of holy ritual, although for it to count as a true and meaningful religious experience for Johnson I had come to realise that some form of alcohol should stand in

264

for the tea.

"I don't know," he said, impatiently, "I told you didn't I?"

"Well," I said, calmly, "you told me that you didn't know, no, I'll correct myself there, you announced that you didn't know, but you haven't actually told me anything about whether you see any future for you and Nicky."

"How about this?" he said, sharply, "I fucked up again, sorry, I'll correct myself there, I fucked up *yet* again. Do I see any future for the beautiful and successful Ms Nicola Pennywell who has the world at her feet with the world's number one screw-up artist who, wherever he goes, whatever he's doing, can't stop himself from treading in dogshit? You know, the one who's sitting in front of you?"

"Do you?" I prompted, "see a future?"

"Do you?" said Johnson, regaining his coolness. "Any more tea in there, or shall we order in some beers?"

"Tea," I said, pouring the last of the pale, insipid liquid into his cup before he could change his mind. "I hope that's enough."

"That's ample."

"I could order some more."

"No, that's fine."

"If you're sure you're OK with that?"

"Doesn't get any better, does it?" he remarked, sourly. "Look at it. The cat's kidneys would be insulted."

"Milk?" I asked.

"Not too much," he assented, "otherwise it'll disappear."

I dribbled some milk into his cup, and was soon halted by a wave of his hand.

"Enough?" I asked.

"You're being very amenable all of a sudden," said Johnson, suspiciously. He picked up a spoon and stirred the floating film of milk into the thin, transparent tea.

"I think I'm always amenable. I've been amenable for the last, Christ knows, how many hours is it?"

Johnson's face broke into his full, joyous grin. He really was quite irresistible when he looked like that. I checked myself, reminded myself of the job.

"Getting to you is it?" he asked.

"No more than it is to you," I replied, stoutly.

"Alright," he said, "you're being very attentive, then."

"We're getting near the end," I said.

"We are, aren't we?"

"I thought it might be time to be amenable, attentive, whatever you want to call it. The thing with Nicky must be hard for you, and I want the ending to be as clean as possible."

"Clean?"

"Might be messy, and we don't want that, do we?"

"I guess not."

"It's really up to you though."

"It is?"

"Doesn't have to be a messy ending," I said.

"No?"

"No," I assured him, "it might not be happy, but it doesn't have to be messy."

Johnson looked as unsure as I had seen him in the past couple of days.

"I don't get it," he said, resorting to the exaggerated rubbing of his fingers through his hair.

"You haven't got nits, have you?" I asked.

"No, I bloody haven't," he laughed.

"Got dandruff though."

"Yeah," he agreed, brushing some dust from his shoulders. "Stress. Put that down to stress."

"How was the diversity audit?" I asked.

"How did you know that's what it was called?" he shot back.

"What?" I said.

"I never used that word."

"Which word?"

"Audit."

"Didn't you?" I asked.

"No, and you know I didn't."

"Anyway, it doesn't matter, session, awareness, audit, doesn't make any difference."

266

"Means you've been snooping," he said, folding his arms, twirling his cigarette lighter between his fingers and gazing hard at the table-top.

"And we were getting along so well," I said, "please don't go into a sulk."

"Well…," he said.

"Come on," Christ this was like dealing with a fractious toddler.

"I don't like the idea of you asking around behind my back."

"You'd better fucking get used to it, hadn't you?" I shouted.

"Hang on," said Johnson in surprise.

"Tell me about the fucking diversity audit and tell me now and then you can tell me the rest, and after that we'll sit round the fireside for the final chapter and then you can read me the fucking epilogue as a bedtime story, and the sooner we get this over with the sooner we can both get out of here. Me, I want to go home. I want a roast lunch in a country pub and a hot bath. I don't know where you're going. Yet. But one thing's for sure, if you don't shape up with some fucking answers it won't be anywhere pleasant."

"Alright," said Johnson, motioning downwards with his hands.

"Amenable? Fuck off. Attentive? Bollocks. I know this is hard, y'see? So what do I do? I try to smooth the way for us, because we have to have this bloody conversation and all you can do is pick fucking nits about awareness or audits or being spied on. Now shut up for five minutes and give me one of those cigarettes."

"I just…"

"Didn't I tell you to shut up, you twat?" I said, lighting up with the zeal of the suddenly-fallen-off-the-wagon smoker. "Do you want a drink?"

"There were twenty of us in this room, it wasn't just me," said Johnson, sliding his palms against each side of the beer bottle, twisting it around.

"Diversity?" I asked.

"Yeah," he said, " I knew I was in trouble right from the off."

"How did you know?"

"Picking on me first, wasn't fair, me being the new boy."

"Who picked on you?"

"Forget the name," he said, "whoever was screwing them for the money for running it, I suppose."

"How did they pick on you?"

"He asked me 'What do you understand by diversity?'"

"And you said?"

"Road closed. Please use this alternative route."

"You didn't?"

"Well, I know that's not what it means, but..." Johnson took one of his long pauses, extended sighs, "Jeez."

"What happened next?"

"Everyone laughed and I sat quietly for the rest of the afternoon, saying as little as possible."

"What was the rest of the session like?" I asked.

"How old are you? It was like Jackanory for beginners. Remember that? Your mum and dad didn't tell you about it? No? Like Play School for the backward, or the differently-abled or whatever you're supposed to say these days. How about Playaway? Trumpton? Tiswas?"

"Tiswas," I agreed.

"It made Tiswas look like The Godfather."

"OK," I said, "seems a bit unfair, but go on."

"You're right," enthused Johnson, warming to his argument. "I wouldn't want to insult anything by comparing it with the crap I suffered to sit through that afternoon."

"Bad?"

"Beyond bad," said Johnson, fists waving in the air, "Cringeing, timorous, cowardly and fearful. Frightened. They were frightened."

"You didn't agree with any of it, then?" I asked, possibly unwisely.

"No need for it," he said, firmly, "one rule, employ the best person for the job. If that means they're all black or all asian or all white, then so be it. You know me.."

"I do," I said.

"I don't have a racist bone in my body."

"I know that, Johnson," I said.

"But it might be taken as such, and it isn't, but everyone's too scared. Ha! Another correction coming up. The white folks are too scared. If you were black, would you want to be given a job on the strength of the colour of your skin? Of course you

268

wouldn't. Or asian, or a woman?"

"Johnson," I said quietly.

"Of course," he said, "but you take my point?"

"I do."

Johnson was off on one of his excursions around the room.

"So, I wasn't exactly off to a good start, and that made me feel guilty."

"Because of Nicola?"

"Because of Nicky," he nodded. "Then I got back to my desk, had a glance at the emails. I hate it when people who send those blanket messages, the ones that begin 'hi all', it's like listening to fingernails scraping down a blackboard. 'Hey everybody!' I can't bear it."

"What did this message say?" I asked.

"Someone was leaving. So this was, 'thanks so much to you all for my lovely card and presents, I've had an amazing time with the most fantastic bunch of people'. So, why are you leaving then? 'Cartwright Blott Spectre is the most brilliant company to work for with a fantastic culture and I've made so many friends here that you'll have to excuse me for wanting to slip away quietly as I'm feeling really choked and tearful right now'."

"Very touching," I said.

"Then, 'I'll be in such-and-such a bar from six PM if anyone would like to join me for a farewell drink'."

"Nothing wrong with that."

"Funny way of slipping away quietly, inviting two hundred people to have drink with you."

"I suppose it is," I agreed. "This didn't tip you over the edge, though? It seems a trivial thing to get upset about."

"No, it wasn't the email in particular, it was the balls-aching diversity thing that started it, the email just irritated me, everything was 'amazing' and 'fantastic' and 'brilliant', and the 'please have a drink with me so that I might exist for a bit longer', and deep down I knew that, hard as I might try to make a go of it, for Nicky really, it wasn't going to work." Johnson was leaning against the wall now, arms folded and head tilted back.

"But you did stick it out."

Johnson banged the back of his head gently against the wall and gentle thudding echoed from the hollow partitioning.

"I did. I tried to make the negative feelings go away. Tried to focus on the work and not be bothered by the extraneous crap. The people."

"Would you say you're anti-social?"

"Not exactly. Who was it that said, 'Hell is other people'?"

"Jean Paul Sartre," I replied.

"Was it? Was it really? I thought it was Eric Morecambe."

"Morecambe was funnier than Sartre."

"But not as clever," said Johnson.

"I wouldn't be so sure about that," I said.

Finally, Johnson stopped banging his head against the wall, he returned to his seat, opposite me.

"Cigarette?" he offered.

"No, thanks," I replied, "I don't know why I had the last one, wish I hadn't now."

"Sorry about that," said Johnson, "my fault."

"No. It's not your fault. I should be able to exercise a bit of control."

"Will power," said Johnson.

"Exactly,"

"I've never had any of that," he said.

"So, you had a bad first day, culminating in a crisis of confidence over your future."

"It wasn't all bad. Brian Rossi was an arsehole, but everybody knew that's what he was, so I could deal with him like everyone else did, by taking the piss out of him. I wouldn't have to listen to a load of diversity-wank every afternoon. I liked Sue, and I was in love with Nicky."

"Even at that early stage you knew you were in love with her?"

"Yeah," said Johnson, thoughtfully.

"And she was in love with you?"

"I think so."

"It sounds like you were in a positive frame of mind, that you had lined up everything in your mind very well, and dealt with it calmly and sensibly."

270

"Sounds like that," said Johnson, "it was like that. I'd pushed the negative stuff to the back of my mind, to the bottom and denied it existed."

"You were in denial."

"No Oprah-speak-bollocks, please," he warned, raising a finger.

"Sorry," I smiled.

Johnson grinned back.

"You want to hear the next bit now?" he asked.

"I hope it's not going to be too sad," I said, sincerely.

"It's not all sad," he said, "some of it was amazing, fantastic and brilliant."

Lucky Bastard

*U*nder Sue's tutelage, Johnson progressed well, and he was soon working independently with his own portfolio of clients. Most evenings, he saw Nicky, although her work often intervened. Tim was an intermittent presence around the flat, he was continuing to work unsociable hours and seemed to spend the rest of his time drinking in the pubs on the market circuit. However, when Johnson arrived home from work one evening, Tim was sprawled on the sofa, watching a pornographic video.

"They are crap these films, aren't they? I mean, has a woman ever said to you, 'come on, come all over my face'," asked Tim.

"Never," agreed Johnson.

"Or over the tits?"

"Once," admitted Johnson.

"Really? Lucky bastard. Who was that, then?"

Johnson shook his head.

"Ever the gent," said Tim. "Was it that Rebecca?"

"No," said Johnson.

"The new one? Whassername again?"

"Nicky," said Johnson, "and it wasn't her."

"I know, Denise, that Denise you went out with for a few weeks."

"I told you, I'm not telling you," said Johnson.

"It was Denise," crowed Tim triumphantly. "Dirty bitch," he said, approvingly.

Johnson shook his head ruefully, but didn't speak.

"Always thought she looked the type who'd be up for anything. What else did you get up to?"

Johnson pressed the remote and the film clicked off in mid-hump.

"I was watching that," Tim protested.

"Well, I'm about to have dinner and I don't want to see anything disappearing into other peoples' mouths while I'm trying to eat."

"Fair one," said Tim, "I've seen it before anyway."

272

"Surprised you haven't worn it out," said Johnson, "particularly that scene in the gym."

"Best bit," said Tim, picking idly at a toenail.

Interview Phase IX

After an hour's break, Johnson and I had resumed our seats around the table.

"How are you feeling?" I asked.

"Fine," he said, brightly, he had showered, shaved and changed his clothes. I guessed the wafts of freshly-scrubbed cleanliness which emanated from his form would last sometime into his second cigarette or his third beer. "Getting harder now, I find," he ventured, "now we're nearing the end, don't you think?"

"I know what you mean," I agreed, "and I'll make it as easy as I can for you, but, at the same time, you've got to help me too. Understand?"

"Deal," he said.

"Do you want anything?" I asked.

"Usual," he said. "Please."

"Pot of tea and the tin of biscuits?"

"Very good," said Johnson, allowing himself a slight smile. "Do you know what the most infected, germ-ridden thing is that's in a hotel room? Your hotel room, my hotel room?"

"I don't," I replied. "Aren't we straying from the point here?"

"Put a proper order in and I'll behave," said Johnson.

"I see," I replied.

"I will not stray," he said, with the precise enunciation which he used occasionally.

I called and put in the order. Yes, a case, please. Chilled if possible, and we'd better have some more cigarettes.

"Sandwiches?" I tucked the receiver into my shoulder as I directed the question at Johnson. He nodded, rubbing his belly and pulling a cheery, chewing face. Strange, how someone could veer from irresistible to tit in such short order.

"So what is it, then?" I asked.

"What?" he asked, looking around suspiciously, gauging his surroundings as if he'd never been in this room before.

"The thing in a hotel room that houses deadly viruses?"

"I didn't say they were deadly, did I?" he quibbled.

"I hope you're not going to fuck me about," I said, "you promised."

"Sorry," he said. "Can't help being a twat sometimes."

"Sometimes?"

"What?"

"Seems you've made it your life's work."

Johnson made a fairly good attempt at looking hurt and upset.

"Dry your eyes princess," I said, "we haven't got time for you to play the drama queen."

"Drama queen?" he said, incredulously.

"Drama queen," I said, adamantly, "I've got sisters like you, so I grew up with it and it doesn't wash, got it?"

"Got it."

The waiter's entrance was preceded by a light tap on the door, so light that we didn't hear it. He set down two trays on the main table and retreated quickly.

"Tinned salmon," Johnson reported with an approving munch, "so much better than that fresh stuff. Could have done with some vinegar, though."

I closed the door behind the waiter and took a slow walk back to the table. I rested my palms on the table top, gave Johnson an unflinching gaze and he met my eyes. He blinked first, attempted to cover it up by pretending that something had fallen from his sandwich, he looked away, scrabbled on the floor.

"We'll do this before we go any further, for no reason other than I just want to know."

"Right," he said, glancing up, head tucked under the table. "Sorry, bit of fish down here somewhere."

"Find it," I said, "or leave it."

"Can't seem to see it," he said, right hand reaching under his seat.

"Leave it," I said, sharply.

"Right," said Johnson, sitting upright.

"What is this thing in a hotel room?" I asked, with some exasperation. "It's the glass in the bathroom isn't it? The one that houses all of the germs?"

"Nope," Johnson said, irritatingly smug.

"I don't want," I said, sliding back into my seat, maintaining my gaze, "to take part in a quiz, I just want the bloody answer."

"OK," said Johnson.

"Which is?"

"The TV remote."

"Ugh," I exclaimed.

"Exactly," he grinned. "Horrible thought, isn't it? All those businessmen, greasy, white-socked photocopier salesmen. In one hand …."

"Alright," I said, quickly, "I can picture the scene. Eurgh."

"Makes you think twice about clicking on CNN, doesn't it?" he said.

"Makes me worried about the state of the pillows," I replied.

We spent five minutes at the window, checking out the passers-by and the traffic.

"Hot," observed Johnson.

"And dirty," I added.

"You know what used to piss me off about going on holiday?"

"No," I replied.

"You'd get out of the shower in the morning, all pink and clean, then you'd have to lather yourself in sunblock. Makes sense, don't get me wrong, so you whack it on and you keep on whacking it on all bastard day long. You come in after your day on the beach or in the town, you might have a little snooze, a cocktail perhaps, maybe a sweet afternoon shag in the heat. I love sex in the hot weather, don't you? When it's really hot, somewhere overseas, getting naked in the afternoon, in the heat. Sweating. When you're both sweating, that's really something isn't it? Intensifies everything, you both smell like sex, that earthy, bodily aroma, you know? I always think it takes you right back to basics," Johnson's eyes took on a dreamy look. "Of course, ideally what you want is a bit of perfume mixed in with all that stink. Bit of Chanel or Kenzo Flower, to set things off properly. Am I boring you?"

"What's the part that pisses you off?" I said, patiently.

"Ah, yes," said Johnson, "almost forgot. Say you've had your day on the beach, or a relaxing afternoon shopping at the market, come back for a cocktail, maybe been lucky enough to slip in and out for a bit."

"You spent too long with Tim," I said.

"Possibly," he agreed, "but I'm just trying to paint you a picture here."

276

"Some of it's attractive," I said. "What's the bit that pisses you off?"

"You shower, personally I like to dress for dinner. Not black tie or anything, but you wear trousers and a shirt, don't you? I don't like it when people go into a restaurant, a nice restaurant, looking like they've just walked off the beach. Then, after you've showered, but before you can get dressed, she says, 'moisturiser?' or 'aftersun?', whatever it is, and you have to slap that on, then your insect repellent. Five minutes ago you were squeaking with cleanliness, and now you're all greasy again and smelling like a tart's handbag."

"Tart's handbag? With insect repellent?" I queried.

"Alright, a zookeeper's handbag, no, strike that, an explorer's handbag," said Johnson. "And there you are, trying to get your slippery hands round the next gin and tonic."

"Doesn't sound too bad to me," I offered.

"I guess not," said Johnson. "Maybe it is perfection that I'm looking for."

He followed me back to the table, where we sat while Johnson opened two beers, he struggled with the opener over the first one, clipping off a brown shard of glass from the lip of the bottle. He opened a second smoothly and handed it to me, keeping the first for himself.

"Be careful with that," I said.

"My hero," he replied.

"When did things start to get shitty at Cartwright Blott Spectre?" I asked.

"Right about now," he replied.

The Big Red Book

"This," said Brian Rossi, holding the red folder high in the air, "is your future. But don't be fooled, your past will be in here too. Along with your present and, of course, your future, as previously mentioned. This is a big red book. The Big Red Book. Your big red book. On the front, as you can see," Brian Rossi pointed to the gilded lettering on the rusty cover with his little finger, "it says, 'This is my Life'. So what does that tell us?"

"Eamonn Andrews has risen from the grave?" suggested one of the older attendees.

"No, no," said Brian Rossi, acidly. "I was expecting this, so can we please get all of your unfunny little jokes out of the way before we get down to the serious business?"

Funny, thought Johnson, when somebody else comes up with the joke, it's a little one that ain't funny.

The room was silent, Brian Rossi continued to wave the folder above his head.

"Anybody?" he barked. "No? Nobody wants to ask where Michael Aspel is? Or say that surely I'm not famous enough? You do surprise me. I'd expected a bit more humorous input. Poor show, Cartwright Blott Spectre people."

"No point," said a quiet voice behind Johnson's left ear.

"Wasted," said one behind his right.

"Over his head," said lefty.

"Stony ground," said the one on the right.

"Right, if nobody is going to speak," said Brian Rossi, taking three steps to the right and then turning dramatically, tossing the book into the air.

"Whooo," said lefty.

"Excitement," said the other.

Brian Rossi missed the catch and the folder hit the floor.

"Butterfingers," said lefty.

"Shame," said the other.

"It is a shame," said lefty, "because now he looks such a pillock."

"He didn't before of course."

278

"Perish the thought."

Johnson adjusted the upper part of his body, slid his arm along the back of his chair and looked behind. Two forty-something women whose names he couldn't remember were the source of the hushed heckling. He smiled, raised an empathetic eyebrow and the three of them were immediately bonded by their shared disdain for the speaker.

"My name's Johnson," he announced. "I've seen you around, but I don't think we've been introduced."

"I'm Wendy," said lefty, she had short blond hair, picked out with darker, reddish streaks, and wore a low-cut top. Johnson maintained eye contact. As Tim would have said, she was a nice bit of old. "This is Sandra."

Johnson turned and smiled. Sandra was older than Wendy, and now Johnson was looking at her directly, he could see that she was stunning. Wedding ring, though, he observed quickly, anyway, Nicky's the one, he reminded himself.

"Nice to meet you," he said, "both of you," switching his gaze back to Wendy.

"If we are all *quite* ready?" Johnson heard Brian Rossi's tetchy tones from the front of the room and he turned back to face him.

"Sorry, Brian," said Johnson. "Just doing a bit of networking."

"OK, fine," said Rossi.

"Bit of team-building, Brian," Sandra called out, and then, quietly, "you twat."

"That's what I like to hear," said Brian Rossi, unable to work out why the trios' shoulders were heaving. "Now, shall we get on?"

"Fire away," said a voice.

"We're ready," said another.

"The idea of the book, this book, is that everything in it will be about you. It will include your quarterly reviews, your targets, notes on how you could do better, notes on the things you have done well. It will build a picture, you see, of your progress, your achievements, your aims. We would like to see testimonials from clients. All of those little 'well done' letters you receive?"

"Oh, I get millions of those," said Wendy.

"This is the place to put them," said Rossi, ignoring her. "Do that, and you will be building a picture. I see it as a three-dimensional overview of target driven aims. We've put everyone's initials on the front as well, can you all see that? BR. That's me."

Nobody spoke audibly, but a slight hum travelled around the room.

"Can I ask a question, Brian?" enquired an unidentified voice form the back of the room.

"Question. That's good. I'll take questions now. What is your question?" Rossi assumed a pose with his thumb resting on the underside of his chin.

"Whose completely brilliant idea was this?"

"First of all," said Rossi, "you're right, it is a completely brilliant idea. It was initialised at board level and became an HR project. Our HR Department are the ones who have shifted into overdrive and moved it into the fast lane. They should really take the credit."

"Yes, but whose idea was it?" asked the voice. Johnson realised that it was Sue at the back of the room.

"It was a board decision," said Rossi.

"Yes, but they didn't all have the idea at the same time, did they?" Sue persisted, "I mean some individual person must have woken up in the middle of the night and thought, 'I know, I know how to justify expanding my department by employing a load more staff and giving them silly things to do', mustn't they? This can't be the work of one evil genius, surely?"

"Can I suggest that if you have an issue with the HR Department that you take it up through the proper channels?" said a slightly flustered Brian Rossi. "Can you all please come up now and collect your folders?"

Johnson, Wendy and Sandra remained seated until the rush had subsided. Then they walked over to Brian Rossi and were handed their folders.

"What are the proper channels?" asked Sue, Johnson hadn't noticed her waiting at the back.

"What is your problem, *Susan*?" asked Rossi.

"My problem, *Bri*, is that this is total bollocks," said Sue, concisely, "but what's the point? Give me the stupid book and I'll see if it works as a frigging doorstop."

Johnson examined his folder as he walked out of the room. The rough edges cut into his fingers, the cheap plastic covering stuck to his palm, and as he peeled it from his hand, some of the gold lettering came away with it.

"Is is my life," he read of what remained of the lettering. "Very profound."

Johnson went to the pub and had a few drinks with Sue, Wendy and Sandra, where they bemoaned The Big Red Book, slated Brian Rossi, disparaged the HR Department, spat bile and generally spread discontent and bitterness all around the saloon bar. Later, Johnson met up with Nicky for a meal.

"Are you alright?" she asked, sipping from a glass of still water.

"Yeah, I suppose so," said Johnson, he told her about Brian Rossi's presentation and The Big Red Book.

"So?" enquired Nicky. "I'd agree that it's bit silly, but surely it's nothing to get worked up about?"

"No," said Johnson, sullenly, rolling a bread stick between his fingers.

"You're not worked up about it, are you?"

"No," said Johnson. The sustained pressure from his fingers caused the bread stick to collapse in the middle. I'm so worked up that I'm about to snap, said Johnson to himself, why can't I tell her? He couldn't answer his own question, but he knew that his state of mind would remain hidden from her for as long as possible.

"You've done really well so far, said Nicky, "I've heard a lot of good things about you."

"You have?"

"Certainly,"

"From who?"

"It doesn't matter from who, I just want you to stay focussed on what you're doing.

"I am focussed," Johnson protested.

"It's just that I know how much you have to kick against the bullshit, and I don't want you straying in to some silly crusade."

"Silly crusade?" asked Johnson. "What do you mean by that?"

"What I said," Nicky said, "what you've got to do is ride the waves and concentrate on the work in hand."

"What I've *got* to do?" mused Johnson.

"Yes," said Nicky, flatly. "We all have to play by the rules."

Johnson pushed his cannelloni around his plate for a while, taking the occasional sip

281

from his glass of Barolo.

"Are you staying tonight?" he asked.

Nicky shook her head, "I've got an early meeting tomorrow."

"You could come back for an hour or two," ventured Johnson.

"I don't think so, not tonight, I've got a few things to do at home."

"Might call it an early night, then," then Johnson, pushing his plate to the centre of the table. "I don't want any more of this."

"I am sorry," said Nicky, reaching for his hand, "I would much rather come back and stay the night, it's just work, that's all."

"It's always work though, isn't it, Nicky?" said Johnson. "It takes over, and you let it take over, every time."

"It's important to me," Nicky protested. "You're important to me too, but I have to, I don't know, juggle."

"I know," said Johnson, "I'm sorry. I should know by now how important it is to you. Let's get you a taxi, and I'll walk home, it's not far from here."

"Are you sure you're alright?" asked Nicky, as they left the restaurant.

"Fine," said Johnson.

"With work, I mean?"

"Oh yes," said Johnson, confidently, "everything to do with work is going to be absolutely fine."

"That's great," said Nicky, as she flagged down a passing black cab. "I'm so relieved. It's all going to work out for us isn't it?"

"It's all going to work out," said Johnson.

Nicky leaned out of the cab window as it drew away from the kerb.

"I love you," she called as she sped away in the taxi.

"Oh shit," said Johnson, quietly, "not now."

As he walked in the humid night air, he considered the events of the previous few months, and by the time he arrived at the flat he had formulated the beginnings of plan.

Johnson and Tim were still seated at the dining table at two AM.

"You want to know what I think?" asked Tim.

"You're going to tell me anyway," said Johnson.

282

"I think you're off your head," Tim advised.

"As you've said every twenty minutes for the last three hours," said Johnson.

"Well, you are," said Tim, exasperated.

"I wouldn't involve you, but I need your help to make it work. I can't do it without you, Tim," said Johnson, pleadingly.

"In which case, I should save you from yourself and have nothing to do with it."

"You're not going to help me?"

"I didn't say that, did I?" said Tim. "For all my life, what I should do and what I end up doing are two totally different animals, Johnners. Now then, we need to make some notes here, or things are going to get complicated. Prior planning and something else prevents piss-ups. No, that's not it. Never mind, get your notepad out and we'll get started."

Johnson and Tim, fuelled with coffee and a box of Black Magic, the chocolates were a previously unopened gift from one of Tim's elderly relatives and were showing signs of ageing themselves.

"What are the white bits?" asked Tim.

"That's the white chocolate," Johnson assured him.

"Oh, right," said Tim, "they mix it in with the dark stuff, do they?"

"That's right," said Johnson, "gives a two-tone effect."

"It's quite an attractive look," said Tim, with a tentative chew, "not sure about the taste, mind."

"Drink some more coffee," Johnson advised, "wash it down."

"Good plan," said Tim.

They reviewed their list.

"You're sure about the location?" Johnson asked.

"Not a problem," Tim replied.

"You do appreciate that we'll need it for a couple of days? Can we have it for that long?"

"No problem. The bloke's sweet, anyway, he owes me and bruv a favour or two. If it's over a weekend, no problem, like I said."

"Right," said Johnson, ticking an entry.

"You're going to handle the initial arrangements, aren't you? I think that's more

283

your department."

"I'll take responsibility for all of that. For the carrot. But I would appreciate you being around for the actual event, I can't handle all of that on my own. In fact, if there's anyone else…?"

"My brother," Tim suggested.

"Great," said Johnson, "and I'll see if I can roust anybody else who might be interested. Two lads from the bright and recent, Goode and Bedford, they might be up for it."

Tim spat the mess of a coffee cream into his hand.

"Shall we seal this with a drink, dear boy?" he asked. "Brandy to take the taste away? Because, strictly between you and me and the stereo, I reckon these chocolates are off. Fucking Uncle Charlie."

"Uncle Charlie?"

"Him that gave me the chocolates. He's one of those relatives, one of those people, that recycles presents. He probably got them off someone a few years ago, put them away, dug them out one Christmas and thought, who can I offload these on as a present? I know, young Timothy, he's the man. There you go son, box of mouldy chocs, season's frigging greetings."

"I've got some relatives like that," said Johnson.

"You don't talk about your folks much," Tim observed, pouring two slugs of brandy.

"No, I don't," agreed Johnson.

"Why's that, then?" asked Tim, offering Johnson a glass.

"Don't know," said Johnson, "I just don't. Now, I'll sort out the personnel, and if your brother can join us that would be great. You're sure about the location. I need to organise the nuts and bolts, of course, but apart from that all I need to do is send out the invitations."

Interview Phase X

"*I*nvitations?" I asked.

"Oh yes," said Johnson, grinning.

"Why invitations?"

"I could hardly send out a summons could I? I worked out that what I had to do was appeal to their vanity, their self-importance, their arrogance."

"If the idea was to get the bitterness out of your system," I said, "I have to tell you that you've failed."

"I might have failed," Johnson said, "but stripping away what you perceive as bitterness was never on the agenda."

"Did you want to be famous?" I asked.

"You have to be kidding," Johnson replied.

"Not fame then?"

"Can't think of anything worse," said Johnson, "than being famous."

"Me neither," I agreed. "What did the invitations say?"

"Well, it's quite obvious that you already know the answer to that. But, in the shell of a nut, they were a bit of flattery, a bit of a teaser, a bit of bait,"

"A bit of a hook."

"Exactly."

"There was a dinner though?"

"Of course, City Banquet at London's famous Mansion House. Chancellor of the Exchequer is the main speaker. All the City knobs are there, all the big boys. Who could resist? You have been selected. You have been spotted as one of this country's up-and-coming business talents. We'll pick up the tab. We'll even send a car for you. Look at this fancy invitation, all embossed in gold, it's got your name on it, look, it says, *you've arrived.*"

"And nobody queried this? Nobody checked?"

"Vanity, you see," said Johnson, "they wanted to believe. They wanted to believe it so much that it hurt."

"They could have checked."

"There was a number on the invitation, a London landline, but any calls were routed to someone's mobile."

"Who's mobile?"

"I couldn't possibly say," said Johnson, shaking his head firmly.

"But nobody called."

"Nobody called," said Johnson, triumphantly. "Vanity took over, you see, and the rest," he finished with an air of resignation.

"So they all came along without a word?"

"All dressed up for the party. They couldn't wait to jump in those strange cars with those strange people. Well, they didn't know how strange at the time, did they?"

"You picked up all of these people from their workplaces?"

"One or two from their homes, actually," said Johnson.

"They expected to be going to a City of London dinner?"

"*The* City of London dinner, please. Major event of the year."

"And instead they ended up in an Essex scrapyard?"

"Sweet, wasn't it?" said Johnson, swilling a beer to the end and knocking the top from another. "So sweet."

"I can't believe that they came along without resisting, when they realised something was wrong and they weren't going to be supping with the chancellor."

"So as he gets in, the driver says, a little Champagne, sir? Oh, thank you, says the passenger, who within five minutes doesn't know if he's been punched, bored or countersunk."

"Drugs?"

"Personally, I don't approve. But, like they say, needs must. I'll stick to my Rothman's anytime, thanks," said Johnson, touching the Bic to another.

"When you got everyone to the scrapyard?"

"Yes?"

"How did you organise things?"

Closure

The area was enclosed by a high fence, fifteen feet or thereabouts, topped with three lengths of barbed wire which raised it by another eighteen inches. It was about half the size of a standard football pitch and was littered with a few wrecked cars, which were mostly stacked together in loose scrap metal arrangements. Like a contender for the Turner Prize. Arc lights at each corner illuminated the scene, it was ten o'clock by now, on a summer's evening and the sky was beginning to darken. An untidy cluster of smartly-dressed people were moving slowly from confusion to anger and frustration.

"Good evening," said Johnson's voice from the PA, "I see that our guests have arrived. Everyone is well, I hope?"

Johnson ignored the shouts of protest.

"No, sorry," he said, pausing for a moment, "can't hear a thing. You can hear me, I hope. Hands up if you can't hear me. Anyone? Good. I do have the advantage of the PA system, I suppose, and whichever way I look at it, I seem to have the advantage all ends up." Johnson allowed himself a gentle laugh, designed solely to irritate. "Now, let me see if everyone is here. I can see Mitchell Turner and Colin Camper from Wink and Kinker. Good evening to you both. Sorry, still can't hear you. There's Mr Flitch, so sorry I've forgotten your first name, Richard Nork from Locked-In Recruitment, hello Richard. I'd like to say it's a pleasure, although, well, actually it might just be a pleasure this time, considering the circumstances. How about that? Isn't that a stroke of luck, Richard? No? Go on, give us a smile. Is Simon Hart with you? Ah, yes. Good evening Simon. Where's Brian? Brian Rossi? Of course, couldn't miss that hairstyle. Hello Bri, how's it going? I almost forgot, of course, we are lucky enough to have not one but two board members from Cartwright Blott Spectre as well. The HR Director and the MD. Helen Stiff is the HR person and the MD is Brenda Rowley. So nice of you to join us. You do indeed honour us with your presence." A further word from Johnson drifted across the yard, which sounded suspiciously like 'bollocks'.

"It seems I'm going to have to remind you again, which doesn't say much about your talent for absorbing the simplest of information and putting it into practice. At least we have something to work on there, though, taking the positives from an abject performance so far. The point is this: DO NOT SHOUT," Johnson's voice boomed through the speakers. "I CANNOT HEAR YOU. WE CANNOT HEAR YOU. NOBODY CAN HEAR YOU. Also, do not forget, that not only can I not hear you, even if I could I would not be in the slightest bit interested in what you have to say. So best you settle down and wait. On the subject of settling down, you will have noticed, at least I hope you have noticed it or you may have to pay a forfeit, that you are completely enclosed by a high fence, which is particularly unforgiving at the top. Where it has the benefit, for its own protection of course, of a not inconsiderable electric current which is being run through it continuously. Outside the fence, you may have heard them, again forfeits may have to be paid if lack of attention to your surroundings is noted, outside are a quite frightening collection of large, ill-tempered guard dogs. I suppose their tetchiness could be put down to the fast that has been imposed on them for the past thirty-six hours, although I'm told that the lack of food is responsible for a quite remarkable sharpening of their senses, and of course, their appetites. Let's hope we don't have to put the theory to the test, shall we? Well, I'll be honest here, I think perhaps it is you, the group that's inside the enclosure that should be doing the hoping. Personally, I don't mind one way or the other, no, no, that's not right, I would have to say that, if forced, I would lean towards the option of seeing the dogs in action. Anyway, I won't force the issue. Not yet." Johnson clicked the switch on the microphone to the 'off' position and let his words hang in the air. He hooked the mike onto the side of the control panel. He could hear perfectly well of course, there were boom mikes concealed outside each corner of the perimeter fence and by using the console he could fade any of them up or down. As he had been speaking, all of them were currently slid to the minimum setting. Johnson was sitting in the cab of a low crane which rested twenty yards from the enclosure. The windows had been fitted with thin plastic sheeting which meant he could see out while remaining invisible to those outside. The crane's usual sole purpose was as a mover and re-locator of scrap, it's main apparatus which hung at the end of a bunch of thick black cables was a bulky electro-magnet. His fingers raised the level of the far right-hand fader and the babble of voices filled the cab. They're just arguing, he thought, fighting amongst themselves already. Simon Hart sounds borderline hysterical, Rossi's trying to tell a joke, Flitch is sitting alone on the ground - twenty feet away from the rest, Mitchell Turner's about to burst into tears, Helen Stiff and Brenda Rowley are making the occasional interjection - but nothing helpful, and Richard Nork and Colin Camper have turned their backs to the group and are having a quiet conversation. Johnson slid the fader down and upped the register of another.

"Any idea who might be behind this?" asked Camper. Johnson could see his ginger hair glowing under the arc lighting. I wonder what it's like, belonging to an ethnic minority, he mused, being ginger. He listened to the conversation which was piped clearly into the cab and watched the incongruous sight of two middle-aged men in evening dress having a serious conversation in the middle of the night while imprisoned in an Essex scrapyard.

"Not a clue," said Nork.

"What line are you in?" asked Camper.

"Recruitment," said Nork. "You?"

"Oil and gas," said Camper.

"Not much in common then," said Nork.

"There must be a link somewhere," mused Camper, "we've just got to find it."

"What do they want though?" asked Nork.

"Search me," shrugged Camper. "What we have to do is establish a relationship with our captors, that's the way things are done in these cases."

"Who are they, though? We can't establish a relationship if we can't see them or talk to them," Richard Nork observed, reasonably.

"We've got to make sure that they do then, haven't we?"

"That they do what?" asked Nork.

"Show themselves and listen to us," said Camper, firmly, "shouldn't be that difficult, you know."

"Really?" said Nork, in an unconvinced tone.

"Not for someone with military training," said Camper, confidently.

"Really?" said Johnson, smiling to himself, and taking an involuntary glance at the inactive microphone.

Johnson left the fader in position so he could continue to listen while he poured hot coffee from a flask that Tim had prepared. Johnson had cavilled at the choice of coffee

289

but Tim had won him over by adding several hefty slugs of brandy to the mix. As Johnson felt the warmth of the coffee and the spirit first hit his throat and then his chest he succumbed quickly to the urge for a cigarette.

"I've got some ideas," said Camper, firmly, "have no worries about that. Oh yes, I've got some ideas alright."

Johnson tuned into another corner of the captives, leant back and put his feet up. He listened idly for an hour, tuning in and out of conversations. The general mood seemed to favour sitting tight and waiting. Johnson was relieved and unsurprised in equal measure that he hadn't overheard the forming of an escape committee. He silenced the incoming chatter, reloaded the tape of vicious dogs barking and gave them another blast, just in case. Tim entered the cab.

"You weren't seen?" asked Johnson, anxiously.

"No chance," said Tim, removing his black balaclava. "I used the crane as cover. What's been going on?"

"Bickering, mainly," Johnson reported, "although Nork and Camper have been trying to get something together."

"A plan?" asked Tim.

"I wouldn't go so far as to call it a plan," said Johnson.

"Nothing to worry about then?"

"No. Where's your brother? Back in the cabin?"

There were a series of Portakabins which served as offices and toilets which sat back from the crane.

"He's, er, gone," said Tim, "He left just after your mates, Goode and the other one."

"Gone?" exploded Johnson. "What do you mean, gone? Gone where?"

"He's gone home," shrugged Tim, "reckons he's done enough and doesn't want to do any more. Anyway, he's on the markets tomorrow. Sussex, early start."

"He won't tell anyone will he?"

"Bruv? Nah."

"The police?"

"My brother talking to police voluntarily? That's a laugh," Tim reached for the flask.

"The papers?"

Tim took a swig direct from the flask.

"Papers? Listen Johnson, he doesn't know what's going on here. He thinks it's a bit of a game. A stunt. A practical joke."

"Well, that's all it is, really," said Johnson, uncertainly, "isn't it?"

"I think you'll find it's gone a bit further than that, dear boy. Kidnap, false imprisonment, administering noxious substances, and that's before we've got started."

"Right," Johnson nodded, "right."

"You're not having second thoughts, are you?" asked Tim.

"Me?" Johnson stated. "No chance."

"Let the games commence?"

Johnson picked up the mike, "Let the games commence," he said, and clicked it on.

"Ladies and gentlemen," he boomed, "it's time to get started. Oh dear, it seems that one or two of you were trying to get some sleep, I am sorry. You'll have to postpone your little naps, I'm afraid. ON YOUR FEET."

"Very good," chuckled Tim, approvingly.

Johnson shot him a look, a deadly serious look.

"Sorry," whispered Tim. Johnson winked at him.

"It is time for the F-U-N to begin. You know what F-U-N spells don't you?"

He picked up the sound of disembodied voices shouting the answer.

"Can't hear you," he yelled, "this is a poor start by all concerned. I can see I'm going to have to start dishing out some forfeits. Mitchell Turner give me twenty press-ups."

He watched Mitchell Turner hit the deck and begin to pump his arms furiously. Twenty press-ups.

"Very good," said Johnson, approvingly, "now give me another twenty with Colin Camper sitting on your back."

Mitchell Turner was at the top of the second one when he collapsed forwards into the dirt, Colin Camper's weight knocked the air out of his lungs before Camper rolled off to the side.

"Unimpressive," said Johnson. "Make note would you?" he said in an exaggerated aside to Tim. "Now, I want you to form yourselves into two teams. Elect a team captain, you know the drill, and I'll be back to talk to you soon."

Johnson reached for the flask.

"How long are you going to leave them?"

"Couple of hours," said Johnson. "An hour or so to argue about the teams and who's going to be captain, a bit longer to try and work out what's going on, by that time a few of them should be asleep again. Just in time to be woken up for some fun and games."

"I'm worried you're so good at this," said Tim, "ever thought about joining the army?"

"No," said Johnson, "certainly not."

"Have you decided on the first game?" asked Tim. "What do you think? Mental or physical?"

"Mental, I should think," Johnson decided, "they'll be mentally tired. They'll be physically tired too of course, but I don't think we want to give them the opportunity of running around, getting the heart pumping and oxygenating the blood, clearing their heads. We want to deprive them of a bit more sleep before going physical on them."

"Stuff up their brains first, then."

"Well put," said Johnson.

After two hours, Johnson addressed his guests once more. He told them where they could find the materials they would need for their first challenge. He watched as the teams ran across the enclosure and searched the rear of what had once been a Ford Fiesta.

"Well done, well found and all that," said Johnson, sounding bored. "Don't open anything, I'll be back to you in a minute." He turned off the mike and slid the faders up.

"Why are we doing this?" asked Brenda Rowley, blond and businesslike.

"Because we don't have a choice," Simon Hart replied.

"Well, we have a choice," Brenda Rowley argued.

"Makes sense to me that we play along, see where that takes us," said Hart.

"To the end?" mused Brenda.

"Anyway, perhaps the winners get out of here?" suggested Hart.

"The problem is, we can't establish a relationship because they are careful to stay out of range," said Colin Camper to Richard Nork.

"What do we do, then?" asked Nork.

"Play the game," said Camper, "maybe the winners will be released."

"You're looking very nice this evening, I must say," said Brian Rossi to Helen Stiff.

"Are you alright down there?" asked Mitchell Turner of Mr Flitch.

"Right, I assume you have divided yourselves into the two teams? You seem to be in two groups of four. Hart, Rowley, Camper and Nork in one team. Rossi, Stiff, Flitch and Turner in the other. One change I am going to suggest, no, I hear you say, well, perhaps I would if I could hear you. But you are correct, 'suggest' is not the right word at all. I should not be suggesting changes, I should be imposing them. Flitch and Nork will change places." Johnson killed the mike and switched to incoming. Shouts of protest filled the cab. Johnson and Tim grinned at each other.

"Nice touch," said Tim.

"I thought so," grinned Johnson.

They allowed the dissenting voices to continue for thirty seconds before Johnson flicked his switches, gave them a burst of the guard dogs and made another announcement.

"Any more of this indiscipline I shall be forced into relocating the dogs over to your side of the wire."

The voices died away quickly and Johnson flicked his switches.

"Tim, I thought we had a headset for this, I need to listen to the incoming without turning off the mike," he said.

Tim reached under the control panel and pulled out a curly black cable which had a jack at one end and a set of heavily padded headphones at the other.

"Why didn't you give me these before?" asked Johnson.

"Thought you liked playing with all the switches," Tim replied.

Johnson grinned, put on the headset and switched on the mike and the incoming speaker.

"Now that you are in your revised teams, we need names for them. What to call them? I know, I know. Team A - that will be Hart, Rowley, Camper and Flitch. Team B is, well you work it out. Now, the game. If one of you will open the briefcase. Good. For each team we have an identical crossword. Cryptic clues, of course. There are plenty of pens and pencils in the case. Off you go, winner is the first to finish. But there is a time limit of one hour, no, I'll give you two hours. How inconceivably generous of me. Shout and wave when you've completed the task and we'll do our best to take notice."

Johnson and Tim watched as the two teams took up position at opposite sides of the

293

enclosure. Team A sat in a row, Team B in a circle.

"See that, Tim?" asked Johnson, "Two opposing systems. How uninteresting."

"You might have missed a trick here," Tim counselled.

"How so?"

"What if one of them is crossword champion? One of those people who can finish the hardest ones in twenty minutes? They have contests don't they? Might work out the clues in no time at all."

"Not these clues, they won't," said Johnson.

"Yeah, but you can't know that."

"Oh yes I can," said Johnson. "The clues bear no relation to the answers, you see. In fact there are no answers."

"No answers?" asked Tim. "But the bloke who made it up, he wrote the clues, he knows the answers."

"I made it up," said Johnson.

"You?"

"It's all completely random. They'll be lucky to get one, and if they do, it'll still be wrong. Did you bring any sandwiches?"

Johnson and Tim watched and listened to the increasing frustration of the teams. As the two hour mark approached, Johnson plugged in the headset and switched on the mike.

"How are we doing?" he asked. "Has anybody finished?"

He heard a voice through his headset.

"Yes, yes. Team A have finished the task. This is Colin Camper speaking, and we have finished."

Johnson heard shouts of 'impossible' from Team B. Well, it was impossible, he knew that, Tim looked at him questioningly. Johnson took a lungful of air and spoke.

"Do I take it from your protests, Team B, that you have failed to complete the task? Shame. I pronounce Team A to be the winners of round one. Well done, award yourself a slap on the back. Scores from each round will be totalled and the eventual winner will be the team with the most points. Now I want you to tear up the crosswords and eat the pieces, as a team, first one to finish is the winner of round two."

Johnson turned to Tim, palms turned upwards.

294

"I wasn't expecting that," said Johnson.

"Trying to get someone down there, wasn't he? Establish contact," advised Tim.

"We don't want any of that," said Johnson.

"Team B's going to win this round are they?"

"I think we want to ensure that level-pegging is maintained, don't you?"

"Exactly," agreed Tim.

"Congratulations to Team B," Johnson announced, although he could see that Brian Rossi still had scraps of paper in his hand. "Honours are now even." He listened to renewed complaints from Team A. "Take a well-earned break. I'll be back on the air with details of the next game, oooh, sometime later."

Tim was leaning on the door, yawning and scratching. Two of his favourite pastimes.

"What's the next thing?" he asked.

Johnson looked at him warily.

"Well, I don't really know," Johnson replied, "I've racked my brains, I really have, but I just don't know. I'm not sure we should stay here for too much longer either. We've had the cover of darkness, but you never know who's going to appear in the daylight."

"I thought you'd planned this out," said Tim, accusingly.

"Up to now," said Johnson, "I have. I thought I might get inspiration from somewhere as we went along. Anyway, I'm beginning to feel like I've been brought down to their level. You know something, Tim? I'm not sure that we continue to occupy the moral high ground, and that's the problem."

"Problem is," mused Tim, reaching for the flask, "we haven't got any kit."

"Kit?"

"You know, ropes, barrels, planks of four-by-two. Certainly haven't got a river to cross or a mountain to climb."

"We haven't," said Johnson, as he reached for the flask.

"All run dry, I'm afraid," said Tim, holding the flask upside down.

"Great," said Johnson.

"Unless you want it without the coffee," said Tim, producing a flat half bottle of Martell from his inside pocket.

"You're a marvel," said Johnson, pouring two fingers into his cup.

"And I think I've had an idea," said Tim, proceeding to elaborate.

"WAKEY WAKEY," crowed Johnson, he watched as the teams stirred. "Team A and Team B are henceforth disbanded. If you feel that the time you've spent bonding has been wasted, then I have to tell you that it has. Never mind. From now on it's every contestant for themselves. You are going to race in pairs against each other. Just running, oh and carrying a wheel each, I think. There's a pile of them in the corner there, look. So, four lengths of your palatial accommodation, winner qualifies for the next stage, loser has to go and sit in the remains of the blue Volvo. First up, Flitch versus Hart, I think, get yourselves ready."

Flitch and Hart lined up against the fence, both clutching a car wheel, and listened for Johnson's instruction.

"When I say, go. GO," he yelled, and the racers set off. "STOP," yelled Johnson.

Tim looked at him with alarm.

"False start. My electronic sensors have picked up Simon Hart going too early. Once more and you'll be disqualified, Hart."

Johnson and Tim watched Simon Hart, arms outstretched, disputing the decision from too far away to make any difference.

"That's enough," barked Johnson, "you don't want a further caution for dissent, now do you?"

The runners took up their positions once more.

"GO," yelled Johnson, and this time he let them go. Simon Hart had hung back, wary of being called for another false start, and Flitch established an early lead. But he was much older, much less fit, the weight of the wheel soon dampened his early pace, and by the finish Simon Hart was a clear winner.

"Hart, stand to the left. Flitch get in the Volvo," ordered Johnson. "Next up, Helen Stiff, don't know much about you, Helen, but I'm going to put you up against, erm, Colin Camper. Ready?"

Helen Stiff and Colin Camper stood side-by-side. Helen Stiff was above average size, tall and quite heavily built, with close-cropped auburn hair. Johnson watched Colin Camper closely, he was poised on his toes, leaning in front of Helen Stiff, edging forwards, trying to gain a fag-paper's width of an advantage.

Johnson called Colin Camper for two false starts and disqualified him.

"There's no point in you jumping up and down like Rumpelstiltskin stuffed full of steroids, shut up, calm down and get in the fucking Volvo, you little rat."

"You enjoyed that, didn't you?" Tim observed.

"Bloody right, I did," Johnson agreed.

"He is like a little rat isn't he?"

"In so many ways."

Eventually Camper climbed into the Volvo with Flitch.

"Hello there," Johnson overheard Flitch's welcome to Colin Camper, and suppressed a guffaw. "I'll budge up a bit, don't sit on that shard of metal, it's a bit sharp." Johnson watched Camper and Flitch organise themselves in the front of the shell of the Volvo. "You want to drive?" asked Flitch. Johnson was beginning to think that he was wrong to include Mr Flitch with the rest of them. Jayston, that was his name, he remembered, and Jayston Jonathan Flitch seemed to have a ripe old sense of humour.

"You want to do one?" Johnson asked Tim. "I could do with a break."

"Alright, then," Tim replied.

Johnson handed him the mike, but kept the headset for himself.

"I need to hear what they're saying," explained Johnson.

Tim nodded, and spoke.

"AAAALRRRRIGGGHHHT," he boomed, Johnson thought he felt the headphones lifting from his ears, and he took a leap and a pace backwards. Tim continued.

"LET'S BE HAVING YOU."

Johnson made dampening motions with his hands, pointed to his ears with an expression of pain and alarm, and mouthed the words, 'too loud', Tim signalled his assent.

"Which one of you twats is next?" Tim yelled a little more quietly.

"You decide," whispered Johnson.

"What?" Tim's voice boomed across the enclosure.

"Mike," whispered Johnson.

"Eh?"

Johnson reached over and switched off the microphone.

"You can't talk to me and leave the mike on," advised Johnson.

"Oh, right," said Tim, "sorry."

"We have to choose two people for the next race. How about Mitchell Turner against Richard Nork? That'll leave Brian Rossi to face his boss in the last. I like the idea of that."

"OK," said Tim. Johnson gave him a questioning look and signalled that he was about to switch the mike back on. Tim blinked in agreement and Johnson flicked the switch and gave him the thumbs up.

"Turner and Nork are the next lucky participants and will first undo their trousers and complete the course like that. With trousers around the ankles. Trouser removal or any attempts at trouser-kick-off will result in instant disqualification. Unbuckle. Unbutton, Unzip. Go," Tim glanced over at Johnson and they shared a look of surprise and delight. "Don't know where that one came from," whispered Tim, although he had switched off the mike. He switched on again. "Come back, come back. You've only forgotten your wheels, haven't you? You unbuckled, unbuttoned, and unzipped, but you didn't pick up, did you? Five point penalty to both contestants and as a further punishment they both now have to carry two wheels each. OK, as before, and don't forget your wheels this time. GO."

"What's the five-point penalty?" asked Johnson, as the runners took off.

Tim gave him an uncomprehending look.

"Don't make out there are rules to this, dear boy, I'm making them up just like you do. Oh no, now I've gone and missed the finish. Who won that one?"

"Who cares?" replied Johnson.

"I think it was the smarmy-looking geezer, what's his name?"

"Richard Nork," Johnson replied.

"Nork stand to one side. Turner get in the car," ordered Tim.

"Time's getting on," Johnson observed, adjusting the faders.

"Right, next pair. Rossi and Rowley. No mucking about. No tyres. Rossi, you've got a one-length start, and I'm about to introduce the dogs to the arena. GO."

"Nice one," said Johnson, approvingly, watching Brian Rossi torn between the possibility of saving himself and the inevitability of upsetting his boss.

"And we have a winner, Brenda Rowley, who somehow pulled that one from the fire," announced Tim.

"What a surprise," said Johnson.

"What now?" asked Tim.

"You know how to work this thing?" asked Johnson, motioning to the crane's controls.

"Yeah, yeah," Tim replied.

"Right," said Johnson, "I want that car in the air. Twenty feet or so should do it."

"With the people in it?" asked Tim.

"Of course with the people in it," Johnson replied.

Tim manoeuvred the magnet close to the roof of the Volvo and engaged the power. There was a dull, metallic thump as the car connected with magnet and Tim swung it into the air. Screams filled Johnson's ears. He picked up the mike.

"The rest of you, the winners, now have your chance to escape. You'll have to scale the fence, but the barbed wire in the top-left corner is loose, none of the fence is electrified, and there are no dogs."

"I know who it is," said a voice in Johnson's ear.

"What?" said another.

"I recognise the voice," said the first.

Tim drove them smoothly through the twisting back roads of the east and the uniform lanes of the M25, while Johnson fretted quietly in the passenger seat.

"It was your idea," Tim pointed out, helpfully.

"So," replied Johnson, "it was my idea."

"Bit late for worrying about it then, isn't it?"

"Alright," said Johnson, "perhaps it is."

"Going to pull in here," Tim announced, "this service station."

"Why?" asked Johnson. "Shouldn't we be getting away?"

"Need some fruit pastilles," Tim explained. "Anyway, I think we're reasonably safe."

Tim slipped the car into a parking bay and eased himself out.

"You wait here," said Tim, "anything you want?"

"Absolutely not," exclaimed Johnson, "fruit pastilles do it for me every time."

299

They drove back in relative silence, soundtracked only by Tim swearing at the radio, and they were soon parked at an Underground station.

"Why have we stopped?" enquired Johnson.

"Catching the train aren't we?"

"We are? Why are we taking the train? We've got a car."

"We haven't got a car. The car belongs to someone else, doesn't it? Gonna leave it here, we get the tube, they can collect it sooner or later, preferably sooner, I should think. Alright?"

They caught the first westbound train of the morning and walked back to the flat in the cool of the morning.

"You're very quiet," Johnson observed.

"Oh, you know," replied Tim.

"I'm sorry," offered Johnson.

"For what?"

"Getting you into all this."

"Not a problem."

"It didn't work out how I thought it would."

"Hold that thought Johnners," said Tim, "you'd better get used to it. Here we are, got your key, have you?"

Johnson, having opened the door, was first to enter the flat and Tim followed close behind, ushering Johnson towards the kitchen.

"Drink, dear boy?" asked Tim.

"I think we deserve one," Johnson concurred as Tim pulled two beers from the fridge. He popped off the tops and handed one to Johnson as they moved through to the lounge.

"Cheers my old mate," said Tim, "I wouldn't have missed it." He tapped his can against Johnson's and flicked on the light.

"You mean it?" asked Johnson.

"I wouldn't have missed it either," said Frank Westlake.

"Oh shit," agreed Johnson.

Tim didn't speak.

"Oh shit, indeed," said Frank Westlake.

Frank Westlake was sitting in an easy chair, dressed, as always, in a dark suit, white shirt and plain tie. The black, leathery hilt of a long, slim-bladed knife was loosely grasped between the second and third fingers of his right hand. He snapped his wrist sharply and the speed of movement meant that Johnson couldn't work out how the knife now came to be held by the blade and between Westlake's finger and thumb.

Tim was unusually quiet and, Johnson noticed, making his way to the door on ostentatious tiptoes.

"Sit down, lad," advised Westlake, tossing over two sets of plastic handcuffs. "Put these on. One set each."

"Alright," said Tim, "front or back?" Tim gestured with his arms.

"With you two I shouldn't think it'll matter, so whatever you like. You sit down," said Westlake, pointing at Johnson, "and you, Tim, isn't it?" Tim nodded. "Before you put your cuffs on you can get me a drink. Vodka. Bring the bottle. Remember, any nonsense and I'll start cutting bits off of one of you. Any preference?"

"You're in charge," said Tim.

"I'd recommend you start with him," said Johnson, "but like he says, you're in charge."

"Funny boy, aren't you?" Westlake said. "And what a lot of fun you've had."

Tim put an unopened bottle of vodka, mineral water and a tumbler on the table.

"Ice?" asked Tim.

Johnson shot him a look.

"Lemon?" Tim persisted. "No?"

"He's funny too, your mate Timmy Tatoes here," said Frank Westlake. "I envy you, you know that? You know why? You'll have to excuse me, I like to talk sometimes, I find it takes the edge off the unpleasantness to come. Yes, funny, that was it, being funny."

Johnson and Tim were both now cuffed, wedged shoulder to shoulder on the sofa and so gave a combined shrug. Frank Westlake rammed the knife-point into the low lounge table and as Johnson and Tim gave a mutual start he snapped the top from the vodka and filled half of the tumbler. He ignored the water and took a gulp.

"Me? I'm not funny. I don't get the opportunity. People I deal with, they aren't funny either."

"How so?" asked Johnson, taking a sharp nudge in the ribs from Tim.

Frank Westlake pulled the knife from the table and rubbed the blade thoughtfully along his jaw line, grinning like he always did, thought Johnson.

"Oil and gas. Dirty business. Well, not the business, as such, not the product. It's not the fault of the oil or the gas, is it? Money. It's the money that brings them out, sucks them in. The chancers, the con-artists, the hangers-on and freeloaders, the greedy, the bone-idle, extortionists, blackmailers, gangsters, the freedom-fighters, fucking freedom fighters! Not much fun to be had there."

"So why....?" Johnson felt another dig in the ribs.

"Because they pay me so much that I can't afford not to. Someone like the firm, like Wink and Kinker, needs someone like to me to protect their interests against people like that. It's what I do, protect their interests against the likes of them and the likes of you."

Frank Westlake drained his vodka and shuddered, he rose to his feet and approached Johnson and Tim.

"I don't really enjoy this bit," said Frank Westlake, "if it's any comfort. I find the cutting and the screaming and the bleeding to be most upsetting. I have been known to suffer with nightmares."

Interview Phase XI

"What did you do?" I asked.

"Apart from scream like Edward the Second you mean?" Johnson replied. He looked wrung out and weary now.

"Edward the Second? He got disembowelled didn't he?"

"With...."

"I remember," I said. "Go on."

"Westlake was walking over with the knife, me and Tim squirming on the sofa, though Tim looked him in the eye which was more than I could manage, then I heard this bang, no, a succession of bangs, and in came well, I thought it was the law, but it must have been..."

"We're all on the same side," I said. "What were you doing? What made you think you could get away with it?"

"The thought never entered my head. The thought of getting away with anything, we were just doing it."

"What happened to you, Johnson?",

"I thought I'd explained all that, Anna, I thought that's what this was all about," he waved his arm vaguely around the room. "What about Nicky?" he asked, "Have you been in touch with her?"

"Yes," I said, "As a department. Officially, you understand."

"Of course," Johnson nodded. "So, Anna, as a friend, officially, does she want to see one or both of my balls hanging from The London Eye? Or, is it the full set?"

"Officially," I said, "I haven't a clue."

"Unofficially, as a friend?"

"Unofficially, I'd say that although you might have a bit of work to do, a lot of work, a lot of sucking up, that all is not yet lost."

Johnson's demeanour lifted visibly at this news.

The door opened, Jeff walked in, nodded to Johnson, and kissed me on the cheek.

"I should have known," said Johnson, ruefully. "Been listening in, have you?"

"Only for the last half an hour," Jeff replied, taking a seat opposite Johnson. "Bit of a mess you've got yourself into."

"I don't regret anything you know," said Johnson, defiantly.

"I'm sure you don't. Caused a lot of trouble though," said Jeff.

I was relieved to have a third party there, relieved that it was nearly over.

"I'll take my punishment," said Johnson, "although I had my reasons and I don't think I've done too much wrong. I've made my point."

"You've certainly done that," said Jeff.

"By the way, how did you know that Tim and I were in the flat with a knife-wielding nut job?"

"Tim called," I said.

"Tim?"

"From the service station," I said.

"Where we stopped for..."

"Fruit pastilles," said Jeff

"I thought that was odd," Johnson laughed, then composed himself and was suddenly serious. "But that means Tim must have known, known what you two do for a living. Whatever it is, I mean I'm still not sure and I've been locked up with you for days."

"He knew a little," I replied, glancing at Jeff.

"He knew more than I did," said Johnson, hurt.

"My tongue got loosened one evening," said Jeff.

"Easily done," I said.

"With Tim," agreed Johnson. "How is he? Tim?"

"On the markets with his brother, or in a pub or a betting shop, I should think," I replied.

"Tim's OK," said Jeff, "they were never after Tim."

"They were after the mastermind," I said.

"Mr Big," Jeff nodded. Johnson looked as if someone had replaced his beer with sour milk.

"One other thing I don't get, small point and all that, but why did you bring me halfway across the planet to have this discussion. Fascinating though it's been, of

304

course," Johnson asked.

I watched Jeff rub his palms together and wince a little as he stared into the middle distance, which, in this case, was me.

"It seemed to make sense to get you away from certain parties who might have decided to take matters into their own hands," said Jeff, in a brief and chilling summary.

"He was arrested wasn't he? Westlake?" asked Johnson. "Arrested and charged?"

"Not exactly. Well, not at all, actually. I mean obviously we spoke to him, but a court case? A court case wouldn't have been in the public interest now would it?" said Jeff firmly. "Or your interest, or anybody's. After all, we are dealing with people who have more people who are in the same line of work, and we needed to protect our...to protect you, do you see?"

"I see," agreed Johnson.

"What do you think's going to happen to you?" I asked.

"I don't know Anna, funny, it seems OK to call you that now, now the formal stuff is nearly over. Prison, I suppose, but I wouldn't know how long I'll get."

Jeff reached for three beers, opened them and passed them round. He threw the packet of cigarettes to Johnson, sat back in his chair, tipping it back on two legs.

"Certain, shall we say, associated government departments have been showing quite a bit of interest in you," said Jeff.

"That's what I need right now," said Johnson, "more trouble."

"No," said Jeff, "you're missing the point. We're not looking at criminal charges here."

"We're not?" said Johnson and I, together.

"Nobody wants to press. In fact we had a terrible job in getting anyone to talk about it at all. Too embarrassed, you see. Too vain, you were right there. Where would their self-regard and arrogance be if it became common knowledge that they spent an evening running relay races with their trousers around their ankles? Or fell for the simplest of scams and got themselves abducted and imprisoned? But the important thing here, the juice, Johnson, here's the juice. The people I've been talking to would be quite keen to make use of your talents."

"My *talents*?" asked Johnson, incredulously.

"The idea is that they will sort out a placement for you in a suitable post, a job, you

305

know, in some industry or other, and, properly channelled, your talents might be of great benefit to this country. Obviously we need to knock off a few rough edges, but the possibilities are endless. Business is so competitive now, and on a global scale, that any little advantage that a country can give itself, well, it makes perfect sense when you think about it. Put you in position and you can do your stuff," said Jeff.

"My *stuff?*" asked Johnson.

"Well, the gentle sabotage was good, we can develop that. We might also get you into promoting some of this nonsense. You know, corporate fun days, psychometric testing, think of the damage you can inflict on resources and morale. I'm excited about this Johnson, I must say."

Johnson, dumbfounded, finished his beer and his cigarette before speaking.

"Where would I be doing this?" he asked, eventually.

"Oh, France to start with, I think," said Jeff, "then Germany, America, let's not forget the up-and-coming, India, China........

THE END